THE RED WITCH

THE RED WITCH

by
Serena Devlin

Pendleton
Books

Published by Pendleton Books
666 Fifth Avenue, # 365
New York, NY 10103

Printed in the United States of America

Library of Congress Catalog Card Number: 00-100095

Serena Devlin/The Red Witch

ISBN 1-893221-04-0

FIRST EDITION

CONTENTS

This book is dedicated

to the memory of

Mary Maloon.

THE RED WITCH

PART ONE

SALEM, MASSACHUSETTS
1995

CHAPTER ONE

"Not too bad," exclaimed Rebecca as she stared into the oval mirror attached to the old burlwood vanity. The lovely piece of furniture was part of a bedroom set that her beloved mother, Magdelene, had treasured for many years. The vanity had many small drawers and secret compartments hidden within its curves and angles. Magdelene had always referred to it as her "altar of beauty." Tucked away in the drawers was anything a girl could wish for in the way of cosmetics or hair accessories. Magdelene had done well by her daughter. The girl had been carefully instructed in most of the feminine arts at an early age. Rebecca was never at a loss when it came to making the most of what nature had given her. She had a natural and uncanny ability to always choose the right look for the right occasion.

It was hard to hit the right mix between the gothic Salem look and the modern Rebecca. Too theatrical an appearance was not her taste, but she owed it to Peter to add a little air of glamour to his moonlight tours. The patrons exploring the ancient walks of Salem expected a bit of the "maid of Salem" look, but Rebecca had never been able to let loose and dress as many of the townsfolk did during the season. The flowing black capes, long black skirts and loose pants sported by many of the worshippers of Wicca were a bit too dramatic for Rebecca. She saw nothing wrong in the unusual garb, it was just that her beliefs ran more to the light than to the dark.

1

Rebecca's favorite colors of cream and pale blue accented the porcelain tones of her skin and deep blue of her eyes. Often to add variety she would include a touch of garnet red. Rebecca's mother had abandoned a lovely collection of garnet jewelry when she left. Included in the collection was an old garnet cross that Rebecca's mother had always referred to as a wedding gift from Rebecca's father, Sean Love. The beautiful cross had been crafted many years ago. It had always puzzled Rebecca that her mother had not taken the cross with her. It had been Magdelene's favorite piece of jewelry. She could never remember seeing her mother without it. When Rebecca had found the necklace inside the envelope that contained the money that Magdelene had left her daughter, Rebecca's fears concerning her mother's return had been eased. Surely Mama would be home soon. She never would have left her beloved cross behind if she was going to be gone long.

Over the years Rebecca had come to believe that the cross symbolized the last thing that Magdelene had cared about on this earth. If she could abandon the lovely art piece, then surely all her hopes and dreams had indeed died.

Rebecca smiled at her reflection in the wavy glass of the old mirror. She had not completely escaped the romantic mysticism of the town. Here she was placing around her lovely throat the heirloom left to her by her mother. The blood red jewels set off her creamy white skin to perfection.

Rebecca's long pale denim skirt and cream colored boots did nothing to conceal the graceful roundness of her hips or smallness of her waist. A cream colored bodysuit with a ballerina neckline enhanced her beautiful shoulders and rounded arms with a simplicity that was both charming and enchanting.

Rebecca looked around the room and realized how much she had missed her little home in the past month. The huge burlwood sleighbed piled high with a thick down comforter and matching white lace pillows looked incredibly inviting right now. Rebecca felt as if she could snuggle in and sleep forever. Perhaps the shock of the past few weeks was beginning to wear off. How proud she had been of being able to handle the arrangements for Magdelene's funeral with a clear head and a cool heart. There had not been a single tear as Rebecca had spoken to the police and the funeral director. She could tell from their eyes that the authorities expected her to break down and sob uncontrollably at the loss of her mother.

But not Rebecca. Rebecca Love had always had to be the strong one. Between mother and daughter it had been Rebecca who had mothered Magdelene. Rebecca had always thought that if her father had lived it would have been different. Rebecca could have been the beloved and coddled child of a brave and strong father and a kind and loving mother. But that was not to be. Rebecca and Magdelene had quite often resembled two survivors on a lifeboat floating in the middle of a vast ocean with no hope of ever reaching shore.

Now however, Rebecca's tempestuous redheaded mother had finally sailed for shore and Rebecca was free at last to chart her own course. At that thought Rebecca felt a strange wave of emotion overwhelm her. Unexpectantly, tears appeared in the girl's eyes and she fell on the bed awash in grief and loneliness. "Why, oh why am I so alone?" she thought. At twenty-two a girl should be flirting with beaus and mastering the world's mysteries. Here she was instead wandering through an ancient seaport town in New England with a man old enough to be her grandfather. It was so unfair! Perhaps she was more like her mother than she thought she was. Her heart was locked away in some mysterious room that no one had the key to.

Even the old museum was part of this illusion. Rebecca spent most of her days locked away in an old room sorting through the objects treasured by the dead souls of Salem. The beautiful rooms and houses, lovingly restored by the historians of Salem, were breathtaking but filled with an eerie stillness.

Where was the life and happiness that Rebecca deserved? Rebecca thought that beautiful though the museum was, it lacked the life and vitality to awaken the sleeping beauty within her.

"And now I'm off to a graveyard," she thought with a touch of irony. How like old Peter she had grown, searching for life amongst the dead, roaming with her dancing form from stone to stone examining the names and dates. Rebecca could just imagine what life had been for the souls buried under the ground in the ancient cemeteries. It was no wonder that she felt closer to her mother in death than she had ever felt to her in life. Now Rebecca was safe to look at the elusive relationship as she would a finished book. The strange waltz that the two women had performed in life was complete and Rebecca could begin to understand why she could not penetrate her mother's far away look or feel the arms that had enfolded her.

It was as if the young Rebecca had been living with a ghost for many years and the strange mist that had lain between mother and daughter had been lifted the moment Rebecca had scattered Magdelene's ashes.

CHAPTER TWO

Several hours before, Rebecca had arrived home from a long flight. The journey from far away Oregon had seemed endless. It had been a sad task to say her final farewell to her mother, but it was finished at last. "Now what?" thought Rebecca, hearing a noise as she sorted through the unruly stack of mail piled high on the kitchen table.

The lovely young woman gracefully brushed a lock of glossy dark hair away from her eyes. In the sultry afternoon sun Rebecca's normally black curls took on a shimmer and brilliance that belied the fatigue in her deep blue eyes.

Rebecca had been attempting to neatly divide the jumble of mail into some sort of order. She was on the verge of total dismay when the metal clank of the mail slot in the hall heralded another delivery.

With a sigh, the young woman went into the front hall of her small Queen Anne Victorian cottage. She checked the rug that lay inside the beautiful entranceway. What Rebecca saw was a familiar symbol drawn on one side of a small piece of folded paper.

The question mark surrounded by a triangle was a part of a secret ritual that Rebecca and her beloved old friend Peter Hawking had made up years ago when Rebecca was a small girl. She had spent most of her time following old Professor Hawking around the dusty Essex Museum, listening to his every word as he spoke about the mysteries and legends that surrounded Salem Town.

The lovely intense little girl had soon been noticed by the old historian. They quickly became accomplices in many a journey through the Salem libraries and museums in search of a way to make the fascinating history of the old city live again.

Whenever a new adventure was at hand Peter would slide a special note through the mail slot. The question mark symbolized a new mystery, and the triangle, the ancient knowledge of the early Celtic sorcerers. Rebecca and Peter had spent one lazy summer afternoon sitting on a carved stone bench, discussing just what their secret signal would be. The bench, memorializing Giles Cory, the Salem witch who had died in 1692, lent exactly the right inspiration to their discussion. The Salem witch memorial was located next to Old Burial Point, the old graveyard on Charter Street, that had been established in 1632.

"Whenever I send this missal to my lady, she is honor bound to accompany Sir Peter Hawking on a new quest."

"But of course my faithful champion, how could I deny you the blessing of my indescribable presence?" giggled the little girl covered with the dirt and chocolate accumulated from a day of mucking through her favorite haunts.

At ten the young Rebecca was already far wiser than her years, both from necessity and as a result of her formidable intelligence.

As the years passed, the two friends had developed a deep trust in one another born out of loneliness and a shared love of beautiful and ancient things.

Rebecca, who had never known her real father, felt instinctively drawn to the old bachelor. She felt that he was the grandfather she would never have. How wonderful it would have been if Rebecca's mother could have asked Professor Hawking to live with them, but Rebecca knew that her wish was only a dream.

Magdelene Love would never have settled for the quiet life of caring for an old man and a young girl. Magdelene needed to dance and sing and create as much noise as she could to drown out the sadness of her yearning soul.

If only Mama could have seen Peter with his eyes aflame, hot on the trail of a new discovery. "Oh well Mama, wherever your soul is, I hope you have found peace at last."

Rebecca had come home one day, five long years ago, to discover that her mother's belongings and few pieces of jewelry had disappeared. At first the high school senior had thought that their small home had been robbed until she discovered a note scribbled in pencil and placed on the small marble mantle next to the delicate pink and white Dresden shepherdess statue that Peter had given Rebecca for her twelfth birthday.

Darling Becca,

I've gone on a small adventure. Please don't worry about Mama, she can take care of herself. You have become such a big girl. I am sure that you can do quite well without me for a few weeks. In this envelope is more than enough to take care of things until I can come home to you.

Stay well and study hard my little bookworm.

Hugs and kisses for always,

Maggie Mom

That note was the last word that Rebecca had received from her mother until a month ago when a telegram had been delivered to the small house in Salem. It arrived on a beautiful September afternoon. As she opened it, Rebecca had already known that her mother was gone. In her heart, the girl had buried her mother several years before. The enchanting Magdelene Love had perished in a car crash in faraway Oregon. The local police department of Cliffside Bend had found a picture of Rebecca in Magdelene's purse along with an address for the small cottage in Salem, Massachusetts.

In shock, Rebecca had packed a blue flowered bag and flown to the faraway Pacific coast. She had seen to it that her mother's ashes were properly scattered out over the ocean. As the last of the ashes disappeared, Rebecca couldn't help but think that finally Magdelene was as free as she had always wanted to be in life.

On the flight back Rebecca had felt nothing but a profound relief that at last she too could begin to find some peace. The weariness that engulfed her was deep yet filled with a certain lightness that the girl had never experienced. Unknown to her, she had been dreading the last chapter of her mother's life for years. Now that it was past Rebecca was free from that sadness that had engulfed both Magdelene and her lovely young daughter.

CHAPTER THREE

Rebecca and Magdelene had settled in Salem many years ago when Magdelene had fallen hopelessly in love with the dashing Sean Love. The result of their tempestuous union had been the lovely little girl with thick dark hair and sparkling blue eyes.

Rebecca's handsome father had been well over six feet tall, with the same abundant curling hair and deep blue eyes that his little daughter had inherited. The small dimple to the left of the rosebud mouth had also been bequeathed to Rebecca by her father. The child's sinuous grace and poise had been a gift from the fascinating red-headed Magdelene.

The result had been the fabulous Rebecca, a powerful force to be reckoned with even as a baby.

When the handsome Sean had been found drowned in Collins Cove one cold October night, Magdelene had sworn never to love again. She had taken all that life could give her in the name of pleasure, but never again had she given her heart to anyone, not even her delightful little daughter.

By the time that Magdelene had left the little house in Salem, her soul had been gone for many years. In a way Rebecca's only family had been the faithful Peter. He had quietly acted as mother, father and mentor for many years.

It was Peter who had helped the girl finish high school early and arranged for a job at the museum. With Peter's help

Rebecca had received a full scholarship to Salem State College and had been able to support herself.

No one had been prouder than the old professor when Rebecca had received her degree in historical archeology. How they had celebrated. Peter's old black spaniel Sable ended the party by jumping onto the table and eating most of the lopsided graduation cake that Peter had painstakingly baked and decorated.

This last summer had passed with the girl and her faithful friend making plans to tour the castles of England and Scotland in the fall.

It had been their precious vacation fund that had financed Rebecca's flight to Oregon and Magdelene's funeral. Peter had insisted that it didn't matter, but Rebecca had seen a wistful look cross his face as he waved good-bye to her.

CHAPTER FOUR

Returning to reality, Rebecca realized that Peter must have been walking by her house as he dropped the note through the slot. "Why hadn't he rung the bell and come breezing in as he usually does?" thought Rebecca as she picked up his note. "Perhaps I can catch him!" Rebecca opened the door and looked up and down the red brick street. The old man had already disappeared. Peter, for all his years, could move quickly when he wanted to.

Of course, this was his busy season. All the soothsayers, psychics, witches and historians in Salem ran special exhibits and tours for the thousands of tourists who crowded into Salem every fall. This year a torchlight parade had been held on Friday the Thirteenth to usher in the unusually busy and festive Halloween season.

Rebecca knew that Peter's ghost tours had been sold out for weeks. Perhaps if business had been brisker than usual they could still steal some time away and realize Peter's dream of his Celtic castle tour. How she had missed their annual prowl with crowds of tourists following in excited anticipation, carrying candles and lanterns in search of an elusive ghost or vengeful witch.

The autumn moonlight usually cooperated by casting eerie shadows across the faces of awed out of towners. Rebecca often felt quite close to these strangers drawn to her beloved city by the same air of mystery that the girl herself loved so much.

"Welcome home, my Lady," read the small note in the young woman's hand. "Salem's premiere seer requests your presence at Burying Point cemetery when the light leaves the sky and the autumn wind is stilled by the spirits of the night, seven o'clock should be good, as that is when all the hopefuls will be gathered in anticipation of an enchanted evening. It is time to begin to lift the veil between this world and the next.

CHAPTER FIVE

"Here we go again," smiled Rebecca. Some things, thank God, never changed, and one of those things was Peter's love of fantasy. Many would have been surprised to discover how whimsical the old professor was. Peter was convinced that every Halloween ushered in a moment when the veil between the real world and the spirit world was so thin that perhaps he could catch a glimpse of all the mysteries he had spent a lifetime studying.

An old sea captain or a diabolical pirate might pick this Halloween to unburden his dark secrets to the esteemed Peter Hawking. Peter was, after all, a direct descendant of Giles Cory, the crusty old New Englander who had been crushed to death between two stones in 1692. Cory had been accused of witchcraft, but refused to utter a word once he was arrested. The brave old man had been a voice of silent sanity in an otherwise insane time. As a result, old Giles had retained the titles to his lands. By remaining silent he refused to accept his fate. The orphaned Cory children, who had lost their father on September 19th, 1692, and seen their mother hanged on September 22, 1692, were allowed to keep their father's land. The mute Giles Cory had only uttered two words as the good people of Salem were torturing him to death between two stones. "More weight, more weight," had been his last words. The man had died knowing that his children would be saved as a result of his bravery. Such were the ancestors of the resourceful Peter Hawking.

Perhaps this would be the year that dear old Peter would finally meet the brave Giles Cory. If anyone could conjure him up it would be Peter.

Rebecca had a secret wish that she had told no one, not even Peter. To her the notorious sea captain, Jamie O'Roarke, had always been the symbol of Salem's great age of sail. Handsome Captain O'Roarke had stood alone against the merchants of Salem when the infamous triangle trade was being born in New England. The merchants were determined to trade their gold and rum for African slaves. Jamie O'Roarke had refused to transport human flesh and as a result found himself a penniless outcast. The once moral O'Roarke had turned bitter and taken to piracy, swearing revenge on the wealthy of Salem Town.

What would have happened to the great merchant mansions on Chestnut Street and surrounding Salem Common if Captain O'Roarke had succeeded in turning the town from the unbelievable profits to be made in slavery and human suffering? "Perhaps," said more than one stout businessman, "it was the hand of the Almighty that had guided the noose around the neck of the Captain of the 'Red Witch.'"

Rebecca could never help but wonder how history would have been changed in New England if Captain O'Roarke could have persuaded the people of New England to abandon the triangle trade. In a way Rebecca's own father had been an echo of the gallant Captain O'Roarke. Both had been dashing Irishmen who had loved the sea and had been taken away in the fullness of life.

Magdelene Love had never spoken to her daughter about the sudden circumstances of Sean's death, but there had been a silent agreement that many questions had been left unanswered.

As the sun set over the Common, Rebecca gazed out the window. The many small lights that the Salem Chamber of

Commerce had strung on the great elms were twinkling into life as the shadows of night chased away the last brilliant red and gold of the late October afternoon. "How beautiful it is," sighed Rebecca as she went back into her bedroom to put the finishing touches on her annual graveyard garb.

CHAPTER SIX

Rebecca closed the solid wooden doors and breathed in the spiciness of the early evening air. Several houses surrounding the Common were burning wood in the beautiful fireplaces designed by Samuel McIntire almost two hundred years ago. Rebecca could smell the aroma of the wood smoke encircling her. It felt like a living, breathing thing, vibrating with an almost electrical energy. Perhaps Peter was right, there was a thinness to the air this time of year that seemed peculiar to Salem. Tonight was All Hallow's Eve and the thick mist of Salem was wrapping itself around the townsfolk with a mystery impossible to describe to an outsider. The many people who traveled to Salem this time of year could never have explained what the magic of the town had to offer to someone who had not been there. Only those initiated into its mysteries could understand.

The red brick sidewalks melted into the lushness of the Common as Rebecca made her way towards the oldest graveyard in Salem. The twinkling trees delicately echoed the murmuring voices of the many visitors as they made their way from one haunted happening to another. Clutched in their hands were black and gold brochures showing the way to Nathaniel Hawthorne's House of Seven Gables and the spooky Pirate Museum. It was not unusual for Rebecca to be stopped by a family from Japan or a visitor from Australia and be asked directions to the Witch House. A shared love of the ancient mysteries of the supernatural enticed many to the small New England town.

On Saturday everyone had set their clocks back an hour so the darkness was even more profound than it had been a week ago.

"Happy Halloween, Miss Love," came a shout as Rebecca passed the basketball court filled with a group of boys from Federal Street School.

"Happy Halloween, Daniel," cried Rebecca, waving as she recognized one of the students she had met as a substitute teacher at the school in early September. Even though she had only spent a few days at the school helping out, Rebecca had come to know and love the irrepressible Daniel. Rebecca had volunteered as a substitute fourth grade teacher until the school had hired a permanent one and there was more than one moment when she wished she could have stayed. Unfortunately she was a girl on her own and the part-time position did not pay her what she made at the museum. Besides there was Peter to think about. What would he have done without her? The pulsating life of the school was in sharp contrast to the dry dustiness of the old museum.

Rebecca had been astonished when she realized that she could persuade a group of nine-year-olds to not only listen to her, but accomplish something. To her amazement she found that she was quite good at it. Oh, she had her difficulties, but once young Daniel had decided that Miss Love was the most beautiful creature that had ever walked the face of the earth, Rebecca's troubles were over. Daniel was a natural leader, and like Rebecca herself had grown up early. Rebecca would often bump into him at the library or at Crosby's grocery store with his little sister in tow. Daniel and his small sister Emily were inseparable. Daniel tried to pretend that he couldn't stand the way six-year-old Emily gazed at him with total adoration, but Rebecca could tell that Daniel would have stepped in front of a bus for the sweet little girl with the huge brown eyes.

"Where are you going, Miss Love?" asked a breathless Daniel as he ran after her. His companions on the basketball court were looking at him in astonishment. After all, Danny was the best player they had and here he was interrupting one of the last warm sunny afternoons in the fall to go running after Miss Love, the substitute teacher. What was the matter with him?

"Miss Love, where have you been? The old professor said you had gone to Oregon and didn't know when you'd be back. My little sister got sick and we didn't know what was wrong with her. The doctor at the walk-in center said she was real sick but we had no insurance, so I took her to Salem hospital. They said she had asthma and pneumonia, but they wouldn't let her stay because of the insurance thing. Ma said we couldn't go back 'cause she was afraid. Emily was so sick you see, so I remembered that you worked at the museum, and went to see you. But you weren't there. Then I told the old professor who likes you what I wanted and he took Emily back to the hospital and raised a stink. So now Emily's okay and she has this medicine that I make her take. Now, where were you?"

"Daniel, slow down, it's all right, I'm here now," said an astounded Rebecca, amazed in the total trust the young boy had placed in her. His rush of words betrayed a fondness that she had never imagined. "I'm so glad your sister is better, but why did you come looking for me, don't you have someone else who would have helped?"

"No one who could have, Miss Love," said the boy with a mixture of embarrassment and defiant pride. "I can take care of my sister. It was that stupid hospital that couldn't. You see, they needed an adult to sign all these papers and they said I wasn't old enough. But I knew you would. You like Emily and you know how it really is. Someday I'm going to be a man, maybe a doctor, and show them all. Ma is just having a hard time now. Her boyfriend left her and she's not feeling so well, she sleeps an awful lot, but she'll be better, I know. So you see

19

I am the adult, only I can't let anyone know or they'll blame Ma and take us away from her. The professor is all right. I knew that he would understand and help us, you could just tell. What does he do there at the museum, undertake or something?"

Laughing, Rebecca gave the young boy a hug. "In a way you're close, Daniel. Why don't you come with me and I'll show you."

"Really, me and you, I mean you and me?" said Danny in red faced excitement. "Wait right here, I'll get my jacket."

Rebecca watched the solid boy run back to his friends, astonished that she had asked him to come along. She never asked anyone to be with her. Even Peter had a habit of appearing when he was wanted rather than being asked. Now to Rebecca's amazement young Danny had caught her when her defenses were down. Here she was about to have to endure his companionship for a ghost hunt through Salem.

"Can't leave this there," said Danny as he ran back to her with a glowing face. Rebecca knew that Danny's black and orange witch city jacket was his most prized possession. He had spent countless afternoons delivering the Salem Evening News to pay for it.

"Miss Love, thanks, this is great. But do me a favor. If you see any of the guys and they mention me going with you, could you kinda tell them it was a school thing?"

"Sure kid," said Rebecca, resisting an urge to give Danny a hug. "We wouldn't want to spoil your reputation."

CHAPTER SEVEN

The whistling boy and the graceful young woman made their way across Hawthorne Boulevard as the last of the red light faded from the sky. In the distance Rebecca could hear the last of the ships in the harbor sailing for home. The eternal foghorns, that even sounded on sunny days, signaled the vessels approaching Derby Wharf and Collins Cove. A tall thin man dressed as a vampire was standing on the corner passing out brochures to Dracula's Castle. The line forming at Laurie Cabot's Crow Haven Corner was already stretched around the block with more people adding to the gathering every moment. Salem was alive with both serious worshippers of Wicca and adults and children reveling in the fun and frolic of All Hallow's Eve in the Halloween capital of the world.

"Miss Love, could we stop at Sweet Scoops? Emily is waiting there for me. I asked Mr. Columbo if she could stay there while I finished my game. She's already gonna be mad at me. I promised to take her trick or treating, but can she come with us? I sorta promised her that she could hang out with me."

"Oh Danny, I don't know," said Rebecca, "we're going to a graveyard. Won't such a little girl be scared?"

"Emily? Are you kiddin'," replied Danny looking at Rebecca with an amused and oddly sophisticated air. "Emily's favorite book is 'Bunnicula,' you know, the story about the

21

vampire bunny. I could recite it to you by heart I've read it to her so many times. The library said she had to let someone else take it out this month, she was hoggin it so much. So you see, I don't think a little graveyard is gonna scare that kid at all."

"All right, Danny, but promise me, if she starts to get quivery, you'll take her home," said Rebecca, hoping she wouldn't regret taking two children along with her tonight of all nights.

As they entered Sweet Scoops, Rebecca spied the pretty little Emily sitting behind the counter with a huge ice-cream cone clutched in her small hand. Mr. Columbo, the owner, had obviously found the way to this small woman's heart.

"Where have you been, Danny?" The little Emily spoke with the imperious air of a great queen perched on an imperial throne. "All the good candy will be gone if we don't hurry up," she said clutching in her other hand a large Crosby's grocery bag already bulging with treats.

"What are you talking about, you little faker? You've already scammed the neighborhood. Look at all that stuff. You're gonna be sick if you don't stop. If you went out alone, I'm gonna tell Mom."

"Mom's asleep, she won't care. Anyway she told me I could go out if I wanted to."

"She did not, you fibber," said an exasperated Danny with an age old sigh.

"Did so," replied his little sister with an air of superiority. "She was sleepin' and I woke her up and asked her. She said 'yes,' and went back to sleep. So you see she did say yes and I didn't bother her or nuthin'. Anyway you can't tell me what to do. You're not my mother."

"No, but Ma said you were supposed to listen to me. I don't want you gettin' killed, do you hear me!"

22

"Okay, okay," said the little girl slipping from behind the counter, knowing that she had gone too far. "I'm sorry, really I am. So how about it, let's go around the block one more time. The Maloons are giving out plastic spiders and flies. I won't eat anymore, I promise. Besides, I don't feel so good."

"No more candy, Emily. Miss Love and I have something important to do," said Danny sounding as adult as he was trying to. "You know the old professor who helped us when you were sick? He needs us to help him in the graveyard tonight, that is if you don't act like a baby and get scared."

"I'm not a baby," said the infuriated little girl, giving her brother a surprisingly hard whack on the shoulder. "Miss Love, I can help, really. Whatever Danny said about me isn't true if he said I was a baby."

" Emily, really, it's quite all right if you come along," said Rebecca, giving up any hope of salvaging any peaceful retreat out of this night. "But remember, the professor will be conjuring up the spirits of the dead. We must be very quiet so that he doesn't make a mistake and bring forth an evil one."

"Oh Miss Love, there really aren't any spirits, they're all just make believe, don't you know that, just like Santa Claus," said the little girl with an all knowing expression. "Danny says there are spirits, but what does he know, he's only a brother."

With that little Emily looked up at Rebecca with heartbreaking earnestness that seemed to invade Rebecca's very being.

"How do you know for sure, sweetheart?" Rebecca stooped down and looked into the child's eyes. "There are more things in heaven and earth than we mere mortals can know," she said mysteriously, hoping to break through the small girl's unchildish cynicism. "Let's go find the professor and find out."

CHAPTER EIGHT

The old graveyard, located a few steps away from the original Salem dungeon that had housed the first "witches" of Salem, was crowded. It was filled with both the merely curious and the awe inspired.

The more serious of the visitors were assembled around a distinguished looking man dressed all in black. Even though he was in his mid-seventies, Professor Peter Hawking had lost none of his awe inspiring height or masculine appeal. The old man had a majestic shock of thick, pure white hair that waved back from his high, intelligent forehead. He still stood, despite his age, over six feet with none of the stoop that could be attributed to most men his age. This was due, in large part, to the fact that he walked almost everywhere he needed to go. His bright blue eyes and ruddy complexion bespoke a man in magnificent health.

The secret of Peter Hawking's seemingly eternal youth was a love of life, his work and a rare purity of heart. He found great joy in journeys through the past and was never happier than when he had a group of earnest disciples gathered around him. Rebecca could tell, by the proud set of his head and the light in his sparkling blue eyes, that tonight would be one of those special nights. Tonight Peter Hawking would set the imaginations and minds of all those listening to him on fire.

"You're quite right, sir," said Peter, addressing a large man in his late thirties, wearing a white knit fisherman's sweater. "All Hallow's Eve was originally a pagan holiday. The ancient Druids would celebrate the eve of the Celtic new year by gathering around great bonfires retelling the old legends. On the eve of Samhein the beautiful Goddess would take her leave and the Celtic wisemen would welcome the protection of the God to guide them through the perilous dark of winter. Then on the feast of Beltaine, known to us as May Day, the Goddess returns to us, in all her glory, to replenish the earth. Many modern day folks think of the feast of Beltaine as a pagan orgy, but it was truly the uniting of the priests and priestesses of Wicca. And speaking of Goddesses, not orgies, let me introduce a quite learned and lovely representative of the museum to you. Rebecca, my dear, how good it is of you to join us. May I present Miss Rebecca Love, the heart of the archeology department here at the Peabody-Essex museum."

The crowd, giving their attention to Rebecca, spoke a collective hello as Peter, standing behind them, looked quite pleased with himself for luring his favorite young recluse out of her home on one of the less intellectual pursuits the museum had to offer.

"Rebecca, my dear, perhaps you can fill our friends in on the rest of the mysteries of Samhein," said Peter, knowing that the girl could never resist an invitation to share her vast knowledge.

"Of course, Professor Hawking, I would be delighted to," said Rebecca with a smile, knowing that Peter had just lured her into being a full participant in his All Hallow's Eve reveries.

"Modern Christianity," began the girl, "has incorporated these festivals into its own religions, specifically with the celebrations of All Hallow's Eve, Christmas and Easter. But even the coming of Christianity could not completely erase the old ways. Merlin the magician was believed to be a Druid high priest and in direct opposition to the new religion introduced by Arthur's Queen Guenivere. The King was a pagan and the Queen was one of the first Christians. For several thousands of years the ancient Celtic religion has been threatened with extinction. Even the people of Salem persecuted the old believers. Today there are still many followers of the Goddess in this very city. They wear black at the time of Samhein because they believe that black is the color that gathers all life force to them. On All Hallow's Eve, the followers of Wicca feel that the veil between the living world and the spirit world grows very thin enabling them to communicate with souls, or ghosts as you would call them. These spirits are as alive as you or I to those who believe in the Goddess. Professor Hawking, whose family never abandoned its reverence for the Goddess, hopes to bring you face to face with several of the spirits who roam on this All Hallow's Eve."

"Thank you, Miss Love" replied Peter eyeing the group formed in a circle around them with a mixture of authority and merriment. "There have been many unexplained mysteries that have occurred in Salem throughout the centuries, and who knows, tonight we may add one or two more. If you will follow me, I will introduce you to some of them."

"Miss Love, does the Professor really talk to ghosts?" Danny suspiciously eyed the friendly old man who had spent a full day helping two children out of the goodness of his heart.

"Why yes, Danny, I think he does, at least I believe that he believes he does. I've known the Professor since I was your age and there has always been something about him that seemed not of this world. If anyone could talk to ghosts it would be Professor Hawking."

"Emily, do you believe in ghosts?" asked Rebecca, still a little concerned that the small girl might become overwhelmed by the tour.

"Of course not," said Emily trying to look very adult. "Stuff about ghosts is just a make believe story like 'Bunnicula,' but I think getting scared is cool. I do it to Danny all the time. You should see him when I hide in his closet and make scratching sounds."

"Ah, I see we have two special guests this evening," said Peter overhearing the conversation. "Well, come along, children are often most useful when attempting to help the spirits travel from their sphere to ours."

"What does he mean, Miss Love? We're not going to be a human sacrifice or nuthin' are we?" asked young Emily, not feeling quite as brave as she thought she was.

"No dear, you're quite safe, I promise. Professor Hawking is just having some Halloween fun, aren't you Professor," said Rebecca with a glare at Peter that telegraphed that he should watch the melodramatics.

"That's quite right, child. No harm will come to you this night. You have my solemn promise."

Emily, intrigued by the professor, moved to his side and took his hand. Her face, gazing up at the old man, shone with a childlike trust that Danny hadn't seen in years. In a way the boy was experiencing an odd feeling of jealousy. Emily had never looked at anyone with such trust, not even him. But of course, the Professor was like a grandfather, and it couldn't hurt to have a real adult around in case she got sick again. Comforted by these conflicting thoughts, Danny gave a sigh and thought, not for the first time, that life with Emily could be confusing, but never dull.

"Now, let us proceed," said Professor Hawking, as the night wind began to pick up. The old elms that encircled Burying Point were making a dry creaking sound that seemed to add an almost lifelike dimension to them. From somewhere in the old neighborhood a dog was howling, sounding more like a lone wolf than someone's treasured pet. The full moon, sailing out from behind the silvery clouds, seemed to cast a shimmering glow on the small band of ghost hunters below. There was a certain heaviness in the air, as if the elements around the searchers were about to give birth to an unholy child. Every once in a while a far off rumble of thunder could be heard, more as a whisper than as a threat. The energized atmosphere infused the tour with an almost sensual anticipation.

Burying Point graveyard, established in 1632, was a treasure trove of early New England history. It was a small area, less than half an acre, but it contained the remains of an original Mayflower passenger, some Puritans, a judge of the famous witchcraft trial, and several privateers suspected of being pirates. Mary Cory, the first wife of Peter's ancestor Giles, was buried there also. As Peter led the intrigued visitors from one stone to the next he experienced a strange feeling of foreboding. The whispers he was hearing were not the result of old age or whimsical foolishness. There were others buried here. Many of the stones had disintegrated or been worn away by time. The stories of the unmarked graves were, to Peter Hawking, the most fascinating of all. Salem was notorious for the witchcraft trials and renown for its place in maritime history, but only a little of its bloodthirsty history of piracy was known. Many the soul of an early governor and merchant of the area had blood on it. The voices of the dead, that were calling to Peter Hawking from the air around him, were very different from what he had experienced before. They were alive with an intensity that he had never felt.

CHAPTER NINE

The Halloween revelers who had earlier been roaming Burying Point were leaving in search of one of the many dances and parties being given in town. All around the Common private homes and the Knights of Columbus Hall and the Hawthorne Hotel were holding costume parties. Hamilton Hall on historic Chestnut Street was known for the elegance of its celebration. A few years ago National Geographic had sent a crew to Salem to photograph the premiere Halloween party in the country.

Burying Point, now devoid of small boys and girls dressed as witches and skeletons accompanied by their parents in equally ghoulish costume, took on a more sinister feeling. More that one participant of the tour wandered away now that the formal information given by the old professor was at an end. The small flickers of the candles were extinguished one by one until only a few serious souls remained. The faithful few consisted of Peter, Rebecca, the children Danny and Emily, and two others. These two strangers were a man and a woman obviously related and as serious about Samhein and its ancient importance as were Peter and Rebecca.

One of the strangers was a lovely woman in her early sixties with pale blond hair that looked almost silvery with the strands of white gray that mixed through her locks. Her huge green eyes would have been almost catlike if it were not for the gentle goodness that radiated from them. Her sensual yet motherly form was draped in the finest of light weight wool in heather colored lavender. The delicate scent that emanated from her made Professor Hawing think of the first day of Spring, not All Hallow's Eve. Just looking at the woman seemed to dispel some of his foreboding. The man accompanying her was much younger, in his early to middle thirties. He was not only large, but massive, with a strangely sinuous quality. His movements, for all his size, made one think of a panther. When Rebecca and Peter had attended the highland games at the old Boston Garden several years before there had been many such men dressed in kilts playing bagpipes and performing the dashing sword dances of bonny Scotland. Even though the man with dark red hair and deep green eyes was dressed in a white fisherman's sweater and dark blue wool pants, Rebecca had no trouble imagining him climbing the craggy rocks of the Scottish shore in full kilt and sword.

"Well," said Peter not at all dismayed that the party had shrunk to the faithful few, "now we can get down to the real business of the night. Since our party has become so intimate, perhaps we should all proceed on a first name basis. My name as you know is Peter, and our young friends are Daniel and Emily, but I do not believe I've had the pleasure of personally meeting you, lovely lady," said Peter to the lavender vision before him.

"Oh, Professor Hawking, how kind of you to ask. My nephew and I have come a long way, hoping for just such an opportunity. Let me introduce us. My name is Arabella MacRae and this is my nephew Ian. We have traveled all the way from the Isle of Skye, in Scotland, to be here tonight. I have been hoping that you might be able to help us. You see our very lives may depend on your being able to solve a mystery that has haunted the Lairds of MacRae Castle for centuries."

"Why, whatever do you mean, dear lady? Nothing could be as serious as all that! Who would want to harm such a gentle creature?" said Peter, utterly forgetting about any voices around him but the musical one of Arabella MacRae.

"Professor, you must help us. Is there a possibility that Captain Jamie O'Roarke is buried here?" Lady MacRae gazed directly into Peter's eyes. "If he is then perhaps we can contact him tonight. You said yourself that All Hallow's Eve is our best chance. Oh professor, we must try!"

"My dear lady, I'm afraid it's not quite that simple. I have been trying all my life to get a spirit to cross over. Even though the veil is thin, ghosts do not appear upon command," said Peter, exasperated by the beautiful lady's complete ignorance of the situation.

"Oh, but we could try couldn't we? If anyone can do it you can," replied the lovely Arabella, touching his arm gently.

"My lady," said Peter astounded at what he was about to say, "if you wish I will try, but please don't be disappointed when all we get is a pleasant evening in an old graveyard."

CHAPTER TEN

"Ah, but this a bonny brae," said Ian MacRae, as he hugged his Aunt. Ian had many other things to do with his time and it had cost him a valuable portrait commission to accompany his Aunt on this fool's errand, but, after all, Aunt Bella was the kindest soul who had ever trod the earth. When Ian's parents had been killed in an accident when he was a child, it had been the beautiful Arabella MacRae who had comforted the frightened little boy and shown him the beauty of the murky brae's of Scotland. Ian's father, the younger brother of Lord Alan MacRae, had never had much use for his ancestral home and as a result, young Ian knew little of his family. Mary and Walter MacRae had disappeared from Ian's life forever the day their small plane had plunged into the waters of the English Channel. The orphaned boy had been too small to remember his parents as more than mere shadows of his half remembered babyhood. Alan and Arabella MacRae had become his real parents.

Aunt Arabella had always been haunted by the old legends of the treasure of Duncan MacRae. The treasure had been captured by the notorious pirate, Jamie O'Roarke, over three hundred years ago. It was this event that had given birth to the "curse of the MacRaes." Ian's dainty but courageous Aunt Arabella was determined that the MacRaes should no longer be victims of the vengeful Captain Jamie O'Roarke.

Ian had been pleasantly surprised as they motored down the New England coast towards the small city of Salem. There was something about the region that reminded him of home. The salty scent of the sea and the rocky coastline were comforting to him. Even the people they met when they had stopped for lunch reminded him of his kin. The wary curtness of the New Englander showed a caution of strangers that Ian could respect. Only a fool rattled off at the mouth. A Scotsman would always get to know the lay of the land before he spent his time or money. These New Englanders were worthy of his respect.

The fog surrounding the town of Salem gave Ian a further impression of a home away from home. Here were people who knew the sea, the mist and the enchantment of both.

Why, even the bonny lassie standing near him now gave him a feeling of comfort. The beautiful Rebecca was having an almost intoxicating effect on him. The usually reserved and analytical Ian MacRae found himself trying to get a closer look at the dark waviness of her hair and her bonny blue eyes. When the charming lass had begun to speak in the educated tones of a scholar, Ian had stopped thinking of her as a possible subject of a portrait and begun to believe that perhaps angels did indeed walk the earth. Was it possible that Aunt Bella's roving nephew could be tamed? It would be intriguing to find out what the beautiful American Miss could teach him about Salem. She was indeed a darling.

Ian's past had been filled with many lovely ladies but none that had the wit and wisdom of this lass. She would be worth more than a whisper in the moonlight. Lips like hers made a man think of true love, and weddings at the kirk in the glen. This beautiful woman was not for light vows made under the moon lasting only until sunrise.

"Come now my cowen, my non-Wiccan friends, it is time to begin our ceremony. The moon has spoken to the earth and the hour approaches."

Peter Hawking felt rather uncomfortable about his role as high priest to this small group, but once he had promised Lady Arabella that he would do his best he was not about to go back on his word. The spirits he had felt gathering around him on this feast of Samhein were giving him stronger powers than he had ever experienced before. Peter felt as if his body were emanating with the glow of their enchantment. What made this night so different from the countless others he had spent in this very spot? Perhaps it was the collection of believers about him. The faithful consisted of two pure souls, Emily and Daniel Martin, the enchanting Rebecca, Lady Arabella MacRae and her nephew, Ian and himself, one of the last true bloods of the old religion. Yes, perhaps it was enough to bring together the forces of All Hallow's Eve.

Peter, gathering the small band around a spot on the darkest side of the graveyard, drew the hood from his black wool cloak over his head. Thinking of nothing but the light within his own soul, he gathered the unseen forces around him into his being. Peter was surprised at the number of murmuring voices that invaded his spirit. Drawing a circle around the great oak that stood beside a crumbling stone wall, Professor Peter Hawking began the ritual spell that had been used by countless worshippers of Wicca since the beginning of time. The powerful chanting rune was only to be used under special circumstance, for to use it was to raise the power of those who had passed beyond the veil. Peter knew there was always a price to be exacted in return for any favor granted from beyond.

Rebecca, sensing that her old friend Peter had taken on the glamour of some ancient mystic, felt herself shiver and draw closer to the strong Scotsman standing beside her. The two children, intrigued and shielded by their innocence, were standing on either side of Lady Arabella enjoying the arm she had put on each child's shoulder. The kindly Lady instinctively gathered the children into the circle of her protection. Lady MacRae may have looked fragile, but that air of delicacy covered up the heart of a Scottish warrior.

Ian MacRae looked sideways at the lovely Rebecca and gave her a reassuring smile. "Don't be alarmed, lassie," he said in a deep melodious voice, "I am sure the old professor's spells are harmless, we'll be out of here safely by midnight."

"Ah, Mr. MacRae, I'm afraid you may be underestimating Professor Hawking. I have seen many things about him that defy explanation. He often knows what is going on around him before the rest of us. I remember once when I had cut my foot the phone rang and it was the Peter telling me to go to the emergency room because I needed stitches and a tetanus shot. How he knew about my injury I can't tell but I do know that I was in shock and not capable of thinking for myself. He has always been more aware than most of us. There are times when it has seemed to me he sees things on a totally different level than you or I."

"Now, Miss Love, I am as open as the next person to the unusual, but do you really believe all this talk about spells and spirits?"

"I hope you won't think me foolish Mr. MacRae, but yes, I believe I do. If you had asked me before Peter Hawking came into my life if I would have answered that way I would have said no, but I have seen too many things that can't be explained away by logic. Anyway let's see what happens. Perhaps your voice of reason will prevail."

"In a way I hope that your belief in spirits is true, Miss Love. My Aunt has placed so much hope in this journey. If it takes the ghost of a pirate to dispel her fears, then so be it."

"Why, Mr. MacRae, you are a romantic after all, just like the rest of us," said Rebecca, closely appraising the undeniably handsome man beside her. There was something about Ian MacRae that made her wish she had bothered to put on some deep red lipstick.

Ian and Rebecca moved closer to each other, feeling a strange attraction that neither could understand. As the wind picked up, blowing the leaves around them, Rebecca felt safe standing next to the powerfully built man from Scotland.

Peter Hawking, glancing around the small circle one last time, gave himself up to the ancient witch's rune.

> *Darksome night and shining moon*
> *East, then South, then West then North*
> *Harken to the witch's rune*
> *For here I come to call you forth!*
> *Earth and Water, Air and Fire*
> *Wand and pentacle and sword,*
> *Work you all to my desire, Hark you all unto my word!*
> *Cords and censor, scourge and knife,*
> *Powers of the witch's blade,*
> *Wake now unto life.*
> *Come now as the charm is made!*
> *Queen of heaven, Queen of hell,*
> *Horned hunter of the night,*
> *Lend your power unto my spell,*
> *Work my will by magic right!*
> *By all the power of land and sea,*
> *By all the might of moon and sun,*
> *As I do will, so might it be!*
> *Chant the spell and be it DONE!*

The "second sight" that Peter Hawking had been blessed with now stood him in good stead as he stepped back quickly from the old oak tree. The Oak King himself could have used such a haven for his winter's sleep. As Peter closed the spell with a raising of both arms to the heavens, a great splintering of wood showered the small group with leaves and wood particles. Miraculously, no one was hurt by the flying debris. Ian, shielding Rebecca with his body, could only pray that Aunt Arabella had moved away from the explosion. There had been no time to protect her from the hail that spewed forth from the old oak. Looking up, he was relieved to see

Arabella shaken but unharmed, gathering the remarkably calm but equally unhurt Emily and Daniel to her bosom.

As the moon sailed from behind a cloud, the small group of stunned adventurers were amazed at what they saw. The immense oak that had stood since before the Revolution was split in two. Surrounding the once proud old tree were the remains of branches and leaves, scattering in the evening wind.

Standing where the mighty oak had stood was the figure of a man. In the dim light Rebecca could tell that he was strong and heavily built. The moonlight shone on his golden blond hair that was tied back with a black satin ribbon. The man's face should have been hideous with the saber cut that ran the full length of his right cheek, but in the case of the apparition before them it only served to enhance his strong chin and chiseled features. The lines around the deep brown eyes bespoke a man in his early forties who had seen the world and weathered many storms.

The long blue coat and the sword at his side were in stark contrast with the sparkling white linen that shown from his collar and cuffs. His strong legs, encased in black leather boots that reached to his mid thighs, gave the impression of a man who could move quickly when he had to. Perched on his head at a rakish angle was a black tri-cornered hat edged in blue. To complete the picture the man sported a magnificent mustache and beard, carefully trimmed and groomed to perfection.

Carefully taking in his surroundings at a glance, the dashing stranger looked straight into Rebecca's eyes and gave a sweeping bow, taking off his hat and brushing the ground with it, as he completed the greeting.

"It is a delight to at last meet you in the flesh, my dear Rebecca," said Captain Jamie O'Roarke.

PART TWO

SALEM, MASSACHUSETTS
1695

CHAPTER ELEVEN

Captain O'Roarke quickly covered the ground that separated the dashing world weary pirate from the beautiful young girl. He took her hand, exhibiting surprising gracefulness, and kissed her fingertips. The handsome O'Roarke's dark eyes never left Rebecca's.

"What a joy it is to feel the touch and warmth of life again. It's been many years since this old pirate has had the intoxicating pleasure of breathing in the perfume of so charming a lady."

"Why, Captain O'Roarke, you quite take my breath away," said Rebecca, who was indeed gasping for breath. The shock of being romanced by so handsome an apparition was a little too much for her.

"My dear girl, I can't tell you how astounded I am to be standing here. I have often glimpsed you from afar, but the mist that separated us was impenetrable. I never hoped to dream that the Gods would again allow me the taste of earthly delights."

Jamie O'Roarke gently captured Rebecca's small hand in his great sea weathered one and smiled at her. "Now my dear, I believe it is time you introduced me to your friends."

Rebecca put her other hand to her hair and pretended to arrange the wind blown locks. Perhaps this would buy her some time. She needed to compose herself. The girl knew that she was blushing furiously and it made her angry. Porcelain skin was not always a blessing. Ever since she had been a little girl, her face had mirrored her feelings. At this particular moment Rebecca could feel the warmth of the blush on her cheeks. This was ridiculous. The Captain was, after all, merely a figure of their collective imaginations. He couldn't possibly be real. He was a fantasy conjured up by the wind and the moon of All Hallow's Eve. Collecting herself, and hoping that her attempt at composure would fool her friends, she turned to the Captain with a sweet smile.

"Come then Captain O'Roarke, let me introduce you to my friends."

The Captain, with serpentine grace, docilely followed Rebecca never letting go of her hand. It was strange, but Rebecca had the sudden feeling that for all his brashness, the bawdy Jamie O'Roarke was not as fearless as he pretended to be. There was a certain feeling in the grip of her hand that reminded her of Danny. He was, after all, in a strange new world that held many dangers for a man who had not trod earth since the seventeenth century.

"Captain, may I introduce myself," said Peter stepping forward and interrupting Rebecca's thoughts. "My name is Peter Hawking. Mine is an old Salem family. Perhaps you knew my ancestors, Martha and Giles Cory."

"Why yes indeed, your grandfather was greatly admired, once all the witchcraft hysteria died down. He was a man of rare good sense, my friend. I'm afraid that I can't say the same of Martha. Never was there a sharper tongue on a woman, God rest her tortured soul. If not for her foul temper, poor old Giles would have been left to smoke his pipe in the corner by the fire and enjoy his old age. Thank the heavens that Mr. Hale of Beverly put an end to all the nonsense. Salem was becoming a grim port to set down anchor in. More than one likely lass with a bright eye was sacrificed to those bible thumping Puritans. I may be a pirate, but I'm a proper Papist, I can tell you that. But look you now, don't breath a word of that. I wouldn't want to scare the ladies."

"I think you'll see that Salem has changed Captain. Anyone may now walk her streets."

"Even an old pirate?" said the Captain raising an eyebrow. "Seeing's believing on that one your worthy. Now, who are the rest of these fine people? I can't help but be a bit curious about you all. If not for you, Eva and I would still be moldering in yonder tree."

"Who is Eva?" said Danny, no longer able to resist the lure of the real live pirate standing before him.

"Why young sir," said the Captain looking at the boy with a gleam in his eye. "Eva be the wood nymph within yonder tree. Her spirit was imprisoned there by the true Crones and Sages of Salem. You see, the good people of Salem were right. There were witches and wizards about, but they were far too clever to be caught by such foolery as went on about Salem Town. Once the hysteria had died down, the ancient believers felt safe to worship as they had always done."

"But what about the fairy?" said Emily joining her brother.

"Not a fairy, young miss, a nymph. There be quite a difference. A dyad, or nymph, is far more playful than a fairy. You never know what she may be up to, if freed. Course 'twas her playfulness that got her imprisoned in yon tree in the first place."

"Oh," said Emily, "what did she do? Was she very naughty"?

"Yes, miss, very. And as to how naughty, I think that is a matter better left alone for now," said the Captain breaking into merry laughter.

Peter, looking at the Captain critically, moved to the shattered trunk of the old tree and grasped a lower limb that lay on the ground.

"Ah your worthy, I see you know something of dyads, then," said the Captain with a newborn respect for the old man.

45

"I only hope I know enough," said Peter, looking the pirate in the eye. Peter took the branch in hand and proceeded to form a great staff out of the wood. When he had finished he leaned against it and tested the staff for strength. Peter turned his back on the party, and spoke a few words into the air while he waved a hand over the staff. The wind, seeming to heed the old professor, swirled a gust of leaves around his feet. As it died down, Emily turned to Rebecca with a wondrous look on her face.

"Miss Love, did you hear that?"

"Hear what, Emily?" said Rebecca holding the little girl close.

"Why the laughing, it sounded like bells!"

"I heard it too," said Danny looking about him.

"No, dear, I didn't hear anything," said Rebecca truly regretting that she had asked the two children here tonight. Some sixth sense told her that the charming facade presented by Captain O'Roarke covered up something far more sinister. O'Roarke had the look of the devil's imp beneath his beguiling smile.

"Why, 'tis the wood nymph Eva, little ones," said the Captain putting a friendly hand on Danny's shoulder. "The professor has captured her spirit in yon shillelagh. And a good thing it is too. There's no telling the mischief she can cause. More than one maiden has reached a foul end because of her silly jealousies. Her favorite trick is to follow a comely maid home and wait until she is asleep. If the maiden is lucky Eva will be content to merely cut the hair from her head. If our little nymph is truly up to her tricks, there is no hope for her hapless victim."

"Captain, please," said Lady Arabella seeing the terrified look in little Emily's eyes, "you are scaring the children with this ridiculous fairy tale. I must ask you to stop."

"Why, my Lady," said the Captain, appraising the mature but charming Arabella with a connoisseur's eye, " 'tis no fairy tale. It is better for the wee ones to be on guard than to be lured with sweet promises by the entrancing Eva. She has wiles that have even defied my strength."

"I can well believe it, Captain," said Peter returning to the center of the group. "Don't worry children. Our dyad is safely contained within this staff, I promise you. As long as she is within my grasp, she must do my bidding. There will be none of her mischievous ways this night."

"Do you really believe all of this, professor?" said Ian MacRae with a critical look upon his face. "I admit that I can't deny the Captain because he stands before me. I've heard and seen enough of ghosts in Scotland to believe that they might exist, but wicked fairies? Perhaps the Captain is playing a game with us."

"Believe me it is no game, my fine sir. You of all people should beware of Eva. She has quite a fondness for fine young gents. By the look of ye I can tell you're a highlander. Would you hale from anywhere near the Kyle of Lochlash?"

"Why yes, Captain, we do," said Arabella, fascinated with the swashbuckling buccaneer. "Our castle stands at the end of Loch Duich."

"Ah, then you would be of the MacRae clan, my fine lady?"

"Yes, Captain," said Ian putting his body between his Aunt and Jamie O'Roarke. "We are of the clan MacRae. I don't often use my new title, but I am the Laird Ian MacRae and this is my Aunt, Lady Arabella MacRae."

"Well then, I am in esteemed company," said the captain sweeping a bow to them both. "It seems that old Duncan's brood survived the terrors."

"Oh, indeed they did, Captain," said Arabella hardly able to conceal her excitement at the mention of Duncan MacRae's name. "They defended the Bonny Prince bravely but still managed to retain the family name."

"And a fine name it is, my Lady," said the Captain with a stunning smile aimed at Arabella. "It seems that ye even have a hardy nephew to add to its glory. How fortunate old Duncan was. I left behind neither kith nor kin."

"Poor Captain," said Emily staring up at the weathered face of O'Roarke. "Danny and I will be your friends. That's the same as kin, isn't it professor?"

"Not quite, Emily," said Peter looking at the two children, "but I'm sure that the Captain would be glad to have you as friends."

"Why to be sure, Lassie, I would be proud to call ye and young Daniel me mates," said the Captain truly touched by the child's sweetness. "Now enough of this blathering about," said O'Roarke, attempting to restore his gruffness. "What is it that has brought me here? Yon tree was never what you might call an easy rest, but at least I could vanish upon my wish. It seems that somehow the good professor has landlocked me in a strange new age."

"Not landlocked you, Captain, summoned you," explained Peter, feeling a bit embarrassed by the whole adventure. "The Lady Arabella seems to feel that you have laid a curse upon her family and she wishes it removed."

"Removed!" thundered the pirate pacing back and forth in an extremely agitated manor. "If her Ladyship wishes the curse removed than let her remove it! I'll have none of it. 'Twas not my wickedness that brought about the curse. 'Twas the wickedness of a MacRae. Do ye not think that I would be content moldering under yon tree? Of course I would. But, thanks to the betrayal of a MacRae my rest never came upon me. For three hundred years I have been condemned to wander the scenes of my greatest joy and tragedy."

" 'Twas the doing of the MacRaes and those ragged gillies Jack and Ezra that brought me to such a pass. Oh no, my Lady. Charming though ye may be, I will not be the one to free a MacRae of the curse."

Lady Arabella, taken aback by the sudden change in the Captain, burst into tears and buried her head on Peter's shoulder. Ian, gathering himself up to the fullness of his height, confronted the Captain.

"Sir, there is no reason to be insulting. Neither my Aunt nor myself has anything to do with your troubles. I myself don't believe in your curse, but my Aunt does. I don't see why it would be so difficult to comfort a grieving widow."

"Ah, Laddie, and the comforting of this widow would also save your handsome neck, now wouldn't it. Captain Jamie O'Roarke will never remove the evil he has placed upon your fine family. It is your curse that all firstborn males shall perish in the sea and it is a proper judgment for bringing about the end of old Jamie. Let you live with it and die of it I say."

"And what if I tell you that I don't believe in your curse, O'Roarke? What happens then? Whatever evil you say you can do will never touch me because I don't acknowledge your power," said Ian standing toe to toe with the Captain.

"Think upon your own father then, fine sir. He was really the eldest was he not, Lady MacRae? Your Aunt only let ye think that your Uncle Alan was the firstborn MacRae."

"Is this true, Aunt?" said Ian turning to Arabella.

The Lady, composing herself, faced her angry nephew bravely. "Yes, my dearest, I'm afraid what the Captain says is true. Your Uncle and I didn't want you growing up fearful of the future so we changed a few facts to protect you. When you were grown you didn't want the care of the MacRae estates so we thought it would be all right to continue the charade. You don't know how many times I have wanted to free myself of the burden of the truth, but Alan wouldn't let me. He was concerned that once you assumed the Lairdship of Castle MacRae that you would fall under the curse and be destroyed. So you see, my burden has been heavier than you could ever imagine."

"Oh, Aunt, I should have never doubted your goodness," said Ian gathering Arabella into his arms. "Please forgive me. I see now why you insisted that we come. Let me share your burden the way you have always shared mine."

"Captain," said Arabella turning to O'Roarke, "could you take me in place of my nephew? Certainly that would pay the debt that you are owed. I beg you to accept my life in place for his."

"Dear Lady," said Jamie O'Roarke truly impressed by the bravery of the grand lady, "I would if I could but it's not that simple. You are indeed a woman of such character as I have never laid eyes on before and deserve a boon. The only possible way to remove the curse is to undo what has been done. If that were brought about I would be delighted to lift the evil threat that haunts your Ian."

"Are you saying that if somehow we could undo your death the MacRaes would be free of you?" asked Peter, musing over the problem.

"That's right me bucko, but only I know the way back through the mists. I would have gone back long ago but for the fact that a spirit cannot travel those roads without an earthly guide. Someone would have to make the journey with me."

"I'll go," said Ian grasping the Captain's arm.

"And who's to say ye be welcome, sir," said the pirate with a wicked grin. "If I'm to be making this journey I would choose a far more pleasant companion than you. A lass is more to my taste, such as the lovely Rebecca here. What do you say my dear? A little adventure on a starlit night might put some roses in your cheeks."

With the Captain's words, a great flash of lightening blinded the small party. As the light faded, only air remained where Jamie O'Roarke and Rebecca Love had been standing.

CHAPTER TWELVE

"How close the stars are," thought Rebecca while the heavens hurtled past her at breathtaking speed. Strange as it may seem the girl sensed no fear as her body and soul were being transported beyond the realm of human experience. Rebecca felt an almost euphoric calm transfuse her whole being. It seemed that less than a moment ago she had been standing in the old Burying Point graveyard safely anchored to the ground. The next moment everything had gone dark.

The blackness that enveloped Rebecca was not a frightening thing. In a way it was almost comforting, like being surrounded by some great celestial womb. The immense, comforting warmth that enveloped her gave Rebecca a strange sense of calmness.

Suddenly, a great burst of light flooded the air around her. Rebecca could see stars and planets rushing past her in a profusion of color. It seemed that all the brilliance of the universe was infusing her body with a Goddess like power. If this is what Peter experienced when he went beyond the realm, it was no wonder that his curiosity in all things celestial was so intense.

"Peter!" thought the girl in what felt like a shattering scream. "Where was he? Where was everyone?" The terrified girl groped madly about her in the vain hope of touching something of earthly substance. Suddenly a strong hand grasped hers.

51

"Now, my Lassie, don't you be afraid. The Captain is here. We are on a fine voyage, you and I."

The words spoken by the Captain seemed to be swirling in Rebecca's mind like phantom thoughts, but the touch of his hand was real enough. "Oh, where are we, Captain?" thought the girl hoping that he could sense her words.

"Why, sailing through time my dear," laughed O'Roarke. "Be ye not afraid. I'll not let anything harm ye."

With that Rebecca could feel herself being gathered up into strong arms. An aroma of leather and pipe tobacco emanated from the muscular chest where she lay her head. The Captain, holding her tightly, seemed to be rocking her in a comforting motion.

"Now my dear, just close your eyes and dream a bit. We should be making for safe harbor soon enough."

Rebecca felt her eyelids growing heavy and actually began to slumber in Jamie O'Roarke's arms. If she could have seen his eyes, she would have been amazed at the look of tenderness that crossed his battle scarred face.

"O'Roarke," muttered the Captain to himself, " 'tis a fine fool ye be turnin' into."

CHAPTER THIRTEEN

Rebecca opened her eyes and looked about. Something was wrong. The girl sat up and gazed at the scene in wide eyed wonder. What she saw would have unnerved anyone. From her vantage point behind an old tree, Rebecca could see bearded men in steeple crowned hats and women either bareheaded or wearing hoods tightly drawn about their faces. The rude market place consisted of three primitive buildings built solely for function. The largest was a wooden structure with a severely peaked roof. Attached to the peak was a wooden cross than someone had lovingly carved. The next building was smaller and far less weather tight. By the two armed men standing before it, Rebecca supposed it to be some sort of prison. In front of the two guards, armed with swords and pikes, stood an immense stocks, large enough to punish ten wrongdoers. Even more forbidding was the gallows that also stood before the prison doors. By the look of the noose attached to the wooden beam, this was a gallows that had seen much sorrow.

The last building, set slightly apart from the other two was a blacksmith's shop. Rebecca could hear the rumble of men's voices coming from within.

The air around her had an oddly tangy taste. The clearness of it almost made the confused girl dizzy. Lying down on the soft moss underneath her, Rebecca shut her eyes and waited for the dream to vanish. When she opened them again she was startled to find that nothing had changed. The men and women in the strange garb of somber hues and the rustic buildings still appeared before her. Sitting up with a jolt, she began to cry out.

A large hand was quickly placed over her mouth. "Now none of that, me dear. You don't want us ending up in yon stocks for lewdness do ye?" Captain O'Roarke looked at Rebecca with concern in his dark brown eyes. "Take a moment to calm yourself. There's nothing to be afraid of. We've just made a bit of a journey. 'Tis nothing to go on about."

Rebecca, furious with the Captain for treating her in such a manner, bit his hand with a ferocity that took Jamie by surprise. He had to muster all his strength not to cry out in pain.

"Now there's no call to be agettin' mean, young miss," whispered the wounded pirate as he gently rubbed his injury. "I was only trying to protect your pretty neck. You have no idea what these people are like. Why they enjoy nothing better than to see such as yourself strung up on yonder gibbet. Forget all the pretty tales the old professor may have filled your head with. The folks of Salem Town are a righteous lot and they don't look kindly on strangers. To them anyone not born and bred here is the devil himself."

"Nothing could be worse than you!" said Rebecca, getting to her feet and brushing the leaves from her skirt. "What have you done! I want to go home now! My friends will be very worried."

Rebecca stood above Jamie with her hands placed firmly on her hips glaring down at the astonished man. No one had ever dared to speak to him this way. Why he was the great pirate captain Jamie O'Roarke. Even those scurvy knaves who had betrayed him had to sneak behind his back. No man faced the deadly sword of Jamie O'Roarke and lived to tell of it. Now twice in one day he had been defied face to face, first by that damnable MacRae and now by this wisp of a girl.

"Look here my fine young miss," said Jamie rising to his full height, "If you don't calm down you'll never get home. Do ye think I can turn this spell weaving on and off at will? Why it was only because of her ladyship's wish that we had the power at all. It was her goodness that made our voyage possible. The truth of it is I'm not sure that I can get you home at all, so you might as well calm down and make the best of it. I'll see that no harm comes to ye."

"No harm!" yelled Rebecca punching the Captain in his well muscled stomach as hard as she could, "why you great fool the only one I need saving from is you. I don't know quite where I am, but believe me anywhere you're not looks good to me."

With that the furious girl gathered her skirts and hiked a few paces towards the direction of the meetinghouse. Rebecca stopped suddenly as she saw two men dressed in black. Between them stood a curvaceous girl bound in chains, weeping as if her heart would break. Rebecca quickly hid behind a tree as the small party passed close by.

"But Reverend Brown, Deacon Williams, 'twas not I that took Goody Parr's shawl. I pray you release me. 'Twas none of my doing."

"Now, Mistress Briggs, we have witnesses that have sworn their word upon the good book that it was you that committed the deed. I will only warn you once not to befoul your crime further by the telling of falsehoods. Be filled with gratitude that the kind woman only wishes her shawl returned. A few hours of repentance will do your troubled soul good."

With these words, the stern looking minister and his deacon locked the buxom blond girl in the stocks that was placed on the high platform in the center of the clearing. Mistress Briggs was poorly dressed and shivered in the cold autumn wind.

"There now, my girl, this will give you a chance to meditate upon the devil's ways. Think upon the kindness of Goody Parr and thank God for it." With these words, the warmly dressed cleric took his leave of the sad wretch.

"So you see, my dear, I know these worthy citizens," said the Captain who had quietly moved to where Rebecca was concealed. "Not for them is the sweetness of your time. There is great fear here that the Church of England and its loose ways will soon put down its roots in Salem. Many believe that they will forfeit all they have if this comes to pass. Yon lass is but an innocent victim of their terror. Your good captain is just trying to make sure that you don't wind up shackled next to the unfortunate Mistress Briggs."

"Oh, Captain, what have you done!" cried Rebecca staring at him with a true understanding of her situation. "I want to go home and you have trapped me in a strange world. I don't know what to do or how to act. I've studied these things all my life, but this is so different than anything I ever expected."

"Whilst now, my dear, Jamie knows how you feel," said O'Roarke putting a hand lightly on her shoulder, prepared to remove it immediately in case of a second rebuff. "I have been a visitor in many places not of my own time. It is indeed a lonely life. Cheer up now, my lass. The Captain is here and we will stay snug and safe as long as you follow my lead."

"Captain O'Roarke, is there any hope of returning to my Salem?" said Rebecca, realizing now that the only possible way out of her situation was a clear head and a calm manner.

"I don't know, my girl. Perhaps if we go about taking care of the business of that damnable curse, there may be a way out. To my way of thinking, the MacRae curse is the key. If we can find a way to save me from the hangman's noose you might find your way home."

"Oh my God! What if we can't stop the curse, I could be trapped here forever!"

"And I would be the same wandering soul doomed to journey my lonely way through the ages with only an occasional drowning of a MacRae to brighten up my bleak existence."

"Captain O'Roarke, you wouldn't still harm Ian MacRae would you? The Lady Arabella is right you know. This has gone on much too long. Haven't you had your fill of revenge?"

"Ah miss, you don't understand much about the spirit world for all your book learning. Once a curse is placed it cannot be removed except by what we are trying to do now. This is the only chance for all of us to live, or die, in peace."

"Well then," said Rebecca gathering her courage, "I suppose we had better get to it. When are you supposed to be captured?"

"Sometime upon the morrow, if me figures be on course, my dear. That gives us tonight to set things straight with those scurvies Jack and Ezra. Tonight's the night that I'm supposed to be meeting them at the Blue Anchor Tavern to lay our plans for the burying of the treasure. Perhaps a pretty lass might be able to change their treacherous course, eh, my dear."

"Not so fast, Jamie O'Roarke, I'm not sure I like what you have in mind. I might be better off stuck in this wilderness than trusting you."

"Now Rebecca, me darling, would I be aharmin' the little lass that I have watched over all her days. When that poor old salt, your father, met his untimely end, 'twas Jamie O'Roarke that watched over you, much like an angel on your shoulder. How joyful was old Jamie when the professor took you under his wing. Besides, yonder Melinda Briggs is more to the taste of those two seafaring men. She's been a serving wench at many a grogshop including the 'Anchor.' What say we pass by her and do her the favor of loosening her bonds?"

Rebecca suddenly felt a kinship with the pirate. Was it true that his presence had always been in her life? On many a stormy night the little Rebecca would awaken, terrified at the wind and rain that shook her little cottage by the sea. On these nights, the girl had often felt the warmth of a phantom touch, not unlike the one that had surrounded her on the journey to old Salem. If that comforting embrace had come from Jamie O'Roarke, then it was true that he could never harm her. What a fool she had been not to have seen it before. Of course it had been Jamie. No matter what happened, she must repay his love. His dearest wish was to be free of the bonds that imprisoned his soul. Rebecca prayed that she could help him.

Putting her arm through his, Rebecca smiled up at the charming Jamie. "Let's get to it then, Jamie me lad," she said with a giggle. "We wouldn't want that poor girl to freeze."

Rebecca and Jamie quietly moved from tree to tree until they were standing directly below the pillory that imprisoned the unfortunate Melinda.

"Hist ye now my girl, can you hear me?" whispered O'Roarke while Rebecca kept a look out for any dour churchmen.

"Who's that now?" said the shivering girl, barely able to get the words out through her chattering teeth.

" 'Tis your old friend Jamie, me girl, come to set you free as a bird."

"O'Roarke, are you mad?" said the shocked Melinda. "Why, if they catch you doin' such a thing it will go hard indeed with ye. Remember the last time you ran afoul of Reverend Brown, it almost cost you your life."

"Aye my dear, and I be aowin' him a return of the favor so to speak. Now stay still while I slip up there and give those chains a turn with me old skeleton key."

With that, Jamie gracefully swung himself onto the platform and released the girl in a miraculously short moment.

"Come on now, let's make for the woods before their worthies have finished stuffing their fat faces at dinner. It's only the poor folk that must practice what others preach."

The three moved quickly towards the woods being careful to leave no trail behind them. No sooner had they disappeared than the Minister came around the corner of the blacksmith shop. With him were two rough looking men in sailor garb.

"So you see your honor," said the heavier of the two men, "I'm sure that O'Roarke will be a tellin' us the place where his stash is. 'Tis always us that does his diggin', ain't that so Jack?"

"Aye, that be so, sir, that be so. An' if O'Roarke's caught unawares, then your honor could be keepin' the treasure for 'charity' while poor old Jack and Ezra go on their way home with a full pardon. What do ye say?"

"I say that you are both despicable, but my parish is in a hard way after the last few years. Doing God's work in Salem has caused many of the farmers to leave their fields. Trials take time and juries must be served upon. As a result there has been much hunger and want in Salem Town. The rewards of finally bringing that foul brigand O'Roarke to justice would far outweigh the pardons granted to the likes of you."

"And to be sure, your honor, none of that gold dust would be stickin' to your fingers now would it?" said Jack with an evil smile.

"Keep your own consul my man or you'll find that Captain Jamie O'Roarke won't be the only pirate hanging from yon gallows."

With these words, the honorable Samuel Brown stormed into the meetinghouse, far too occupied to notice the disappearance of one small tavern wench.

CHAPTER FOURTEEN

The three fugitives halted behind a large oak to catch their breath just as the minister and his cohorts came into view. Jamie motioned to Rebecca and Melinda to be quiet. What they heard terrified the two girls but seemed to amuse the world weary pirate.

"Now my girls, don't worry about Jamie. Melinda, my lass, could you stow us away until I can set things straight with me mates. This is my 'niece' Rebecca, newly returned from the Carolinas. As you can see she needs something a bit more fitting to wear. I would be grateful if you could see your way clear to helping us."

"Ah Jamie darlin', it won't be the first time I've hidden you beneath me skirts, but upon my word, I must admit that your 'niece' lends a new twist to things," said Melinda appraising Rebecca with a look that made the girl quite nervous.

"Come along now, dearie, Melinda knows just the place for the two of you. I hope you don't mind a bit of rough talk. By the looks of ye, Jamie has got himself a lady for a 'niece.'"

"Thank you, Miss Briggs," said Rebecca, taken aback by the obvious familiarity between the dashing O'Roarke and the lusty maid. "I can't tell you how much we appreciate your kindness. I hope we aren't causing you any hardships."

"Eh now, I knew you were a lady, dearie, old Melinda can't understand your strange speech, but your manner is pleasant enough. Come now then before old Brown decides to check the stocks. I'm countin' me blessings that he was thinkin' more about O'Roarke's treasure than my hide or I might have had a bit of a battle keeping the old lecher's hands off me. Last time I spent an afternoon with yon minister he was far more friendly. What say we stop by the parsonage and entertain Mistress Brown with tales of her husband's wandering ways? That would serve the old hen fair and proper."

"Another time, me lass," said Jamie, giving the well padded Melinda a pinch. "I'll be delighted to escort you to Reverend Brown's very doorstep anytime, but for now I think we best be traveling out of sight and quickly. No telling when our fortune may turn."

"Well spoken, Jamie lad. Just follow me. There is a small path not far from here that will be aleadin' us to the cove. There must be a dory or two laying about that we can borrow to take us to the Blue Anchor. Ye haven't forgotten how to row now have ye, me boy?" said Melinda giving Jamie a tickle under the chin.

"Why, you just lead the way and I'll have you there faster than a nor'easter at Christmastide," laughed O'Roarke heartily as he grabbed the confused Rebecca's arm and hurried her down the lushly overgrown path.

Rebecca was amazed by what she saw around her. Not even being born in Salem and studying its history could have prepared the girl for the unbelievable difference between Rebecca's world and Jamie's. The clearness of the air and the lushness of the foliage was only one aspect that astounded her. The citizens of Salem had indeed civilized a primal wilderness. Only an occasional rude structure or cleared field relieved the impression of an eden like forest. If what she had read was true, there were even more elaborate homes that housed the wealthy of Salem Town. Beyond the seashore, in the center of town, were the brick residences of the wealthy complete with imported finery from England. It was unbelievable what the citizens had wrested out of this new world jungle.

"Come along now, don't be draggin' your feet Miss," said Melinda with a scornful glance back at Rebecca. "It's easy to see that you have been raised delicate like, but we mustn't tarry."

"Don't worry about me, Melinda," said Rebecca, trying to keep the exhaustion out of her voice. It was obvious that both O'Roarke and Melinda Briggs were far hardier than Rebecca, but she would rather die than give Mistress Melinda the satisfaction of taunting her with jibes about her strength. The hardships of old Salem built a stamina that was unknown to any twentieth century marathoner.

At last the dense forest began to give way. Rebecca could see shafts of sunlight between the trees as they followed a swiftly flowing stream. The ground sloped downward as the water took on speed and energy. Just as she felt that she was making progress, Rebecca tripped over the large root of an old tree. With a cry of frustration she fell flat on her face.

Laughing, O'Roarke halted Melinda and they retraced their steps to where the girl had fallen. "It looks like it's time for a bit of a rest my dear. It won't do us any good if I have to carry you the rest of the way."

Stooping beside Rebecca, he gently lifted the girl and propped her beneath the trunk of the old elm.

"Easy now, lassie, there's no danger here. A few moments in the woods won't spoil our chances."

"Hah," said Melinda looking down at Rebecca with a look of triumph. "You're a fool, O'Roarke, bringing such a girl to a place like this. You should know that a lass of your own kind would be more fitting. This is what you get for lookin' above your station."

"Now, Melinda, me girl," said Jamie gathering the wench into his arms and holding her tight. " 'Tis not what you think. This lassie truly is an acquaintance of the blood, so to speak. Your bearings are right concerning her upbringing, but she is in as tight a spot as you or I. She is not here by her own choice and we owe her protection. Now be a good girl and show some of that kindness you are known for. If you will sit and rest with us I'll grant you a wish."

"Any wish?" said the maid thoroughly charmed by Jamie O'Roarke.

"Any wish, I swear on the sails of the 'Red Witch.'"

"Oh now, don't go to swearin', it's a heathen practice my lovey, just take out your knife and prepare yourself," said Melinda teasing the pirate.

"My knife! I'm warnin' you now I'll not commit a foul deed, promise or not."

"'Tis no foul deed but a token of affection I wish, Jamie," said Melinda smiling up at him with love shining in her eyes. "My wish is for you to carve our initials in this great tree for all the world to see. Then I'll know that you're not ashamed of humble Melinda Briggs."

"As you wish, my lady," bowed Jamie trying hard not to let his embarrassment show. Women were indeed strange and mysterious creatures. Here was a lass without a farthing to her name and not knowing where the next one would come from. Only such as Melinda would have asked for a love token when she knew he had a bounty of doubloons for the asking.

"Go ahead, Jamie, do it," said Rebecca from her resting place. "I think it's a sweet idea. Why don't you sit next to me Melinda and we can both take a rest while the captain works away."

"Why, Mistress Rebecca, I do believe you are a true lady and I'm thankin' you for your kindness. It's certainly time we acquainted ourselves. It looks to be a long day. Hop to now, Jamie my lad. M.B. entwined with J.O. would do nicely, wouldn't it, Rebecca lass?"

"Quite nicely," said Rebecca as the two girls lay against the tree chattering like old friends.

"Now, me lovely burdes," said a voice that interrupted Melinda and Rebecca a few moments later, "I've done with me labors and it's time to be gone."

"Not so fast, Jamie," said a merry Melinda aching to see the bit of foolishment O'Roarke had carved.

"Yes, let us see your fine work, Captain," said Rebecca equally curious to check on O'Roarke's handiwork.

"Well, and there it is," said Jamie taking his large hand away from the spot where he had carved the finely wrought initials held together with the flowers and leaves of the beautiful woodbine. "Wherever the woodbine twineth shall be Jamie O'Roarke forevermore. You are one of my dearest mates, Melinda lass, and I'm proud ye asked me for such a boon."

"Oh Jamie, how truly lovely," said Melinda putting her arms around Jamie's neck and giving him a passionate kiss full on the lips. "You are indeed a wonder, O'Roarke."

" 'Tis nothing but a bit of scrimshaw, lass," said O'Roarke in an attempt to cool the lusty Melinda down. "What say we move on a bit and make for the Blue Anchor. I seem to be in need of a noggin of rum."

Rebecca, looking from Melinda to Jamie, smiled as she stood up and stretched. They were indeed two of a kind. Both Mistress Briggs and Captain O'Roarke belonged in this strangely treacherous world that Rebecca found herself in. It made her feel unbearably homesick just to look at them. Where were Peter, and Ian and Arabella MacRae? Would they be wondering what had happened to her and was there anything that they could do to help? With a wistful sigh Rebecca paused to look at O'Roarke's artwork.

Astounded, Rebecca recognized the fantastic piece of artwork that Jamie O'Roarke had carved for Melinda Briggs. This was the carving that had always fascinated her as a child. The last remaining elm tree on Forrester street stood in front of Rebecca's own neighbor, Mary Maloon. As a little girl,

Rebecca could remember lovingly tracing the almost invisible carvings on the side of the tree. The delicate flowers and indecipherable lettering had remained a mystery to her until now. That beloved carving was the love token requested by Melinda Briggs!

She was home, Rebecca was truly home, but it had all vanished. The wetlands leading to the Common had been filled in over two hundred years ago, but that was still a hundred years from where Rebecca stood now. George Washington had just been declared the first president of the United States when the citizens of Salem had decided to enlarge their city by filling in the stream and clearing this land. Rebecca stood underneath Mrs. Maloon's tree and gazed at the section of forest that stood where her own cottage would be built someday. How eerie it all was.

"Come now, Mistress, we must hurry," said a far kindlier Melinda pushing Rebecca in front of her. "There's no telling when the magistrate may feel the need of a bit of sea air and stroll down to the cove."

With that, Rebecca came fully to life. There was no use in yearning for what wasn't here. If Captain O'Roarke was right, she may never see her Salem again, but that didn't make life any less precious to her. No matter where she was, Rebecca wanted to live.

CHAPTER FIFTEEN

The surf roared along the cove as Jamie steadied the small boat while the girls climbed aboard. The cold bitter wind of the late afternoon promised an early winter with long hard frosts and heavy gales. The ripples lapped on the stones calling their siren song to the men of the sea. For all its cruelties, Rebecca loved the harsh tempest of the ocean. No matter what else had changed, Rebecca's beloved Collins Cove had remained the same.

"Look sharp now, lassies," shouted O'Roarke over the roar of the sea. " 'Twill be a rough crossing. Hold on to the side while we round old Marblehead."

A laughing Melinda drew a fine blue cloak from beneath her skirt and wrapped it about both Rebecca and herself. The two girls, huddled tightly together underneath the closely knit wool, were almost warm as Captain O'Roarke skillfully headed the tiny boat toward Lynn harbor.

Rebecca pushed the cloak away from her face and breathed in the salt air with an exuberance that she had never felt before. The intoxicating wind and rocking of the boat were having a strange affect on the girl. It was as if her soul were following her body back into the past. She was a different Rebecca. The girl she had left behind was but a frail shadow of the woman she felt being born within her on the open sea. It was not until this moment that Rebecca had truly understood the attraction of the past, with its lust and passion. In this world you had to live all you could today. No one could count on tomorrow in a world where death lurked around every bend.

"Land ho," shouted Jamie as he turned the boat toward shore. "Let us pray that this be a friendlier shore than the one behind us." With an expert turn of the wrist, O'Roarke guided the small boat into harbor with surprising gentleness. As they approached the old dock he whistled to a small boy who was fishing. The boy, with a smile that revealed several missing teeth, caught the rope that O'Roarke tossed to him and handily tied it to the dock.

"Here now, me lad, help the ladies up," signaled O'Roarke, tossing a large gold piece to the delighted youngster. The happy boy quickly ran to the edge of the dock and reached down to assist Melinda and Rebecca up the rickety wooden steps.

"To be sure, sir, 'tis a pleasure," said the child with an even wider grin.

"Off with ye now and look lively, my lad," said Jamie tossing the child another gold piece.

"Whist now, O'Roarke, you shouldn't be doin' that. What if the lad shows those about. No child could come by such treasure honestly. They'll be sure to track ye down."

"Now don't go on so, Melinda, he's a barin o' the docks and knows better than to blab about any such windfall. Why I was much the same at his age. Now suppose you smuggle us off to your quarters at yon tavern and we'll all be abreathin' easier."

"Aye aye, Captain," said Melinda with a salute and a nod of her head to Rebecca. "This way to a snug harbor."

CHAPTER SIXTEEN

The low murmuring of voices, along with the warmth of the thick down filled mattress, quickly lulled Rebecca into a childlike slumber. In her dreams she felt the strong arms of a man entwine themselves about her. He was drawing her towards him with a strength that she was powerless to resist. Rebecca felt her body being raised towards this strangely magnetic entity. The blackness that surrounded them both was deep and comforting. She felt his soft warm lips through the tickling of his beard laying a seal upon her mouth that seemed to claim her for his own. Just as she was about to be enveloped in a cloud of unlimited passion, Rebecca gave a cry of terror. The spirit pressed onward in hopes of fulfilling his passion, oblivious of his victim's fears. Underneath his desire, Rebecca could sense something else, an evil force that was subtle yet insidious. The stirring desire within her was suddenly twisted into a burning terror that infused her being. As she struggled to break free of the spirit's iron grasp, a bright light infused them both. Rebecca became aware of a benevolent force placing itself between her and the dark power of the seductive spirit.

A voice was calling to her, from within the cloud of light, with a lilt that was both familiar and enchanting. Another spirit emerged from the shining cloud and moved towards her. As he came closer, the dark entity raised an arm and attempted to destroy the shining being that kept moving toward him. For a moment, Rebecca could feel the power of the nightmare-like being threatening to overtake them all and drag them beneath the universe to a place of unspeakable horrors. An emptiness filled the air in which no living thing could breath. Just as Rebecca felt herself being smothered by the heavy darkness, the light-filled spirit broke through the night, shattering the evil one's power. The beams of light that radiated from him infused those around him until even the dark spirit became harmless in the glow of the sacred light. Rebecca, raising her arms to embrace the kind entity, was aware that both god-like men were now united in a singular quest. Never could either spirit rest until the dark one had achieved redemption and absolution for the unnamed horrors that lay within him. As they moved towards her, she was filled with their energy and longing. The girl knew that without her strength, both spirits would remain forever in battle with one another, doomed to replay the struggle of light over dark throughout eternity. Somehow her small soul could be the passageway through which both the brilliant and somber spirits could at last achieve true peace and harmony.

Rebecca grasped a shaft of light emanating from the golden god and floated towards him. Her feet touched lightly on the sunbeam cloud that now sustained both men. As she took her place between them they were drawn upward towards some unspeakable ecstasy that was not of any world that Rebecca had ever known. The benevolent nothingness that surrounded them all seemed to unite their three souls into one powerful force that entwined around their bodies and radiated into the air above them. Never before had Rebecca experienced such total passion and energy. The two men, holding her tightly, seemed to be paying homage to her for her great love and kindness. The girl, enveloped in the light suffusing her, reached out to them both and was just about to form a caress when a cold iciness broke the spell.

"Mistress, Mistress, you must wake. The sun's been set for nigh on an hour and the Captain has much to do before the dawn."

Rebecca felt herself gasping for air as she struggled to answer the insistent voice that was calling her. How she wanted to stay where she was and travel between the two spirits forever. How dare this voice call for her and drag her back into the other world. Try as she might, Rebecca could not resist the pull of the lovely voice calling her back.

"There now, Miss," said Melinda as Rebecca sat up and groggily rubbed her eyes.

"Why I thought ye might never wake by the looks of ye. O'Roarke must have led you a pretty chase for you to be in such a state. A nice noggin' of rum and Melinda's cornbread will fix you right up. Wake now and we will find you something of a more fittin' nature to wear."

"Oh, Melinda," said Rebecca shaking her head, "I just had the strangest dream."

"That's no wonder, Mistress, with the company you've been keeping. You're not the first maiden that's had a few dreams about O'Roarke and you won't be the last. Tell me which was it, the answer to a maiden's prayer or one of those black nightmares?"

"That's the strangest part," said Rebecca shaking her head. "It wasn't either of those. I'm not sure I know what sort of dream it was. For that matter, I'm not entirely sure it was even a dream. It felt so real."

"There now, Miss, don't be worried. You've just been through too many adventures this day, 'tis all. Sit up now like a good girl and eat your bread."

"Melinda, you have been so kind to me. Thank you for the shelter and the food. What would we have done without you?"

"Many have said the same thing, Mistress, but I'm athankin' you for your manners. 'Tis pleasant to hear such gentle words here about. Say now, perhaps you could be ateachin' Melinda a thing or two about being a lady. The gents always seem to settle down with such as the likes of you and leave poor Melinda behind crying into her apron."

"Oh, that can't be true, Melinda, and please, call me Rebecca. You're a wonderful girl and I'm sure there must be many men just dying to make you their sweetheart."

"A sweetheart for sure, Miss, but never a wife. Who would make a home for such as I?"

"Melinda, where I come from, we don't think like you do at all. Women can be free and independent and still be respected and loved for their wonderful ways. You should never think less of yourself because you must make your own living. As a matter of fact, you're quite a catch."

"Ah, Rebecca, you must come from a very strange land indeed. Any place I've ever heard of fancies a lady who languishes upon a couch and gowns herself in silks and satins. Couldn't you just see me entertainin' at a fine party with a cup o' tea in me hand. Why I'd probably spill it on the Lord Mayor's wife and disgrace myself. It's all very well for you to speak as you do. You've never had to go to sleep hungry or make a promise on a moonlit night to a cad just so ye can have a bit of shelter and a full belly. It's a lady bred and born ye be and that's a fact. I'll bet you can even put a name to your own parents." With that, Melinda sat on the bed next to Rebecca and began to munch noisily on the delicious cornbread.

"Well, Melinda, I do know you're wrong about one thing. I have had to make my own way. My father died when I was a baby and my mother was practically mad with grief until she died. I know what it's like to be alone. If it weren't for good friends, I could have very well found myself where you are now. The only difference between us is luck."

"See there," said Melinda tapping Rebecca's leg, "what did I tell ye. No matter what you say you are a lady, not like the Goody's around this place who would see a girl hanged for the borrowing of a shawl. Ye be the real thing lass and there's no mistakin' it. How I wish I could be like you."

"But you can!" said Rebecca excitedly swinging her legs over the side of the bed. "All you need is a bit of polish and some pretty things to turn the heads of the men about here. I'm sure that if you really wanted it, Captain O'Roarke would be glad to give you some gold for clothes and schooling. From what I've heard he has more than enough to spare."

"The Captain, Mistress, I mean Rebecca? Why I would never dream of askin' him for such. He'd just laugh at the likes of me and make some foul merriment out of the whole thing. It would cut me to the quick to be the brunt of his jests, I can tell ye that. No, mayhap it's better just to remain simple Melinda than to face that."

"Oh, I think you're mistaken. Beneath that rough exterior lies a heart as kind as any, I'm sure. The Captain has been quite nice to me despite everything."

"Mistress Rebecca!" said Melinda standing up and looking down at the girl with an expression of exasperation. "Never trust O'Roarke. He has the charm of a snake and he can be twice as cunning. I've seen him smile at a man while cutting his throat. It's a scoundrel he is and no mistakin' it, for all his fine words. I may take him to my bed, but I'd never make the mistake of turnin' me back on him."

"Now, Melinda, he can't be all that bad. He saved you from the stocks and carved your initials in the old elm tree. There must be some redeeming qualities to him. I can just feel it."

"If O'Roarke has some of them qualities, I've yet to see it, Rebecca, but I will be atellin' ye that despite his cruelties he's always been the only one for me, God curse him. He's gotten to my heart like no other and there's no diggin' him out. There are times when I think I'm dying over the feelings I have for him. 'Tis a hopeless love, but true."

Rebecca looked at the girl with astonishment. The heartrending confession touched her. Taking Melinda's hand she gently drew the maid back down onto the bed beside her and gave her a hug.

"Don't you worry now. Perhaps there is something we can figure out to make O'Roarke stop thinking of you as a shipmate and start seeing you as a woman. It's time he stopped playing with your heart and acted like a real man."

"Rebecca, I thank you for your kindness, but don't you go a runnin' off on a fool's errand. 'Tis you that O'Roarke wants and there's no denying it. You don't see the way he gazes at you when you're not lookin'. 'Tis enough to break my heart, but it's true. When a man looks like that there's no stoppin' him until he plunders the ship. And I'll bet me cap that you're not some light maid to give in without a ring on your finger and a fine house waiting. 'Tis the way of things and there's no denyin' it, more's the pity."

"But I'm sure you're mistaken, Melinda. Why Captain O'Roarke's old enough to be my father. He couldn't possibly think of me in that way."

"Dearie, as long as there's breath in that pirate, he'll be a thinkin' of a pretty face and the swish of a skirt, that's the truth. Now don't you go on so. I'm used to O'Roarke disappointin' me. 'Tis nothing but his nature. I know what's what and still care enough about my own hide not to ruin me day over it. Come on now and let's see to putting you in something that won't get ye in trouble."

Melinda walked over to a great wooden sea chest and began to rummage through a surprisingly colorful collection of clothing and what could only be described as gewgaws. Hidden amongst the folds of her wardrobe were the momentos and treasures that she had collected over a lifetime. As Rebecca moved from the bed and began to help the Salem maid place her bounty on the bed, the girl from the twentieth century couldn't help but be amazed at the curiosities in Melinda's sea chest. Amongst the stockings, bodices and skirts that lay before her were jumbled a hand carved wooden doll, a lovely broach, several gold doubloons and many objects that bespoke the everyday life of a tavern wench of Salem's 1695. An enormous whale's tooth with intricately wrought scrimshaw would have brought a fortune in Rebecca's time. Here was a treasure chest right before her scholar's eyes that made O'Roarke's everyday booty look pale. This was the stuff of real life that Melinda loved and Rebecca treasured.

"There now, that's the lot. I'm afraid ye be a bit smaller than me, but all we need to do is pull the laces tight," laughed Melinda heartily as she watched Rebecca surveying her gear.

"I'm not sure where to begin," said Rebecca picking up a dark red bodice with a series of laces threaded across the front."

"Ah then, the fine Mistress doesn't know everything now, does she. Let me help ye. Divest yourself of that strange garb and we'll have ye lookin' like one of us before ye know it," said Melinda attempting to make some sense of the Zipper and Velcro that held Rebecca's blue denim skirt together.

"Sure and this is a strange contraption. Better not let those about here see this or they'll be callin' you out for a witch. I'm becoming right fond of ye and would hate to see that."

Rebecca laughed and quickly drew the Zipper down and detached the Velcro fastening. The whoosh of the fastener amazed Melinda as she took the skirt from Rebecca.

"Now then what's this? I swear it might be real enchantment," said Melinda as she playfully kept pulling apart and reattaching the Velcro strip that held the waistband of the skirt together. "And what is this strange fabric. Seems a wonder to me. Why something like this could weather a gale and still be pretty as a picture."

"If you like it that much you can have it," said Rebecca smiling at the girl's wonderment. "As a matter of fact let's trade. My clothes for yours. Perhaps the Captain would like your new look."

"Oh I couldn't, Rebecca, why, your things are for a rich girl, not for the likes of me. See the fine knit of your strange bodice and the leather of your boots. I would be jailed for stealing such things. No one would ever believe that I came by such pretties in an honest way. And look at your stockings. Never did I see such fine weave and in so strange a manner. Tell me do they really go from waist to toe?"

"Yes they do," said Rebecca finding herself caught up in Melinda's excitement. "They're called tights, or pantyhose, and where I come from everyone wears them, even girls with little money."

"Oh that must be a wondrous place indeed. Say now, I wouldn't mind kicking the dust from my feet and seeing such a place. Whereabouts is it, Rebecca? Would it be a far journey?"

"Farther than you could ever imagine," said Rebecca wistfully. "I may never see home again unless a miracle happens." Rebecca fought vainly to keep the tears from her eyes but her feelings could not be denied. With a soulful look at Melinda, Rebecca burst into tears as the sturdy maid kindly put her arms around the homesick girl.

"There now, Rebecca, it's not so bad here. Mayhap we can get the Captain to settle down and build ye that fine house. Seeing as he's not for me I can't imagine anyone more fittin' for him to set his cap for. Cheer up now and we'll quickly have you in these things and downstairs for a real supper. There's not much a warm fire and a full belly can't make better." With that Melinda went about her work with a deftness that amazed Rebecca.

"Whist now and ye do look more fittin'," said Melinda stepping back to look at her handiwork. Rebecca's transformation was truly miraculous. In place of the modern twentieth century girl now stood a maid of old Salem Town. Rebecca kept staring down at her bosom not able to believe the curves created by Melinda's bodice. You could say all you wanted to about the wonders of the modern age, but there was something undeniably alluring about the fashions of Puritan Salem. Rebecca reached into the pocket of her abandoned skirt and pulled out a small compact. The small mirror reflected her image as she ran it down the length of her body. Yes, it was truly amazing.

"What a wonder you are Rebecca," said Melinda taking the small mirrored compact from Rebecca's hand. "Why I've never seen the like."

"Take that too, if you wish," said Rebecca generously. "I won't be needing it here, and you're right. My strange things might cause some trouble."

"Thank you, Miss," said the delighted Melinda adding the compact to her pile of treasures. "That bodice certainly shows off your lovely cross. 'Tis a pity the people of Salem Town see such things as Papist. 'Twould do them good now and then to hang a pretty around their necks rather than hanging each other."

"Do you think I should take it off?"

"Oh no, Rebecca, such a pretty suits you. It's plain to see that you're a stranger here. There be no rule against outsiders indulging themselves now and then. Wear your jewel and enjoy it I say."

Rebecca touched the cross and looked at Melinda. Closing her eyes she prayed that somehow this talisman would guide her home.

CHAPTER SEVENTEEN

The din from the tavern below startled Rebecca as she and Melinda made their way down the old wooden steps. Rebecca found that she had to squint her eyes to see into the darkness. The candles and lanterns that served as the only source of light cast eerie shadows on the patrons of the Blue Anchor tavern.

From a dark candlelit corner Rebecca could hear the deep voice of Jamie O'Roarke raised in uproarious laughter. "There now me lads, don't give me any of your willywas. 'Twas as much the crew's doin' as me own that brought down old Duncan MacRae and his treasure, and that's the long and short of it. Why yerselves had quite a hand in it. Jamie O'Roarke swears by this noggin o' dark rum that ye will all have more than your fair share."

"Our fine Captain better be speakin' a bit more quiet like or there'll be no treasure to share," said a laughing Melinda pushing an embarrassed Rebecca in front of her. What had been an amusing dress up costume in Melinda's chambers felt far more daring now. Rebecca could feel the eyes of more than one lustful pirate follow her across the room. This was a dangerous place and Rebecca was frightened.

"Why and what have we here?" said O'Roarke taking in Rebecca's transformation.

"Just a bit of my handiwork you old snake," said Melinda jabbing O'Roarke in the ribs, "but don't you be forgettin' that Mistress Rebecca's a lady. You'll have me to answer to if any harm comes to her."

"Yes, Ma'am," said O'Roarke, rubbing his side gently, surprised at the power in the tavern maid's thrust.

"May I offer you a seat and a noggin, Milady? Perhaps yon wench would be good enough to fetch us more rum."

"Why thank you, sir," said Rebecca daintily arranging herself on the rough wooden chair Jamie offered her.

"Melinda, me girl, off with ye now and bring us a cask while I introduce this fine young Mistress to me mates," said O'Roarke, slapping the tavern wench on the backside as a payback for the beating his ribs had taken.

Melinda, giving a smile and a conspiratorial wink to Rebecca, turned and hurried on her way, praying that her new friend was not entering stormy waters.

"Now then let me have a look at ye," said O'Roarke. "Why 'tis a fine wench ye make, don't she lads?" O'Roarke glared at his two mates and looked back at Rebecca. "But don't ye be makin' any mistake about it. What that Melinda says is true. Mistress Rebecca is a lady and I'll be makin' sure that's she's treated as such, won't I, my dear," said Jamie taking Rebecca's hand and fondling her fingers in a less than protective way.

"Hey now, Captain," said the old sailor in a tattered sea cloak, "If you say she's for you than that's the way of it. I've no need to battle with you even over such a tasty wench as that."

"She's not for me either, you scurvy dog," roared O'Roarke leaping to his feet with his hand on his sword. "The first swab who touches the lady answers with his life, do ye hear, and that goes for any other rum soaked knave in the place. She be my niece and due the respect owed one of me own and that's the end of it."

"Settle down, O'Roarke" said the younger of the two sailors, "we have enough trouble this night without you shoutin' loud enough to raise the dead. Here now, let's get to the plans and leave the lady to herself, pleasant though her company may be. 'Tis none of my business if you want to do a bit of lootin' and give the pretty burde a token from old MacRae's treasure."

"What are you speakin' of? Be ye daft?" said O'Roarke with a puzzled expression.

"Come now Captain, yon bauble hangin' around her neck is part of MacRae's booty and we all know it. But who are we to be arguing about a Captain's prerogative, so to speak."

"That's a boy, Jackie, you always were smart one and that's a fact." said Jamie O'Roarke staring at Rebecca. Damn the rum. He should have seen the thing right away Now here he was trying to pretend that he wasn't as startled as Jack and Ezra Love by the sudden appearance of the famed MacRae cross gracing Rebecca's lovely neck. The last time he had seen the jewel it had been wrapped in cloth of gold and placed at the bottom of the sea chest that the pirates planned to bury tomorrow night. Here was a mystery that even the clever O'Roarke could not solve.

"Now then, maties, let me introduce the lady to ye. Mistress Rebecca, these be my mates, Jack and Ezra Love. They've traveled many a sea with me and know all my secrets."

"Not all, Captain," said Jack, amused at the formality of the introduction. "There be a few that ye've kept to yerself and that's for certin'. This fine lady is one of them and I'm sure there's more. Many's the time old Ezra and I have had a hankerin' to get ye in your cups and squeeze out all the mysteries you've kept to yerself."

"Now, Jackie, don't be ateasin' the Captain, he might think you're serious like," said Ezra with a warning glance at his young impetuous brother.

"I was just having some fun and the Captain knows it, now don't you, sir."

"Of course, matey, of course," said O'Roarke smiling a toothy grin that reminded Rebecca of a killer shark. " 'Twas the rum talking, 'tis all. Now then let's get down to cases and get old Duncan's treasure underground before Cotton Mather wanders in and gives us a stroll down Prison Lane."

Rebecca had been astounded when Jamie O'Roarke had introduced the two sailors to her. Jack and Ezra Love! Rebecca herself was descended from these two scurvy pirates. Her mother had often spoken of Sean's pride in his ancient Salem heritage. The cross around her neck had been a symbol of that lineage. How surprised he would have been to find out that the honorable Love family could claim two such as these, destined for the hangman's noose, as its founders. Her beloved cross was nothing more than pirates bounty stolen from Ian MacRae's family long ago. Rebecca felt herself growing dizzy with all the confusion of past and present and gratefully accepted a large noggin of rum that Jamie O'Roarke put into her hands.

"There now, me darlin', why don't you settle in and relax whilst we plan the stowing of MacRae's boon?"

"Captain, do ye think it's wise lettin' her in on it? Meaning no disrespect, but the less that knows our secrets the better," said Ezra Love, eyeing the beautiful newcomer.

"Why, Ezra, you can trust her like your own daughter and ye have my word on it, isn't that so, Mistress Rebecca?"

"Yes, Jamie, dear," said Rebecca amused by the Captain's appreciation of irony, "there's no reason why not. I swear upon my father's grave never to reveal your secrets."

"There now and that's done. Now let's get down to business, lads."

Lowering their voices to a whisper O'Roarke and the Love brothers began their discussion of when and where to stow the loot of old Duncan MacRae. Rebecca found that following their conversation was almost impossible. Whether it was the powerful rum that she had gulped down to cover her nervousness, or the closeness of such dangerous company, she found herself unable to concentrate on anything but the flicker of the candle placed on the table. Jamie O'Roarke's beautiful melodious voice was caressing her mind like a sensuous lullaby, rocking her into oblivion.

The three buccaneers, making their plans to smuggle forth the treasure in the dark of the moon, seemed to recede to some dreamlike place. All Rebecca could think of was the storm tossed sea and how wonderful these men were for braving it with little more than their courage to protect them They had no idea how truly masculine and romantic they were. Even old Ezra, with the touch of hoar frost in his beard, would have put many a modern man to shame. These were men who had a sense of their purpose and destiny.

Had old Duncan MacRae been like Ian, but flavored with the intensity that set these adventurers apart? If he had been, then it was no wonder that the pirates relished the capture of his treasure. What if Ian MacRae had lived in these times? How well the handsome stranger from Scotland would have fit in. All he needed was a cutlass and leather breeches to grace the Captain's circle. Where was he now? Would she ever see any of her friends again or was she destined to find her way in this wilderness forever?

"So now you see, laddies, it's quite simple," said O'Roarke pouring Rebecca more rum. "You just wait until the right moment, smuggle the treasure off the 'Red Witch,' and let her down easy as we've done before."

"What about setting the seal on it, Captain? Shouldn't we be atakin' the young mate along to rest in peace with MacRae's treasure."

"You do and I'll hang ye myself, Ezra Love," said Jamie O'Roarke, meaning every one of his words. "I've never cottoned to such practices and I won't be startin' now. Slitting a young boy's throat so's his ghost can protect the treasure is mere foolishness, I say. Any who believe in ghosts and spirits is a fool I tell you. Isn't that so, Mistress Rebecca?"

Rebecca, trying very hard not choke on her rum, gave a giggle that turned into a laughing frenzy. Somehow through her gasps she sputtered, "yes Captain," and then gave herself up to her merriment until tears began to roll down her cheeks.

"Well then, it looks like this lady has had enough of us for an evening, lads," said Jamie attempting to quiet Rebecca before the curious glances around her raised unwelcome questions. "Until the dark of the moon then, mates."

"Aye, Captain, we'll be aseein' ye at Collin's Cove," said Jack with a look at Ezra who was nodding his assent.

"And one warning, my friends," said O'Roarke eyeing them both with an understanding that terrified the Love brothers, "if anything happens betwixt and between 'twill not be my soul to answer for it. Not this time. Begone now and may the Devil bless ye."

O'Roarke quickly turned his back on Jack and Ezra, dismissing them with his silence. As the two pirates glanced back, what they saw was their dashing Captain sitting beside the beautiful young lady, the candlelight reflecting the tears in his eyes that he was too proud to let fall.

CHAPTER EIGHTEEN

"Oh, Jamie, how could they?" said Rebecca resting her head on the Captain's shoulder.

" 'Tis the way of the sea lass. Ezra's been me own mate since I was a boy. When all went afoul, 'twas he took me aboard and schooled me in the life. He was the father I never had, Rebecca, and that's the truth of it. That evil Jack is to blame for all this, to my way of thinkin'. He thinks he's better than he is and lusts for the gentleman's life. I'll warrant that he gave poor Ezra no peace until the old salt fell in with his plans. 'Tis a pity that Ezra's blind to young Jackie's ways. He was a good soul and I'll miss him."

"But, Jamie, he wants to see you hanged. He deserves no pity whatsoever. I can't believe that you can even feel sorry for the old scoundrel."

"Ah girl, the sea can do strange things to a man and I've seen them all. Ezra's act is not the worst deed I've come across. And who are you to be asidin' with me over your own blood? Have ye no loyalty, girl?"

"You beast," laughed Rebecca delighted that Jamie was attempting to brighten their mood. "You could have at least warned me."

" 'Twas more fun to see the high and mighty Mistress Rebecca Love brought down a peg," laughed Jamie, reliving Rebecca's discomfort.

"Well, you're still a beast," said Rebecca snuggling into Jamie's shoulder, enjoying the smell of tobacco and rum mixed with the heady aroma of Spanish leather.

"Now, me girl," said O'Roarke putting his arm around her and enjoying the results of Melinda's costuming, "what are we going to do? So far all has gone on as before, the result of which was yours truly hanging at rope's end. Surely we can change that one little thing, but how? I've a feelin' that you might even be amissin' old Jamie if Jack and Ezra have their way."

"Oh, Jamie, it can't happen now, can it? You know what their plans are and all you have to do is get to Reverend Brown first. Offer him the treasure as your gift to the church and I'm sure they'll let you alone. Why, he might even help make you mayor," giggled a very tipsy Rebecca, stroking Jamie O'Roarke's sleeve.

"Give him the treasure! Are you mad, girl? Why that old skunk doesn't deserve MacRae's treasure. Why should that pious hypocrite receive the bounty from the labors of Captain Jamie O'Roarke?"

"Because if he doesn't he's going to help hang you, that's why," said Rebecca, exasperated at the pirate's attitude.

"Women! You all like to see such as Jamie tied up in fancy little knots that only you can unravel, now don't ye. I'll not be agivin' up me treasure and that's the end of it, do you hear. There must be a better way. All I have to do is puzzle upon the problem a bit."

"Don't puzzle too long, or Jack and Ezra will get to the magistrate and he'll wind up with the treasure," said Rebecca feeling decidedly dizzy. "This dark rum is far more powerful than anything I've ever had before. What do they make it out of."

"Only the finest of spirits me dear," said Jamie looking down at her and holding her close. "Come now let's not quarrel, 'tis too fine a night for it. By God it feels wondrous to be home."

"Does it really feel like home, Jamie? I would have thought after centuries of wandering you might have been disappointed."

"No, lass, there is no disappointment. This is old Jamie's home. Even if it doesn't have the fancies that you find in your world, I prefer it. Here a man knows where he is at and doesn't have to act like some bemused hag ridden fool."

" Are you saying that women like me don't value our men?" said Rebecca sitting up and glaring at O'Roarke.

"Now, lass, settle down, that's not what I meant at all. It's just that here it's easier for a man to prove himself. There are scarce chances for that in the world ye came from, that's all. Besides, perhaps I'm mistaken. I don't understand your world at all. This is a place that respects such as I. Snuggle in now and let's toast to Jamie's world."

With that, Jamie poured himself and Rebecca a generous helping of rum. He gave a sigh as he leaned back in his chair, surveying the room about him. Here were men whom, for better or worse, he could understand. The profound loneliness of the last three hundred years was something that Jamie would never be able to explain to the sweet girl beside him. Anything, even oblivion, would be preferable to the terrors of nothingness that Jamie had felt when he had first awakened in the dark world of damned spirits. The curse he had laid upon the MacRaes and the Love family was nothing compared to the terrible revenge exacted by the fates themselves. Once heaven or hell has granted a mortal's vengeful wish, that mortal's soul must see to the enactment of it. As a result, Captain Jamie O'Roarke had become his own victim, doomed to wander in loneliness through all eternity until the last of the MacRae and Love families had been destroyed. At least his innocent prey could find some comfort in the peace of the afterlife but poor Jamie was sentenced to forever roam the earth unless he could undo the evil that had been done.

And now there was this beautiful pure girl beside him wearing around her neck the precious gift that she had received from her dead father, the father whom Jamie himself had drowned in Collins Cove. Pray God that she never found out. Fate was indeed crueler than any could imagine. Unknown to Rebecca, Jamie's curse had also included the treacherous Jack and Ezra. How was Jamie to know that someday a lovely young girl might have to suffer for the foul deeds of a pirate band. If Jamie could not stop tomorrow's events, both he and Rebecca would find themselves embroiled in a dance of death that neither would have the power to stop. He must find a way, he must, even if it cost him his immortal soul. It was indeed a laughing God that had filled Jamie's heart with love for the innocent Rebecca.

"Now lass, go a bit slower on that," said Jamie looking down at Rebecca with a guarded eye. Was she feeling as lost as he had been? If so, it was time that old Jamie cheered her up a bit. There was no more to be done this night except treasure the company around him.

"I'm trying, Jamie, but this stuff slithers down my throat too easily. Don't you people ever drink water?"

"Water? Why 'tis foul liquid around here my dear unless you carry it from a stream. None of your easy ways to be had in old Salem Town. Every precious drop must be loaded on someone's back and paid for dearly. Besides, if you're to be a pirate's wench 'twould look odd indeed, this hankerin' for water with good rum flowing by."

"Still, I think I would prefer it, I don't know how to handle your rum and I feel quite strange."

"Just sit back and rest easy, lass, what you need is a good supper to brighten your spirits. 'Tis a rude fool I am not to think of it."

Jamie, motioning to Melinda, found himself searching his mind for what had pleased his stomach when he had been a mortal. It had been three hundred years since he had eaten solid food and he suddenly found himself delighted with the prospect.

"Shiver me soul, girl," said Jamie as Melinda sidled up to him brushing her leg against Jamie's in a suggestive way, "why haven't you brought us some food? Do ye want yon girl to faint from hunger? Why look at her, she's pale as a ghost."

" 'Tis all the drink you've been pouring' down her, O'Roarke, and you know it. Don't blame me for your evil ways, I'll not be havin' any of it. Now then, what's it to be?"

"I don't know, some beef or pudding, anything that's hot and good. You know your trade, girl. Bring us the best ye've got and lots of it," said O'Roarke feeling strangely irritated at his own confusion. What if what Rebecca said was true. Could he ever truly be happy here again? What if he had changed? What if there was no place for such as Jamie O'Roarke?

"Whist now and ye're a sharp one tonight, Jamie, settle down and I'll bring you some fine beef pies and fresh Indian bread. And if that isn't enough for ye there's even hot apple pie with clotted cream for the likes of ye. Rebecca could use some nice fresh cream to put the roses back into your cheeks now couldn't you, dearie?"

"What? Oh yes, Melinda, anything would be lovely, thank you," said Rebecca, rousing herself for a moment and then sitting back again.

"Hurry now, girl, and there'll be a doubloon in it for ye," said Jamie smiling at Melinda fondly.

"It's not a doubloon I crave, O'Roarke," said Melinda sticking out her tongue saucily, "but it will have to do until you come to your senses, you old pirate," said Melinda with a swish of her skirts as she hurried on her way.

When she returned a few moments later she carried an enormous pewter tray groaning with food. Rebecca had never smelled anything so wonderful. Melinda set before her a huge meat pie with steam rising from the holes cut in the delicate pastry. Beside the pie was a cake-like piece of bread that must have weighed a pound. In the center of the table, Melinda made room for an apple pie simply bursting with cinnamon and nutmeg. The pitcher of clotted cream she set beside it was as thick as ice cream.

"My goodness, we can't eat all this!" exclaimed Rebecca staring down at the food.

"Yes we can and yes we will," said O'Roarke tickling her under the chin. "It's been a long time since I've had such, and I crave your company while I'm doing it. None of your foreign nibbling ways here. While before ye know it we'll have changed you from a scrawny pale creature to a blooming beauty like Mistress Melinda here. Eat hearty now, girl, this is indeed a meal fit for a queen."

"Now don't ye go makin' her sick, O'Roarke, ease up on her a bit," said Melinda watching the dainty way Rebecca picked up her spoon. "She could teach the both of us something about fine table manners and the like. You eat what you want, mistress, and I'll make sure the poor kitchen knave bundles the rest up for his children, it won't go to waste, I promise."

With that Melinda laid a key on the table. "Here you old rogue, 'tis the best I could do on short notice, but it's good enough. Don't be astealin' my gear. There's plenty of extra blankets for you to make up a bed on the floor while Rebecca uses mine. Don't be gettin' up to any foolishness or you'll have Melinda Briggs to answer to, do you hear me?"

"But, Melinda, we can't take your room, where will you sleep?" said Rebecca amazed at the girl's kindness.

"Oh here and there, Mistress, don't you worry about me. There's plenty here would be glad to grant me lodging's for the night. Better for me to ask about then you, I say. Young Davy over yonder appears to be more than willing to help out a poor girl."

"A sad choice if you ask me, girl, why a strong gale would have him down in no time."

"Well and who's askin' you, O'Roarke?" said Melinda tweaking his beard. "Just make yourself cozy and stay out of sight 'till cock's crow, my friends." With that the lusty maid chuckled and went on her way whistling an old Irish sea chantey.

"What a wonderful girl she is," said Rebecca looking after Melinda.

"I suppose that's one way to look at it," said Jamie, mystified at the moods of all women. "Give me the sea and a fine ship over such as that. 'Tis much easier to fathom."

"Oh, we are not so hard to understand, Jamie. Most women just want love and companionship, along with a little security, of course."

"Spoken like a true female. And what if you get all that, why I would bet my boots that in a fortnight you'd be lookin' for more. No Rebecca, what a woman really wants is a dangerous man like yours truly, Jamie O'Roarke. I've had many a Salem lady set her cap for me when her fine fat husband is up in Boston Town on business. They have all that they need but they crave more. Only Captain Jamie can give them excitement and danger. What good is a carved wooden bed and satin quilts if there is no one to share them with?"

"And what good is a beautiful wife if she isn't true, Jamie? Oh, how sad that is, why can't we have both? If only we could all have our heart's desire."

"Oh, but you are a sweet soul, Rebecca, one such as you may just find your true love, if we get out of this mess. I can promise you that Captain Jamie will do everything in his power to make your wishes come true."

"Why, Captain O'Roarke, what are you talking about? You've already been more than kind. I want you to know that whatever happens I forgive you for bringing me here. I know that you were desperate and took the only way out. Don't you worry. We'll get home, I know it."

"But what if we can't, Rebecca, then what? What if we save my life and remove the curse and still find ourselves marooned here? You must see the way it is. God help me but I'm afraid this old pirate has fallen under the spell of the beautiful Rebecca Love."

"Jamie," cried Rebecca, "you can't be serious. I must admit that I'm attracted to you, but our worlds are so very different. We could never hope for happiness. You're a pirate and I'm an archeology assistant. Besides, look at the difference in our ages, why it must be," and Rebecca looked at Jamie, "over three hundred and twenty years," she said as a series of girlish giggles emitted from her smiling lips.

"There, you see, girl, we do have something in common. We both love the strange and unusual. Tell me now, haven't ye always been fond of Jamie even when he was nothing more than a page in one of your dusty old books? Jamie O'Roarke in the flesh has been something you've dreamed about for years. Here I am standing before you, smitten with love as I've never been before, and askin' for a bit of a kind word from ye. I'm not askin' for a promise and five bairns, just a chance 'tis all."

"Why, Jamie, please don't look so sad. You are one of the finest men I have ever known. You forget I know all about you. I've thought quite often about the poor little boy raised in Lynn with no father, and a mother forced to sell herself to get bread for her child. The fact that you became a ship's captain through your own determination is nothing less than a miracle. I remember crying when I read of how the merchants of Salem Town betrayed you because you refused to carry their cargoes of suffering slaves from Africa to the Caribbean. I don't blame you for your bitterness and your need to revenge yourselves on them. I loved your spirit then and I do now. It's just that I don't know if I love the man. I haven't known him for very long and you must admit this is a strange way to carry on a courtship."

"Right you are then, lass, what yer sayin' is that you need to get to know Jamie, that's all. Why then fear not. I'll have ye mad for me in no time and that's a fact. Come now let's bundle ye to bed before the rum takes its toll and I disgrace myself for another eternity."

PART THREE

ENCHANTMENT

CHAPTER NINETEEN

"By God he's gone and done it," said Professor Peter Hawking staring at the space where, until a moment ago, Rebecca had stood next to the dashing Jamie O'Roarke.

"Where are they, Professor Hawking? I swear if that foul O'Roarke has harmed that lovely girl I'll kill him."

"I'm afraid it's a little too late for that, Ian," said Peter desperately trying to gather his wits about him.

"What's happened to them?" said little Emily, grasping Peter's hand tightly, while desperately trying to still her quivering lower lip. Halloween was supposed to be scary but this was carrying things a bit too far. Emily adored the beautiful Miss Love and often fantasized that her mother could be just like her. Surely nothing really bad had happened to her!

"Don't you worry, Emily," said Peter looking down at the small girl. "Nothing has happened that can't be undone. I just need to make a plan."

"I think I know what's up," said a breathless Danny, his eyes staring at the spot where Rebecca and Captain O'Roarke had stood. "The Captain whispered something just before he disappeared."

"Well, what is it, laddie, speak up now," said Ian gently shaking the boy who seemed to be in a slightly trance like state.

"He said 'revenge' and laughed. Then the lightning flashed and they were gone. What did he mean, Professor?"

"I'm afraid I don't know, Danny," said Peter looking over the boy's head and into Ian MacRae's fearless eyes, "but I think we had better hurry."

"Professor Hawking," said the Scotsman, "whatever you mean to do must include me. It's my fault that this whole thing has occurred and as a man of honor I must see to Miss Love's safety. There is something that you may not know. Many years ago my Aunt read me an account of Duncan MacRae's life and death. It seems that the Laird of MacRae castle did have his revenge on Captain O'Roarke. The MacRae family appealed to a certain Reverend Samuel Brown of Salem for aid. It seems that this Reverend Brown enlisted the help of two pirates named Jack and Ezra Love to recover the MacRae treasure and bring O'Roarke to justice. Unfortunately, the Love brothers were also hanged without revealing the location of the treasure. Captain Jamie O'Roarke swore eternal revenge not only on the house of MacRae, but on Jack and Ezra Love and their descendants. So you see, Rebecca is in as great a danger as I am."

"I'm afraid that what my nephew said is true," said Lady Arabella, brushing back her silver gold hair. "That lovely girl must be found and quickly."

"I have often felt the danger around her myself," said Peter, finding himself trying to not not be mesmerized by the beauty of Arabella in the moonlight. "Her father and mother both died under suspicious circumstances. Pray God we find the girl in time."

With that Peter Hawking grasped the great staff he had formed from the shattered oak and raised his powerful arms. His body, blocking out the moon, cast a shadow over the graveyard that seemed to envelope the souls captured within. Raising his clear blue eyes to the heavens he gave a great cry and braced himself as a white light filled his body. The staff he was holding began to move with a light of its own until it emanated with a shimmering green gold presence. Peter, attempting to retain control of the staff, felt himself trembling. With his last surge of strength, he grasped the staff with both hands and planted it in the ground. As the wood touched the earth the company was delighted by a sound of bells. The sound began as a delicate whisper and soon surrounded them until the magical sound infused their very beings.

Emily, hypnotized by the sound, began to walk towards the staff. She was totally unaware of the ground beneath her. The earth itself was shaking with the vibrations caused by the staff and several cracks had appeared on the surface.

"Emily, come back," shouted Danny attempting to cross the shaking space that lay between his sister and himself.

"Do not worry, young sir," came an unspeakably beguiling voice from the staff. "The little one is pure of heart and can come to no harm. Come here my precious one. It has been a long time since I beheld a child."

"None of that, dyad," roared Peter placing himself between the green gold mist and Emily. He gently scooped up the little girl and deposited her in Ian's arms.

Peter, turning back to the shimmering presence, drew himself up to his full height. He stood tall and majestic in front of the light. "I am your master and you will do my bidding. The nymph Eva, I presume?" said Peter turning back to the blinding light.

"Why yes, handsome sir, that is what I'm called. Believe me, I wish the little one no harm, I just crave the touch of her hair and the sweet smile on her lips."

"I know what you wish, Madame, and it has nothing to do with kindness. If a dyad can find one such as this innocent young girl to take her place, she becomes free to roam the earth spreading her evil mischief. If you had your way, our little Emily would soon find herself imprisoned in some ancient elm crying for help. Heed me now. I am your master and unless you do my bidding this ancient wood will find itself in flames."

"Oh no, master, please. 'Twas an innocent game 'tis all. I swear that I will harm no one. Please do not destroy me. I can bring you glory and wealth beyond your wildest dreams. Just name your desire."

"I know the cost of your granted wishes, Madame. There is always a price to be paid and I am prepared to do so."

"Ah then, sir, you have knowledge of sorcery. My greetings to you as a brother and a sage. What is it you wish, master?"

"My wish is not for myself but for another. We have a friend who must be returned to us. She has been spirited off this very night. If you are truly as powerful a nymph as I have heard, it should be a simple thing to grant my request."

Peter Hawking bowed before the beautiful vision, hoping against hope that all he had heard about the vanity of the dyads was true. It was believed that their only vulnerability was their vanity. If the story he had heard was true then this particular nymph had been lured into her enchanted captivity by the husband of a lovely young girl she had destroyed. The nymph Eva had been unaware that the enchanting young man she lusted after was also a powerful sorcerer more than willing to trade his own life for revenge upon the evil nymph. It was said that the handsome sorcerer had been found breathing his last beneath the shade of the old elm. Clutched in his hand had been a small locket containing a picture of his beloved Elizabeth. Such was the treachery of a dyad. But her power could not be denied. Peter could only pray that his magic was stronger than hers.

"It should be a simple thing master. Just tell me where she is and she will be returned. Traveling the earth is as simple as the wink of an eye for a dyad."

"Ah but can you travel the ages, that is the question Eva." Peter moved towards the staff and touched the face of the smiling nymph. "It seems we have need of all the power you can summon. Our Rebecca has been taken to a time long ago. She should be standing in this very spot, but the year would be 1695."

"You wish me to bring someone from the past into the present! It can't be done, master. There is no one to show her soul the way. To travel such roads is a delicate matter. Many have become lost, doomed to wander throughout eternity in the nothingness of time already past. What you ask is impossible."

"It can't be," cried Peter holding the nymph by both shoulders and looking into her eyes. "There must be a way. Rebecca didn't travel alone. There was someone from that ancient time that spirited her back with him. You must be able to do something."

"Calm yourself, master. There are often many ways to conjure, but I must know all. What sort of being could do such a thing? He must be powerful indeed. Is he some witch who wishes you evil? If so just say the word and we will conjure up a spell to defeat him."

"It is not as simple as that, Eva. The man we must deal with was once a mortal."

"Then it should be a simple matter to defeat him. There has never been a mere mortal that could resist the temptations of a dyad. Just mention his name and your girl is as good as home."

"Thank you, my lady, rest assured that we will all be grateful to you. You are indeed the most powerful and beautiful of nymphs," said Peter Hawking kissing the fingertips of the lovely vision. "The man's name is Captain Jamie O'Roarke."

"O'Roarke! Oh no, it is not possible! Master, Jamie O'Roarke is the foulest man that ever walked the face of this earth and I would be thrilled to make him suffer unspeakable torments, but there is nothing I can do to harm him. He has been my fellow prisoner in this place for an eternity and there are celestial laws that prohibit my interfering with him. Believe me when I say that I am powerless against his spells."

"But there must be a way, there must. Every second we stand here talking, Rebecca's life is in danger. You must know of something we can do."

"Tell me all, master. Perhaps there is more than one way around this. There is nothing I would rather do than bring a bit of mischief to that old pirate."

With that, Peter, with several interruptions from Danny, who had wandered close to Eva fascinated by her loveliness, recounted the entire tale. At the end of the story, the old man took a silk handkerchief out of his pocket and wiped his brow. The exertions of the evening were beginning to tell on him.

"So, O'Roarke still has some human foolishness left to him. How fascinating," said the nymph giving her bell like laugh and sending the trees around her into a swirl of movement. "There is something we can do, but you must be prepared for some risk yourself. It is possible to send you back to save the girl, but I cannot promise your safe return. There are many events that may prevent you. If you are willing to take the risk then I will be glad to be your guide."

"You'll not be going alone, Professor. Rebecca's safety is my concern as much as yours," said Ian MacRae entering Eva's enchanted circle.

"And who might you be, sir?" said Eva, running her small pink tongue over her full red lips.

"He is not for you, Madame," said Peter, laughing at the transparency of the nymph's desires. "This is the Laird Ian MacRae. He too owes O'Roarke some mischief and must be regarded as a fellow adventurer."

"If Ian goes than I go," said Arabella putting her arm through Peter's. "If the MacRaes are to perish then let it be to the last man, or woman in this case. You cannot deny me the privilege. Besides if we become trapped in the past, I must be there to look after any great nephews or nieces that might come along."

"Aunt, I won't hear of it. Professor, this is madness!"

"I think that yon lady could be quite helpful, master," said Eva, eyeing Arabella and taking in her mettle. "You have no idea how different old Salem Town is from anything you have ever known. The lady would lend you both an air of normalcy and make your task easier. I can get you there but I won't be of much help once we are upon that ancient sod. The citizens of Salem Town know me well and have longed to have me burned for years."

"Well then, it's settled. But Eva, I have your promise that once our task is done you will try to get us home."

"I swear upon yon Lairds lovely locks, sir," said the nymph with a mischievous smile. "It would be a great boon, however, if the children could remain here as a celestial link for us. If they are standing where the old oak stood, then perhaps we could find our way back to them."

"Sort of like they do on 'Star Trek,' Professor, you know," said Danny delighted to be included in the magic.

"Yes boy, but you must be in exactly that place or we could become lost. One male and one female might be enough to satisfy the source," said the Professor.

"The source?" said Danny, his curiosity overcoming his shyness.

"Yes, the source of all things, Danny," said Eva to the intrigued boy. "Everything must be in balance to create the right passageway from old Salem Town to here. You and Emily might just help us to create the power needed." said the nymph.

"But, Danny, do we have to stay here alone?" said Emily looking about her. Halloween night was fun if you could end it in your own warm bed, but this was too much. She wanted to go home and wake up from this bad dream.

"It's all right, Emily," said Eva smiling at the little girl. "I'll weave a spell about you both and the next thing you know the sun will be shining. You and Danny will feel better than you have ever felt before."

"A spell," said Emily looking at Danny, "then I suppose it will be okay. I've never had a spell put on me before. It might be nice."

"It's very nice, I promise. You'll be safe and warm. Now just lay down on the grass and close your eyes," said Eva like some benevolent fairy godmother.

With that the two children walked over to the remains of the elm and made themselves comfortable. As they closed their eyes a gentle breeze enveloped both of them in its embrace. Arabella watched as the two children seemed to fade from view.

"Why, where have they gone!" she exclaimed totally alarmed.

"Oh don't worry, they are still there, dreaming happy dreams. I just thought that it would be better to shield them from sight so that no harm could come to them," said Eva with a casual shrug of her shoulders. "Now then, it is time for our journey. If what you said is true, we have no time to lose."

At her words, a great shimmering mist enveloped Peter, Arabella and Ian. Feeling an unbelievable lightness in his soul, Peter grasped Arabella's hand and smiled at her. "I feel like a boy, my dear, like a boy," were his last words as they disappeared into the vast eternity of Salem Town.

CHAPTER TWENTY

The brilliance of the blood red sunrise almost blinded the Laird Ian MacRae as he opened his eyes. He had awakened many other mornings in strange places not knowing where he was with his head pounding and the taste of scotch still upon his tongue, but this was entirely different. Taking the place of the muddy fog that usually accompanied his forays into the dens of Glasgow or Aberdeen was a feeling of incredible lightness. It seemed as if the weight of the world had been lifted from his shoulders. As Ian shifted his body so that his resting weight was propped up by his elbows, he gazed about him taking in the lay of the land.

The crispness of the air assailed his lungs and he found himself gulping down great amounts of the intoxicating stuff. To his left lay his Aunt Arabella cradled comfortably in Professor Hawking's arms. The two gentle souls were fast asleep.

Many a time Ian had roamed the Scottish highlands attempting to capture the beauty of the moors and lochs on canvas, feeling always as if his meager talents were not equal to the job. Now he took in the beauty of Salem Town at sunrise and once again felt an insatiable hunger for brush, colors and canvas. Before, when he had felt overwhelmed by such desires, he had fled to the cities of Scotland and buried himself in the security of portrait work. It was much easier to record the smile of a lovely young wife or old merchant on canvas than it was to try to capture the enchantment of the highlands. The trouble was, that even though Ian MacRae was a good portrait artist, his heart lay in the soft heather of his Aunt Arabella's beloved highlands. The praise he received for his work, along with the caresses of many a lovely lady, had been enough to convince the handsome Ian that he was happy and fulfilling himself as an artist. But deep within his soul Ian knew it was a lie. Fame and fortune lay in Glasgow, but his soul's yearning for the true greatness of the highland wilds could not be denied. Once he had accepted the first falsehoods of his existence, many more followed. He had convinced himself that he was happy with his many light loves and had ceased searching for a true soulmate. The loneliness in his heart and soul he filled with too much drink and too many late nights until he found himself grateful to be able to dab a few brush marks on a canvas and call it a work of art. His patrons never complained about his works because the truth of it was that Ian MacRae's portraits were the finest ever known in Glasgow. Ian was blind to the fact of his own genius and only a miracle could save him from his downward spiral to mediocrity.

Aunt Arabella had wept many a tear for her beloved nephew as she watched him squandering his health and talent. Many times she had pleaded with him to come home and find some fine village lass to share the highlands with, but Ian had never heeded her words or her tears. The fear that lay deep within the powerfully built Ian MacRae threatened to destroy him.

It was Arabella MacRae who had loved and understood Ian from the first. Many years before, the lovely Arabella had married the persistent Alan in hopes that he would save her from her own demons. The young Arabella Taylor had dreamed of becoming a poet and after several years of giving herself fully to her first love, Arabella had abandoned it all in a fit of despair. When Alan MacRae had asked for her hand she had resigned herself to the life of lady bountiful caring for a great castle and the villagers who surrounded it. It was not until the three year old Ian had arrived that Arabella had felt her heart awaken again. How she had adored the brave, stalwart little boy full of passion and artistic desire. It was Aunt Arabella who had put the first crayon in his small chubby fist and been amazed when instead of childish scribbles the young boy had recreated a perfect likeness of his dead mother. She had run excitedly to Alan and insisted that the child must have the finest of teachers and any supplies he needed. Alan had laughed indulgently and told her to do anything she wanted to for the boy. Within a few years Ian was amazing the local townsfolk and the guests at the castle with his pictures. What others saw as mere cleverness or a parlor amusement, Arabella knew to be real genius and encouraged Ian to follow his dreams. How she had felt her heart break a second time when she saw the deadly fear she knew so well overtake and threaten to destroy her beloved Ian. As his mind became more muddled with fear and scotch, Arabella could only stand helplessly by praying for a miracle.

That miracle had already happened, but neither Ian nor Arabella were aware of it. Through the love of his Aunt and a beautiful pair of blue eyes, Ian MacRae had been drawn back into the enchantment of old Salem Town and had been purified in the sunrise of an autumn morning.

"Come, my boy," said the deep voice of Peter Hawking rousing Ian from his thoughts, "we had better get to work if we are to find Rebecca. There is no telling what that foul O'Roarke has done with her."

"Right you are, sir," said Ian getting to his feet and moving to where Arabella was sitting. "Come, Aunt, if you feel anything like I do there just may be enough strength in us to get this task done. Why I haven't felt so fine in years."

"Truly Ian? Well, then, so do I," said Arabella taking the hand Ian offered and springing to her feet like a young girl.

"Why Professor Hawking, I do believe we have discovered the fountain of youth. I haven't felt like this in years." With that Arabella proceeded to begin to spin in circles and laugh like a young girl.

"Halt! Who goes there?" said a muscular man dressed in leather and carrying an ancient but deadly looking pike.

Arabella stopped in mid twirl and quickly took refuge behind Peter.

"Why 'tis none but visitors from yon Salem Village to the west," said Peter praying that his voice had at least some of the characteristics of those that this strangely dressed man was used to hearing.

"Well, and I know most of the folks of Salem Village and I've seen none of your like about."

"We're but relatives of those who once lived there," said Peter drawing himself up to full height in an attempt to impress the smaller man. "I am Peter Hawking, relative to Giles Corey, and this is Goodwife Hawking with our son Ian. I have learned that my cousin and his wife recently passed away and I have come here in hopes of paying my last respects."

Peter drew in a breath and silently prayed that the man would believe his tale. Grounding some of it in the truth made him feel that at least he may have sounded convincing. Arabella looked in the yeoman's direction and gave him an appealing smile, displaying an earnest yet wistful look.

"Yes, fine sir," she said, "we were grieved to find that Giles and Martha were no more, but we feel that it is our Christian duty to see to their memory before we take our leave of this lovely town. Would you kindly tell us where they have been laid to rest?"

The man, looking down at his the buckles on his shoes shifted his weight first from one foot to the other. "Well now, Goody Hawking, that would be hard to say. Most of the folks what were hanged were tossed into a pit below Gallow's Hill, I'm sorry to say. 'Tis an unsavory place to take your sorrow I'm afraid. 'Twould be better if we spoke to the Reverend and let him show you the place himself. The doings around here were none of my affair. I'm just mighty grateful that neither myself nor none of mine were touched by the madness."

The yeoman looked at Arabella with heartfelt pity and placed his pike over his shoulder. As the sun rose behind the visitors, a startled expression replaced the one of sympathy when he realized that there was something far odder about these pilgrims than their faces. The lavender of the lady's dress was a hue that he had never seen before except in the flowers of the field at high summer. That combined with the tweed sports coat of Peter Hawking and the watch on Ian's wrist alarmed the simple man.

"What is this now. Ye are not of the ilk of the Coreys. To be sure your dress is the oddest I've ever seen. Come along now and don't be arguin' with me. I don't know what this bodes, but this is a matter for higher than such as me to judge upon."

The man quickly pointed his pike at Ian's back and nudged the party towards the rough looking building that stood next to the stocks that had earlier held the prisoner Melinda Briggs. With a determined nod of his head, the yeoman motioned Peter and Arabella to follow him.

"Well, now, my good man, this is no way to treat guests in your fine town. You can be sure that the governor will hear of this," said Peter attempting to keep up the pretense and hoping he was impressing the man with his importance.

"You wait right here whilst I fetch Reverend Brown," said their captor, securing Ian in a set of chains that hung from the wall. "There now, I feel you'll be going nowhere without this fine young man. Bide ye here and wait for his honor."

With that the man quickly went out the door, relieved that the strangers would soon be in the hands of his superiors. The authorities of Salem Town were hard enough to deal with since all the trouble a few years back. The last thing Isaiah Wolf wanted was any more trouble hereabouts. Best to deliver up the strangers and put some distance between himself and the doings.

"Oh, Peter, what are we going to do!" said Arabella, pulling on the chains that held Ian fast to the wall of the stoutly built prison.

"The first thing to do is to not panic," said Peter sitting down on the earthen floor that had been tamped down by the many feet that had trod upon it.

"Are you in any discomfort, Ian?" said Peter, attempting to deal with his surroundings in as logical a manner as possible.

"Actually no, Professor," said Ian trying to keep as calm as possible. Aunt Arabella must not be alarmed further no matter what his discomfort. He gave her a reassuring smile and rattled his chains.

"See, Aunt, I can give a fine imitation of Dicken's 'Marley.' Don't be aworrying. I'm sure the professor has something up his sleeve."

"Of course, my boy, of course. All we need to do is convince the honorable Reverend Brown that we are distant relatives of Giles Cory. Perhaps if we promise to not hold the entire town responsible for the unjust torturing of my 'cousin' they might let us go. If memory serves me correctly, it was sometime around now that all the victims except Rebecca Nurse were completely exonerated of any wrong doing. Let us just hope that I have my facts straight."

"Peter, why wasn't Goody Nurse forgiven her crimes, surely she must have been innocent too?" said Arabella touched by the plight of the Salem woman.

"Of course she was, but Rebecca Nurse was a member of the Salem Town parish rather than the Salem Village parish. It took the townsfolk a lot longer to admit the error of their ways. That is why we must be very cautious. People around here are very sensitive about what went on. I'm sure that there are still a few that would like to justify their actions with a few more hangings."

As he spoke, the heavy wooden door was pushed open by Major Isaiah Wolf. Following him were two distinguished men in clerical garb.

"Now then, Isaiah, what is all this about? You know that Deacon Williams and I dislike being interrupted during our morning devotions."

"The only devotions you were attending to were over fish and potatoes, Reverend Brown," laughed the man in armor.

"I'll remind you to keep a civil tongue in your head, Major Wolf. You've been much too lenient with the prisoners of late. Remember it was on your watch that Melinda Briggs slipped away," said Samuel Brown, straightening the spotless white color and cuffs that adorned his deep black jerkin.

"And that was a bit of foolishness, sir, if you don't mind my saying so. Mistress Parr was just being spiteful and that's the truth of it. To punish that simple girl was a pure act of cruelty. It's time that those about here practiced the Christian beliefs they speak of so loudly," said Major Wolf throwing his scarlet cape over his shoulder.

"Now then, what is all this bother, Wolf?" continued the minister. "These strangers don't look so strange to me."

"I thought I should turn them over to you, sir. You said yourself that I was to notify you of any suspicious characters hereabouts."

"That was only concerning the pirates anchored off Collin's Cove, ye dolt. But I suppose 'tis better you summoned us than not. Release this man immediately."

The major turned to the hapless Ian and quickly unlocked his chains.

"My apologies to you and your parents, sir. May I be the first to welcome you to Salem. I take my leave now. I am sure the Reverend can point you in any direction you may need."

With that the gallant major left, relieved to be rid of both trouble and clergy. Life in Salem was becoming far too tame for the adventurous Major Isaiah Wolf. He often dreamt about leaving the oceanside town far behind him and setting out to explore the unknown regions that lay to the west. There had been many rumors of untold riches just waiting for a brave man to reap. Perhaps it was time to resign his commission and set out before any more trouble occurred in this place.

"So you see, your honor," said Peter as the clergymen escorted the travelers from the prison, "all we wish is to pay our respects and be on our way."

"I wish I could be more helpful to you, sir," said Samuel Brown," but I have no idea where old Giles and Martha rest. Many lay in unmarked graves hereabouts and I'm afraid that your cousin is among them. So you see your journey has been a fruitless one. Please accept the hospitality of our town as long as you like, with only one request. It would be wise if you attempted to follow our customs and garb yourselves in something more suitable. I'm afraid that your lady's costume is a bit too daring for our simple town. Men are not used to the sight of so fair an ankle and the display of a woman's hair."

"Well," said Arabella startled at the disapproving look from the righteous Reverend Brown, "I'll be more than happy to comply with your customs, but I'll have you know I'm a lady and not used to such treatment."

"Be that as it may, Goody Hawking, you must find more suitable cover or face the wrath of our womenfolk. They would not take kindly to such boldness."

"Calm yourself, my dear, I am sure that we can find something for you. Your beauty would outshine any attempt at drabness to be sure," said Peter warming to his role as husband. In the spirit of the moment he gave the delighted Arabella a warm hug and a kiss full on the lips.

"Sir," said Major Wolf blustering through the door in search of his hat, greatly alarmed by Peter's gesture, "I regret that I must place you under arrest for public lewdness."

CHAPTER TWENTY-ONE

"Arrest! But why? This lady is my wife!" countered Peter as Major Wolf clasped the iron cuffs around his wrists.

"That makes no difference in Salem Town now does it, Reverend Brown," said the major secretly glad that he had an excuse to keep the odd visitors under his watchful eye a few more hours. Something about them did not make sense to the world weary soldier. He had seen many new places and unusual costumes, but those worn by the "cousins" of Giles Cory were unlike any he had ever encountered. As he was about to depart for his daily inspection of Salem, a flash of intuition had sent him hurrying back to the prison, praise be for his forgotten hat. It was the bright gleam of gold that had caught his eye. The strange circular band around Ian's wrist intrigued the well traveled soldier. What was there about it that was so unusual? The sundial inscribed on the clear surface seemed to move in an almost magical way, surely this was not a trinket that could be found upon the person of any man of Salem Town. Yes, there was something definitely different about the family of Peter Hawking and it was his duty, troublesome though it may be, to investigate these odd folk further. How fortunate it was that he encountered such a display of public lewdness as he rounded the corner. Not even the Right Reverend Samuel Brown could deny Isaiah Wolf the pleasure of placing the old man in the stocks for a few hours. Why, it was the pious cleric's own rule!

"This is preposterous, I've done nothing wrong!" exclaimed Peter as Isaiah gently prodded him with the tip of his sword.

"Mount the steps now my man. A few hours in Salem's stocks will do ye no harm. I'm afraid I have no choice, do I, Reverend?"

"I'm afraid not," said Samuel Brown glaring at the soldier with an evil eye. "The laws of Salem are very clear about public displays of affection. I very much regret the inconvenience sir, but you must see how it is. If we allow such as yourselves to escape the justice of our laws we would soon have nothing but anarchy in our small community."

"Captain Wolf, please see to it that yon gentleman is released at the stroke of noon. We can at least be kind to him regarding the length of his punishment."

With that Samuel Brown beat a hasty retreat in the direction of the church. Damn that cursed Major! The Reverend would have liked the strangers to leave town as quickly as possible. There was too much confusion gathering around this day as it was. What with the meeting between himself and the "Red Witch" pirates, along with the untimely escape of Melinda Briggs, Reverend Brown felt that things were not as neatly arranged as he would have liked them to be. There were too many loose ends laying about town just now and a pack of strangers asking questions would only complicate things further. Why couldn't the honorable Isaiah have relaxed the rules just this once. Perhaps the good Major Wolf had a suspicion of what Reverend Brown was up to! It was not impossible that the minx Briggs had some knowledge of the pirates' doings and had spilled her knowledge to Wolf!

"Get hold of yourself, man," muttered Samuel under his breath, "if you go on like this you'll soon be jumping at shadows and declaring the devil has returned to Salem Town. I know it is all in my mind, but I'll be the happiest man on earth when O'Roarke is safely hanged and his body thrown to the dogs."

"Still," he thought, "it would do no great harm to arrest Mistress Briggs until this whole affair was over. It might even be amusing to question her in his own special manner regarding any knowledge she may have of the despicable Jamie O'Roarke."

Turning heel, he returned to the clearing where Major Wolf was just finishing his odious task.

"Captain, seeing as how the prisoner is secured, I have one more errand for you. The matter of Mistress Briggs has been weighing heavily on my mind. Her untimely departure from yon stocks must not be overlooked. As you said yourself, an example must be set or all will be chaos. Please fetch the burde to the prison so that I may question her as to the manner of her escape. She could not have accomplished it alone and we must find out who has been flaunting our laws. This transgression must not be allowed."

"Yes, sir," saluted Isaiah, looking regretfully back at Peter locked in the stocks. Ian and Arabella sat on either side of him trying to distract the man from his humiliation with light jokes. How intriguing it would have been to pass the allotted punishment time in conversation with the strangers. Leave it to that pious black crow to spoil his plans. Isaiah could only hope that the rumors of Samuel Brown's discontent with Salem Town were true. The fine Reverend yearned for greater things and was quite eager to shake the dust of provincial Salem from his heels. As the whole town knew, the grandeur of Boston and an appointment from Cotton Mather were more to Samuel Brown's taste. His new appointment could not happen soon enough for Isaiah. But until then Samuel Brown was his superior and must be obeyed.

"It was a fine mess they made when the clergy chose to rule over the magistrates here about and that's a fact," thought Major Wolf mounting his black stallion and heading off towards the Blue Anchor tavern. Perhaps the lovely Mistress Briggs would be feeling more kindly towards him if he promised to do what he could to save her from the lecherous grasp of Samuel Brown. What a fine sturdy figure of a woman she was. Isaiah Wolf had fantasized more than once about placing her on his black stallion and heading west with only the wind and the sun to set the rules. It would take a brave lass indeed to venture where she could lose her scalp or die of hunger at any time. But then again, if anyone had the mettle it was Melinda Briggs, who could fell a man with one shot and have the musket reloaded before a man could turn around. What a woman!

CHAPTER TWENTY-TWO

"Oh, Peter, you must be so uncomfortable," said Arabella rubbing his large brown wrists with her small white hands.

"Why, not at all, my dear," said Peter attempting to erase the concern from the lovely Arabella's brow. "I find this experience quite fascinating. It's a lovely day and the air is really very invigorating. My only regret is that this will delay our search for Rebecca, but it is becoming quite clear that unless we move cautiously we may borrow even more trouble for ourselves. We must have a plan. Luckily, it seems that the good Major Wolf will be out of our hair for awhile. I wonder who the unlucky Mistress Briggs is and what has she done? Poor girl. I wouldn't want to find myself in the clutches of either of those two rogues."

"But, professor, if we don't find Rebecca soon, she may come to harm. You said so yourself that O'Roarke is a dangerous man. If what I've read about him is true we don't have a second to waste."

"Quite right, Ian, but look around you. Where would you start, a strange man in a strange land. Arabella, hand me my livewood. Perhaps our dyad may still be lingering here abouts."

Arabella quickly climbed to the bottom of the pillory steps where, in the confusion, Peter had dropped the great staff fashioned from the old oak. Thank heavens it had not been lost or confiscated in the last few moments!

Giving it to Peter, she helped him balance it between his two hands that were bound by the wood of the sturdy stocks. The professor smiled at her as he managed to create a rubbing motion with the wood that resulted in a bright shower of sparks. Peter closed his eyes and prayed in a combination of pagan and biblical thoughts for the nymph Eva to appear. Just as he was losing hope, the party felt a warm breeze engulf them. Ian peered down at the staff and was amazed to see a miniature version of the fascinating Eva. This small enchantress stood only about thirteen inches high and glimmered with a soft golden light. It was in this way that she eluded the prying eyes of the Salem townsfolk.

"What is it, Master? I implored you not to call upon me here. Any knowledge of our unholy union and old Brown will be toasting our toes. He has been lusting after the capture of my soul for years. 'Twas not my fault that the fool's son ran afoul of me. Served him right too. Anyone who can pass up my charms deserves punishment. But enough of me, what is it that you summoned me for, Master? Let us resolve the matter quickly."

"My lovely Eva, I do apologize for disturbing you, but I'm afraid it can't be helped. You were quite correct when you warned us of the strangeness of this land. Our quest is to find our friend Rebecca, but I'm afraid it is becoming more difficult than we realized. You can see for yourself that our ignorance of the ways of Salem has already resulted in a slight delay."

"A delay!" exclaimed the nymph. "Why I bet 'twas Samuel Brown stuffed you in there! See what I mean! They think nothing of torturing us body and soul. Would you like to be freed, Master?"

"Yes, but don't, please. It would only arouse more suspicion and we can't afford that. Better I should be seen as an erring, but penitent citizen. It will only be a short while until my release. But we can't afford to waste any more time. Is there any way you can help us discover Rebecca's whereabouts?"

"Well, your worship, I can and I can't," said Eva creating a mist of shimmering green about her. "I can tell you that I see O'Roarke with her and they are departing from a rough looking building. They can't be far away, as I am sure that the smell I detect is that of the sea. Whist now while I try to hear their thoughts."

Taking on a quizzical look, the miniature nymph seemed to stop breathing as the stillness around her became profound.

"I have it! They are heading back to Salem Town in search of a man called Jack, whoever he may be. It seems that the Captain is more interested in slitting his throat than he is in harming your girl. One thing, however, I feel something else in that foul O'Roarke. I would search out your innocent Rebecca and quickly or he may have his way with her if you know what I mean," said Eva winking at Ian in a wicked way.

"I'll kill him," shouted the Scotsman totally forgetting where he was.

"I think you would have to wait in line to do that this day, my Laird," said Eva smiling in a self satisfied way. "My guess is that if you just bide your time in Salem Town your girl and the pirate will soon appear."

"Then, that is what we will do, my dear, and thank you. As you say you must not linger here a moment more than is necessary so off with you now. And Eva," said Peter with a smile, "I must say you look quite charming today."

"Why thank you, your worship. Perhaps later we can spend some time under a shady tree. I believe that you could teach a nymph a thing or two now, couldn't you," said the dyad as she disappeared in a symphony of twinkling bells.

"Why I never," said Arable moving towards Peter in a protective manner. "You stay away from that evil little fairy or you may find yourself locked in an oak tree, Peter Hawking."

"But, my lady, whatever do you mean?" said Peter, delighted to find himself the object of not one, but two charming lady's affections. This adventure was beginning to be quite a pleasurable experience for the lonely old professor.

"You know very well what I mean," said Arabella exasperated at how easily a pretty smile could turn a man into a fool. "She just looks upon you as a way out of that staff and you know it. Watch her, she's a dangerous minx who will seduce you into an eternity of misery."

"You are quite right, my dear, quite right," said Peter rousing from his delicious reverie, "and many thanks for warning me. You are indeed one in a million, Arabella."

"And one who is becoming quite fond of you, Peter Hawking. That nymph is not the only one around here with a few feminine tricks. When this is over, perhaps you and I can explore more than the graveyards of Salem."

"Why, Aunt, what a time to be talking like this," said Ian both shocked and delighted to see the sparkle in Arabella's eyes.

"Did you think I was dead, nephew?" said the lovely Scottish lady looking at Ian. "Never forget that as long as there is breath in our bodies, we deserve happiness. Isn't that so, Peter?"

"Yes, my sweet lady, indeed it is," said Peter completely enjoying his morning in the stocks.

"Now then, Ian, let us formulate a plan for luring our lovely Rebecca away from that scoundrel O'Roarke. There is no guessing what he has told her to get his way."

CHAPTER TWENTY-THREE

"Well now, my dear, that was a closer call than I would care to have twice in one day," said O'Roarke as he and Rebecca skirted the perimeter of Salem Town. "I say that it was quite unfair of that honor bound Isaiah Wolf to arrest Melinda a second time. After we're finished with that scurvy Jack we must see to spiriting our Melinda aboard the 'Red Witch' and setting the girl down in some safer harbor."

"Oh, Jamie, that would be wonderful," said Rebecca slipping her hand into the Captain's weathered one, "I just know that Melinda would love to travel a bit. Do you think it would be possible for her to be taken someplace where she could live like a lady?"

"A lady! That buxom burde!" laughed O'Roarke until the tears were running down his eyes. "Why, Rebecca me girl, you do amuse me!"

"I don't see anything funny in what I said, Jamie O'Roarke! Melinda Briggs is as good as you or I and don't you forget it. A little humility couldn't hurt you, Captain high and mighty." With that Rebecca turned her back on Jamie and began to walk towards the clearing. As she strode stubbornly away from the pirate, Rebecca heard the sound of horses hoofs thundering towards them. Jamie ran up behind her quickly and grabbed the girl around the waist. They both tumbled down a shallow ravine, praying that they had not been noticed. If Jamie and Rebecca were discovered now, everything would come to naught.

Looking up, Rebecca and Jamie saw the flash of Major Wolf's black stallion. The unlucky Melinda was riding in front of him, holding on for dear life. As the two broke into the clearing ahead, Rebecca ran up the ravine.

"Jamie, do something! There is no telling what may happen to Melinda!"

"Go slow now, lass," said Jamie staring after the dusty tracks of the Major. "If we are discovered and arrested there is little hope for Mistress Briggs. We must keep cool heads or we all may find ourselves at rope's end. Lay low now while I survey the lay of the land."

Jamie, climbing a small hillock covered with trees, positioned himself so that the town presented itself below him. With an expert motion he removed his small brass telescope from within the depths of his great coat and looked about. What Jamie saw changed any immediate plans he may have had for throttling the scurrilous Jack while trying to talk some sense into old Ezra.

Below him, Captain Jamie spied a party of unhappy prisoners on the pillory, one of whom was locked securely in the sturdy wooden stocks. With disbelieving eyes, Jamie refocused the telescope and realized that it was the old professor. "Thank the devil for Major Wolf," he muttered as he quickly snapped the telescope shut and hurried back to the waiting Rebecca. To be sure, perhaps all would have to wait now. Captain Jamie had not lived this long without being able to change course in midstream. His only choice, if he wanted to save his hide and keep the beautiful Rebecca by his side, would be to abandon all hope of a quiet life in Salem Town and head for the high seas. If only that damned Wolf had not gotten his hooks into that lusty burde of a Melinda. No telling what they would do to her if they discovered that she had helped Captain O'Roarke escape their clutches, treasure and all. Why those pious pigs were sure to hang her, or worse yet, burn her at the stake for some foul foolishment that she had never had a part in. "No," sighed Jamie as he quickly grabbed Rebecca's arm and began to lead her down a path overstrewn with autumn roses, he could take to the sea, but only after both Melinda and Rebecca were safely aboard the "Red Witch." " 'Tis a fine sentimental fool I am and that's a fact," he said to the whispering trees as he sat down beneath a bower of blood red roses, warmly drawing Rebecca to his side.

"Why do you say that, Jamie?" said Rebecca glad to get away from the main road. The look on Jamie's face was one that she could not fathom. It seemed to be a mixture of pain and love as he looked down into her clear, innocent eyes.

"Rebecca, me darlin', I'm afraid our plans have changed, damn the luck. It seems that there is too much going on about the town to risk my staying here, even though I promise you that the blackguard Jack will taste the edge of me cutlass before I breath my last. It is time to take to the sea awhile and bide our time until we can return in safety. I cannot risk your life along with mine. It has become even more precious than all the treasure I have hidden here abouts."

"But, Jamie, what of Melinda, we can't abandon her! She is only in trouble because of us. There is no telling what may happen to her!"

"Well spoken, my girl. Aye and you are right, but this is a risk I must take alone. I plan to get her out of that dank prison somehow, but first I must see you safely aboard the 'Red Witch.' It would do well to bide here a bit until all is calm in yonder town. Then we can follow the path to Collin's Cove. Lassie, do ye know how to handle a skiff?"

"Do I know how? Why, what a question, Captain O'Roarke, I was born right here and have been sailing around the cove my entire life. Don't you worry about me, Captain. Unless you've laid one of your drowning curses upon me I should be just fine."

"Well now then, that's me girl," said Jamie drawing her head down upon his shoulder and savoring the nearness of the beautiful Rebecca. If he were to die this day, he could think of nothing better than spending his last hour here with Rebecca in this secret bower of perfumed roses. All his life he had been a sentimental fool, fight as he might against it. How fitting it was that the ferocious Captain Jamie O'Roarke might meet his end this day, not on the end of some soldier's cutlass, but saving not one, but two lovely ladies. Perhaps then it was supposed to end this way. It was a plan the blessed virgin herself would have smiled at.

"Oh, Jamie, there have been moments during the last few hours in which all this seems more real than anything I have ever experienced before."

"How so, lass?" said Jamie putting his arm around the thoughtful girl. Many was the pretty young wench he had taken to his bosom, but none had been like this fair lass. She was not only beautiful, she was made of the same steel that Jamie himself had been fashioned. Jamie felt in his desire towards her a confusing tumult of conflicting emotions. One moment he wanted to take her in his arms and experience the bliss that he knew could only be found in Rebecca's arms. The next moment he wanted to spirit her away from the glare of the dangerous world and wrap himself about her like some great protective entity. Forgotten were his first plans of revenge upon the girl. The avenging spirit, who had shadowed the innocent child awaiting an opportunity to plunge her into the deadly waters of Collins Cove, had died the moment he had resumed his all too human form. Thank heaven that Peter Hawking's sixth sense had protected the girl or Jamie would have followed through with the cruel demands placed upon him by his own words. It was an evil day that had brought about such venom from his lips.

"Rest now, my love. 'Twill be a long day indeed and there is nothing to do but catch our breath. Though this may seem like a dream, I'm afraid that it is all too real."

"Jamie, what did you see in the clearing? Is Melinda all right? I would never forgive myself if anything happened to her."

"Whist now and it was nothing, my girl, just several of the poor townsfolk being locked up for spitting in public or some such crime. But by the mood down below I think it would be better to wait until things are a bit quieter if we are to spirit Melinda away without raising a fuss. As soon as the shadows grow long we shall part, you for the cove and me for the prison. That way all the worthies here abouts should be occupied with the filling of their ample stomachs. There is the one thing I know we can count on above all else. Reverend Brown has never been known to let his duty get in the way of his comforts."

" But what of Melinda, she must be scared. Will she be safe? It seems that Reverend Brown holds some sort of grudge against her."

"Aye that he does, lass, but I think that Major Wolf will see that she comes to no harm. The history of it is that old Brown has been trying to get the lovely Melinda between the sheets for years, but the lass will have none of it. Try as he might she has turned his every trick against him, and he can't forgive her that. It seems that his worthy believes that everyone in this town belongs to Reverend Brown with or without their consent. But never fear. Isaiah Wolf has cast longing eyes of true love towards the girl. I wouldn't be surprised if he uses this opportunity to confess all to our darlin' Melinda. No, I don't think any harm will come to her while there is still light in this sky. 'Tis the night that concerns me. There is no telling what our venerable Reverend will be up to under the cover of darkness and if I don't miss my guess, this could be Melinda's last chance. If she refuses him again she will burn, and not for her crimes."

"But that's horrible, Jamie! How can such a thing be, are there no laws against such things?"

"Ah, but ye are an innocent, my Rebecca. No, there are no such laws that protect such as Melinda Briggs, not now nor in your world either."

"Oh, but you're wrong, Jamie. Things are much better in modern times, I know they are!"

"Are they now? Did anyone question your own mother's death? Everyone assumed that since she was a woman alone, taking her pleasure as she wished, her death was of no consequence. What guarantee do you have that her accident was a true one?"

"But it must have been, Jamie, what else could it have been?" said Rebecca shocked at his inference.

"Nothing else, my angel, I just wanted to make a point. Even in your 'safe' world things may not always be as they appear. Who knows what evil may lurk around the next corner?"

"Jamie, you're scaring me. How am I to go on if things are as you say? I don't understand this place or these people. It seems that life counts for very little here and death is hiding behind every tree. If anything were to happen to you I don't know what I'd do. Please be careful when you go for Melinda, I know you must, but it doesn't make me any less afraid."

"Only a fool would not be afraid, dearest," said Jamie cupping his hand underneath her lovely chin and looking deeply into Rebecca's bonny blue eyes. Jamie felt a calmness come over the girl as she gazed back at him with shining trust. Overwhelmed with passion, Captain Jamie O'Roarke pressed his strong full lips against those of the beautiful Rebecca Love. He held his breath as he silently prayed to the God that he had almost forgotten. "Please let her return his feelings." If this were so then Jamie O'Roarke could begin to make some sense of the last three hundred years and begin to live as a man again, filled only with joy and hope.

As Rebecca's lips moved under his, he heard her moan softly in gentle assent. Jamie, growing bolder, parted his lips and tasted the delights that only the trembling girl beneath him could have surrendered. What was there about this girl that made him feel as if he were a young boy tasting the pleasures of love for the first time.

The truth was that Rebecca was the first and only love Jamie had ever known. All the other women before her had been used to fill the terrifying loneliness that icily creeped into his soul when he found himself alone. Any companion was preferable to the dark terrors that lay within Jamie O'Roarke. From a very tender age his mother had taught him that the pleasures of the flesh were to be used as a means of survival. Anyone who fell in love was a fool only to be used for profit. Little Jamie had learned well. It was not until this very moment that he realized what true love could mean. Gone was the fear, the terror, that flooded his soul when he felt the touch of a woman weakening his heart. Filling him instead was the joyous peacefulness that comes with knowing that a man has given his heart to a woman he can trust.

As Rebecca drew him gently down upon the soft earth covered with rose petals, he felt himself engulfed in an unknown ecstasy for which there were no words. The seducer became the seduced, and the innocent wise, in the sunshine of that brilliant autumn day.

CHAPTER TWENTY-FOUR

"Isaiah Wolf, you handle me more gently or I swear I'll scratch your eyes out," yelled Melinda Briggs as Major Wolf attempted to lower her from his horse.

"Now you know you're not being fair, Mistress Briggs. If you had only ceased your squirming the ride could have been quite a pleasant one."

"Nothing could be pleasant about a journey to the prison of Salem Town and you know it, Major. What is it that the bastard of a Brown wants of me now?" said Melinda tossing her curls in a haughty manner.

"He just needs you to answer a few questions, I'm sure," said Isaiah as he dismounted and held Melinda's arm tightly. "Perhaps if you are cooperative you may escape a night in yon jail. Believe me I do not relish the thought of you languishing there, Mistress."

"Why, Major, I do believe you mean it," said Melinda looking up into his earnest brown eyes. "Well then, all right, I'll try to be a model citizen, but I'll have you know that if old Brown gets up to any of his special tricks, there will be hell to pay."

"Hush now, Melinda, don't speak so or it will go badly with you. The Reverend is a man of the cloth and holds all womanhood as sacred, I assure you."

"Much you know of it, Isaiah, you are a great fool like all men. Your precious saint Brown has had his hands wandering over me more than once, I wouldn't mind it so much but for his foul breath. Oh, I could tell Mistress Brown a thing or two and that's a fact."

Isaiah stared at the girl, hoping what she was telling him was wrong, but knowing in his heart of hearts that there might be some truth to it. Many was the time that Reverend Brown had sent him on an errand just as some lovely young prisoner was to be questioned. Perhaps Melinda Briggs was speaking the truth. Isaiah Wolf had served Salem Town for many a year and disliked the idea that lechery may have been occurring under his very nose. As much as he hated to do it there was only one way to resolve the matter. When the good Reverend came to question Melinda, Major Wolf would be listening outside. As much as he disliked the deception, a bit of cautious listening would do no harm, that is if the Reverend were truly innocent. If things were really as Melinda said, then he would be there to protect her, no matter what the consequences.

"Get along now," said Isaiah trying to hide his feelings for Melinda Briggs by the gruffness of his voice, " 'Tis well to get this over with quickly. I am sure that ye will be resting in your own lodgings come sundown. I must make my rounds now, but I'll return quickly to claim you."

"Whatever you wish, Major," said Melinda squaring her shoulders and walking resolutely towards the prison door. She could only pray that Jamie and Rebecca had enough sense to take for the high seas.

As she entered, Melinda squinted in an effort to make some sense of the dank, windowless surroundings. What she saw filled her heart with a foreboding that she had never felt before. Melinda prided herself on being able to wiggle out of any situation, but as soon as her eyes focused, Melinda knew she was in a battle for her life, one she might not win. The faces of Jack and Ezra Love gleamed up at her, telling

Melinda Briggs that she was in far deeper than was good for her heath.

"Eh now, lads," she said pulling up a chair and touching shoulders with Jack, "and what brings you here? I bet 'tis some silliness the Reverend has cooked up."

" 'Tis not silliness and you know it, you hussy," snarled Jack, pulling his chair away from her as if her very breath might infect him with guilt. "It's all up with you, Melinda Briggs, so you might as well come clean. The Reverend is in a hanging mood and if he finds himself without O'Roarke's neck to stretch, I'm willing to wager that yours will do."

"Now, Jackie, what do you mean? I'm just an honest girl making her living where she can. What do I know of O'Roarke's plans?"

"Enough to get ye hanged, my burde," said the good Reverend Brown as he entered the small room and shut the door behind him.

"It seems that these two fine sailors saw you cozying up to our traitorous Captain only last night. They say that they overheard O'Roarke telling you where his treasure was to be buried. Perhaps he offered you a share in exchange for 'services' eh, my girl?"

"Why you're all daft and that's a fact," said Melinda leaping to her feet realizing that this whole thing was a trap.

"Now then boys, grab her," shouted Reverend Brown as Melinda flew to the door in a desperate attempt to escape.

Jack and Ezra leaped to their feet and quickly secured the struggling girl to the damp wall with the same irons that had so recently held Ian MacRae.

"There now, my girl, perhaps you should tell me all you know. I promise this is only the beginning. Unless you answer my questions satisfactorily, 'twill go very hard with you indeed. These two worthy seamen have already told me they know nothing of O'Roarke and his treasure. Why, they have even been cheated out of their fair share of wages due them by our tricky Captain. So you see, my fine lady, it is all up to you. Tell me where O'Roarke plans to hide his treasure and I promise you will be freed."

"Oh, and they are foul liars, sir," said Melinda struggling against her chains. "Why 'twas they that were sitting at table last night and that's a fact. They were planning it all, I know. All O'Roarke said was to bury the booty in the 'usual spot' 'tis all. If they've told you anything else 'tis a tale that only a child would believe." With that Melinda, taking expert aim, spat on Jack Love's left shoe.

"Now, my girl, calm down, perhaps we have misjudged you," said the Reverend with a backwards glance at the two sailors.

"If you could tell me where O'Roarke is now, I am sure the whole matter could be cleared up. Boys, Mistress Brown has baked some fine apple pies that I am sure you would enjoy. If you would be so kind as to return after you are finished, I am sure the good Melinda and I will have sorted out the details."

"Right you are your worship," said Ezra as he pulled his brother towards the door. "Come along now, Jack, and let the Reverend get to the bottom of this."

"I think I'd rather stay and watch the merriment," said Jack leering at Melinda while he wiped his shoe with his sleeve.

"Off with you now, my good man," said Reverend Brown, ignoring the unsavory sailor's implications. "And take your time. Mistress Briggs doesn't sound like she will easily give up O'Roarke."

Melinda stared at the closing door with a sinking heart.

CHAPTER TWENTY-FIVE

"Now then, Melinda Briggs," said the worthy Reverend straightening his collar and smiling at the retreating footsteps of Jack and Ezra. "It is time that you and I settled down for a friendly chat."

"Samuel Brown, I swear that if you lay a hand on me I'll raise a fuss loud enough to raise the dead," said Melinda attempting to kick out at the Reverend as he approached her.

"There will be none of that my girl," said Brown as he nimbly moved away from the girl's reach. "I believe that it's time that you remembered who I am and where you are. I have the power of life and death over you, and if you don't give me a few honest answers, you'll lose far more than your questionable virtue."

"But I swear that I know nothing of O'Roarke's treasure. 'Twas that evil Jack along with his grizzled brother what were making plans with the Captain, and that's the truth of it. They only lied to save their own skins. I know enough to tell you that it's them that should be questioned, not me. They're the ones that do the dirty work for O'Roarke."

"Melinda, my girl, I just wish I knew whom to believe," said Reverend Brown coming close to the chained girl's cheek and whispering in her ear. "On the one hand, I have two respected men of the sea telling me that you hold the key to the trouble that O'Roarke has caused, and on the other hand there is you, as brazen a hussy as ever set foot in Salem, telling me that they are lying schemers intent on mischief. Perhaps it is time that you convinced me of your good intentions. I could be persuaded to let you go if you took it into your mind to be cooperative. Think how much more pleasant it would be to spend the afternoon in some sunny glade discussing O'Roarke's whereabouts."

" 'Tis not whereabouts you're interested in you son of Satan," said Melinda as she attempted to twist out of the way of Samuel Brown's questing hands. As she struggled, he managed to pin her against the wall and began to lightly run his fingertips down the lovely breasts.

"There now, my girl, isn't that much more pleasant than the feel of the scourge on your tender skin? I promise you that if you reveal O'Roarke's hiding place, you'll find yourself with not only the pleasure of my company but with a bit of gold in your pocket to boot."

"Why, 'tis an evil one you are and that's a fact," said Melinda as she struggled under Samuel Brown's grasp. "I swear that if you do any harm to me there will be hell to pay."

Reverend Brown, releasing his victim, turned and made his way to the far corner of the room where a smoldering brazier was kept. From among the hot irons he drew a beautifully fashioned piece of work. At the tip of the iron was a delicately fashioned fleur de lis. The good Reverend smiled at Melinda as he retraced his steps towards the hapless girl.

"Now then, good sir," said the terrified Melinda attempting to buy some time, "there is no need to joke with me. What would a fine Christian man as yourself be doing with such a thing?" she said nodding at the flame red branding iron in the Reverend's hand.

"My duty, 'tis all, my girl. There are times when the flesh must be mortified if the soul is to be saved. Believe me this is not something that I enjoy, but for the sake of your immortal soul, you must submit. Ask any whore in France how they have been marked with such as this pretty flower. 'Twill not only chasten your soul but 'twill also protect the good folk here abouts from your sordid lechery. Once you have been marked with the fleur de lis, all will know you as the whore you are and use you accordingly."

With that, the cruel Reverend Brown laid the hot brand upon Melinda's breast. The maniacal sparkle in his eye as Melinda Briggs screamed told the true depth of Samuel Brown's depravity. This man that held the souls and laws of Salem in his hands was a disciple of all that was evil. Wiping the spittle from his lips, Samuel stepped back to admire his handiwork. "There now, my girl does it not give you a cleansing of the soul to have the wantonness burned from you?" Brown, with a self satisfied look, gently touched the soft burned flesh that now displayed the cruel brand.

"If you do not wish another touch of yon brand, it would behoove you to entrust O'Roarke's hiding place to me. Remember, my dear, that I am the only law in this fair town."

"But, sir," cried Melinda, the tears of anguish running down her cheeks, "the only place that I know of is O'Roarke's bower and he only uses that for trysts, 'tis not a place to hide in."

"Tell me then and quickly, girl, or you'll feel the warmth of this instrument," said Samuel Brown turning the brand in the fire and lifting it again. As he came towards her intent on another assault, Melinda felt madness grip her very being. "Forgive me, Jamie," she prayed as she fastened her eyes on the delicate fleur de lis.

"No more, I beg of you, sir. I know only of the great rose bower on the path leading to Collins Cove. Captain O'Roarke often takes his rest there of an afternoon. Whether it will do ye good or not I have no notion, but 'tis all I know, I swear."

"Now then, that's my good girl," said Samuel Brown placing the brand back in the fire. " 'Tis not as hard as you believed to begin your reformation, now is it, Melinda?"

Reverend Brown approached the helpless girl and gave her a benevolent smile. "Now there remains but one necessary duty that must be fulfilled. You see, my wayward Melinda, to cleanse the flesh, it must first be mortified. I look upon it as my sacred duty to restore your immortal soul, even if it puts my own in peril."

"Oh please, sir, no!" begged Melinda as Samuel Brown approached her, unbuttoning his fine wool breeches.

"Stop right there, Brown," thundered a deep voice from the prison entranceway. Samuel Brown, quickly making himself neat, turned to face Major Wolf.

"What is this now, Isaiah, you were supposed to be at the cove keeping watch over O'Roarke's ship. This is a deliberate disobeying of orders. I'll see you flogged for this."

"You'll do nothing of the kind if you know what's good for you, Reverend," said Isaiah, pushing his pastor aside and unlocking Melinda's chains.

"There now, Mistress Briggs, I can only pray that you find it in your heart to forgive me. 'Twas my doubt of you and trust in the Reverend here that caused you such misfortune. I only wish I had turned back sooner. Come now, I've had enough of this place to last me a lifetime."

"I'll have you arrested for desertion if you take one step further, Major Wolf," shouted Samuel Briggs as Isaiah and Melinda headed towards the door.

"Try that and I'll see you hanged for lechery, my man," said Isaiah holding Melinda tightly around the waist. "There are many in this town who would secretly like to see you punished for all the trouble here abouts, and that's a fact. Bide your tongue until we are safely clear of this place and I'll bide mine. Now then, Mistress Briggs and I will be relieving you of your fine white mare for our journey. Remember, mum's the word now, eh Reverend?"

"Isaiah, I'm so afraid," said Melinda as the athletic Major swung her onto his stallion. "Surely the Reverend will have us followed and arrested?"

"That, my darling Melinda, is very unlikely. I am sure that the good Reverend Brown would just as soon never hear from me again. I know too much. No, I think it would suit his plans nicely if the two of us headed west and were never seen in Salem Town again. What say we start a family to keep us company in the wilderness?"

"Why, Isaiah Wolf, are you proposing to me?" said Melinda catching her breath and looking into the man's honest brown eyes.

"Well then and what would you be callin' it?" said Isaiah holding Melinda tightly. Coming so close to losing her this day had crystallized the feeling that the rough Major had been harboring for the girl. His happiness would have been complete if he could have sliced the Reverend Brown in two, but his first thoughts must be for Melinda's safety. She had been through too much this day. Better to get her far away from this place before worse befell them both.

"Will we be married good and proper?" said Melinda tickling Isaiah in a playful manner.

"Good and proper, I promise," said Isaiah placing his hand upon his heart.

"Well then and what's keeping you?" said Melinda kicking the side of the stallion. "Let's be off on our fine adventure. I only regret that the Reverend forced me to tell of O'Roarke's hiding place in the rose bower near Collins Cove. His lass, the girl Rebecca, was uncommonly kind to me."

"Now don't worry your head about it, my dearest," said Isaiah smiling down at Melinda, " I am sure that your friends are resourceful enough to avoid capture. Remember, Reverend Brown no longer has Isaiah Wolf to do his bidding. Come now and let's be off to fetch that mare while our luck still holds."

With a thundering of hoofs, Isaiah Wolf and Melinda Briggs set off in the westward direction of Salem Village.

CHAPTER TWENTY-SIX

"Peter, did you hear them? That girl has seen Rebecca," said Arabella, breathlessly pulling on the old Professor's arm.

"I know, thank the heavens that she is still alive," nodded Peter. "I am quite familiar with the place she spoke of, it is on the way to the Cove where Rebecca lives. If what that soldier said is correct, I'm afraid our Rebecca may be in some danger if she is found in the company of Captain O'Roarke. We must get to her first."

"Professor, just tell me how to get there. You can't go now and Aunt Arabella, resourceful though she may be, would only slow me down," said Ian, looking about for some sort of weapon to take with him. Along the side of the prison he spied several cutlasses hanging loosely in readiness for defense if the settlers should suffer a sudden Indian attack. Running down the steps of the scaffold, he quickly grabbed one and was fastening it to his belt as he rebounded down the steps two at a time.

"Good thinking, my boy, no telling what you may run into along the way," said Peter, wishing he could join Ian in his adventure. "Now then, let me tell you a short cut I know of that will take you to the bower. We can only hope that the paths that I am familiar with have been around for three hundred years."

As Arabella and Peter watched Ian disappear in the thick underbrush leading towards Collins Cove, Reverend Samuel Brown opened the prison house door. From the agitated manner in which he called two yeoman to his side, Peter and Arabella knew that it had only been a stroke of luck that had sent Ian ahead of the soldiers to rescue the unsuspecting Rebecca.

CHAPTER TWENTY-SEVEN

Ian MacRae was well equipped for his journey through the heavy foliage that covered the trail that Peter had described. His many forays throughout the highlands of Scotland had been through tangles of briar and bramble of incredible thickness. As he used his sword to cut away the greenery blocking his path, Ian felt an unbelievable surge of energy enter his soul.

What spurred him on was the memory of the lovely lass with eyes as bright as stars. Try as he might to deny it, Ian MacRae had fallen in love. Gone was the cynicism that had marked his days in Glasgow. He swore that if he found Rebecca alive, that he would fall on his knees before her and speak his heart. Ian let out a great laugh as he thought of the picture he would make. None of his old acquaintances at McKenzie's pub would believe this of him. Well, let them waste their lives in their cups, Ian MacRae had awoken to a brilliant new world washed clean by the smile of a wee lassie.

" 'Tis a fool ye are, MacRae, and there is no mistaking it. Come now and stop your musings before there is no lass to save." The thought of Rebecca being led back to the square in chains like that poor Melinda was more than Ian could bear. With renewed energy he hacked away at the shrubbery before him. At last a path became clear and Ian ran like one possessed by the devil. Behind him was the sound of horses making their way with caution through the dense thickness that covered the path leading to Collins Cove.

"Oh God in heaven, let me be savin' the lass and I swear you can do with me what you will," breathed Ian.

CHAPTER TWENTY-EIGHT

"Why 'tis an old custom, my girl," said Jamie handing an apple peel he had just carved from the windfall fruit that lay about them. "If you throw yon peel over your shoulder it will land in the form of the initial of he who is to be your wedded husband."

"Oh, Jamie, that is just a superstition I am sure. How can some piece of fruit determine a girl's fate?" laughed Rebecca.

"Right you are, lass, 'tis almost as fantastic as saying a fair lass could find herself in old Salem Town sitting beside the likes of Captain Jamie O'Roarke." Cradling the girl in his arms, Jamie gave her lovely lips a passionate kiss. The spell wrought by Rebecca Love had indeed bewitched Jamie O'Roarke. How right he had been to spirit her away from her friends. No telling what may have happened if she had seen the meddling old professor and that damnable Ian MacRae. MacRae had eyes for Jamie's Rebecca, there was no doubting that. What chance would the old captain stand against such as MacRae, a man younger than himself and from Rebecca's own world to boot. No, he had a right to even the playing field and that was a fact. Rebecca would be far out to sea before dawn and they would sail the world together adventuring where they wished. Let Professor Hawking search for Rebecca in vain. Jamie would hide her in some far corner of the earth, safe from her meddling friends. Rebecca was the dearest treasure of his life and if he dammed his immortal soul through his deception than so be it.

"Jamie, the sun has moved well across the sky, shouldn't we be carrying out your plans?" said Rebecca looking up at the pirate, full of trust.

"Just a few minutes more, lass," said Jamie reluctant to release the girl from the haven of his arms. "It never pays to be hasty about such matters, I have found."

With a sigh, Rebecca settled back into Jamie's arms, tossing aside the apple peel he had handed her. "Right you are, Captain. I can't remember when I have been more at peace."

CHAPTER TWENTY-NINE

"Rebecca, Captain O'Roarke, make haste, Reverend Brown's men are at my heels!" yelled Ian MacRae as he burst forth from the underbrush, his sword flashing in the afternoon sunlight.

"Ian, my God, what has happened, how did you get here?" cried an astonished Rebecca leaping to her feet and looking frantically at the wild eyed Scotsman.

"There is no time for questions now! The King's men are directly behind me. A girl named Melinda was forced to reveal your bower, Captain, and now there's hell to pay."

"You take the lass, Ian, and make for safety. There is no sense in seeing her hanged beside me," said Jamie O'Roarke with a grim look on his face. "Go along now the both of ye. She'll need protecting this day and that's a fact. 'Tis your duty to save the girl, MacRae," said Jamie with a look at Ian that brooked no argument.

The expression on the Scotsman's face was one of a man determined to stand beside Jamie O'Roarke and fight to the death. A MacRae never ran from a fight. To leave Jamie now was against everything Ian held dear, but he knew that the O'Roarke was right.

"No, Jamie, I won't leave you," screamed Rebecca as Ian nodded and picked her up in his great arms. Swiftly he made for the safety of the woods beyond. As he and Rebecca were about to reach protection Ian turned and looked upon Captain Jamie O'Roarke. The Captain, with a smile, beckoned them to go. In turn Ian grasped his sword and saluted Jamie in the ancient form used only by Scottish highlanders to a foe of equal mettle.

Just as Ian and Rebecca disappeared into the safety of Salem woods, Reverend Brown's men crashed through the underbrush. Even though there were six mounted men, Jamie O'Roarke stood his ground determined to buy Rebecca the time she needed to escape the destiny that he now knew he must embrace. Leave it to the fates to give Jamie O'Roarke a taste of the bliss he might have known, only to snatch it away from him at the last minute. Surely he must have been born with the mark of Cain upon his brow. Giving a thunderous yell, Jamie O'Roarke turned to embrace his attackers with the taste of Rebecca Love's kiss upon his lips.

CHAPTER-THIRTY

"Ian, we can't leave him, we can't!" said Rebecca as Ian set her down.

"We have no choice now, lass. Hurry now and we'll circle back through the woods. No one knows that you were with Captain O'Roarke this day so I think you will be safe. The only hope we have of saving him is to see what they've done with him. We can only pray that for now he is unharmed."

"But you're wrong, Ian. O'Roarke's two mates saw me with him at the Blue Anchor tavern last night. Surely they will betray me to the Reverend."

"I think, lass, that you had better tell me everything that has happened since we were parted. When I came upon you and O'Roarke under the roses, you didn't seem to be putting up much of a struggle."

"Why, Ian MacRae! I do believe you're jealous," said Rebecca, laughing despite their desperate circumstances. Here they were trapped three hundred years in the past with Jamie O'Roarke sure to be hanged, and Ian's greatest concern was what had occurred in the rose bower. Men were really exasperating sometimes. Rebecca, smiling at Ian, made the resolve to lock within her heart forever the tender moments that she and Jamie had shared. It was none of Ian's business if Rebecca chose to return Jamie O'Roarke's affections. If he were to die this day then she could only rejoice that she had granted the lonely pirate's heart's desire.

"Now, Ian, don't be so silly, we were only resting. There was nothing more to it than that. As to the everything else, you are right. You need to know what has been happening."

Rebecca and Ian shared the events of the last day as they made their way back along the tangled paths. Both were astounded at the great adventure in which they found themselves emeshed.

"I can't believe that you actually met two of your own ancestors," said an amazed Ian. "How did you ever manage not to give away your secret? One thing is clear, you must hide that garnet cross. If anyone finds it on you, it could be used as evidence. Why don't we stop at the tree where the Captain carved his initials and bury it there?"

"Why Ian, what a wonderful idea!" said Rebecca, entirely forgetting the seriousness of the situation in the momentary pleasure of the thought of burying her own heirloom beneath Mrs. Maloon's old elm tree. How ironic it all was. Perhaps that is where one of her father's ancestors had found it! When they came upon the tree, Rebecca and Ian swiftly buried her small treasure and covered the neatly patted earth with golden leaves.

"There now, I think it will be safe for you to make an appearance at my side, Mistress Love," said Ian putting his arm through Rebecca's. "It would be safer by far if you pretended to be my wife. That way no one will question your sudden appearance. From what you tell me, those two sailors can't mention that they've seen you before without putting the noose around their own necks. Let's hurry and see if we can save the brave Captain. Don't forget, if he dies this day, the curse goes on."

"Oh no, Ian, I had forgotten the curse. If the Captain is hanged then you will be in great peril as well. How could I have been so careless? You should have stayed and fought with Jamie! If you had, than perhaps you would have both been saved. I was only in the way. If I hadn't been there, then you both might have escaped and been free!"

"Don't be silly, girl!" said Ian grasping her around the waist and looking into her beautiful sea blue eyes. "What would life have been worth for either of us if something had happened to you. I've seen the way O'Roarke looks at you. He is a man in love and there is no mistaking that. As for myself I can only tell you, Miss Rebecca Love, that Captain Jamie O'Roarke is not the only man to hand you his heart. I present you mine as well this fine day. Pray keep it well and honor my gift," said Ian MacRae kneeling on the ground before Rebecca.

"Why, Ian, we barely know each other," said Rebecca, astonished at the way his declaration took her breath away. It was as if all the years of study and grief had been washed away by her two dashing suitors. Jamie O'Roarke had awakened within the girl a passion for love and life that she had never suspected. As for Ian MacRae, from the first moment she had seen him, she had felt that he might be her true love.

"I am so confused, Ian," she said praying that he could not hear the wild beating of her heart. How could she have such feelings for him, with Jamie being dragged off to such a terrible fate. What was wrong with her? Perhaps this was what Melinda had been trying to tell her about a woman's heart. Whatever her feelings were for Jamie O'Roarke, her love for Ian MacRae could not be denied.

"Don't answer now, my lovely lady," said Ian rising from his knees. "There will be time soon enough to speak our hearts. Just let me know that there is hope."

"Oh yes, my dearest Ian, there is indeed hope," said Rebecca gravely placing her hand in his as they entered the clearing.

PART FOUR

THE HANGMAN'S NOOSE

CHAPTER THIRTY-ONE

Arabella gently smiled at Peter as he climbed down the pillory steps. He was rubbing his wrists gingerly, attempting to restore the circulation that the stocks had so cruelly cut off. How handsome he is, she thought, as he bounded down the last few steps with the agility of a man half his age.

"Well now, that's a great improvement," said Peter stretching his arms and feeling the back of his neck. "I wonder who invented the stocks and why?" he said looking back up the steps.

"Once a historian, always a historian," laughed Arabella, attempting to hug him.

"None of that or we'll both wind up in the stocks for another three hours!" said Peter as he jumped away from Arabella's inviting arms.

"Oh my goodness, I forgot," said the lovely lady, horrified at what she had almost done. "Time travel certainly isn't easy. All those books people write about visiting the past are nothing like this. They always have special gadgets that they can use in the 'nick of time' if they find themselves in trouble."

"My dear, please don't be upset," said Peter trying to imagine what the events of the past few hours must be like to someone who had not spent a lifetime immersed in the folklore of Salem. "You forget that we have a few gadgets of our own," he said taking the great staff from her.

"Your staff is no gadget," said Arabella looking at the livewood with anxiety. "Don't forget, Peter Hawking, that I am a Scot. Witchcraft was born there. You have only to read 'MacBeth' to know that. All your Puritan ancestors did was to transport our beliefs to this side of the sea. I know how dangerous magic can be. For every wish that is granted a price must be paid. It sickens me that you are already in the debt of that dangerous little minx. There is no telling what she may demand in return."

"Yes, my lovely," said Peter touching her hand gently, "but don't forget that I know a thing or two about Mistress Eva. I think that I am a match for her. Besides, even if I'm not, we had no other choice. If we hadn't made the journey both your Ian and my Rebecca would have been destroyed."

"Right you are, my brave lad," said Arabella with a twinkle in her eye. " 'Twas a Hobsen's choice indeed. But mark my words when I say if that little lady tries to lure you away from me she'll have the fight of her life on her hands."

The staff, as if to answer Arabella's challenge, began to tremble in Peter's hand. The ground about them began to shift slightly and Peter was astounded to see something that looked like smoke curl around Arabella's feet.

"There will be none of that now, Miss," Peter said to the staff, as Arabella leapt quickly from the steaming spot. In answer, the staff shook violently, trying to release itself from his grasp. The sweat poured down Peter's face as he attempted to subdue the powerful dyad. With a final twist of his wrist, he managed to strike the staff upon the ground. The sound that came from deep within the wood resembled an unholy scream. The anger in the sound could not be mistaken.

"Now then, you wicked girl," said Peter laughing in relief, "a promise is a promise. Break your word to me and this will be your home forever. If you behave, my dearest Eva, then perhaps we can see to it that your next thousand years can be lived in freedom. What do you say to that?" In answer, the air was filled with the sound of a delicate wind chime.

"You can't mean to set that dreadful creature free!" said Arabella bending down to see if her shoes had been scorched by the hotfoot Eva had given her.

"But of course I do," said Peter looking at the staff sadly. "Most of this young lady's trouble is that she has been used unjustly. Through the ages, dyads have been thought of as a great prize, something to be captured and enslaved. Imagine if someone wanted to keep you bottled up like a genie? Wouldn't you become angry and resentful? I doubt that Eva has ever been free long enough to have any of the fun she desires. It would be fascinating to see what she would do with a bit of happiness."

"You're mad, Peter Hawking," said Arabella fondly. "I suppose I can only pray that you are right," said Arabella looking at the staff with an almost maternal kindness. "Eva, if you can hear me, believe me when I say I wish you no harm. Let's say we declare a truce until this whole thing is over."

As if in answer, the ground that had smelled like brimstone suddenly returned to its former greenery with not a trace of scorched earth.

"There now, you see, she's not so bad," said Peter stroking the head of the staff, pleased but still cautious. Confident as he might appear to Arabella, he still had a sneaking suspicion that Eva's magic might prove to be more powerful than his own. "There is nothing to worry about as long as we all remain friends."

"Oh my lord," said Arabella, her hands flying to her cheeks as she looked towards the direction of Salem woods. "Look, Peter, he's found her!"

CHAPTER THIRTY-TWO

In answer to her prayers, Arabella watched as her beloved nephew walked towards her, hand in hand with the beautiful Rebecca. How right they were for each other thought the Scotswoman as she saw the tenderness in Ian's grasp of the girl's hand.

Peter looked first in Rebecca's direction and then back at Arabella with satisfaction. The expression on the woman's face could not be denied. Peter had been the object of many a matchmaker in the past and if he was not mistaken, Lady Arabella MacRae had just made up her mind about the young couple walking towards them. Well then, so be it. He would hate to lose Rebecca, but it was about time the girl had some happiness. But was Ian MacRae the type to settle down and make her happy? Peter resolved that he would have a serious talk with the dashing Scotsman before another sun set.

"Peter!" cried Rebecca as she ran up to her dearest friend. Before he could stop her, Peter found himself smothered in kisses that covered his entire face. "I thought I'd never see you again! However did you find me?"

"Settle down now, 'Becca," said Peter delighted at the girl's display of love for him, but alarmed that they were exposing themselves to prying eyes. There were still many dangerous obstacles that must be overcome if they were to reach home safely.

"Come rest beside me, Rebecca," said Arabella patting the spot beside her as she gratefully sank to the tender grass.

"Oh, but we can't waste a minute," said Rebecca looking at Peter imploringly. "Captain O'Roarke has been captured and must be rescued. It was only because he gave himself up to the soldiers that we escaped at all!"

"Now, Rebecca, you must remain calm," said Peter forcing her to sit down. "Tell us everything that has happened since you disappeared. We can't rush into anything until we have all the facts. We must tread carefully."

Rebecca, trying to quiet her racing heart, quickly told her friends what she had been through since they had parted, leaving out only her delicious moments with Jamie beneath the bower. She hoped that the burning blush she felt creeping over her cheeks didn't reveal her secret thoughts. What girl wouldn't be flustered at the thoughts of the last twenty-four hours spent with Jamie O'Roarke!

"So you knew the girl that Reverend Brown had here for questioning!" said Peter, astounded at all his quiet protege had been through. He had always known that Rebecca would make a woman of great depth, but he had never expected the transformation to happen so quickly. The face of his darling little girl had changed into that of a woman overnight. She had always been undeniably pretty, but now she had an unearthly beauty about her that quite took his breath away. No wonder Ian MacRae could not keep his eyes from the enchanting vision that sat beside him.

"Yes. Melinda is the reason we didn't immediately make for Captain O'Roarke's ship. We couldn't leave without her after all she had done for us. When Jamie saw that she was being taken to jail he formed a plan to save her. I was to make for the ship while he rescued Melinda."

"How did he know that Melinda was in the prison?" asked Ian, with a peculiar tone creeping into his voice. "I'd always thought that the old custom was to question any single woman in the presence of some matron of the village. By rights she should have been taken to the Reverend's home where his wife was!"

"Why," said Rebecca puzzled by Ian's curious look, "Jamie climbed to the top of a small hill and used his spyglass to check the clearing. That is when he returned to me and we decided on our plan. Whatever is the matter?"

" A great deal," said Ian with a look of anger clouding his features, "Captain O'Roarke must have seen us too. The stocks stand directly in front of the Salem prison. By God! That foul pirate never intended that you should know that we were here looking for you. Don't you see, Peter? He meant to have Rebecca safely aboard his ship without ever telling her about us!"

"But, Ian, that makes no sense at all," said Rebecca, unable to believe what the Scotsman was saying. "Why would he have faced the soldiers alone if he were so evil? You must be wrong!"

"Don't you see, darling," said Arabella gently taking the girl's hand in hers, "the Captain loves you. When Ian appeared with the soldiers at his heels, Jamie knew it was all up with him and the only thing left that he could do was to save you. It does look like Ian may be right. Why else would he so conveniently forget to tell you that he had seen us? We were in plain sight. There was no way he could have missed us if he saw Melinda being escorted to prison. Try not to think too harshly of him."

"Oh how cruel of him!" said Rebecca. If what her friends said were true, and how could it be denied, then everything that had happened between Jamie and herself was nothing but empty lies. He had only wanted his way with her. Jamie O'Roarke couldn't possibly care for her true happiness if he had done such a thing. Crushed, Rebecca buried her face in her skirt and sobbed as if her heart would break.

"There now, lass," said Ian pressing her face against his shoulder. "Don't take on so. It's only his way. Jamie knows no better. I'm sure he meant well."

"Don't try to defend him, Ian MacRae!" said Rebecca feeling a depth of anger she had never felt before. "I hate him! I hope he does hang!" she cried bursting into another torrent of sobs."

"Now then, rest easy. Yours is not the first heart he must have broken you know. We must remember that if Jamie dies at the end of a rope the curse will never be lifted. I'm afraid that we must be practical and try to save O'Roarke whether he deserves it or not," said Ian hoping that his appeal to reason might calm the girl. He had not realized how deeply Rebecca cared for Jamie O'Roarke. If O'Roarke died, Rebecca had it in her to love his ghost until her dying day. The only hope for Ian was to win her love fairly. O'Roarke must be saved. No one, not even a Scotsman, could compete with a ghost.

CHAPTER THIRTY-THREE

"Leave me some feelings in me arms, damn you," said Jamie, with a scornful twist of his lips, as the soldiers tightly bound his arms against his body. The leader, yeoman Benjamin Webb, had been waiting a long time for this moment. Many years ago, Jamie O'Roarke had seduced his young sister Sarah, bringing shame upon his family.

"Now then, O'Roarke," said the yeoman, mounting his horse and prodding Jamie with his pike, " 'tis all up with ye and that's a fact. 'Tis more than the rub of a rope around yer fine body ye'll be a feelin' this fine day. Along with ye now. The town's been waitin' for just such a sight."

With that, the horsemen made their way back through the woods. The proud Jamie O'Roarke did not look so grand now, thought Benjamin Webb, as the pirate stumbled over a rotting tree branch and fell forward.

"Up with ye, O'Roarke," said Webb as he stood over the man laughing.

"Ah, Webb, I wouldn't be a countin' me out yet," said Jamie struggling to his feet and glaring at the yeoman. "Captain Jamie O'Roarke has as many lives as a cat and that's the truth. Think upon it and remember that O'Roarke always pays his debts."

"The only debt that you'll be paying is the one that waits for you at the end of a rope and that's for sure," said

Benjamin, moving Jamie along, trying not to let him see that the pirate's words had shaken him. 'Twas true indeed that O'Roarke had escaped more than one scrape that would have destroyed any other man. Perhaps there was something to the rumor that O'Roarke was a witch. Benjamin would rest much easier when Jamie's neck was true and rightly stretched at the end of the rope.

As the soldiers broke into the clearing, Jamie saw a sight that heartened him greatly. There on the grass was his Rebecca safe and sound. The afternoon sunlight that shone upon her curls gave him the courage to lift his head and cover the ground that lay between himself and the prison gate. As they passed by her, it almost broke his heart to turn his face away so that she could not see the tears of humiliation that suddenly sprang to his eyes. Damn his hot heart! 'Twould do no good for the great Jamie O'Roarke to carry on so. Squaring his shoulders, he ushered forth a thunderous laugh that he hoped would hearten Rebecca and boldly marched through the open prison door like the King of Tara himself.

CHAPTER THIRTY-THREE

"Oh, Peter, we must help him!" cried Rebecca as she watched Jamie vanish behind the heavy oak doors. Forgotten was all her anger against the proud pirate. His deception had been in the name of love. If he died now, Rebecca felt that her heart would die with him.

"Whist now, girl," said Ian attempting to quiet the frantic girl. "If anyone hereabouts learns that you are in alliance with O'Roarke we'll all find ourselves in a clamjamfry."

"My nephew is right, Rebecca," whispered Arabella in an attempt to soothe the girl. "It will do the Captain no good if we are captured too. His only hope is us, and we must be free if we are to rescue him. Remember, I want him to escape, too. If Captain O'Roarke dies, Ian dies. We must liberate him, but I don't see how."

"It's obvious that the 'good' Reverend is as much interested in O'Roarke's treasure as he is in the pirate. I think Jamie will be safe until Brown learns where that is," said Peter trying to keep a calm manner.

The stakes were high indeed. Not only Ian, but Rebecca would perish unless the decisions he made in the next few moments were the right ones. The heartbroken look on Rebecca's face was almost more than Peter could bear. If he could have taken O'Roarke's place at this moment, Peter Hawking would have gladly given his life for her happiness, but that was not possible. It was O'Roarke, the brave Captain of the "Red Witch," who must be saved, but how? If he called on Eva one more time, Peter knew that her power against him would begin to grow beyond his control.

Unknown to the others, the wily nymph had been weaving a spell about Peter. He could feel the tendrils of her insidious power slowly creeping through his spirit. Peter knew that each time he summoned her, those tendrils made there way closer and closer to the center of his being. If he fell under her spell then all was lost. Eva cared little for O'Roarke except as an old sparring partner. As for Rebecca and Arabella, there was no telling what she would do to them to amuse herself. Ian would be safe for a time until she tired of him, but woe unto him if he attempted to free himself from her loving grasp. The only possible answer was to attempt to save Jamie without Eva's help.

Peter knew that he would have to summon her one more time if they were ever to return home, and even that was very risky. Pray God that if she demanded the sacrifice of the "Great Rite" it would only be Peter Hawking who paid the price.

"What we need to do first," said Peter turning to the others, "is find out what they intend to do with O'Roarke. Perhaps there will be a few minutes when he will be left in a cell alone. If that is the case then we might be able to free him. You were quite right Arabella when you volunteered to come along. Two ladies might be able to visit the Captain in his cell. You could pose as curiosity seekers wishing to view the famous pirate."

"It just might work!" said Ian getting into the spirit of the adventure. "Even if the worst happens and they are denied entrance, they might learn something that we can use. What do you say, Aunt, to a bit of the Flora MacDonald!"

"Why," said Rebecca, glad to be planning some sort of action, "what is a Flora MacDonald?"

"Flora MacDonald, my dear, was the noble Scottish maid who saved our Bonny Prince Charlie and made off with him to the Isle of Skye," said Arabella with pride in her voice. Turning to Peter, Arabella nodded her head. "Yes, it is a good plan and the only possible one under the circumstances. Let us make haste. I have a feeling that there may be no time to waste."

CHAPTER THIRTY-FOUR

Jamie O'Roarke looked about him. The dim light that filtered through the narrow cracks in the wall cast shadows about him. The twilight only served to make his surroundings even more depressing. How well he remembered this! Once before Jamie had sat in this very cell, pondering his fate. What a cruel twist of destiny it was that brought him back once again. Surely no saint in heaven had ever been asked to suffer martyrdom twice. The very thought of it made Jamie's blood boil and his soul cry out for revenge. Curse that Brown! Jamie could only imagine what poor Melinda must have suffered before she gave Jamie up.

"If I am to die again, I swear upon all that is holy that I'll be acursin' the right man!" cried Jamie to the empty walls. In a mixture of anger and frustration he began to pound furiously against the heavy wood planks until his hands bled. Finally, exhausted, Jamie sank to the ground in defeat.

"At least it will be quick," thought Jamie as he lay down and shut his eyes in an attempt to dispel the gloom. The worst thing that anyone could do to a man like Jamie O'Roarke was to shut him away from the sea and sky. Better death than to be locked away in a dark cage!

Unable to quiet himself, Jamie got to his feet and began to pace back and forth. Surely this was no way for the great Captain Jamie O'Roarke to act! Where was his spirit, his courage! The first time this had happened Jamie had held out hope that some miracle would save him. This time he knew that there was no such miracle for the likes of old Jamie. Die he would upon the morrow in a cruel reenactment of his first death. What irony it was that this time he should feel such pain. Only a man in love could feel such agony. This time he was leaving behind him the beautiful Rebecca Love.

"Rebecca," cried Jamie's soul in utter despair, "please don't forget your Jamie, please know that his love was true." If there was a God, then perhaps He would carry Jamie's words to his lost love and comfort her.

As he closed his eyes in an attempt to see her lovely face, Jamie could have sworn that he heard Rebecca's wonderful laughter. It was so real that he could feel the warmth and comfort of the sound wrap about him. With a start he sat up. This was no dream! From somewhere beyond his prison door, Jamie could make out the dearness of her voice broken only by her lilting laugh.

What was the meaning of this? Jamie pressed his ear against the thinnest part of the wall in an attempt to make out her words, but it was hopeless. Why, from the sound of it, his beloved Rebecca was in a merry mood. How could that be with Jamie facing certain death? What could possibly account for her lightness of heart?

With a coldness beyond the grave, Jamie was filled with a certainty that made his rage against Brown seem like a child's simple tantrum. Somehow, from the beginning that evil MacRae had planned this! It was obvious that he wanted Rebecca for his own! The old sorcerer had been enlisted to summon up Jamie so that the MacRaes and the Loves could enact a final revenge upon Jamie in payment for their dead. Why else would they all have been assembled there so neatly in the graveyard. They had planned it all from the beginning, counting on Jamie's fondness for the ladies. Rebecca had acted as a beautiful decoy to lull Jamie away from the truth. Now the sudden appearance of Rebecca's friends in old Salem Town made sense.

As the sound of Rebecca's magical laughter echoed through Jamie's damp cell, he swore that nothing would stop him from laying upon both Rebecca Love and Ian MacRae a curse such as had never been uttered before in the underworld. Let his soul be damned twice over. "They will pay!" said Jamie O'Roarke with a sinister smile upon his twisted lips.

CHAPTER THIRTY-FIVE

"Why, Miss, I'm afraid that it would be impossible for me to let you see the prisoner," said Benjamin Webb quite taken with the charming vision before him. The flush on her cheeks and the roundness of her hips was indeed a tasty combination. What a shame that the pious old Reverend had left orders that anyone who meddled with the prisoner would find himself at the end of a rope.

"But, kind sir," said Arabella placing herself between Rebecca and the hungry looking yeoman, "do we look like dangerous highwaymen? All we wish is to view the famous Captain O'Roarke. Think what a story it would be for us to bring back to our neighbors. We can tell how the brave soldiers of Salem Town bested the ferocious Jamie O'Roarke in battle. How strong you must be to have brought down such a vicious beast," said Arabella lightly touching yeoman Webb's biceps.

"Why, 'twas nothing, Mistress," said Benjamin, finding these ladies more charming with every passing moment. " 'Tis nothing that we don't face everyday what with cutthroats and savages around."

"Oh my," said Rebecca taking her cue from the older woman, "you have Indians in Salem! How very frightening," she said with a quiver in her lips and a heaving of her rounded breasts. Thank God Melinda had costumed her in the becoming bodice. It might be a bit embarrassing to walk around in the tightly laced garment, but from the look on the simple yeoman's face, its affects might just open a few doors.

"Yes, my lovely burde," said Benjamin trying to position himself closer to Rebecca. "There are many dangers lurking about the town. Savages and pirates be but a few. Surely you have heard of our troubles the past few years. Why 'twas myself, Benjamin Webb, that was responsible for bringing many a witch to this very jail."

"How thrilling, Master Webb," said Rebecca choking back the urge to laugh. The pompous little soldier looked just like a fat partridge in his puffed up importance.

"Do tell, sir," said Arabella, "how did you ever manage to escape their evil spells?"

"Wasn't easy, milady, and that's the truth. I had more than one close call. I recollect a young lady, Eva Munroe by name, that managed to escape our grasp. It was like she vanished into thin air leaving only the body of a poor young lad behind her. So you see, like it or not, we can take no chances. Who's to say yon pirate is not in league with the devil. He has the look of it for sure. It's protectin' you I am by making you keep your distance."

"There now," thought Webb with a smile on his face, that was neatly done. Perhaps the beautiful Miss might see her way clear to thanking the brave Benjamin for saving her from the devil's own imp.

"Why thank you, sir," said Rebecca breaking forth in a merry laugh that she could no longer withhold. "What would we have done if we had found ourselves spirited away by yon dangerous criminal! Please accept our gratitude."

"No need to thank me" said the yeoman leveling his gaze and staring at Rebecca's bosom in what she thought was a most insulting manner. "But 'twould be pleasant to share a bit of rum with you ladies," he said drawing a flask from within his deep coat pocket.

"Why to be sure we would be delighted, wouldn't we, Rebecca?" said Arabella staring down the girl's furious glance. At this moment all Rebecca wanted to do was to escape from the odious man's disgusting glare. Whatever could Arabella be thinking of? As these thoughts passed through her mind, she suddenly had a vision of Jamie O'Roarke mounting the scaffold on Derby wharf. With a gasp that she hoped the yeoman took for pleasure, she turned back to his lustful eyes and gave what she hoped was a seductive giggle.

"We would be indeed delighted to share a bit of your refreshment, sir. How very kind of you," Rebecca said, sitting down at the rough wooden table.

Benjamin Webb, delighted at the turn of events, sat closely beside her and took a long drink from the flask before wiping the mouth of the bottle with his sleeve and handing it to Rebecca. The girl, having encountered the affects of Salem rum the night before, tried to give the appearance of taking a great gulp. She actually managed to keep most of the liquid from flowing down her throat. A good thing it was too. Even the few drops that escaped her blocking tongue burned hotly as the dark gold rum flowed through her body.

"There's a girl!" said Webb as Rebecca passed the bottle to Arabella. If the older woman would only take her leave, Benjamin believed he might find a way to get closer to this lovely lass. As Arabella took a long drink of the powerful rum, Benjamin Webb had visions of the older woman snoring in her chair while he dallied with the girl. Little did he know that Arabella MacRae, dainty though she might appear, had a leg as hollow as any in Scotland. The fair lady had been raised with whiskey in her milk. A little rum could hardly fell such a highlander.

"Tell me, sir," said Rebecca looking at the yeoman seductively, "what are they to do with yon Captain? Surely they do not mean to keep him caged in that dark room forever?"

"Why no, Mistress Rebecca," said Benjamin as he felt the strong rum relaxing his tongue, "they mean to bring him to trial this very day. Two of his scurvies that hail from Salem mean to put the noose around their own Captain's neck. We must thank providence that Jack and Ezra Love have stood forth like two brave blades and invited the wrath of the pirates code. 'Tis the black spot for them both and that's for sure if any of O'Roarke's mates hear of their betrayal."

"And what is this black spot?" said Rebecca attempting to keep the panic out of her voice.

"Why 'tis only what their mates believe those two deserve for betraying their own. Once a seaman has turned traitor he must watch day and night for fellow pirates. The instant a bloke manages to slip him a bit o' paper with a black spot drawn upon it, the man knows his time is up. 'Twould indeed be easier to be hanged at rope's end, than to suffer a death dealt out by such as Captain Kidd, and that's the truth of it," said Webb leaning back in his chair, thoroughly enjoying impressing these two ladies with his vast knowledge of pirates.

"And is the Captain to be kept here until the trial?" said Arabella sensing that the yeoman's guard was down.

"But of course, Mistress, until that very moment, protected by yours truly. None shall get past my blade."

"Yeoman Webb, what is the meaning of this!" came a soft but menacing voice from behind them. The Reverend Samuel Brown, who had quietly opened the door in the hopes of catching Webb drinking on duty, swooped down on the hapless Benjamin like an angry black raven.

"Guards," he called summoning the two watchmen who had been stationed outside the door. "Take yeoman Webb and lock him in the stocks until his head clears, then escort him to the edge of town. Just be grateful, sir," said Brown turning on Benjamin in fury, "that I have too many worries this day to see you properly tried for dereliction of duty! And as for these two ladies," said Samuel Brown as he turned to face the poor Webb's companions, "why, where have they gone!"

"Frightened away by the likes of your ugly face, your worship," said Benjamin Webb as his fellow soldiers dragged him towards the door hoping that they could keep him quiet long enough to save his neck. Webb had been a right sort and the least they could do was see that he was sent off with no worse than a stiffness in his joints and a few coins in his pocket. It was not the first time that such a thing had occurred. That despicable Brown was always sneaking around hoping to catch them in some wickedness.

" 'Tis the devil's own work afoot this day if I am any judge of it," said Brown sinking wearily into the creaking chair. "First Melinda Briggs and that traitor of a Major Wolf trick me and now those two hussies escape. 'Tis a pity that their faces were turned from me. There was something very familiar about them."

Musing upon the days events, the Reverend looked about him and picked up Benjamin Webb's abandoned flask. As he swallowed the remainder of the fine rum, Samuel Brown closed his eyes and dreamed of the treasure that would soon be his.

CHAPTER THIRTY-SIX

"According to what I've read, O'Roarke is tried the day of his capture and hanged the next morning at dawn," said Peter trying to deal with the information that Rebecca and Arabella had brought back. "It looks as if everything is repeating itself," he said sadly.

"How can you be so calm! We must do something!" said Rebecca afraid of the despair she felt. What was the matter with her! Less than forty-eight hours ago her life had been a calm, well ordered series of events. True, it had been filled with the sorrow of her mother's death and her own lonely existence, but it had been predictable. Now, no matter how hard Rebecca tried to make some sense of her surroundings, she felt herself spinning out of control. The emotions she had for Jamie O'Roarke were beginning to frighten her. It was as if he had spun a gossamer web around her that was threatening to enmesh the girl forever in its deadly grasp. How clean and honest were her feelings for Ian MacRae by contrast. Jamie O'Roarke was a deadly flame that drew her like a moth to its heat, while the miracle of Ian's love bathed her with a purifying light. Unknown to her, a dangerous spell had been cast over Rebecca. Only her friends arrival had saved Rebecca from the dark forces gathering strength around her.

"I agree with Rebecca, Professor Hawking," said Ian looking at the girl's tortured face, "but I don't see how we can possibly free O'Roarke from the jail without endangering both ourselves and the ladies. Sooner or later we would come under suspicion for our very strangeness and find ourselves hanging beside O'Roarke on the gibbet. That would do no one any good, least of all O'Roarke. If he is to be saved at all we must tread carefully. One mistake would mean the end for us all."

"What of the dyad you spoke of, Peter, couldn't she help us?" said Rebecca, grasping at any hope.

"That's not as easy as it sounds, my friends," said Peter setting his jaw. "The lady Eva must be called upon only as a last resort. Each time she is summoned her power over me grows stronger. If I lose control of the dyad, there is no telling what may happen. There are far worse things in the spirit world than a mere curse. We may lose any hope of ever returning home if our nymph escapes the livewood."

"Not to mention the revenge she will take upon you, my dear," said Arabella touching Peter's cheek in an unmistakable display of affection. "To see you locked away in some old tree silently screaming in agony would be more than I am willing to bear. Certainly the four of us can liberate one pirate from the grasp of Samuel Brown?"

"Wait, I think there may yet be a way," said Ian, looking around the clearing. "It's obvious that to try to break O'Roarke out of jail would be foolhardy, but it wouldn't surprise me if what Samuel Brown really wants is the treasure of Duncan MacRae."

"That's quite true my boy, quite true," said Peter surprised that he hadn't thought of it himself. "According to legend, O'Roarke would have been granted a pardon if he had given up the treasure to the town of Salem. But he died rather than give Brown the satisfaction. It was pride that really killed Jamie O'Roarke. I'm afraid that there is little hope that he would tell you where it is even if you could get in to see him."

"But there might be another way!" said Rebecca with a gasp. "Captain O'Roarke's mates are supposed to bury the treasure tonight in Collins Cove. Reverend Brown's men will discover it if they don't. Jack and Ezra Love will be at Collins Cove tonight with the treasure!"

"That's it then! We'll surprise them and seize old Duncan's booty. Then we can use it as a bribe to win O'Roarke's freedom!" said Ian, glad at last to have a plan involving action.

"Not so fast, lad," said Peter, "it would be far safer to wait until they bury the treasure and leave. That way Rebecca can go with you to guide the way and still be safe. It's just a matter of watching to see where they bury the treasure. It's my guess that they will board their ship and make to the open sea as soon as O'Roarke is sentenced and the goods are hidden. Even if they are stopped there will be no treasure on board to incriminate them."

"It will work, I know it will," said Rebecca throwing her arms around Ian's neck and smothering him with kisses. "Oh thank you for not minding about the treasure. You are so wonderful."

"My pleasure to be sure, lassie," said a delighted Ian MacRae holding the grateful girl tightly in his arms.

CHAPTER THIRTY-SEVEN

"Candlelight and all's well," came the cry from somewhere in the dusk. Jamie, despite his determination to stay alert, had drifted off into a slumber as dark as night. The voice that awoke him brought the unwelcome news that soon he would be summoned to trial.

"Candlelight already," sighed Jamie as he sat up in the soft darkness. Hard though it was to fathom, the small cell was growing gloomier. Soon Jamie would be denied even the small pleasure of the gray shadows that surrounded him. Oh, to hear the sound of the ripple lapping softly upon the shore one last time! But Jamie knew that even that small wish was to be denied him. Through the hundreds of years that he had journeyed as a spirit, not once had he been granted those things that the mortals about him were blessed with. The ghost of Jamie O'Roarke had been forced to exist in a vacuum devoid of touch or fragrance. Not for him were the pleasures of the earth. The smell of the sea and the bliss of the wind in his hair had been denied to Jamie O'Roarke from day he had been hanged.

How sweet it had been to experience ecstasy just once more. In a way, the journey had equaled the price. Mistress Rebecca Love be damned, the adventure had been worth the risk. Let her be just one more wench that had crossed Jamie's path. 'Twas not the first time that Jamie had been tricked up by a fair maid. At least her hips had been round and her lips soft. With a chuckle Jamie leaned back and thought of the delicious moments he had spent in the beautiful girl's arms. Oh, she should pay for her betrayal, but the more O'Roarke mused upon the memory of her lovely smile, the harder it was to be truly angry with the lass. 'Twas the doing of MacRae that had brought Jamie low. The lass must have been duped by that spawn of old Duncan. Her sweet smile and precious kisses had been genuine, of that Jamie was sure. So be it. Let the fullness of his wrath fall upon Ian MacRae.

"Ah then, here's the brave Captain O'Roarke playing the fool again. How well it suits you, Jamie me lad."

Jamie leaped to his feet and turned towards the beguiling voice that had spoken. How well he knew its mocking tones. "And what brings you here, my little Daughter of Satan? What a wicked wench ye are to taunt old Jamie at such a time. If ye can't see your way to relieving me of my chains than begone."

"What! And miss all the fun?" said the lovely Eva filling the cell with the radiance of her green gold light. "Why, Jamie me darlin', I wouldn't dream of denying myself such a pleasure. Perhaps this time you will see your way clear to being a bit more pleasant to me. Who's to say that I might not take it into my head to free you and set your course for the open sea?"

"And who's to say you have the power to do it, you deceitful sprite? What of the old sorcerer's spell? Well, I know your tricks, lass, and this is just another way you've thought up to torture me. You may be able to appear before me, but any power you have is imprisoned in the shaman's staff. As long as he holds it in his hand you must do his bidding. Float about all you wish making your empty promises, I'll have none of them. 'Tis a day too full of falsehoods for me," said Jamie sitting down with his back to Eva. Let her torment him all she wished. Jamie was in the mood for neither a pretty face nor a beguiling promise.

"Come now, laddie," said Eva moving next to Jamie with a motion that was as soft as a sigh, "don't look so forlorn. We had some fair times in our old wood, strange though they might have been. Your company was welcome despite your foul moods. I swear that you are the most amusing man I have ever met. Do you remember the time you lured that fat burgher, Ebenezer Love, into the graveyard for some sport? He'd just come from the dedication of Hamilton Hall and was full of good port. What a figure he made as you pricked him with your cutlass. Oh how he spun in circles looking for the source of the stings."

"Hah, and well I remember him running off into the night. 'Twas not my fault that he fell into a shallow puddle and drowned himself, but 'twas a fitting end," laughed Jamie despite himself. Trying though she might be, yon nymph and Jamie O'Roarke were cut of the same cloth. Mayhap she was right. Better to give up all thought of redemption than to suffer as he was now. Lady MacRae's tears had awakened something fine deep within him that he had painfully abandoned long ago. His hopes for salvation were not to be. The goodness that lay in Jamie had been cruelly crushed by the death of his dreams. Why not give himself up to the joys that Eva found so enchanting? At least she was not taunted by unattainable visions of a pure love and noble deeds.

"That's better, O'Roarke! I was beginning to fear that you were going soft on me. It was sad I was to see you simpering after that little maid with your tongue hanging out. 'Twas not the proud Jamie I knew and that's a fact. Come on now me bucko, cheer up. Once this unpleasantness is over we can have some fun. I'll make sure the sorcerer and his mates get back to their home and then we'll see what's what. One more wish from the old codger and the balance of power will shift in my favor. Well he knows it, too. Thank Beelzebub that he has no choice but to enjoy my talents. Even if it means the end for him, Peter Hawking would never let his precious Rebecca or the enchanting Lady Arabella languish here forever. So you see, my fine Captain, there be amusements ahead to dispel your gloom," said the nymph with girlish pleasure.

"And what of the loneliness, my girl? Do you never long for a loving touch or a tender word? I myself would gladly trade all eternity for the blessings of a peaceful sleep," said Jamie. It was strange, he thought, but the miracle of Rebecca's tenderness had awakened the true Jamie O'Roarke. Gone was the fire within him that could only be quenched with cruel deeds. In its place lay a deep peacefulness that felt like a calm cool breeze. The old Jamie would not have forgiven anyone who had maneuvered him into such a spot, but the renewed heart that now lay within him thirsted for purer waters. The pleasures the dyad had to offer no longer held any allure for him.

Many years ago, a small boy had run along the shores of Lynn beach and Collins Cove filled with dreams of being a great privateer. How he had played at being a fine sailor, master of his own ship, respected by all who knew him. The taunts of the other wharf rats had no effect on the young boy as long as his visions of wealth and power lay before him. What matter that his father had abandoned him and his mother was a whore? The great Sir Jamie O'Roarke, knighted by the King, would show them all! Someday he would return to Salem Town and build the grandest house ever seen in New England. Aye, and marry a fine lady to boot. He would be a gentleman for all to see.

When his sweet dreams had been crushed by the evil schemes of the Salem merchants, Jamie had taken up arms against them. Better to be an honest pirate than walk upon the bones and drink the blood of African slaves. Never had he boarded a ship that had been in honest trade. It was the slavers that were Jamie O'Roarke's meat and drink. With the laughter of revenge, Jamie O'Roarke had slit the throat of many a fine "gentleman" captain who traded in human misery. It was only after he had seen the poor devils in the hold to some safer shore that Jamie had helped himself to any booty.

Old Duncan MacRae's ship was to have been the last sunk by Jamie. With the great Scottish treasure buried safely in Collins Cove, Jamie would have at last been able to realize his dreams of wealth and respectability. It was his own innate goodness that had scuttled him. Jamie had been a fool to trust anyone, even his dutch uncle, Ezra Love. His old mother had always said that blood was thicker than water and how right she had been. Jamie's respect and love for the old man had meant nothing next to Jackie's appeal to the blood. An orphan he began and an orphan Jamie would end, with everyone's hand against him. Hang him they would, of that there was no doubt, but the secret of MacRae's treasure would die with him. Jack and Ezra would be forced to bury it, what with every man jack searching for it, so at least it would do them no good. The Love brothers would find out soon enough that the false promises of Samuel Brown would bring them to rope's end.

"Now, Jamie, where have ye gone, me lad," said Eva, used to O'Roarke's musings.

" 'Tis a place you can't follow for sure, lass," said Jamie tickling her under the chin. "Off with you now before someone sees you and has us both burned for a witch. 'Twould be a fitting end to an unusual day for sure, but not such a one as I would relish."

"All right then, Jamie, as you say I will be off, but don't lose heart, darling, I'll be waiting for you."

Eva's light slowly faded with the last of her words returning Jamie to his gloom. The man, giving into utter despair buried his face in his weathered hands and wept silently as he had done as a boy.

CHAPTER THIRTY-EIGHT

"That's right, lads, take a seat, take a seat," said Samuel Brown, quickly hiding Benjamin Webb's now empty flask beneath his coat."

Jack and Ezra Love looked about nervously. To be sure this was the only time they had ever spent time in Salem jail on this side of the prison door. Ezra kept glancing nervously towards the stout wooden planks that were the only thing that lay between him and Jamie O'Roarke.

If he had it to do over again, Ezra Love would have let his greedy brother hang before he would have betrayed the Captain. Curse the dark rum that had always been his downfall. And curse his wicked brother who always lusted after that which belonged to others. But what was done was done. There was no turning back now. It was the black spot he deserved, no doubt about it. It had been the young Jamie O'Roarke who had leapt into the storm tossed sea and saved old Ezra's skin that time off the port of Jamaica. And how had Ezra repaid him? By betraying the finest Captain a scurvy had ever known. Well, here he was, and there Jamie was. They were both in too deep to ever escape what might happen in the next few hours. Perhaps, thought Ezra, if he changed his tune he could yet save the Captain. But one look at Jackie's face told the tale. Ezra knew from long experience that once his younger brother was set on a course, he would toss anyone he needed to overboard just to stay afloat. The thirst that never left Ezra for very long, burned like a fire within him. Oh for the blessed oblivion brought about by a keg of rum. The thought of Jamie swinging at the end of a rope through Ezra's own folly was more than he could bear when sober.

"Now then lads, I asked you here to get a few things straight before O'Roarke is brought to trial. I want no mention of the MacRae treasure. It would only serve to inflame the townsfolk further against the prisoner. Is it understood that any knowledge of the treasure will remain our secret?"

"Oh to be sure, your worship," said Jack grinning widely, revealing a set of jagged teeth that reminded Samuel Brown of a hungry shark. "We wouldn't want the good citizens here abouts digging up the town in a frenzy, now would we, Ezra?" said Jack elbowing his brother in the ribs.

"No, we wouldn't," said Brown moving his chair away from the unwashed pirate. "Whatever knowledge O'Roarke may have of the treasure is to be kept in strict confidence between himself and the authorities. That way I can see to its administration for the good of the town. Remember, any pardon I may grant can be rescinded if you break our agreement."

"Now, sir," said Ezra, afraid that Jack would get them both hanged. "I swear upon our dear Mother's bones that we are men to be trusted. Just give us our bit of paper and we'll be on our way."

"You're forgetting, my fine fellow, that without your testimony and without the treasure, I have no hard evidence against O'Roarke. Make sure that you appear in an hour's time before the magistrate and I promise you that you shall receive full pardon. Back out on our agreement and there will be justice to face at the end of a rope," said Samuel Brown, holding the two pardons signed by both himself and Cotton Mather just out of arms reach. As he glared at the pirates, Samuel Brown fanned himself with the two parchments.

"Now then, I believe our business is concluded for now. If you do all you promise there will be an escort waiting to accompany you wherever you wish to go."

"Let us shake on it then," said Jack Love offering a grimy hand to the Reverend. "It's a done deal, and may we both be glad of it."

Samuel Brown, hiding his disgust, grasped the pirate's hand and shook it heartily. The treasure of Duncan MacRae was well worth it.

"One hour left," thought Jamie as he listened to the heavy oak door close behind his two mates.

CHAPTER THIRTY-NINE

"What a beautiful place this is," sighed Arabella, breathing in the crispness of the autumn air about her. "This is really quite an exciting adventure. I only wish that it were not ours."

"Now, my dear," said Peter, carefully looking about before he slipped his arm around her waist, "I'm sure that in a few hours time all our problems will be solved and we'll be snug in our own beds."

"How boring that sounds," sighed Rebecca, stooping to pick up a flaming red leaf. "It must have been so romantic to ride the seven seas as Captain O'Roarke has, burying treasure and seeing the world. How lucky he is."

"If you call ending your days hanging at the end of a rope lucky," said Ian, feeling very uncomfortable about the look on Rebecca's face. "And don't forget, Jamie O'Roarke has spent the last three hundred years roaming through the land of the undead like some unholy angel."

"At least he didn't suffer from hunger or thirst," moaned a famished and footsore Lady Arabella. "However do these people manage to get a bite to eat?"

"I have read that after the Salem witch trials many went hungry in Salem Town. It seems that everyone neglected their fields during the panic. It took several years to recover from their losses," said Rebecca as the small group followed the path towards the meetinghouse where Peter had said Jamie O'Roarke would soon be brought to trial.

"Surely there must be some goodwife with a bit of bread and cheese to sell. Why don't the Lady Arabella and I ask about while you and Ian try to rest?" said Peter concerned about the dark circles that had appeared under Rebecca's eyes. If she was to make it through this night she must be alert!

"There is a sheltered group of trees right over there that look quite comfortable," said Ian, seeing Peter's worried glance at Rebecca. "We'll wait there while you scare up some food. It wouldn't do to leave a lady alone in these wilds. No telling when an Indian attack might occur."

"Oh thank you," laughed Rebecca, "I feel safer already."

"Take my cloak, dear," said Arabella handing the girl her light wool cape, "the air is really turning quite chilly."

"But what about you, won't you be cold?"

"You forget, my dear, that I am a highland lassie born and bred. Why, this is like midsummer's eve to such as me. Besides, I'm sure the Professor has enough wits about him to keep us both from the chill."

"That I do, my lady," said Peter motioning to Ian to take shelter beneath the trees. "Run along now children and take your nap while we still have time."

"All right, all right," said Rebecca kissing both Peter and Arabella lightly. "But be sure you come back for us soon."

CHAPTER FORTY

"I still can't believe we're really here," said Rebecca resting her head against Ian's shoulder. "All my life I've studied these people, but now I realize that no book could actually describe this. It's so different from anything I could have ever imagined."

"I think I know what you mean, lass," said Ian holding Rebecca tightly in his arms to ward off the sudden chill of twilight. "The treasure of old Duncan MacRae has always seemed like a fairy tale to me, something you would tell a child as they drifted off to sleep. To be on the verge of seeing it, touching it, is a wonder beyond belief to me."

"Oh, Ian," said Rebecca snuggling deeper into his arms. "I always thought I would love going back in history and visiting all the places I have read about, but it's so different. Why, do you realize that a girl like me with no father would have been forced into a life of poverty? If I had been lucky, I would have ended up like Melinda Briggs, but I think it might have been worse. The widow and daughter of a sailor would have had no choice but to beg for their very existence. There is no telling what my mother would have had to do to survive. I would have had no more than Jamie O'Roarke."

"Poor Jamie," sighed Rebecca, "he never had a chance. First a child of the streets and then betrayed by everyone he trusted. It's no wonder that he became an outlaw. It was the only thing left to him."

"You don't really believe that do you?" laughed Ian as he patted her glossy black hair.

"But of course I do," said Rebecca, irritated at his condescending tone. "Jamie tried to follow the rules and laws of his time, but the merchants of Salem made it impossible for him to make an honest living. They wanted him to use his ship for the slave trade. When he refused, they blocked him at every turn, giving their business to others."

"But that doesn't condone his foul murdering ways, darling. Jamie O'Roarke had choices, just like we all do. He could have found another way to earn his bread. Why, he could have even gone west and sought his fortune there. Instead he chose to become a thief and a cutthroat. Duncan MacRae and his crew carried only good honest wool aboard the 'Golden Fleece' and they received no mercy. Captain Jamie O'Roarke threw them into the sea and watched as they were eaten alive by sharks. According to my ancestors, he had one of his scurvies pipe a lively tune as he toasted their bloody death. That is your 'saint' Jamie for you. If it weren't for my Aunt Arabella, I would be more than happy to see him hanged a second time. It would be worth watching my back for the rest of my life to see O'Roarke swing."

"Ian MacRae, I don't believe you!" shouted Rebecca as she struggled out of his arms. "Jamie never killed anyone but slavers who had tortured poor innocent souls. He told me so."

"Of course that's what he told you, girl. He's in love with you and would tell you anything to have his way with you. Don't you realize that? Only a fool would believe his fairy tales. You can't tell me that Stewart Mackenzie, the ten year old cabin boy aboard Duncan MacRae's ship, had done anything to deserve his fate."

"That's a disgusting lie and you know it," cried Rebecca battling her own doubts. How dare this man call her a fool! What did he know of Jamie O'Roarke and his sad smile and tender ways?

"Well then, think what you want," said Ian with a shrug of his shoulders, "but don't say I didn't warn you." With that he closed his eyes and prayed that somehow Rebecca's Captain Jamie would slip up just once. If he went to his grave with her believing him an innocent, any chance Ian had of winning Rebecca's love was dead. No one could fight the romantic legend of Jamie O'Roarke.

Rebecca was too agitated to sleep. She sat down on the soft brown earth a few paces from Ian. Her mind was a swirl of confusion. It seemed that every time she thought she knew the truth a new twist appeared. Whatever Jamie had done, he still had goodness within him. It was with great relief that she saw Peter and Arabella walking towards her swinging a lantern and carrying a straw basket full of simple, but delicious food.

CHAPTER FORTY-ONE

The strained silence between Rebecca and Ian was interrupted by the twilight picnic. Arabella chattered gaily as she laid the simple feast out on the rough cloth that had been woven by a local farmer's wife. It was not the first time she had to endure her nephew's moodiness during a meal, but she was surprised to find that the lovely Rebecca was also silent. Giving Peter a smile, Arabella proceeded to chatter away as if nothing were wrong, hoping to dispel the gloom.

"Such lovely clotted cream, and look, Ian, scones! What luck we had in finding a goodwife whose mother hailed from Dumfries. I must say that for a lowlander she handles a ladle well. Oh my, why there is even bread pudding. Eat up you two, there is no telling when we may get the chance again."

"I don't think I'm hungry," said Rebecca, glancing at Ian beneath her lashes.

"Well, I am," said Ian taking a scoop of cream and spreading it on the fragrant scone. Let her act like a little fool if she wished to. Ian MacRae went hungry for no lass, not even Rebecca Love.

"Look," cried Rebecca as several lantern lights flickered at the entrance to the prison. "It's Jamie! Where are they taking him?"

"To trial, my dearest," said Peter, gently putting a protective arm around her.

CHAPTER FORTY-TWO

Jamie O'Roarke marched into the Salem meetinghouse with his head held high. No chains could subdue his pride or quench the fire in his soul. He was the great Captain O'Roarke, scourge of the seven seas. So he had lived and so he would die if that was what the fates had ordained. He would never humble himself before this rabble. Looking about, Jamie was amazed at the size of the crowd that had come to witness his humiliation. The good Puritan folk of Salem were dressed in shades of black and brown. They reminded Jamie of a flock of vultures waiting eagerly for their chance to feast on the slaughtered carrion. If these ghouls were here to watch Captain Jamie beg for his life then they would have to wait until hell froze over!

Jamie took his seat near the judges table with a flourish of his frock coat. Just as he was about to turn his back on the crowd Jamie spied Ian and Rebecca slipping through the heavy oak doors. Peter and Arabella followed and the small party had some difficulty finding room to stand. All of Salem must be here, though Jamie wryly. The least he could do was to give them a bit of entertainment. Grasping his great feathered hat, Jamie turned towards the crowd and waved it. His eyes searched out those of Rebecca. To his great surprise, she gave him a smile of encouragement and tears shone in her eyes. "Perhaps he had been wrong about the lass after all," mused Jamie as the constable beside him pulled at Jamie's chains forcing the pirate to his chair in an ignominious fashion.

The honorable Cotton Mather rose to his feet and surveyed the crowd with a stern glare. It seemed only yesterday that Mather had entertained these same folk in this same place. Three years had passed since the last Salem witch had been hanged, but Mather still thought of the place with a mixture of pride and resentment. The ungrateful townsmen had been making attempts to remove themselves from the proceedings that Mather had conducted in 1692. What simpletons they were to think that perhaps the trials had been caused by nothing more than the moody vapors of a group of pubescent girls. Of course there had been witches in Salem! Had not several witches confessed to dealings with the devil? 'Twas only guilt that caused the people of Salem to regret their actions. Perhaps, thought Mather, all the witches had not been rooted out of this small haven. He made a mental note to reexamine several folk that had seemed suspicious to him several years before. But first this O'Roarke business must be concluded. What a pity that O'Roarke's treasure had not been found. He was such an amusing fellow and would be sorely missed at the Blue Anchor Tavern.

Despite his thoughts, the righteous Reverend Cotton Mather knew his duty and was quite prepared to do it. If O'Roarke was a pirate than he must hang, that was the law. Facing the accused, Cotton Mather adjusted his heavily starched collar and banged the heavy wooden gable on the massive trestle table that served as a judges bench. "Captain Jamie O'Roarke, you are summoned to trial. Present yourself before the court, sirrah."

Jamie, struggling to his feet under the weight of his chains, faced the honorable Cotton Mather and gave him a nod of his head. At least the detestable Samuel Brown had been relegated to the far end of the table for the trial. Only such a man as Cotton Mather could be judged as important enough to preside over the trial of Captain Jamie O'Roarke. It seemed but a moment ago that Jamie and Mather had been sharing a noggin of rum at the Blue Anchor. Little did old Cotton know that while Jamie had been entertaining him downstairs, one legged 'Jambe de Bois' was escaping out the upstairs window and making for the coast and the warmer climes of St. Lucia's Pidgeon Island. "Oh to be there now with a bevy of beautiful Caribe girls wrapped about me," thought Jamie with a wistful smile.

"Captain O'Roarke, you must answer the charges against you. They are grave indeed and carry the highest punishment of all, death by hanging. 'Tis a grave matter, sir, and not one that should be regarded lightly. I fail to see what you find amusing about this trial."

"I beg your pardon, your honor," said Jamie rousing from his reverie of the Caribbean. "I seemed to be lost in thoughts of happier days. Now what is it that I am being accused of, your Reverence?"

"Of piracy on the high seas and the cold blooded murder of innocent seafaring folk," replied Mather gazing sternly at O'Roarke."

"But your Honor, I am merely a humble privateer, traveling from port to port with what goods I can. It is a humble living but one that I have always conducted with honesty and pride. I have done no more than any respectable merchant of Salem, peddling his goods from town to town seeking only a fair profit in return. What is this slanderous talk of piracy! I am indeed shocked that anyone would bring such charges against me. Reveal the blackguard. I will defend myself against any man. More's the pity if they come up lacking I say." With that Jamie took his seat and refused to be brought to his feet by the constable.

"Stand before your betters, O'Roarke," yelled Samuel Brown from his seat at the far end of the table.

"I will when I see one, you hypocritical lecher," retorted Jamie putting his feet up on the table before him despite the discomfort of his chains.

"Order, I say, order," said Cotton Mather banging his gavel upon the table and motioning to Samuel Brown to remain silent. "I'll not have this trial be conducted in such a manner. Captain O'Roarke, if you can't find it within yourself to give the officers of this court the respect due them you will have to be tried 'in absentia', do you understand?"

"Quite well, your honor, I must present my apologies to you and this esteemed body," said Jamie with a scornful sneer. "I am but a simple man of humble origin and must abide by your rules. As for Reverend Brown, I needn't challenge his politics or inclinations. All about know him as a fine upstanding gentleman with an impeccable character. Why, I was speaking to Mistress Melinda Briggs only yesterday of his faithfulness to hearth and home. My deep regrets for having disturbed the proceedings, sir."

"Reverend Mather, are we to accept this impudence?" said Samuel Brown as he attempted to regain his composure. "The sooner O'Roarke was swinging from rope's end the better," thought the lecherous man of God.

"Now then, I believe we would all do well to remember where we are and pray to the Almighty to grant us wisdom. Let us bow our heads and entreat His blessings."

With that Cotton Mather led a prayer as the yeomen lit the torches in the darkening room. The hellish red and black shadows cast by the setting sun made Rebecca shudder with fear.

CHAPTER FORTY-THREE

Jamie could feel hundreds of eyes behind him boring into his soul as Cotton Mather loudly intoned the power of his Puritan God. The torchlit room was almost as he remembered it. The one small change filled Jamie with a bit of unexpected comfort. To the right of where Samuel Brown sat was a familiar glow of green and gold that Jamie had come to know intimately over the past three hundred years. Eva! She had come after all to watch poor Jamie's punishment. Despite himself, Jamie felt amused by the soft tones of her aura. Any friend in this pit of righteousness was a welcome one, even the mercurial siren.

"Now let the trial of James Patrick O'Roarke commence," said Cotton Mather with a light tap of the gavel upon the table, "and please remember disturbance will not be tolerated in this courtroom." Cotton Mather settled himself into the great captain's chair that had been brought from the governor's house for his comfort. As he stroked the supple brown leather of the chair, Mather couldn't help but think of his accommodations with a bit of scorn. The people of Salem were becoming distracted by the comforts of the devil. Of that there was no doubt. One had only to look at the fine lace collar that enhanced Mistress Brown's neck to know that. Where had a man of the cloth such as Samuel Brown come upon such a luxury for his wife? If even the Minister's wife had succumbed to such fripperies, then what hope was there for the simple folk? The devil was indeed abroad again in Salem Town. Perhaps the trial of Captain O'Roarke was a divine sign from heaven that Cotton Mather should once again take up the cudgel of the Lord and smite down those who had gotten above themselves. Was not a discontent with one's lot in life a sure sign that the devil was at work? Look at Jamie O'Roarke. If he had contented himself with the lowly station that had been ordained to him by God, he would not now be on trial for his life. But then again what could be expected of him? O'Roarke was a bastard of the waterfront, a child claimed by no one and left to scrounge out his existence from the bounty of others. "Better that he had never been born," thought Mather with a look of disdain as he viewed the arrogant set of O'Roarke's jaw. What right did the scurvy have to hold himself proudly as a nobleman. If he had shown some humility towards his betters, then Mather might have had some sympathy or pity for the man, but as matters stood, the sooner the town was rid of him the better.

"Captain O'Roarke," said Cotton Mather rankling over the fact that he must give the man the title of captain, "what say you to the charges before you?"

"What charges, your worship?" said Jamie with a grin. "I have heard no charges, nor do I know why I am brought before this assemblage. All I know is that I was surprised sleeping beneath a rose bower in the middle of a fall day and brought before you. The only thing I might be held guilty for is sloth or perhaps laziness. Beyond that I am indeed curious as to the charges against me."

"You know very well what they are, you blackguard," said Samuel Brown rising to his feet in fury at O'Roarke's feigned innocence.

"You, Captain O'Roarke, have caused the good folk of Salem Town to live in fear of your evil deeds for years," said Mather. "There has not been a fortnight that has passed without some new tale of wickedness on your part. The shame you have brought upon the place of your birth, that nurtured and protected you, is abominable. A true penitent would be on his knees imploring this honorable assemblage forgiveness for the manner in which you have sullied our peaceful haven."

"Peaceful haven is it my lords?" said O'Roarke letting forth a great laugh of scorn. "Why this small town is known and feared around the world as a hotbed of intolerance and greed. What other town would have hanged such a saint as Rebecca Nurse and her goodly sisters? My only regret is that I was not here at the time to offer them the solace of escape upon the 'Red Witch.' When many of your fine citizens had turned their hands against a small hungry boy, 'twas Goody Nurse who invited me to share the warmth of her hearth and a crust of bread. For shame upon you I say, sir, for her cruel murder and the many who followed her path."

" 'Tis not we who are on trial here, O'Roarke, but you," replied Brown glancing about the room uneasily. What O'Roarke had said hit too close to home for comfort. Even now there were rumblings amongst the townsfolk about the strange occurrences that had transpired a few short years ago. Many of the afflicted girls who had accused the dead witches now deeply regretted their actions and one by one were quietly seeking forgiveness from their victims. Why it was even rumored that Ann Putnam Jr., a leader amongst the girls, was having second thoughts. "That would not do at all, not at all," thought Samuel. If the townsfolk regretted for one moment their actions then Samuel Brown's authority over them would be destroyed.

"And why is it, Captain, that you feel such kinship for those who perished through their own deeds? Is it perhaps that you too, spawn of a whore and a thief, are himself a wizard? Only such a one would dare defend such wickedness."

"Why you bastard," shouted O'Roarke attempting to overcome the weight of his chains and lunge at Brown, "my mother was the greatest lady that ever lived, sacrificing herself body and soul so that I might live. 'Twould not surprise me if your own father might have contributed to my welfare. Think well upon that, sir, before you condemn an innocent woman whose only crime was being born simple and loving." With those words on his lips, O'Roarke was wrestled to the ground by three yeoman who proceeded to chain him to the heavy oak chair at the defendant's table.

"Gentleman," cried Mather rising to his feet and staring down Samuel Brown. "If these proceedings are not restored to order instantly then the room will be cleared and Captain O'Roarke will be taken to Boston. Do you hear me!" With that Cotton Mather wearily took his seat and prayed to God for the strength to see this trial through. For a long time he had wanted to replace Samuel Brown as the minister of this fair town and tonight's proceedings were beginning to strengthen his resolve. It was obvious that any clergy who could not control and inspire fear in his flock was not worthy of such an appointment.

"Call your witnesses, Reverend Brown, and let's be done with this matter."

"Yes, your worship," said Brown, bowing to Mather in a toadying fashion. Try as he might, Samuel Brown could not help but feel uncomfortable at the way Cotton Mather was ordering him about.

"I call to the stand seaman Ezra Love of the sailing vessel 'Red Witch.' Master Love, you are summoned to court."

CHAPTER FORTY-FOUR

Ezra Love pulled uncomfortably at the freshly starched collar around his throat as he walked down the aisle that led to the witness chair. How did landlubbers stand all these fool geegaws? The itch of the wool of his new black suit was nothing compared to the torture his poor feet were going through. The tight leather shoes may have been the finest Reverend Brown could afford, but to Ezra Love they were nothing more than a sign from hell that he was damned. Oh, for the taste of the sea and the feel of a deck beneath his bare feet! Why, oh why, had he let Jackie persuade him into betraying the Captain? Perhaps it was not too late to save him. Jack might never forgive him, but Ezra could see no other way out of it. The Captain was as fine a man as any who had ever sailed the seas and he deserved better than what Jackie was about to hand him. 'Twas a bonny time old Ezra and Jamie had shared before Jackie had come upon the scene. Ashamed he was and that was a fact, but now here was his chance to redeem himself and save the Captain. Squaring his shoulders, the grizzled old sailor walked toward the witness stand with more nobility than a prince of the blood.

"Your name is Master Ezra Love, is it not?" said Samuel Brown as he took his place before the citizens of Salem in his position of prosecutor.

"That's right, your honor," said Ezra feeling strangely intimidated by his surroundings. The closed in space of the crowded meetinghouse was having an almost suffocating affect on the small man used to the open seas and blue sky.

"And you have been with Captain O'Roarke for many years, have you not," said Brown.

"Aye sir, I have, and may I say that never has there been a finer man or a more generous Captain."

"In what way has he been generous with you, Ezra?"

"Why in all ways, your worthy. When our stores ran low, many's the time I've seen the Captain give up his bit of bread to a weaker man. Always the gentleman he was and that's a fact."

"That's not what you told me before, sir," said Samuel Brown moving closer to the old sailor in a menacing manner. "What you said was that Captain O'Roarke had been the cause of many cruelties upon the high seas. Why have you so suddenly changed your tune? Is it that perhaps you are under some threat?"

"Oh no, your honor. I know I said many things last night when I was in me cups, but the truth of it was I was just braggin' a bit, trying to make out I was more important than I really was. 'Twas the rum speakin', your honor, I swear!" said Ezra feeling very uncomfortable about the whole proceeding.

"This is not what your brother told me, sir!" shouted Samuel Brown coming up the the edge of the witness stand and breathing in old Ezra's face. "Your brother Jack shall testify here this evening, Master Love. He has sworn that Captain O'Roarke has committed many foul deeds of murder and theft, including the piracy of the great MacRae treasure. Jack said that both you and he pleaded with Jamie O'Roarke to spare the lives of the poor souls that the Captain so cruelly tossed into the sea. He said that you heard the terrified young cabin boy plead for his very life and you watched in horror as the child was tossed into the jaws of a waiting shark. Is that not true, Master Love, or were you and your brother part of these foul crimes? If this is so, then you both deserve to hang alongside your Captain."

" 'Tis not the way it was at all, your honor," said Ezra becoming alarmed at the way the Reverend was twisting his words. "The boat split in half and before we could save any of the crew of old Duncan's ship, they were seized by the monsters. I swear it."

"That's not the tale told by your brother, Ezra Love, and you know it. You are a foul liar and as guilty as your Captain. Admit it now and throw yourself on the mercy of this court. I am sure that the benevolent Reverend Mather would be more than happy to grant you clemency. You are but a poor working sailor following orders, is that not so?"

"Why sir, I don't know, I mean yes, yes that's right! I never murdered no boy I swear! None of us did, at least I don't think so," said Ezra feeling dizzy as the room closed in upon him. In a flash of intuition Ezra realized that Reverend Brown didn't want the truth, he wanted to do away with the Captain and unless Ezra watched his step it would be too late for all of them! How he wished he had a cutlass in his hand so that he could cut the brigand down, but that was not the way of it in Salem Town. Leave it to these prisoners of the land to use deceit and treachery on the Captain. The only thing to be done was to try and save his own skin. It was too late for Jamie.

"Your honor, said old Ezra with tears in his eyes, "you know the truth of it and so do I, but I can see now that we simple seafaring folk are no match for your great wisdom. Forgive me, Jamie," he said turning and facing O'Roarke with a bow, "but there's no help for it now. Through me own folly you are to see the rope's end and all I can do is beg your pardon."

"That you have and gladly," said Jamie, smiling at the old man. " 'Twas not your fault that your trusting heart led you astray, Ezra. Not to worry, I'll be standing beside you in paradise."

" 'Tis true, 'tis true, matey," said Ezra smiling back at Jamie. "Now then, your worship, what is it you wish to hear?"

"The truth from your lips, that's all," said Samuel Brown with triumphant gentleness.

"Then all you say is right, sir, about the sharks and booty and all, if that's what will make me a free man."

"Very good, my man, very good. Let it be recorded this night that Captain Jamie O'Roarke cruelly plundered the ship of Duncan MacRae and sent the crew to their death," exclaimed Samuel Brown in triumph. "You may step down now, sir. The citizens of Salem thank you for the great service you have rendered."

As Ezra stepped slowly from the witness stand he hesitated. Before his eyes flashed the picture of the twelve year old Jamie O'Roarke come to him for employment. How straight and fine a lad he had been, and what a man he had grown into. Stopping by the defendant's table, old Ezra put his hand upon Jamie's shoulder.

"Is it true that we will see paradise together, Jamie?"

"Aye, matey, 'tis true," said Jamie putting his chain laden arm about the old man. "Don't be afraid, you'll be there long before Jamie. I'm counting on you to smooth the way for me."

"Then all is well between us, eh laddie?"

"It always was, my friend," said Jamie giving Ezra a kiss upon his weathered cheek.

Samuel Brown seeing the tender exchange between the two men was alarmed to hear murmurs of sympathy from the townsfolk. Surely they must see that O'Roarke was guilty. How could they doubt their own ears?

"Reverend Mather, it is time to hear our next witness," said Samuel hoping to dispel the air of sympathy filling the room. "The hour grows late and I am sure that these good people would like to take their leave."

"Yes, I suppose you are right, Reverend Brown," said Mather watching as Ezra Love quietly left the courtroom. Mather was becoming quite uncomfortable with the proceedings and if it had not been for the fact that there was only one more witness he might have declared the trial finished. The evidence presented by the old sailor was at best inconclusive and not enough to be used to sentence a man to death. But never let it be said that Cotton Mather was not a fair and thorough judge.

"Let Master John Love be called to testify," said Samuel Brown with a knowing smirk upon his face.

CHAPTER FORTY-FIVE

In contrast to his older brother, Jack Love swaggered into the courtroom with an air of confidence and bravado that made more than one feminine heart flutter in anticipation. This was what they had been waiting for. Jack Love was the pirate of their midnight dreams, dark and dangerous.

As Jack passed his Captain, Jamie O'Roarke made a sound of disgust and muttered so softly that only Master Love caught his words. " 'Tis the black spot for you and that's for certain. Beware my faithless friend."

Jack Love, visibly shaken by O'Roarke's message, took the stand and attempted to stare down his former mate.

"Now then, my good man, what is it you have to tell the court," said Cotton Mather, determined to take control of the situation before another scene broke out. Mather had been through enough court disturbances in Salem Town to last him a lifetime. Why, just this spring, Increase Mather, Cotton's own father, had through his authority as head of the ecclesiastical council of Boston, managed to depose that annoying Samuel Parris as the head of the Salem Village church. Unfortunately the obstinate villagers were being very uncooperative. Even now a petition was being circulated on Parris' behalf. What ungrateful fools these people of Salem were, thwarting the good work of their betters at every turn. Mather would never forget Parris' words in September of 1692. "The city of heaven, provided for the saints, is well-walled and well-gated and well-guarded, so that no devils, nor their instruments, shall enter therein." What boldness to compare Salem with heaven and the good Reverend as its self-appointed protector!

"Why, your honor," said Jack Love facing the esteemed Mather, "I have come here so that ye may know the truth and act accordingly. I can't tell you how it grieves me that through doing my Christian duty I must bring down me Captain, but I know my duty, indeed I do."

"And what does your sense of Christian duty compel you to tell us, sir?" said Mather taking in the cut of Jack's clothes and the scars on his face. Somehow, Mather was getting the distinct impression that the wrong pirate was on trial here. For all his foibles, Jamie O'Roarke had always seemed a good man, quick with a favor or a tale to lighten the heart. This skulking blackguard made the hairs on Cotton Mather's neck stand up. Here was a man who would just as soon cut your throat as look at you. Mather had seen his ilk many times before, but this was the first time he had ever seen one taking the witness stand prepared to do his "Christian" duty.

" 'Tis but a short tale, and a sad one, I'm afraid," said Jack shaking his head woefully. "Yon Captain, for all his pretty wit is nothing more than a bold desperate blade who has shipwrecked a score of vessels and cut many a throat just to fill his own pockets with gold pieces. Me mates and I were ill pleased when we realized his plans, but there was nothing to be done until we made for safe harbor. 'Twas old Duncan MacRae himself that handed me this here watch as he was being thrown into the sea. I don't know enough to scratch me own name, so I never figured out its message. Perhaps you can read it for me, your worthy, if you wouldn't mind the trouble."

"You black dog," said Jamie as he struggled in his chair. "You yourself lightened MacRae of that watch as you ran him through. Your honor, I can no longer remain silent while this man slanders me. I was all for leaving the passengers and crew of the 'Golden Fleece' on a nearby island and such were my orders, but my third mate, who stands before you now, went behind my back while I was taking my rest. By the time I took my stand on deck it was too late. I saw with my own eyes the murder of Duncan MacRae by this man. I beseech you to hand me a cutlass and let us do battle over this matter. Why not let God himself determine who is innocent."

"Captain O'Roarke, please remember where you are," said Cotton Mather desiring above all else to make an end of this business. "Reverend Brown, please bring the watch to me."

Samuel Brown, a bit chastened by his smaller role in the questioning of Jack Love, made haste to quickly transport the gleaming watch from Jack's weathered hand to the soft one of Cotton Mather.

The watch was a heavy affair with intricate etchings. It shone in the torchlit room. Cotton Mather carefully touched the delicate spring that opened it and examined the inside. On the upper sphere was an inscription made with love. "To my beloved Father from your adoring daughter on the occasion of your fiftieth birthday, Mary Ann." As Mather read these words aloud, they ran through the courtroom like a beacon in the night. No matter what had been said or how kind and dashing Jamie O'Roarke might appear, he was the Captain of the "Red Witch," the ship that had sunk the "Golden Fleece." It was Jamie who had murdered the innocent souls aboard. Captain O'Roarke must pay for his crimes.

"Captain O'Roarke, as much as it grieves me to sentence any man to death, I fear that I have no choice," said Cotton Mather gazing sternly at the prisoner. "There can be no doubt of your guilt. I hold the conclusive evidence in my hand. Pray God that he will accept your life as atonement for your crimes and grant you the solace of his mercy. As for those others who may have had a hand in these crimes, woe unto them if I discover their guilt. The reach of the law is a long and vengeful one."

"No, oh please no, your honor!" came a tortured scream from the back of the room. Rebecca was desperately trying to remove the arms that Ian had placed around her in order to restrain the girl. Nothing could be done for O'Roarke, and if Rebecca made herself known now, she would only be placing herself in danger.

"What is this disturbance? I'll have none of it do you hear!" said Cotton Mather as he drummed his gavel on the judges bench to restore silence.

"Captain O'Roarke, do you have any last words you wish to say to the court?"

"Only that I should have expected no better than this from the fine folk of Salem Town," replied Jamie as the constable released him from the chains that bound him to the chair. "All my life you have turned your hand against me and wished me ill. It must be such a comfort to you all to know that you have finally rid yourself of old Jamie. Beware, my good friends and neighbors, for one such as I will not go quietly. A curse upon this town I say, and a curse upon all those that have brought me down. Oh ye may raise yourselves to great heights, but beware of the spirit of Jamie O'Roarke. He will haunt your seas and your coves searching for his victims and bringing tears to the goodwives of Salem Town. It is upon the blood of my father and the soul of my mother that I make this promise and if I am to be doubly damned then so be it!"

With that Jamie allowed himself to be escorted from the room looking neither left nor right. No one noticed the small glow of greenish gold that seemed to hover about his shoulders.

"Be it known that yon prisoner shall suffer his punishment at the first light of dawn upon the morrow," said Cotton Mather strangely chastened by Jamie O'Roarke's words. Would a guilty man have had the courage to make such threats or entertain such anger? Only God himself knew.

PART FIVE

THE TREASURE

CHAPTER FORTY-SIX

Rebecca fought to free herself as Peter and Ian dragged her away from the Salem meetinghouse.

"I must see him, I must talk to him. He looked so alone, so friendless. He has to know that we are going to try and save him," she cried in a frenzy of grief.

"Hush now, lassie," said Arabella attempting to soothe the distraught girl. "The folks here about are in a mood for hanging and it would behoove us to make as little spectacle as possible if we are to help the bonny Captain."

"You must see that the less the Captain knows of our plans the better," said Ian drawing the sobbing girl to him as the small party took refuge in what looked like an abandoned lean-to. "Remember that the whole town is now against him and any who might care for poor Jamie."

"Well, I do care for him and I'm not ashamed to admit it," sobbed Rebecca. What was happening to her? Where was the little girl who carefully guarded her heart and calculated every move so as to not give away her feelings? Little by little that girl had been disappearing and in her place stood the new Rebecca, the real Rebecca, cleansed of all the old cynicism and twentieth century hardness. What had taken its place was something that Rebecca had buried beneath the surface on the day her mother had left. The vulnerability that O'Roarke had awakened within her now shone from her very being. But she was strong too, make no mistake about that! The day this lovely girl learned to use her strength would be a formidable one indeed. The brittle, bruised looking aura that she presented to her friends covered the heart of an avenging angel.

"I will see him, do you hear me, Ian MacRae, even if it does put me in danger. Jamie O'Roarke is my friend and he's all alone. I would no more abandon him than I would you or Peter. How could you even dream of not giving him some comfort to see him through this dark night? A man of such good heart should have been treasured and nurtured by the town, but what did they do? They murdered him for his gold. There he sits, betrayed by the man who was like a father to him and facing an eternity of sadness with not a friend in the world. If it costs my own life, then so be it. At least in some way I will be atoning for the wrong done to him by my family."

Rebecca, standing before them in the moonlight with the magical beams flashing through her raven hair, reminded Ian of some ancient warrior goddess preparing to do battle for hearth and home. How precious she was to him at this moment. If Ian MacRae was ever to claim this beautiful Diana then he must grant her desires. The young woman who looked at him now with eyes glowing like midnight sapphires would accept nothing but the finest that he had to offer. Not for Rebecca Love were excuses or blundering. She would ask of a man the finest he had to offer and reward him with a touch of paradise. So be it. Anything less than everything she asked for would result in her scorn and pity. O'Roarke held the lovely lass in the palm of his hand. Ian MacRae knew that he would have to show his mettle if he ever hoped to hold Rebecca in his adoring arms. She must be released of the pirate's spell. Her heart must be appeased and her soul comforted.

"Never you mind then, lass, I'll do what I can. But promise me that you will be careful," said Ian looking at the girl with a mixture of love and exasperation.

"Oh Ian, I knew you would help, I just knew it," said Rebecca with gratitude shining in her eyes.

CHAPTER FORTY-SEVEN

Jamie O'Roarke paced his cell like a caged panther. What a fool he had been to ever believe he could escape his fate. Damn his pride. The only thing it had gotten him was a repeat of the most tortuous moments of his life. In his fury he kicked over the small three legged stool that stood in the middle of the dank room.

"Watch it, laddie," said a merry voice from under the fallen stool. "I wouldn't be mistreating your only friend if I were you," said the sparkling tones that were coming from the gentle greenish gold light that now filled the room. As Jamie watched, Eva gradually materialized into the form of a life-size woman and sat upon the newly righted stool.

"I hope you don't mind it if I take the liberty of sitting down. All that flitting from place to place gets very tiresome after awhile," she said as she modestly arranged her gossamer skirts about her. The loveliness of her green cat's eyes and the spun gold of her hair brought a lightness that Jamie O'Roarke welcomed.

"Well here we are again, old girl," he said with a laugh as he sat at the lovely dyad's feet.

"Yes, my love, just Jamie and Eva traveling down eternity's vicious road once again," giggled the nymph as she playfully ruffled Jamie's silver gold curls. "You know, me lad, we haven't had such a bad time have we? Of course there have been long spells when everything was much too quiet for my taste, but on the whole you have been quite amusing, what with your lovely way with a sword and a cudgel. Why I'll never forget the time you splashed Shane MacRae into the Hebrides and we watched as he tried to make for the shoals with his pockets loaded down with gold. What a fool! If he had let those coins sink to the bottom of the sea he would have made it to safety to land with breath to spare."

"Ah lassie," laughed Jamie catching her wicked mood, "you forget he was a Scotsman. Better to sink to the bottom of the sea than to live without a doubloon."

" 'Tis a pity though about that lovely young lad, Eben Love. I don't see why you had to do away with him so quickly. There I was with a full evening of fun planned and no one to play with."

" 'Twas a mercy killing and you know it, lass. What you think of as fun would have had the poor laddie praying for death. I've watched you toy with more than enough unfortunate fellows to know that."

"But I've never toyed with the great Jamie O'Roarke and that's a fact," chuckled Eva as her mind ran gleefully over the adventures the two damned souls had shared together. "And don't be amakin' yourself out to be St. James of Salem either, Jamie O'Roarke. You're as guilty as me and you know it. Why you must have been daft to ever believe that these pompous bible thumping Puritans of this unbelievably boring little burgh would ever let such as you roam amongst their fair wives and daughters as free as the wind. They're afraid of you, Jamie. What lady would ever look at her fat rich husband the same after a night of swooning in the arms of Captain O'Roarke? You've caused a bit of mischief of your own and don't deny it."

" 'Tis true, 'tis true," said Jamie with an amorous smile, "there will be more than one beauty hiding her tears behind a veil tomorrow. Why I ever thought I could live cheek by jowl with these landlubbers is beyond me, Eva darlin'."

" 'Tis because you fell for a pretty face, you fool," said Eva tickling him under the chin. "Next time I'll be sure to remind you of your folly, Jamie me boy, before you get in over your head."

"I'm sure you will, lass," said Jamie looking up at Eva fondly. "I've often wondered what it would have been like if we had met in human form, my dear. Do you think we would have stood a chance?"

"Us! I don't think so," said Eva looking at Jamie sadly. "We would have probably ended by killing each other out of passion or in a jealous rage. No, Jamie, we were never meant to share the same heart."

"Or the same tree," sighed Jamie putting his head in her lap.

"Oh I don't know. I can't imagine anyone who I would have rather spent the last three hundred years with, sweetheart," said Eva smoothing his brow. " 'Twas not as joyous as freedom, but we had our moments, and we will again. Think upon that tomorrow and not on the hangman's noose. I'll be waiting for you, laddie, to take your hand and guide you just as I always have."

"But Eva," said Jamie getting to his feet and standing before her with his hands upon his hips. "You can't know what it's like to be a mortal. The sweetness of it fair takes my breath away. I'd almost forgotten the touch of a hand and the feel of the wind in my hair. The first time was bad enough when I didn't know what I would be giving up. This time the cruelty of it will be beyond words. Your dear companionship is but a shadow when compared with the bliss of even the simplest human moment. Oh, to feel the deck of the 'Red Witch' beneath my feet as my fine crew sets sail for the West Indies. There is nothing to match the sight of her sails unfurling in a fair wind with their black crosses striking fear into any that should cross our path."

"Well, I like that," said Eva standing nose to chest with the tall Captain. "Here I am offering you more comfort than I can stomach and what do you do with it. Put me second to an old rotting boat and a crew of smelly knaves. It's a wonder to me, Jamie O'Roarke, that you ever managed to seduce so much as a frog without my tutoring."

"Now, me girl, don't get in such a huff," said Jamie as he sat down on the stool and drew her onto his lap. "Ye are the fairest lady that ever graced the underworld and that's the truth. Forgive old Jamie his temper. The events of the past few days have gotten me more than a bit confused. We are indeed cut from the same cloth, you and I. The gratitude I hold for you in coming to me in my hour of need is boundless. By this time tomorrow we shall once again be locked in each other's embrace, like it or not, so let's make the best of it."

"Right you are, laddie," said Eva with a twinkle in her eye. "And this time, can I have just a little more playtime with young Eben?"

"Off with you now, lass!" roared O'Roarke merrily as he aimed a light blow at the mischievous nymph's enticingly rounded bottom.

"I'll make it worth your while, I promise," said a voice lost in the twinkling golden beams that had taken the place of the succulent form before him.

"I'm sure you will, lass," said Jamie as the beams of light faded against the earthen walls.

CHAPTER FORTY-EIGHT

"I can't believe you talked me into this," said Ian as he and Rebecca made their way towards the small but sturdy building that housed the condemned Jamie O'Roarke. "What must I have been thinking of?"

"Oh, Ian," said Rebecca putting her small hand into his, "can't you see that I have no choice? If not for my ancestors Jamie wouldn't be where he is right now. Jamie must know that at least one member of the Love family believes in him. We have no guarantee that our plan will work. If Jamie is to go to the gallows tomorrow, he must know that my heart was with him. Against all odds he raised himself from the dust of a disgraceful beginning. Neither of us can possibly understand what that must have meant to a man of the seventeenth century. What Jamie did was impossible and to be cast back into disgrace and hanged is an unbelievable act of cruelty. It's as if the people of Salem were taking their revenge upon Jamie for the unpardonable act of rising above his station."

Ian was so moved by the girl's passionate speech that he stopped and faced her. Gently putting his hand under her chin the tall Scotsman tilted the dear face towards him. Ian looked down into her sparkling blue eyes. He knew that at some point soon it would come down to either him or O'Roarke for Rebecca, but to ask her to choose now would only lose him any chance of his ever possessing her. The thought of returning to the darkness of an existence without Rebecca was impossible.

"My dearest, there will be a time when this storm has passed. All I ask is that you guard yourself so that we may see it together. Pray God that everything we planned goes well, but if we fail, you must be prepared to go on. The world here is cold and real and this storm we are walking through cares not who it destroys in its wake. Beware of the feelings you have now for they may change when we return to our time."

"I don't care if we ever go home," said Rebecca looking at Ian with fury. "How can you speak of such things now with poor Jamie alone and friendless. Wherever we are we at least have hope and the comfort of each other. He has nothing, no parents or children, not even the comfort of some sort of religion. These people have stripped him of everything but his pride. If I could return to that time when I lived in ignorance of the true Jamie O'Roarke, then perhaps I could find some peace. Don't you see that now that is impossible? It was better when I didn't know his laughter or his tears. Now I know all and I must bring him comfort whatever the cost."

Ian put his arms around Rebecca. He could feel the heat that suddenly filled the air around her. Surprised, Ian backed off a step. Whatever was emanating from Rebecca was setting off some sort of electrical charge. It was as if her passion was taking actual form and swirling about him. Perhaps, thought Ian MacRae, who had grown up believing in the tales of Scottish witches, there was more power in this Salem girl than even she realized. No matter what happened to O'Roarke, Ian realized that he must get Rebecca away from Salem as quickly as possible. If any others chanced to experience what he just had, the lovely girl would be destroyed in this place where brimstone fell from the sky. The pain of O'Roarke's damnation and his sad existence had been ordained long ago through no fault of theirs. No matter what the girl might believe, they were not responsible. Ian made a silent vow that if it came down to Jamie or himself, Ian would fight with everything he had to save Rebecca's soul. It was a fight he mustn't lose.

"Whist now, girl, don't you worry. We'll bring comfort to your Jamie I promise. Don't lose heart."

"I'm sorry," said Rebecca realizing how ill she had been treating the compassionate Scotsman. "It's just that I'm tired and feeling a bit dizzy. I don't know what's come over me, but I feel faint."

"Sit ye down," said Ian pressing the girl to the soft grass. "What do you mean faint? There are strange illnesses here about that neither you nor I have ever had, such as smallpox and the like. Are you really feeling ill?"

"Not ill exactly, just dizzy and a bit sick to my stomach. Perhaps it was the bit of cheese we had earlier. Don't worry, I'm sure the fresh air will soon revive me," said Rebecca getting to her feet, touched by Ian's sweet concern. "There's nothing wrong with me that seeing Jamie and reassuring him about our plans won't make better."

"All right then, my stubborn barin," said Ian fondly taking the girl's arm, "let's make haste. The rising of the moon must see us awaiting O'Roarke's henchmen in the cove."

———

"Halt, who goes there?" said the fully armored yeoman as he spied two strangers approaching the prison door. Reverend Brown had left strict orders to be doubly vigilant this night. The simple yeoman, Jeremiah Jacobs, did not relish his dangerous duty and would be profoundly grateful when this night was over.

"Why, kind sir," said Rebecca coming up to the man and giving him a smile of heartbreaking sweetness, " 'tis but two pilgrims in need of your help."

"My help, Mistress? Why whatever can such as I do for you?" said Jeremiah finding the lovely girl's closeness a rare distraction.

Rebecca put the small handkerchief that Melinda had given her to her eyes and looked at the man with distress.

"My poor brother lies within, alone and condemned before the world without the comfort of those he loves about him. I beg you, kind sir, to grant me a moment with him so that he may know that his family believes him of kind intent and shall pray for his soul."

"Ah Mistress, I would if I could," said Jacobs firmly, "but it would cost me the skin off my back. The Reverend Brown has threatened me with a public scourging if anything goes amiss with yon prisoner. Besides, O'Roarke himself said that he wished to see no one."

"But how can that be? Surely there must be some mistake! He wouldn't turn me away," said Rebecca looking to Ian for help.

"Oh, but Mistress, I do believe he must have meant you especially when he spoke," said yeoman Jacobs as he studied Rebecca. "The Captain stated that he wished to keep solitary vigil this night and wished to be disturbed by none. His very words were, 'let none be brought into my presence, especially any young lady with eyes like midnight and hair like a raven.' So you see, even if I could, 'twould go ill against me if I ignored the last wishes of a condemned man."

"I thank you, sir," said a crestfallen Rebecca as she backed away from the guard. Why had Jamie turned her away? Did he no longer care for her? Had she just been the diversion of the moment, or was he afraid for her safety as Ian was? If only she knew.

"Come then, Goodwife," said Ian turning Rebecca quickly from the curious stare of the yeoman. " 'Tis overtime for supper and I am hungry."

As they hurried away from the prison, yeoman Jacobs eyes followed the two suspiciously. Strangers hereabouts were a rarity. Especially those claiming kinship to Captain Jamie O'Roarke. He carefully made note of their forms and features.

CHAPTER FORTY-NINE

"Why wouldn't he want to see me?" asked Rebecca as Arabella attempted to calm the distraught girl.

"Perhaps he didn't want you to view him in the prison gloom, darling," said Arabella attempting to put the best face on things. "Remember the Captain is a proud man. For you to see him humbled may be more than he can bear."

"But I need to see him! What if I never get a chance to see him again?"

"Whist now, dearie," said Arabella holding the girl at arms length. "There is no need for such talk. My nephew and you shall succeed and Jamie O'Roarke will be freed. I feel it in my heart. Hurry along now the both of you. There is nothing like a bit of action to clear the head."

"Yes, Rebecca, it is time to go," said Peter as he handed Ian the lantern and the last of his matches. "You will need this to find your way back through the woods to the cove. And take this too," said Peter as he drew an ancient pistol from beneath his coat.

"Where did you get that?" said Ian in surprise.

"Why, I always carry it with me when I roam the graveyards of Salem. It belonged to Giles Cory," said Peter with a wistful look on his face. "Many years ago I had a dream that one day I would be transported back to a place where this gun would come in handy. I remember waking to a voice softly whispering in my ear to get up and place it in my coat pocket. The dream must have been over ten years ago, but I can still remember the haunting feeling it left me with. The voice was a man's, deep and lilting. It was not until last night that I heard it again."

"Well, I'm certainly glad you listened to it," said Arabella stroking Peter's sleeve. Off with you now, Ian lad. Don't forget that your life as well as O'Roarke's depends on your success. If the Captain lives then we will be free of the banshee forever."

"The banshee?" said Rebecca looking at Arabella in puzzlement.

" 'Tis the legendary harbinger of doom to all Scotsmen, Rebecca," said Arabella in a respectful whisper. "The night they brought the news of Mary and Walter MacRae's death the cry of the banshee could be heard echoing through the highlands. 'Twas but a few days later that the babe Ian arrived. My Alan swore then that if he could save the wee one from the curse he would. Unfortunately, he died before he could make the journey to Salem. It is up to you now, Ian lad, to realize your Uncle's dream of freeing the family from doom. Good luck to you and may the spirits of the MacRae clan guide your steps."

Arabella stood on tiptoe and gently kissed her nephew's rough cheek. He would never know how proud she was of him at this moment.

"Well then, times awastin'," said Ian gruffly trying to hide the storm of emotion that suddenly welled up within him. "Are you ready, Rebecca?"

"As ready as I'll ever be," said Rebecca drawing herself up to her full height and taking the lantern from Ian. "Let me take this so your hands are free. We don't know what may be out there."

CHAPTER FIFTY

"May the Goddess protect them," said Arabella as she and Peter watched the flicker of the lantern light slowly fade into the darkness.

"I believe they may already be protected by something they don't realize," said Peter leaning down and putting his hands on the earth where Rebecca had been standing. "Did you feel it?"

"Yes," said Arabella quietly.

"It was really quite something, wasn't it?"

"Almost more than I could stand," said Arabella lifting her face to the sky. "I wonder what awakened it within her. 'Tis young for the girl to achieve such power. And to think she knows nothing of it."

"I'd often had my suspicions about Rebecca but I'd never been sure until now," said Peter smiling at the tiny Scotswoman. "Most of the tourists who come to Salem think that the witchcraft hysteria had no basis in fact, but we who follow the old religion know differently don't we?"

"Indeed we do. I've been a crone these many years and it never ceases to amaze me how easy it is to practice our ways right under people's very noses. How Alan and I used to laugh at the blindness around us."

"You miss him a great deal, don't you?" said Peter with a look of sympathy.

"More than I can say," said Arabella with a sigh. "If only he had consented to the 'Great Rite.' He used to laugh and say that his deathing was preordained. He would look at me with his glowing green eyes and tell me that I was to seek out another sage once he was gone. He said that I was to be joined with one who was a great shaman."

"He sounds like a good and wise man. And one who truly loved you," said Peter.

"Aye, that he did. That is why Ian must succeed. This journey was not only for my nephew's sake. It was Alan's last wish that the MacRaes be freed from O'Roarke's curse once and for all. I promised Alan that I would do everything in my power to grant his desire. 'Twas he who felt that only in Salem could the mystery be solved. Tell me, Peter, do you think we were wise to send the children into the night?"

"Who can say if we were right or wrong? I only know that we had no choice. If Rebecca remains here much longer, others will begin to sense her power. And then what would happen? There are forces here that are beyond even me."

"I thank the Goddess that Ian is as of yet unaware of his, but it is only a matter of time. Did you see the way he touched Rebecca's hand when she took the lantern from him? He feels something. The longer he is in this place and under her spell the thinner the veil becomes. I have protected him with everything I have, but once his god is awakened it must be heeded."

"Arabella, my dear," said Peter gently taking her arm, "could you ever find it in your heart to love again?"

"Peter, once you have loved and are awakened to the bliss of sharing your heart with someone's soul, there is no stopping it. My heart longs for another, even though I know I shall never be able to replace what Alan and I had together. That was his gift to me, don't you see? Wherever he is now I am sure that his spirit is not lonely. Alan used to say that love must never be denied."

"Then what would you say to the joining of our spirits?" asked Peter.

"Why what a pretty picture the two of you make," laughed a bell like voice behind Peter and Arabella.

"Eva, my dear, however did you manage to free yourself?" said Peter alarmed by the vision that met his eyes. The calm face he presented to the nymph belied the tumult within him.

"Well, old man, it seems that the forces here about favor such as I. There I was all cramped in that nasty staff of yours wishing I was free, when suddenly whoosh, I found myself floating above your head. I hope you'll forgive me for not telling you sooner, but I've been visiting an old friend."

"Very amusing, my girl, but now I'll thank you to resume your proper place. It won't do at all for us to have you roaming about. Remember what happened to you the last time? It's for your own good, Madame Bubble."

"Don't call me that," said Eva stamping her foot in fury. "Ever since that fool John Bunyan wrote about me in 'The Pilgrims Progress' people have been making fun of me and calling me by that ridiculous name. What utter rot!"

Peter, pleased at throwing the devious Eva off balance continued. "Wasn't it that same author who wrote:

> " 'Twas she that set Absolom against his father, and Jereboam against his master. 'Twas she that persuaded Judas to sell his lord; none can tell of the mischief that she doth. She makes variance betwixt rulers and subjects, betwixt parents and children, 'twixt neighbor and neighbor, 'twixt a man and his wife, 'twixt a man and himself, 'twixt the flesh and the heart."

"And he also had that fool character of his, 'Great heart,' call me a witch. Little did he know. The man had no knowledge of his subject."

"Right you are, darling," said Arabella keeping her distance. "We all know you are a dyad, a being far superior to a humble witch."

"Thank you, Mistress," said Eva looking at Arabella with new respect. "I can see you are a lady of breeding."

"Come now, Eva," said Peter attempting to take advantage of the mercurial nymph's sudden good mood, "get back into the livewood and I'll see what I can do about freeing your soul from its grasp."

"Not so fast, sorcerer," said Eva backing away from Peter. "First I want a promise from you."

"And what is that?" said Peter realizing that the flickers of gold around her feet meant that Eva was losing the power battle between them.

"I want O'Roarke. He belongs to me. You know that. We've been together a long time and it was quite unfair of you to take him away from me. If you give me back O'Roarke, I'll be a good girl and rest within your staff. What's more I'll make sure that you all return home safely."

"And what about the curse, dear?" said Arabella sensing that together she and Peter had more than enough magic to imprison Eva within the staff.

"What of it! Let the MacRaes and Loves fend for themselves. Neither of you belong to either house by blood. Why should you be concerned about it?"

"Never mind why, Eva, just accept that which you can't understand. Now I command you to return to the livewood!" Arabella and Peter forcefully raised their hands to the moon as Eva attempted to back away from them. She realized too late that she had misjudged their combined power. In a flash of lightning she disappeared and Peter's staff glowed with her fury.

"Now, my little friend, let's discuss our plans," said Peter. "Once Ian and Rebecca have restored O'Roarke's honor and you have returned us to our Salem, I will be more than happy to discuss your freedom. Who knows, we might even become friends."

"Watch your step, old man, a dyad never forgets," whispered the angry nymph.

CHAPTER FIFTY-ONE

The eerie light of the moon shone down upon the vast thickness that was Salem woods. As Ian hacked his way through the underbrush, Rebecca couldn't help but be terrified by the sharp black branches that seemed to be reaching out for her.

"I'm frightened, Ian," she said in a little girl's voice.

"Now lassie, there's no reason to be afraid," said Ian turning to comfort the girl. " 'Tis the same woods that you ran through but a few hours ago."

"But it all looks so different now. Melinda was telling me that they have even been threatened by unfriendly Indians around here. This is not the Salem I know. This is a dark and dangerous place."

"Are you forgettin' that the Laird Ian MacRae is here beside you ready to fight to the death to protect you? Whist now, lass, if we give into fear than all is lost. Where's that courage that I've seen flashing in those lovely blue eyes?" With those words Ian gave Rebecca a smile that would have heartened an army of adventurers.

"Right you are," she said ashamed of her timidity. "It's just that the night is so dark here. I'm not used to such utter blackness."

" 'Tis true indeed," said Ian as they continued making their way stealthily through the thick wood. "Not even in the highlands have I seen such a sight. We have no idea how light fills our world do we? These people must live by the rising and setting of the sun. What misery the cold winters must be for them with only a candle's flicker to cheer their souls."

"Yes," said Rebecca looking about her. "Imagine living in such gloom. It's no wonder that the people in Salem became quarrelsome and superstitious. You can almost feel their fear."

"I think there is more to it than mere superstition," said Ian looking at Rebecca warily. "Haven't you sensed something here that lies beyond human understanding? I know I have."

"I thought you would think I was silly if I said something," said Rebecca. "But now that you've brought it up, yes, there is something in Salem Town that is beyond the norm. Look at Peter's heritage and how he calls the powers of the supernatural to him. Where else but here would such talents flourish? And what of Jamie O'Roarke?"

"Not to mention his little friend the nymph," said Ian with a shudder. "There must have been quite a trade in rabbit's feet and good luck charms to ward off such spirits. It makes you wonder what has happened to them in our modern world. Have they disappeared behind a veil or do they still exist? Perhaps such wonders as were commonplace in old Salem still exist."

"But would the modern Salemite recognize such things?" said Rebecca pondering what Ian had said. More than once Rebecca had felt the glimmer of something not of this world in Salem but she had dismissed it as foolishness. And what of Peter? It was not until she had found herself magically transported back to Salem that Rebecca had truly believed in his powers. If such things had escaped her, then they were indeed well hidden.

"You know," she said as they entered the clearing where O'Roarke's bower was, "the aura surrounding the town did not end with the witch trials. In 1702 there was a terrible story about one of the sons of the most prominent family in

Salem. It seems that the young man had left Salem Town to go to sea and had been murdered and eaten by his mates."

"That just sounds unbelievable to me," said Ian shaking his head.

"Many denied the rumor," said Rebecca nodding in agreement, "but it has always seemed to have the ring of truth to me. And then there was the story about a rainstorm of brimstone releasing itself over Salem in 1700."

"Brimstone!" said Ian with widening eyes.

"Yes, brimstone," said Rebecca.

"The town does seem to attract more than its share of odd happenings doesn't it?" said Ian taking a late autumn apple from a nearby tree.

"Oh look," said Rebecca as the moonlight shone through the branches of the gnarled old tree. "Here is the apple peel I threw over my shoulder this afternoon. It seems like that was a thousand years ago."

As she looked at it Rebecca remembered the folklore that had inspired her action. Jamie had said that the shape the peel fell in would reveal her true love. And now here was the answer to her hearts desire. Rebecca gazed at the apple peel and felt a desperate energy infuse her soul. What good would such things do her now if Jamie died? In a burst of anger Rebecca kicked the innocent peel and glared at Ian.

"Come on now, let's hurry. We may yet save Jamie if luck is with us!"

"Coming, my dearest," said Ian with an exasperated sigh as he watched the erstwhile kitten show her lions claws. "Wait for me!"

The "Red Witch," anchored off Collins Cove, was a magnificent sight in the moonlight. Rebecca gave a gasp as Ian roughly grasped her arm and dragged her towards a small cave.

"Careful now, girl," he said as soon as he was sure they were hidden from sight, "You wouldn't want any of O'Roarke's mates spying your pretty face. It would be all up for us if they did."

"Oh my goodness, how could I have been so careless," said Rebecca, her annoyance turning to gratitude as she rubbed her arm.

" 'Tis only natural to want to see the sight. Such a ship as the 'Red Witch' makes a man envy Jamie O'Roarke. There isn't one amongst us that wouldn't give ten years off his life to be captain of such a ship." The look on Ian's face as he and Rebecca gazed at the "Red Witch" from the protection of the cave, was one of a man having a magnificent dream. "Just imagine what it would be like to stand on the deck of such a vessel shouting out orders as the crew unfurls the sails. What a feeling it must be! Why, it would be worth an early death."

"Oh look!" exclaimed Rebecca as a shooting star streaked across the velvet sky. Rebecca gave an involuntary shudder as it disappeared from sight. "A spirit passes but a star is born," she whispered ominously.

"What foolishness is that, my darling?" said Ian putting his arm around Rebecca.

"It's what my mother always said about a shooting star. Every star that falls foretells someone's death."

"That's just a superstition," said Ian.

"No more superstition than a banshee foretelling a Scotsman's death," said Rebecca quietly. "At least we've heard none of those so far."

"Well," laughed Ian trying to lighten the mood, "the night is young. Who knows what we may see or hear before the light of dawn."

"Don't even jest about such things," said Rebecca sitting down on a large moss covered rock. "My mother may have had her faults but she was always right about such things. She used to tell me that someday I would know more about this world and the next than most. I never understood what she meant until I found myself here. Lately I've had the feeling that the practical world I believe in merely masks the true realities about us. It's what we can't see or touch or smell that really exists. Look at Jamie. He is a ghost, but in many ways he is more real than any man I have ever known."

"In what way, Rebecca?" said Ian, determined to hear what he must. Better to know the truth that lay within her heart than to agonize over his uncertainty.

"Why his love for life, for one thing," said Rebecca with shining eyes. "Jamie grasps life and makes it dance to his tune. He feels everything down to the center of his being. He can't understand the dullards who only see life as survival. To Jamie life is pure joy. Without it there is no life for him."

"And has he found his joy in his one true love?" said Ian unable to keep back his words.

"I don't know, Ian," said Rebecca looking into his eyes, hers glowing with honesty. "I don't even know if there is just one love for a man like Jamie O'Roarke. You see, his greatest love is his freedom. If not for his kind heart he might have been miles away from here already turning the 'Red Witch' to the open sea. Without freedom he will go mad and die like Bothwell, who gave up his freedom for Mary Queen of Scots. It would be worst than death for Jamie to be locked away in some dark hole."

"And what of his heart? You can't tell me that the proud Jamie hasn't presented his heart to you," said Ian.

"He has, my dearest," said Rebecca with a sad nod of her head, "but that doesn't mean I have taken it. Jamie O'Roarke's first love will never be a woman and I come in second for no man."

"Poor Rebecca," said Ian smiling at her. "What confusion this must all be for you."

"I'm not confused, Ian," said Rebecca gently taking his hand in hers. "Far from it, my darling. I might have been carried away by the moment today, but I see now that perhaps it was for the best. You see, Jamie O'Roarke is like a fever that enters a girl's heart. When that happens there is nothing to be done but to let the fever run its course and burn out. Strange though this may sound, the fever that consumed my soul just a few hours ago has freed my heart. I now see my way clearly."

"And am I included in your crystal vision?" said Ian moving breathlessly close to the beautiful girl.

"You are the vision, my darling," said Rebecca with a sirens smile on her lips as the two lovers embraced.

CHAPTER FIFTY-TWO

Rebecca and Ian could make out a the sound of a sailor's hornpipe as they lay side by side in the moss covered cave. It seemed as if all the songs of the sea were embodied in the haunting tune that echoed from the "Red Witch."

"How beautiful it is," sighed Rebecca as she lay back in Ian's strong arms. "I will never forget this magical night."

"And it's not over yet," said Ian gently placing Rebecca's head upon her arm and moving to the mouth of the cave. "If I'm not mistaken, I see a lantern light coming towards us."

"Whoever could it be?" said Rebecca quietly joining Ian.

The bobbing light moved tantalizingly from side to side as two dark figures approached. Rebecca let out a small gasp as she recognized the Reverend Samuel Brown and the worthy Deacon Williams. Ian motioned her to retreat a few steps so that their forms were enveloped by the darkness of the cave.

"Here now, sir," said Deacon Williams as the two men stopped directly in front of the small cave, "shouldn't they have been here by now?"

"Quiet, fool, not so loud," hissed Samuel Brown kicking the sand with his toe. "According to the mate Quinlan, those two pirates should have been here and gone unless we've been tricked!"

"Right you are, sir, I bet it was a trick," said the chastened Williams anxious to retreat from the deserted beach as soon as possible. There was no telling what was lurking hereabouts. If the pirates weren't enough for one man, than the thought of some savage scalping him for pleasure was.

"You idiot! I don't know why I ever listened to you."

" 'Twasn't me, governor, and you know it," said the Deacon having had enough of the damp night. "I'm heading back to me own bed and I advise you do the same."

"Well if you must, be sure you keep your wits about you and your lips sealed," said Brown with a threatening glower directed at his Deacon.

"You can count on me, sir," said Williams as he beat a hasty retreat, disappearing into the woods with lightening speed.

"God cursed fool," muttered Brown as he watched Williams' disappearing form. "I should have known better than to trust him." Overhead a great white owl circled boldly, curiously eyeing the parson with hunger. As it swooped towards him, Samuel Brown decided that, indeed, he was on a fools mission and quickly followed his hapless assistant back through the woods.

"What was that all about?" asked Rebecca gasping for air. In her fright she had forgotten to breath.

"I think that the Love brothers are not the only ones who know of O'Roarke's treasure," said Ian with a frown.

"Who is Quinlan?"

"Whoever he is," said Ian, "I'll bet you odds that he is now laying at the bottom of the sea courtesy of the Love brothers."

"Oh," said Rebecca, her hands flying to her mouth to stifle an involuntary scream. "But now what? Do you think they will still bury the treasure?"

"I think they will, darling, they have no choice. The treasure will be seized if it remains on the 'Red Witch' much longer. They have no alternative but to bury it. No cove but this one is safe enough. They will appear, I'm certain. I'm sure they were waiting to see if the Reverend would show his face. Now that he has and has given up the watch, all is clear for the pirates."

"I hope you're right!" said Rebecca feeling a return of the queasiness that had assailed her earlier. As she groped her way back to the warmth of the cave, Ian followed her with concern.

"Are you sure you're all right?"

"Just let me lay down a moment and I'll be just fine," said Rebecca attempting to make the cave walls stop spinning.

"Tell me," she said, "what did you think when you came upon Jamie and me in the rose bower?"

"I don't know what I thought," said Ian cautiously. Their love was still such a new and fragile thing.

"Surely you must have some questions?" pressed Rebecca delicately. If she and Ian were ever to have an honest and deeply fulfilling love she must tell him all.

"Well," said Ian quietly, "as I came upon you my first thought was thank goodness you were still alive and had not been murdered by the foul pirate who had kidnapped you. But when I saw you entwined in his arms, I almost went mad. What chance would an innocent girl like you have against the wiles of an experienced seducer like O'Roarke? I know that it was not your fault."

"It was no one's fault, Ian," said Rebecca knowing that the next few minutes might result in her losing him forever, but realizing that she must continue. "It's not what you think at all. Jamie didn't seduce me. In fact he did his best not to. What happened in the bower was something that we both wanted. At the time I thought I'd never see you or my home again and the solace of his embrace gave me both hope and courage."

"I would say that's a mighty strange way to gather your strength," said Ian moodily as he paced back and forth in the small cave.

"Oh, Ian darling, you simply must understand!"

"The only thing I understand is that within the space of twelve hours you have declared and given your love to two men, and expect us both to believe in your loyalty. What am I supposed to think? My darling Rebecca, I know you are a modern girl, but I am an old fashioned man. I love you with all my heart, that I can't deny, but don't ask me not to feel something when I imagine you in that pirate's arms swooning with love."

"Would it be any comfort to you if I told you that I love you and you only?" said Rebecca rising dizzily.

"Of course it would, my love," said Ian taking her in his arms," but don't ever let me catch you alone in any bower with Jamie O'Roarke again."

"I swear on my honor that from now on I will swoon only in your arms," laughed Rebecca as she held onto Ian for dear life. The light around her was becoming dim. Rebecca sank to the ground oblivious to all but the swirl of color that glowed behind her eyelids.

Terrified, Ian laid her on the moss covered ground that had so recently been the scene of their mutual ecstasy. He smoothed her brow gently.

"Dear God in heaven," he prayed, "don't take her from me now. If you must have someone take me instead."

"Well spoken, my lad," said Rebecca, her lips smiling sweetly as her eyelids fluttered open. "I don't think either of us are going anywhere, but I'm beginning to think that we may have more than mere memories to remind us of olden Salem Town."

"Hush now, don't speak," said Ian cradling the girl and looking into the deep blue eyes that shone as clear as rainwater. "Whatever has happened or will happen has nothing to do with our love. I'm sorry I was so upset. I vow that from now on I will trust you no matter what."

"As I trust you, my love," said Rebecca touching his cheek.

"It's almost as if there was something in the air bewitching anyone who breathes it," said Ian keeping a careful watch on the beach. "The moment we landed here we have been surrounded by a heightened sense of awareness. Life and death lay side by side here. Even the townsfolk know it. There is a strange acceptance of the unusual around here as if they have lived with it all their lives and know of nothing else."

"Are the occurrences here so unusual, Ian?" asked Rebecca reflectively. "All my life I have heard talk of witchcraft and the occult mixed in with tales of the seafaring folk from around Salem. My neighbor, Mrs. Maloon, even has an old penny shop that was built on the side of her house by the wife of a Salem ship's captain. The woman would sell useful odds and ends to make a shilling or two while her husband was at sea. The wives of Salem never knew if their husbands would return to them or be drowned at sea. Even after the hysteria of the witchcraft trials died down it remained an unusual community. People from Salem Town have always been a bit different, I would say. I've heard tell of more than one woman awakened by the ghostly specter of her drowned husband many months before actual news of his death would reach port. It's no wonder they believe in otherworldly events. They have lived with them for centuries."

"And what of you, my little Salem witch, what do you believe?" asked Ian treading carefully.

"I used to believe only in what could be proven by a camera or a book, but ever since I arrived here I have experienced the strangest sensations. It's as if something buried deep within me has been awakened. There have been moments when I have felt my mother guiding my hand and heart. I have heard her voice in my dreams and felt her touch on my soul."

"And what does she say, my love?" said Ian looking into Rebecca's bewitching eyes.

"That mine is not an easy destiny but it is a great one. I must be strong and let no one come between me and my power."

"What power?"

"I don't know," she said quietly. "There are times when I feel an odd trembling within me and the air seems to rush by, warmed by some celestial force. I thought it was my imagination, but now I'm not so sure. When I am at peace it lies dormant, but...."

"When you get angry or upset it leaps from you and electrifies the air with energy," finished Ian.

"Why yes, how did you know?"

"Because I have felt it," he said. "It is the same thing I remember coming from my mother as she held me as a babe. No matter how tired or unhappy I was, one moment in her arms would be enough to calm and energize me. I always thought it was merely her loving touch, but now I know that it must be some sort of magnetic link between astral souls. The Goddess of Ireland, Scotland and Wales is not to be denied. It seems she has even traveled to this strange new world and found a home in Salem Town. The old religion, as Peter calls it, claims its priestesses for eternity. My Aunt has often spoken of how a priestess never dies, she just takes on a new form in another life."

"And what of the shamans? Do they come back too?" said Rebecca with newfound understanding in her eyes.

"I'm sure they do," said Ian thinking of Peter's heritage and power.

"Do you think that priestesses and shamans are drawn to each other?" said Rebecca.

"I don't know," said Ian, "but it would certainly explain love at first sight. I always thought that was impossible until I met you."

"And now you believe in it?"

"With all my heart, my love, now, and for eternity," said Ian with wonder.

CHAPTER FIFTY-THREE

The great white owl that stood guard at the entrance of the lovers cave gave a mournful hoot as he viewed the two intruders that had taken over his lair. As he gave another cry, the man came to the entrance and looked out. The man then settled himself near the entrance away from the sleeping girl, and took a piece of paper and a charcoal pencil from his coat pocket. He soon became entranced with the sketch he was making of the "Red Witch." Old Nicodemus the owl realized that at least for the moment the intruders were not about to abandon his home. He gave one last annoyed hoot and flew away.

Inside the cave the sleeping girl dreamt peacefully. The visions that came to her were ones of comforting wonder. She found herself wandering through a lush rain forest. The sunlight that filtered through the trees seemed to be beckoning Rebecca towards some sort of abandoned ruin. She was robed in a diaphanous gown made out of what seemed to be cobwebs. The colors of gold and silver that shot through the fabric were echoed in the threads of the delicate sandals that encased her feet. She was gliding over the forest floor, her feet never touching the ground. The perfumed air around her was both intoxicating and invigorating. It filled her with an unearthly energy that infused her entire being.

In her dream Rebecca was freed of any of the concerns that normally troubled her. Gone was the need for food or water.

In its place was a divine peace that shone like the sun from her face. As Rebecca approached the foot of the ancient pyramid, she felt a myriad of eyes watching her. The warmth of the love generated from these glances filled her with courage. Rebecca placed her foot on the first step and felt herself being lifted towards the top of the great structure.

Looking down, she saw that the ground below her was very far away, half hidden in misty silver clouds. Rebecca placed her arms protectively around her to shield that which grew within her from harm.

Rebecca alighted from the topmost step and moved towards the presence that held out its arms to embrace her. Around the beautiful presence's neck was a cross made of gold and garnet, the twin to the one that lay buried beneath the old tree.

"Come, my Daughter, we have been waiting for you," said the voice that filled Rebecca with love.

"Yes, Mother, I have journeyed far and am glad to be home at last."

"You must understand," said the spirit that had taken on the form of Magdelene Love, "that you cannot stay. You are only here to receive our blessings and protection for your babes. Your journey is not yet finished. We must all serve our moments on earth between the fallow times. Yours is a sacred trust as was mine when I carried you. If not for the evil being that swept me away before my time I would have stood beside you to protect those who will follow," she said with a nod towards Rebecca's womb. "Now we must seek another way to protect them so that they may grow to the fullness of manhood."

"But Mother, they will have me to protect them," said Rebecca fearing that any touch of the spirit world might harm her precious trust.

"Your journey will be filled with peril and these are not ordinary babes. They are born of a shaman and a damned spirit. They will have much laid before them. One is of the sun and the other the moon. They will be the dark and the light that will fill the world. Many will seek to destroy the dark one, but without him the child of light will perish."

With these ominous words, Magdelene drew a veil over Rebecca. When she opened her eyes Rebecca saw an alter with the shades of Jamie O'Roarke and Ian MacRae standing on either side. Gone were their everyday garb and in its place were the sacred vestments of the two great kings of the Goddess. Jamie attired in the dark reflection of the Holly King stood on the left, while Ian standing to the right of the alter, was resplendent as the Oak King. He held the gifts of summer's bounty in his hands.

Rebecca approached the alter with the dignity of a priestess carrying not one but two sacred vessels. The power that was hers came not from evil but from the great goodness of the Goddess and her sister spirits. Before her stood the two that protected the female spirits in the time of their fertility and birthing. These were the gods from whom all life found fulfillment. They were the Goddess's greatest glory. The symbol of man at his finest.

The gods moved forward and gently picked up the girl. They placed her on the altar with reverence. A mist came over Rebecca's mind as the room was filled with chanting and music. Deep within her the babes stirred restlessly and filled with the life of the spirits around them. Gone was any terror that Rebecca may have had and in its place was the great peacefulness granted by the gods and goddesses about her. She wordlessly told those about her of her total acceptance of her great mission. It would be countless years before Rebecca would see this place again, but the great Goddess had filled her with the strength she would need to return.

Rebecca heard the music about her change as she was carefully lifted from the alter. In the place of the gentle tones that had filled the room was the sound of pipes and drums in an almost warlike beat. Many arms reached for the girl and

Rebecca found herself swirling to the primitive music with an abandon she had known only once before. The heat of the music almost drove her into a mad frenzy of desire and she reached out for the two men on either side of her.

"Rebecca!" came an insistent unwelcome voice, "wake up. I see the reflection of two lanterns on the water. It must be the pirates."

With a cry of disappointment, Rebecca opened her eyes to the face of Ian MacRae. Where was the warmth and beauty that had seemed so real?

"Can you stand?" he said concerned. Rebecca's gaze seemed to be focused on some faraway place that Ian could not be a part of.

"Give me a moment," said the girl realizing that the world she had just been called back from was as real as anything she had ever known. "I just need a moment to find myself."

As she looked up at Ian she saw the reflection of the Oak King in his eyes.

CHAPTER FIFTY-FOUR

Rebecca and Ian could hear the sound of muffled oars as the small boat rapidly approached the cove. The tiny vessel was being tossed roughly from side to side as Jack Love attempted to head for the shore. Collins Cove was deceptive. It gave the appearance of a peaceful inlet, offering safe harbor to any in need. In reality it had many hidden shoals and breakers just waiting to scuttle a small ship.

"Hold it steady now, Jackie," yelled Ezra over the crash of the surf.

"That's what I'm trying to do," growled his younger brother with a scornful twist of his lips. Jack was sick and tired of Ezra always telling him what to do. It was high time the doddering old fool realized that Jack Love was a man fully grown and far more able than the simple minded Ezra.

"Heave ye to starboard," yelled Ezra helping Jack pull the line as they narrowly missed a large rock jutting out of the water. "There now," said the older brother settling back, "that should bring us safely to shore. 'Tis a treacherous spot for certain."

"Then why are we chancing the swords of the King's men and that meddling parson to bury the treasure here?" said Jack losing patience with the whole idea. If it had been up to him he would have gathered together a few of his cronies and taken over the "Red Witch." It would have been quite simple to slit the throats of the scurvies still loyal to O'Roarke and head for the open sea with the treasure. What a fool he had been to listen to Ezra.

"Because, Jackie," said Ezra in the tone of a father explaining something to a young child, "we wouldn't have made it as far as Boston. The 'Red Witch' is a marked ship. We would be boarded for sure. I have no wish to end my days swinging from a rope on Scarlett wharf."

In annoyed silence, Jack jumped from the boat as it ran aground on the beach. Ezra, looking about, nodded towards a stand of trees that hid an old cave from view.

"Best to stow our gear in there. No tellin' who may be wandering about tonight. I can smell restlessness in the air."

Rebecca and Ian, in a panic realized that Ezra and Jack Love were heading straight for them. Ian drew his pistol and motioned for Rebecca to take cover behind him. Rebecca shuddered as she watched the two pirates approach their hiding place. She silently prayed for a miracle.

"What in hell was that!" screamed Jack as he fell to the ground. The side of his face had been raked by a set of talons. Overhead, old Nicodemus was screeching at the intruders angrily and preparing to continue his battle.

"Take cover, Jackie," yelled Ezra over his shoulder as he attempted to outrun the enormous white owl. The burden in his arms almost strained the man to the breaking point as he struggled to reach the protection of the trees. Jack snatched up the lantern and shovel and followed Ezra's advice. Old Nicodemus saw that his prey was vanquished and silently flew to the entrance of the cave. The triumphant owl perched on his favorite overhang and continued to stare at the two pirates with an angry glare.

"I guess this will have to do," said Ezra as he and Jack quickly covered their gear with leaves.

"Let's just hurry up and get out of here," said Jack becoming more and more wary of the strange place that was Salem. Ever since they had approached Collins Cove things had gone wrong. Many's the tale he had heard of the great white owl that guarded the cove, but he had never believed a bit of it. And now here he was bearing the damned creature's mark upon his face.

"Patience now, Jackie me boy," said Ezra as he lit the lantern and scrutinized the shoreline with an experienced eye. "I'd say it would be a fine idea to give yon demon a moment to settle."

"Do you really think that was a demon?" said Jack touching his cheek and then drawing away his fingers as if they'd been burned.

"There's no telling, my lad, But better safe than sorry I always say."

"Right you are then, Ezra," said Jack looking at his brother. The man was old, but he knew his business, that was for sure.

"Where did they go?" whispered Rebecca cautiously.

"I'm not sure, but I think they are near us. I heard one of them say something about the trees," said Ian trying to relax his clenched muscles.

Rebecca, who was still reeling from her strange dream, sank to the ground and took a few deep breaths. How real that dream had seemed. So familiar and yet so foreign. It was clouded in the same mist that she and Jamie had shared on their journey back through time. The only difference was that when she had first felt the swirling power around her the complete Rebecca had woken up in a strange new time and place. This time her mind and soul had journeyed beyond the mist but had left her body behind. It was almost as if she could travel at will, leaving all earthly encumbrances behind her.

Old Nicodemus left his perch and flew past the entrance of the cave a few times. He then gracefully alighted on a branch growing inside. Rebecca held her breath as he looked first at her and then Ian. The bird opened and closed his great eyes three times, gave a gentle cooing sound, and settled himself down for a nap.

"How strange," said Ian whispering quietly so as to not disturb their feathered landlord. "I could have sworn he knew us."

"Perhaps he does," said Rebecca smiling at their protector.

CHAPTER FIFTY-FIVE

Jack and Ezra emerged from the woods and looked about. It seemed as if that devil of an owl had disappeared, but it paid to be careful.

"Come on now, Jackie," said Ezra straightening his creaking frame. "Let's get on with this. The sooner we are relieved of this burden the better," he said as he hoisted the heavy sea chest containing Duncan MacRae's finest treasure. The two pirates carefully made their way down the shore as Ian and Rebecca watched. The lantern, reflecting on the water, gave an unearthly glow to their faces.

"Come on now, lass," said Ian to Rebecca. If they didn't move quickly the Love brothers would soon disappear from sight.

"But won't they see us?" said Rebecca.

"Not if we stay low. Thank God there is a full moon to guide us." With that Ian motioned Rebecca to follow him and they cautiously kept their distance as Jack and Ezra led the way.

"Poor old Ezra," thought Rebecca as she watched the aged sailor struggle under his heavy burden while his robust younger brother held the lantern. What a bitter way to spend your golden years. Ezra deserved better than what Jack was handing him.

As she watched, the pirates stopped by a circular rock formation.

"This is the place. It's just like the Captain said it would be," said Ezra wearily placing the chest on the ground and wiping his brow with a brightly colored rag. "Give me a moment to catch me breath, Jackie. 'Tis a beauty of a night and that's for sure. Why look at those stars. A man could almost reach out his hand and touch them tonight." Ezra lifted his hands to the sky with a look of childish wonder on his face. "You see, Jack, there's the big dipper as bright as I've ever seen it and look how the north star is glowing just waiting to light our way home. I wonder if you can still see the stars when you pass on? What must it be like to be an angel up in paradise and livin' among them? It must be a fine thing indeed."

"That's one thing you'll never see," said Jack with a growl. "It's hell for the likes of you and me. Your soul is as black as mine."

"Ah now, Jackie, that's not true. I say me prayers and I've tried to do as right as I could under the circumstances. And when I haven't been quite up to snuff I've said I'm sorry, like I did with Jamie. He forgave me and I bet he would forgive you too if you could see your way clear to it. That along with prayin' to our mother for mercy should be enough to secure me a berth up yonder."

"You're a simpleton," said Jack getting to his feet and handing Ezra the lantern. "The only heaven or hell is the one right here. Now hold that damned light higher so that I can see what I'm doing."

Just as Jack had his shovel poised over the spot he had marked the autumn wind carried a strange chant-like sound that sent both men scurrying for cover.

"What was that, Ian?" said Rebecca from their flimsy hiding place made up of scrub bushes.

"I don't know, but it sounded like singing."

"Not singing, chanting," said Rebecca as she held her breath so that she could hear.

Coming slowly towards them was something that sounded like a toccata to the damned. The ominous tones first raising and then lowering in pitch reminded Rebecca of a dark angel's chorus. Rebecca saw Jack and Ezra take cover behind the largest of the old stones as the music floated towards them. A moment later a group of dark figures robed black as midnight approached the clearing. They stopped only a few feet from where Jack and Ezra hid.

The largest of the figures reverently took the hand of a smaller one and led her to the center of the circle of stones. As the moon shone down upon her face, the small woman in the velvet robe removed her cowl.

Rebecca gave a gasp as an incredible tumble of red hair released itself and surrounded the woman's face with its fiery glow. "It can't be," she said, her words muffled by the muted drums and chanting of the worshippers of Satan.

"Who is it?" asked Ian looking around for any safe path of escape. Things were quickly moving out of his control and the dark group that stood before them was obviously up to no good.

"I think it's the notorious witch, Catherine Deshayes, known as La Voisin. Louis XIV had her burned at the stake in 1680 before she could name his mistress, Madame de Montespan, as a poisoner and practitioner of the occult. I've seen a portrait of La Voisin and I'm sure it's her. But that's impossible! She's been dead for fifteen years!"

"I don't think anything is impossible here," said Ian holding Rebecca close and watching as the large figure threw off his cloak to reveal the face and form of Samuel Brown.

"I knew it!" said Ian as they watched the parson and the witch bestow their blessings on the kneeling crowd that surrounded them. "And I have a feeling," he continued, "that most of the town of Salem is up there. Whatever goes on around here is no secret. Look at how many there are. It's unbelievable."

Ian and Rebecca watched as the priest and priestess finished their dark rite and gathered the faithful in a circle.

"Bless us Beelzebub in this our new coven," said Reverend Brown. "Gather to us the forces of evil and grant us your power to vanquish all those who do not follow your way."

With that final benediction, Samuel Brown drew his cloak tightly about him and motioned his followers to retreat into the dark of Salem woods. As they disappeared both Rebecca and Ian exhaled and held each other close.

"I can't wait until dawn," said Rebecca shivering in Ian's arms.

"Neither can I," said Ian hugging her close.

CHAPTER FIFTY-SIX

"Hurry up," said Jack as he and Ezra crept back to the stone ring. "Now I can see why O'Roarke said this would be the perfect spot. It's protected by all the demons from hell. What could be better."

"I don't like it, Jackie. It's not right," said Ezra with fear in his eyes. "It's an evil place."

"And so is our business," said Jack rubbing his hands together. "Hand over that chest and we'll soon have it protected by Old Nick himself."

Jack Love dug furiously as Ezra nervously held the lantern high. The old man was moving his lips in silent prayer. The night about them grew darker as the only sound that could be heard was the scraping of Jack's shovel and the distant hooting of an owl. Even the waves of Collins Cove had taken on a gentle caressing tone. Ezra looked up at the stars sparkling overhead and continued his prayers. As he gazed at the sky, the laughing face of Jamie O'Roarke appeared before him. Oh what a beautiful young man he had been, full of life and courage. Jamie O'Roarke locked away in some dark hole was more than Ezra could bear to think of.

"Stop digging, Jack!" said Ezra in a commanding tone.

"What's the matter?" said Jack climbing out of the hole covered with dirt.

"We can't do this, lad," said Ezra with an assurance that Jack had never seen before.

"Can't do what, you old fool?" said Jack angrily.

"Captain Jamie has been like the son I never had, Jack. We can't leave him to the hangman. Don't you see, it's not right, by God it's not right at all. I can understand if ye don't want to take the risk, but I've got to. All they want is the treasure. I could read it in Cotton Mather's eyes. He was of half a mind to let Jamie go. If they had a sack of gold to run their fingers through Jamie O'Roarke would be set free for sure. I could say I found it in the Cove. Then Jamie would be free to sail away."

"And what of us, you idiot?" said Jack growing more angry by the second.

"It doesn't matter what happens to me, I'm old and I've had my fun. As for you, you've never liked the sea anyway, Jackie. This is a grand country just full of opportunity for a bright lad like you."

"Now listen to me, Ezra," said Jack looming over the old man, "I've heard more than enough to know that you've finally gone daft. A man without gold in his pocket is dirt here just like anywhere else. I never intend to be poor again. Your life may be over but mine isn't. We're sticking to the plan. After we've got our pardons and things have grown calm we're commin' back here to get the treasure."

"And what of Jamie O'Roarke?" said Ezra quietly.

"Let him hang, I say," said Jack turning his back on his brother and picking up the shovel. As he moved towards the treasure, Jack felt the point of Ezra's cutlass touch his shirt. He whirled around in an attempt to grab the older man's arms, but Ezra jumped out of his way with surprising agility. As he backed Jack towards the largest rock at the center of the ring of stones there were tears in Ezra's eyes.

"I mean you no harm, Jackie, but I must do what is right. It won't be comfortable for you to be tied up here but you've left me no choice. You have to see how it is. You tricked me, I know that now, but you couldn't help it, 'tis your nature. I'll send someone to find you, I promise. The night is fine and you shouldn't be here long."

"Now Ez'," said Jack looking about him as he desperately searched for a way out, "I was just having a bit of temper. Why, I was climbing down that hole to get the treasure for ye. Don't you see? You can't blame me for being a bit disappointed, but I know ye to be a good an honest man. You're right, it's time I changed my ways and made for the straight and narrow. I can't be athanking you enough for showing me the error of me ways."

"Jackie, ye make me proud," said Ezra as he gladly put down his sword and wrapped his arms around his brother. As he held Jack tightly, Ezra Love's expression changed. The clasp-knife, held by his brother Jack, entered Ezra's heart.

"Oh Jackie, how could ye?" he said as he sank to the ground, his hands grasping the tarnished silver crucifix that hung around his neck. As Ezra Love looked up at his beloved sky one last time, a brilliant shooting star made its path across the velvet darkness. Ezra smiled up at it and breathed his last.

"There now, ye won't be bothering me any more with your damned goodness," muttered Jack as he dragged Ezra's body over to the freshly dug hole and threw it in atop the treasure. "Dead men tell no tales," he laughed with bitter mirth.

"But live ones do," said Ian MacRae standing behind Jack holding Ezra's sword in his hand.

The moonlight shining on Ian's hair gave it the glow of a flame as he advanced towards the pirate. The sparkle of his cat's eyes struck terror in Jack Love's heart. Here was no feeble man ripe for the taking. This Scottish warrior meant to have his blood.

"Now sir," said Jack Love in a wheedling voice, "you must have seen how it was. I was defendin' myself 'tis all," said Jack as he stepped into the shadows and retrieved his cutlass from behind the rocks. As he advanced on Ian with a shrill battle cry Jack Love knew he was in for the fight of his life. Slashing first this way and then that, he quickly managed to dominate the battle. Ian MacRae had great heart but how could he be a match for a man born with a sword in his hand. Ian slashed desperately as the determined Jack used every bit of his skill and cunning to advance on the Scotsman. Ian, taking in some of Jack's techniques, quickly adapted what he had learned to Jack's style and to the surprise of both of them abruptly parried and then thrust, wounding Jack in the shoulder. In return Jack angrily slashed at Ian, tearing his shirt and drawing blood from his chest.

"Stop, stop!" came a scream from behind them as Rebecca ran to the circle clearing in horror. Neither man heard her as both furiously battled for his life.

"So ye think ye are a match for Jack Love?" laughed the pirate as he lunged towards Ian and left a scratch upon his cheek. " 'Twill be sweet indeed to savor the lady's charms once I have done with you."

Ian, in blind anger, advanced on the pirate and began to slash at him like a madman.

"What's the matter, Scotsman, can't bear the thought of someone touching your lady?" said Jack in an attempt to distract his opponent. As he laughed, the earth beneath him began to shake with an otherworldly tremor.

"See for yourself how helpless the lady is," said Ian realizing that Jack had triggered some deep power within Rebecca.

Jack quickly jumped from the shaking earth to the safety of a rock. He leapt upon Ian in a final attempt to overcome him. As he struck the Scotsman, Jack gave a cry. Old Ezra's sword had found its way home.

Ian stood over the body and gave a great sigh. He wretched the sword from the dead man's chest. A savage triumph filled his soul. Ian MacRae gave the ancient cry of the Scottish warrior and lifted his sword to the heavens.

CHAPTER FIFTY-SEVEN

"Ian, the treasure!" screamed Rebecca as the earth beneath them continued to shift and rumble. The hole that had been dug by Jack Love was rapidly disappearing. Ian leapt to the crevice and jumped in. A smaller man would have never been able to grab the heavy chest containing Duncan MacRae's treasure. He threw the chest upon the sand and turned and hoisted Jack Love's body into the shifting ground.

"There now, may they both rest in peace," said Ian as he and Rebecca watched the earth cover the two pirates.

As the ground began to calm itself, Rebecca looked at the spot that covered her two ancestors. Never again would she be able to walk Collins Cove without thinking of them. For better or for worse they were hers, a part of her heritage. Rebecca walked over to the spot that until a moment ago had held the bodies of Jack and Ezra Love.

"Do you think Ezra found his paradise?" she said, gently stroking the ground.

"I don't know, darling," said Ian, touching her hair. "I do know that he was a good man, despite his trade." Ian gave Rebecca his hand and she slowly rose from the spot. Ian carefully hoisted the treasure chest over his shoulder as they turned towards town.

"Look," cried Rebecca as a group of lighted torches advanced towards them. It was Reverend Samuel Brown followed by a lovely lady in forest green and the faithful of his parish.

As the party advanced towards them Rebecca's head began to swirl. Was it only a few moments ago that she and Ian had seen these same citizens robed in black and swearing allegiance to Satan? Or had it been a dream? They appeared so normal now. The look on Samuel Brown's face was one of concerned annoyance. It was the expression any community leader might have.

"What is the meaning of all this noise?" asked Samuel Brown as he glanced about him. "The screams we heard were enough to wake the dead."

"Oh, I'm so sorry," said Rebecca demurely. "I couldn't help it. You see my husband and I were taking a stroll along your lovely beach when we happened upon this old sea chest."

"A sea chest?" said Brown eyeing Rebecca with suspicion. What had these two strangers seen while they were taking their evening walk? Samuel Brown had assumed when he had seen the old man and woman quietly resting, that their two younger companions were not far away. It boded no good that these two had been wandering about sticking their noses into things that were none of their business. What a fool he had been to not make sure they were safely lodged for the night. The unexpected appearance of his cousin, the beautiful Catherine Deshayes, had utterly robbed him of his reason.

"Why this sea chest, your worthy," said Ian praying that now was the time and place to gamble everything he had for the life of Jamie O'Roarke.

"Why sir, wherever did you find it?" said Catherine quite taken with the handsome Scotsman. It had been a long time since she had seen a man worthy of her charms.

"Right here on the beach," said Rebecca moving closer to Ian. The look in Catherine's eyes was quite alarming.

"Yes, my wife and I were admiring your lovely shore when we happened upon this sea chest. I do believe that according to the law of the sea anything found upon a beach belongs to the finder."

"Quite right, sir, quite right," said Reverend Brown relieved that the stranger man's attention had been taken up by whatever paltry loot he might find in the abandoned old chest.

"What say you, your Worship," continued Ian "if we look inside?" With that, Ian MacRae drew out a great string of black pearls held together with a heavy diamond clasp. The crowd gave an awed gasp as the jewels sparkled darkly in the moonlight.

"Sir," said Samuel Brown realizing what the Scotsman had discovered, "that is the treasure of Duncan MacRae, of that there is no doubt."

"I am quite aware of that fact, Reverend Brown," said Ian looking down at the man from his intimidating height. "And as you say here in Salem Town, 'to the finder go the spoils.' I believe that there are many witnesses here that could testify to your word."

"Aye, 'tis true, but you must see that this is a special case," said Brown trying to think his way out of this damnable mess.

"Of course there is," said a voice behind him. Isaiah Wolf and Melinda Briggs stepped sprightly from the misty forest and walked towards the spot where Samuel Brown stood. "I believe this is yours, sir," said Isaiah as he picked up the chest and heaved it to Ian. "In Salem there are many that hold the law sacred and would wish to see those that don't on their way. I am one of those men. Just this very day I have seen yon Reverend commit two foul deeds. No one is above the law, not even you, Samuel Brown."

"I *am* the law, you traitor," said Brown turning upon Isaiah Wolf with fire in his eyes. "How dare you show your face in this town after what you have done? This man," said Brown turning towards the crowd, "has committed foul acts of treason. He has aided in the escape of a known thief and prostitute and has abandoned his post."

"Not so fast, Reverend, I would ask you to speak more kindly of my wife," said Isaiah drawing Melinda under his protective arm.

"Your wife! But you posted no banns, there was no service."

"Not in this town. I would hardly expect you to give your blessings to the lady and me after all we've been through together," said Wolf in a menacing tone.

"And what do you mean by that?" said Samuel Brown with dignity.

"Perhaps," said the melodious voice of his cousin Catherine, "some things are best discussed in private. I am sure the good folk of Salem wish to return to their warm hearths and comfortable beds, Samuel."

As he looked around, Samuel Brown realized Catherine was right. More than one man among the crown had been a lifetime friend of Isaiah Wolf and knew him to be an upstanding citizen. As for Melinda Briggs, many a lady in the village had come to her for help when there was a delicate matter to be discussed. Melinda was wise in the ways and needs of women and in this godforsaken place that counted for a lot.

"You are right as usual, my charming cousin, what say we invite our friends and the newlyweds back to town for a cup of rum and a bit of chat."

"Quite wise, Samuel, but don't you have any decent French wine?" said Catherine linking her arm through Samuel's and dismissing the crowd.

"Come along now, my friends," she said over her shoulder, "I am sure that everything can be sorted out."

CHAPTER FIFTY-EIGHT

"Now sir," said Brown addressing Ian in a respectful tone, "what is it you wish of us? You know as well as I that yon treasure is too great to be held by one man and should by rights be put to use where it can do the most good."

"And that would be in your pockets now, wouldn't it?" said Isaiah winking at Melinda.

"Of course not, Major Wolf," said the Reverend attempting to remain calm. "There are many in this town on the verge of starvation, facing the winter before us without hope of food or shelter. Your gift to the people of Salem would be a godsend."

"A godsend now is it?" said Ian looking Samuel straight in the eye. "Well, yes, be that as it may, I am a Scotsman you may have noted and I love to bargain. If I gave you the treasure of Duncan MacRae, what would you do for me?"

"Why anything you like," said the Reverend beginning to sense a glimmer of hope. "A house, your own farm, why even my two matched bays come this very month from England."

"But earthy rewards are not what I desire," said Ian beginning to enjoy the game. "If that was all I was after, I would have taken the treasure and been on my way. No, what I seek is of a more personal nature."

"And what is that?" said Brown warily. He was beginning to think it would have been better to have run the Scotsman through when he had the chance.

" 'Tis not much, just a few small requests," said Ian smiling at Melinda Briggs-Wolf in a charming manner. "First of all I would like to see Major Wolf reinstated and raised to the office of Captain, with a house and stipend to match."

"Done," said Samuel relieved that nothing more weighty had been asked of him.

"Second, there is the matter of Captain Jamie O'Roarke."

"What about O'Roarke?" said Brown warily.

"You have it in your power to free him and grant him full pardon. After all, you said yourself that you *are the law.*"

"Free that brigand! Are you mad? Jamie O'Roarke is a cold, fiendish murderer who belongs in hell. I say he will hang on the morrow and find himself dancing with the devil!"

"It seems hell must be full of those from Salem Town now isn't it," said Ian glancing at Catherine and giving her a mischievous smile.

"Come now, Samuel, what will the freeing of yon O'Roarke cost you but a king's ransom in treasure," said Catherine seeing the wisdom of cutting their losses before Ian MacRae delved any further into their personal lives.

"But Catherine, Jamie O'Roarke! It galls me greatly to see the brigand set free. 'Tis not right."

"Samuel, me darlin', you can make amends by helping the poor of Salem," said Melinda plopping herself down on the Reverends lap. "Come on now, sweetie, be a dear and old Melinda will keep your secrets. That's a promise."

"Come along, Cousin, sign the pardon," said Catherine taking quill and ink from the cupboard behind him and drawing a piece of parchment from a shelf underneath. "If what I hear about this Jamie O'Roarke is true, you may yet have your day with him."

"As you wish, my dear," said Samuel Brown brushing Melinda from his lap and picking up the pen. "As you wish."

Rebecca held her breath as Samuel Brown scratched the words on the parchment that would set Jamie O'Roarke free.

"There now," said Brown as he handed the paper to Ian, "is that good enough?"

"It will be when you put the King's seal upon it, sir," said Ian as gravely as a judge.

"All right then, have it your way," said Brown as he removed his great seal from the cupboard behind him and put flame to the hot red wax. As the glow of the lantern lit his face, Samuel Browns lips twisted into a sinister grin. Let them have their way for the moment. None escaped his grasp for long.

PART SIX

IAN

CHAPTER FIFTY-NINE

"Damn!" muttered Rebecca as the keys to Jamie's cell fell from her hands a second time.

"Here, let me try," said Ian as he took the keys from her. Ian inserted the rusty device into the rustier lock and managed with some difficulty to turn the key. As the door swung open Rebecca and Ian peered inside. In the reflected candlelight Rebecca could make out the form of Jamie O'Roarke sleeping with the innocence of a child.

Ian reached out to stroke her hair as Rebecca moved away from him. A fear like none he had ever known before filled him as all he grasped was air. Aunt Arabella had often said to him that a man who fears nothing loves nothing and has no joy. For the first time Ian understood what she meant. In the past few hours Rebecca had given him the greatest love and joy that he had ever known. Now as he watched her run to Jamie O'Roarke, Ian knew the meaning of true fear. The radiance of her beauty was so bright it lit the dark prison with an unearthly glow. The bell that Ian could hear tolling off the passing hours seem to be knelling the death of his dreams as well. "No dream lasts forever," he thought as he quietly closed the unlocked door on Jamie and Rebecca.

"Jamie, wake up my dear friend, you are free, free at last," whispered Rebecca as her satiny hair brushed his face.

Jamie, feeling the touch of angel's wings upon his cheek, opened his eyes slowly, fully expecting to find himself in paradise. The sight that met his eyes was even more welcome.

"You're like a statue come to my life, my beautiful 'lady of the roses,'" he sighed as he sat up and attempted to get his bearings.

"You're free, Jamie, do you hear me, free," said Rebecca putting her arms around the pirate and helping him get to his feet. "Ian did it! He destroyed the pirates, saved the treasure, and forced Reverend Brown to pardon you," she said in a lilting voice.

"Did he now, lass?" said Jamie, grasping her shoulders and looking at her as if he couldn't believe she was real. "Rebecca, me darlin', during this long night there have been moments when I would have given my life for the sight of you and now here you are standing before me tellin' me that great hulk of a Scotsman has given me back my freedom. You're not foolin' old Jamie now are you? Could it be that the grief has driven you mad?"

"It's all true. I swear it," said Rebecca happily as she grasped his hand. Jamie gently drew her to him and enfolded her in his great cloak. The pirate turned her lips to his and engulfed them both in a kiss of breathless passion. The very air about them seem to shimmer with the magic of their embrace.

"Jamie, no," whispered Rebecca as she tore herself away from him. "I can't."

"And what is this foolishness, lass?" said Jamie tipping her face towards him, seeking some sign of merriment in her words. "Ye know that we are meant for one another no matter what your fool head may tell you. Forget who you are and do what you want to do here and now, who knows what the morrow may bring."

"Oh, Jamie, if only it were that simple," said Rebecca trying desperately to keep her voice from trembling.

"It's that Scotsman who has brought this about isn't it?" said Jamie with a calm that belied the turmoil in his heart.

"No, Jamie, it's not just that " said Rebecca softly. "It's everything that has happened. Until a few moments ago I thought I'd never see you alive again and now here we are. I'm so confused. I don't know what I want anymore. I do know that you are free and Ian MacRae almost died to save your life."

"Did he now," said Jamie moving away from Rebecca and drawing himself up to his full height. Turning to her with a brilliant smile, Jamie took her hand and led her to the door. "Come now, lass, I'll not kiss you again until you ask me to. 'Tis time now to thank the fine lad who freed old Jamie from these prison walls. After all he braved the gauntlet this night."

Jamie O'Roarke flung open the heavy door with a great thrust and strode into the candlelit room. Ian MacRae, not daring to look at Rebecca's face, moved toward the valiant pirate and handed him his pirate's sword.

" 'Tis no longer my rapier but yours, sir," said Jamie handing the cutlass back to Ian. "I ask you to accept this along with my homage and gratitude, Laird MacRae."

The sword glowed in the flame and cast a brilliance upon the countenance of Captain O'Roarke. Rebecca watched anxiously as the two men stood face to face.

"It is only in serving others that we are truly set free ourselves," said Ian as he handed the sword back to Jamie. "You may yet need this, O'Roarke, to save another of your nine lives."

CHAPTER SIXTY

"Rebecca, thank goodness we've found you," said Arabella as she thrust the door open and hastened towards them. Peter, who followed, looked equally grateful.

"If it hadn't been for the sour look on Reverend Brown's face, we would have never guessed you were here," said Arabella dropping into the nearest chair and fanning herself with Jamie's pardon.

"He had right reason to have a foul look upon his face," said Isaiah Wolf, placing his arm around Melinda's waist. "He was so angry about the freeing of yon Captain that he threw me the keys and fairly fled the place."

"Congratulations, Captain O'Roarke," said Peter Hawking striding up to the handsome pirate and shaking his hand vigorously. "I can't tell you how pleased I am that you are free. I wish that we could celebrate in proper fashion but time has suddenly become short. Rebecca, my dear, you and Ian need to say your farewells quickly. That Jezebel of a dyad has once again managed to find a way to have us dance to her tune."

"What do you mean, farewells?" said Rebecca grasping Jamie's hand tightly.

"We simply must be at Burying Point by midnight if we are to ever see home again," said Peter giving Jamie O'Roarke a stern look. "Lady MacRae and I went to the top of Charter street and located the exact spot that we were standing on when we were transported here. I then summoned Eva. With her help we were able to fix the celestial signs that would align themselves into a bridge between this world and ours. Unfortunately in doing so, I had to let the dyad stand free of the livewood."

"And as usual," interrupted an exasperated Arabella, "the little minx took advantage of your kindness. Once she was free of the wood, she demanded rather than obeyed."

"What does she want?" said Jamie raising an amused eyebrow.

"Her freedom, of course," said Peter wearily. "She stands free of my staff, but she must still remain in my power in a nominal way. She can wander only a short distance using what power she can summon that is not absorbed by the livewood, but she refuses to cooperate past helping us this night. Her magic is diminished, but still formidable. The nymph says that only during the cycle of the moon directly following All Hallow's Eve can such forces as the one that can return us home be summoned. The veil between the two worlds must be very thin and if we wait any longer it will be too late."

"If that's what she says, then I would believe her," said O'Roarke looking at Rebecca grimly. "Eva is an ancient dyad and wise in the ways of the stars. Many's the time I have scoffed at her to my sorrow. If she says that your time is short, you would do well to follow her lead."

"But we need more time," pleaded Rebecca looking about her frantically and lightly touching her waist.

"Rebecca, darling, surely you see that we must go quickly," said Arabella not unsympathetic to the girl's plight. The Lady MacRae had lived long and well, and the thought of being torn between two such attractive lovers was enough to cause agony in any female heart. "Perhaps you would like a moment alone to say your good-byes to Captain O'Roarke. After all," she said with a glance at Ian that brooked no opposition, "you have shared quite a few adventures in the past few days and have become close comrades." With those words she ushered everyone but Jamie and Rebecca towards the door. "Hurry, dear," Arabella said as she gave Ian a final shove.

"I can't believe you did that," said Ian furiously as Arabella slammed the door behind her.

"Ian, I love you, but honestly there are times when you can be such a fool," sighed his Aunt in an exasperated tone. "Let them say farewell and be done with it. The worst thing that can happen is a good-bye kiss or two."

"But what if he talks her into staying with him?" said Ian in a strangled voice.

"There are too many things that draw her home, my boy. Trust your Aunt and give the girl time to say a proper good-bye. It is far better to have her leave with no regrets," said Peter putting a sympathetic arm around Ian's shoulder.

"I suppose you're right, but I'll certainly be glad when we have a bit of modern ground beneath our feet," said Ian as he strode over to an overgrown holly tree and sank to the ground. The exhausted Scotsman propped himself up against its gnarled trunk and closed his eyes. As he drifted into uneasy slumber the voice of his long dead mother came to him crooning a lullaby of exquisite beauty. She held in her arms a small boy, the image of her own son but for his bight blue eyes. "Be not afraid, lovedy," she murmured. "You will yet embrace yon bairn," she said as she gently rocked the babe. Strangely comforted, Ian turned on his side and fell asleep.

CHAPTER SIXTY-ONE

"I can't go, Jamie, not yet," cried Rebecca as she flung herself into his arms with the tears streaming down her face.

"Now what's all this," said Jamie fondly wiping her face with the edge of his cloak. "Where is the reluctant miss who held me at arms length but a few moments ago?"

"Gone forever, I swear," said Rebecca sobbing quietly. "I can't leave you, Jamie, it's too soon. There is so much I have to say to you."

"Whist now, lassie, and what have you to say to me that you haven't already? Old Jamie will come along with you to Burying Point and send you off with a smile. Don't forget that a part of me will always be with you and a part of you will always be with me. No matter what else happens we will always have that."

"Then you know," said Rebecca quietly.

"I've known from the first," said Jamie ruefully, "and I also know that your destiny lies beyond here in that strange place you call home. My heart you will always have, darling Rebecca, but part we must. You have given me back my life, but more than that you have restored my soul. No matter where I roam or what my end may be, I know that once there was a lady whose love for me was pure and true. Carry our love to your land and guard it well for my sake."

Gently kneeling before her, Jamie clasped both her hands and kissed them fervently. She drew him to her and lightly stroked his silver-gold hair as the last of the candle sputtered out leaving them in darkness.

"Come now, my love," he said rising to his feet. "It is time to go."

The moon shone brightly overhead as the small party made its way towards Burying Point. The sound of fluttering wings surrounded them as old Nicodemus, out for his nocturnal flight, followed along at a distance. Peter looked up and signaled the great owl. To everyone's amazement he swooped gracefully through the night sky and landed lightly on Peter's outstretched arm.

"Well, old man, it's been a long time," said Peter gently stroking the glossy feathers of Nicodemus the hunter. "My thanks for guarding my friends this night."

Nicodemus turned his head in what looked like a complete circle, gave a low pitched hoot and then flew off. The stir created by his enormous wings scattered the leaves that lay at the travelers feet.

"A fine friend you have there," said Jamie slapping Peter's back in a gesture of respect. "Most fear yon creature, but I have always felt a certain kinship to him. Many's the time that we have rowed ashore dodging his attack. He's a bold one to be sure."

"Nicodemus should be," said Peter sadly watching the shadow of the owl cross the moon. "He holds the soul of a brave man within him."

"It's the soul of Giles Cory isn't it?" said Rebecca looking at Peter in wonder.

"Perhaps, my dear, perhaps," said Peter fondly putting his arm around the girl. "Come now, we must hurry. I don't like the look of this fog. It's becoming dangerously thick. Please everyone, stay on the path," said Peter as he raised the lantern high in an attempt to see around him. As the light reflected the forms of his companions, Peter was amazed to see Arabella and Jamie under a tree fast asleep. The mist that curled about him seemed to be entering his mind and confusing his thoughts. Peter whirled around and searched frantically for Rebecca. To his astonishment she now lay at his feet in a confused stupor. Ian groped towards them, his hands desperately trying to find something to steady himself with.

"What's happening, Professor Hawking?" said Ian in a desperate attempt to remain awake.

"I don't know, lad," said Peter as the sound of bells filled the air. "I've never seen anything like this before. But it's not of this world. Of that I am certain."

Peter and Ian fought desperately to remain awake, but the insidious mist that engulfed them was too powerful. In a last desperate attempt, Peter gave a whistle towards the sky, praying that old Nicodemus would hear and come to watch over them.

CHAPTER SIXTY-TWO

Arched torches, reflected in the moonlight, moved slowly towards the group as a chorus of dark angels sang a toccata to glorious death. A tall figure halted in front of the sleeping Rebecca and motioned to his followers to gently pick her up and place her on the litter they carried. The girl moaned as she was lifted onto the mossy bed. The tall man bent down and placed a kiss on her parted lips.

"To win a kiss from such a lady is always a pleasure," he murmured softly as he ran his hands down the sleeping girl's body. Satisfied that she would be a fitting gift, he turned his attention to the remaining slumberers.

"Dispose of the rest," he said ominously gesturing to the men who stood by his side holding swords. "And remember, bury the bodies at the foot of Gallow's Hill. 'Twill be a fitting end for Peter Hawking," said the Reverend Samuel Brown as he motioned for the litter bearers to depart.

"Shouldn't we wait for them to finish the job?" said his cousin Catherine stroking Rebecca's brow languidly.

"I've no wish to see the end of O'Roarke," said Eva. "He was a fine companion for all his difficult ways. Your price for my freedom is high, Catherine."

"But more than fair, don't you agree?" said the witch with a merry laugh. "Think what fun we'll have sacrificing this lovely bit to the dark one."

"Aye, there is much comfort in that," chuckled Eva as she linked arms with the witch Catherine Deshayes.

"I don't see why we always have to do the dirty bit," said Moses Coffin as he stood over the sleeping form of Peter Hawking.

"Well like it or not it's got to be done and quickly if we want to get back in time for the fun," said his companion.

"Right you are, Josiah. You and Archie take the pirate and the lady while I finish off the gents here," said Moses drawing his sword from his scabbard. "I hear this one is a sorcerer. Best to cut off his head. That's the only way to make sure he doesn't come back for you."

Moses steadied himself and raised his sword above his head. As the moonlight struck the blade a tremendous blow knocked the man off his feet. He screamed in horror as the blade meant for Peter Hawking entered his own heart.

"Did you see that, Archie?" whispered Josiah as he crawled towards his companion's motionless body.

"That I did," said the man glancing about him. " 'Twas some sort of flying creature struck him down."

"Well, there's no hope for it now. We'll bury him with the rest. The Reverend will make us pay dear if we don't finish this up." The man sighed and took out his knife. He moved quietly towards Arabella. "Perhaps the lady will be more gracious."

Josiah Beadle, the town's blacksmith, gently lifted the sleeping Arabella's head and cradled it in his lap. " 'Tis a shame to kill this one. She's prettier than a summer's day for all her years. Ah well, it can't be helped."

As if to belie his words, a fiery pain seared across his own throat as the talons of the great hunter sank into his flesh. "Archie, help me," screamed the dying man as he struggled in vain to release himself from the claws of old Nicodemus. The owl gave a thundering war cry and ripped at the struggling man until he heard the death rattle in his throat. The bird then released his victim and turned his attention to the hapless Archibald Knight.

"No!" screamed Archie as the avenging spirit advanced on him. The great owl gave a scream of triumph as he pounced on his prey.

CHAPTER SIXTY-THREE

"What was that?" said Eva as the worshippers approached the circle of stones held sacred by the coven.

"Merely the cry of an owl, my dear," said Samuel Brown, "nothing to be afraid of. How skittish you've become."

"You forget that I've spent three hundred years locked hand in glove with the pirate O'Roarke," said Eva shaking her head. Something felt strange about this night. Try as she would, the dyad could not escape the feeling of foreboding that filled her usually cold heart. 'Twas a shame that the price of her freedom had been Jamie's life. But there was no help for it now. What was done was done. How she wished she could have stayed to watch that old sorcerer Peter Hawking breath his last. He was indeed a true son of that foul tempered Giles Cory. Despite herself, Eva gave a merry laugh.

"What's so amusing, darling?" said Catherine Deshayes removing her cloak as she motioned the true believers about them to lower their cowls and reveal their faces to the demons of the night.

"I was just thinking of how that wicked old man Giles Cory died," said Eva barely able to contain her mirth.

"It was a wonderful time, wasn't it?" said Samuel looking at the nymph fondly.

"Oh, do tell me about it, Samuel," said Catherine as the trio watched two of their minions place the sleeping Rebecca on the largest stone that lay in the center of the sacred circle.

"It was right on this very spot, three years ago, wasn't it, Reverend?" said Eva savoring the memory.

"Yes, lovely," said Brown with a misty look in his eyes. "First we staked him to the ground under heavy planks of wood and then one by one placed stones upon the planks. He was a stubborn one all right. It took him two days to die."

"Oh, and do you remember about his tongue?" said Eva savoring the forgotten moment.

"Why yes, it had quite slipped my mind until this very moment," said the Reverend turning to his cousin. "The best part was when the terrible weight caused his tongue to protrude from his mouth. I used my cane to stick it back in. If the damned fool wasn't going to confess and forfeit his property to me then of what use was his tongue? By rights I should have ripped it from his throat."

"What grand times those were," said Eva wistfully, "when a bit of spectral evidence could be used to hang the innocent folk of Salem Town. It used to be so easy to convince the magistrates that anyone could leave his body and do evil deeds."

"You must admit, Eva," said Samuel, "that in a way Dorcas Good was our finest moment."

"Who was Dorcas Good?" asked Catherine caught up in the merriment.

"Eva here," said Samuel Brown proudly putting his arm around the nymph, "actually convinced the judges and that pompous Cotton Mather that a four-year-old child could be a witch."

"Oh, no," cried Catherine, her hands going to her mouth to still her giggles."

"Yes, it's true, I did," said Eva humbly. "But Sammy here helped. They threw her in jail along with the rest and there she remained until that meddling Reverend Hale from Beverly managed to convince the townsfolk that they should stop the whole thing."

"But it should be a great comfort to you that she came out damaged beyond repair," said Brown in a comforting tone.

"She did?" said Eva.

"Oh, I forgot, my dear, by that time you had been imprisoned yourself in the oak tree up on Burying Point. What fun you missed. Little Dorcas was finally released through the petitions of her father but she has never had the wits she should. Her mind is still that of the four-year-old child that stepped across the dark and dirty cell that she should have died in. Why she stands right there next to our sacred stone. See for yourself."

"Dear Samuel, how grand! Is it really her?" asked Eva jumping first this way and then that in excitement.

"The very same. She is moving on now to eight years, but has no more wits than a babe. The child often follows us about. She only feels safe in the dark."

The delighted Eva ran swiftly over the earth to where the child stood staring at the lovely Rebecca, who was by now strapped to sacrificial stone. Eva clapped her hands in the little girl's face and was rewarded by a whimper and the sight of the girl taking her thumb and placing it in her mouth. With a cry of mama, Dorcas ran away from the shimmering nymph and fled into the woods.

"Thank you, Samuel. It comforts me greatly to know that at least all our hard work was not in vain," said Eva in a satisfied voice as she watched the fleeing child.

"No evil deed is ever forgotten," said Catherine Deshayes turning to the faithful worshippers who were eagerly awaiting them.

"My brothers and sisters!" said the powerful witch embracing each faithful servant with her eyes. "Tonight is the moment that we have been waiting for. With the blood of this sacrifice we will consecrate a new order in this virgin land. Europe has

301

grown old and weary in our service. It is time to bring our religion to this place, the land of freedom and opportunity. Are we not persecuted and killed for our beliefs? Are we not punished for merely holding our own dark Lord sacred? What is our reward for our faithful worship? We are hunted down and slaughtered by the thousands. Enough of this I say. It is time that we established a new order, one so powerful that no mere human can destroy it. This night, when the veil between our world and that of the netherworld grows thin we shall summon the demon to live with us in this land and transform it into a hell on earth!"

With an embracing gesture, the priestess motioned the faithful of Salem to kneel before her as Eva quickly unlaced the ribbons of Catherine's gown. Stepping out of her garments, Catherine Deshayes stood before the alter with only the silken tresses of her fire red hair as adornment. Samuel Brown, with eyes downcast, knelt before her and offered Catherine the sacrificial knife that was forged from a single shaft of onyx. The moon rose from the mist and shone down upon them. It illuminated the stirring Rebecca in its glowing beams.

"I present this sacrifice to you high priestess as a symbol of my homage," said Eva as she ripped open the bodice of the victim's dress. Beneath the garnet-colored cloth lay the frantically beating heart of Rebecca Love. Rebecca, awakened by the sudden movement, regained her senses.

"No, oh please, no," she cried as she saw the red headed woman standing over her with the hungry dagger.

"Quiet her, Samuel," whispered Catherine angrily.

Samuel Brown quickly tore a length from Catherine's abandoned gown and tied it around Rebecca's mouth, stifling her terrified screams.

Rebecca's eyes frantically looked about for salvation and prayed silently to the heavens for help.

"Oh Father of hell, accept this our humble sacrifice as an offering from your faithful servants. Grant us your blessings and gifts this night of nights and protect us in all our endeavors, remembering always that what we do is for your sake and everlasting glory. Bring unto us the powers of evil and make us your servants. Let not any of our enemies escape retribution. Grant us the wealth of the world and the blood of the innocent so that we may delight in its strength."

"Praise unto Satan," said his cousin taking Eva's hand and facing the throng.

"Praise unto Satan," repeated the towns folk as Catherine poised the knife directly over the struggling Rebecca.

CHAPTER SIXTY-FOUR

"What in Hades!" exclaimed Jamie O'Roarke as he removed the severed arm of Archibald Knight from his face. The pirate wiped the blood from him with fragments of dark brown cloth that were scattered about him.

Jamie, alarmed by the bloody pieces of body parts strewn on the ground, leapt to his feet and searched frantically for his companions. Many the time he had come to in just such a bloody scene but never in so pastoral a setting.

"Ian lad, wake up!" he said as he rudely shook the highlander to consciousness. Jamie was relieved to see that both Peter and Arabella were also groggily coming to. But where was Rebecca? It was only by summoning up the experience of a lifetime that he was able to remain calm. If he lost his reason now there was no hope of ever finding the missing girl. To his grim relief, Jamie noted that none of the scattered remains resembled his beloved. The only garments on the ground were the coarse dark cloth favored by the men of Salem.

"What happened?" said Arabella ruefully rubbing her forehead trying to dispel the hangover left by the fog.

"I believe that the dyad wove a spell about us," said Peter, his eyes meeting Jamie's. "The last thing I heard was a chorus of bells. It's a sure sign that she has been at work. Is there any sign of Rebecca?" said Peter getting to his feet and scanning the area with his hawk-like eyes.

"None," said Jamie grimly touching what remained of Moses Coffin with his foot. "Use whatever magic you have left old man. I have a feeling that if we don't hurry Rebecca is doomed. There are many in this town that want their revenge upon us."

"Peter, you must find her quickly," said Arabella panicked by Jamie's words.

Peter put his fingers to his lips and gave a shrill whistle. He raised his face to the moon. In swift reply he was rewarded by a rustle of wings and the welcome sight of Nicodemus. The great bird landed on a nearby branch and surveyed the bloody scene triumphantly.

"My friend," said Peter hastening to where the owl had settled himself, "our thanks for all you have done this night. Unfortunately, your work is not yet finished. Lead us now to our Rebecca before it is too late."

The great owl looked at Peter with wise eyes. He gave a screeching hoot and turned his head first to the left and then to the right. Then he took wing and landed on the ground in front of where Ian and Jamie stood.

"He wants you to follow him," said Peter gratefully. "We'll come behind as quickly as we can, won't we Lady MacRae?"

"Yes, of course. Hurry lads before it's too late," implored Arabella as they watched the impatient bird take wing and circle above their heads.

"It's up to us now, Ian lad," said Jamie fastening his sword tightly to his side and throwing Ian his pistol. "Let's see what ye are made of, Scotsman."

CHAPTER SIXTY-FIVE

"Satan guide my hand and make it true," cried Catherine Deshayes as she thrust her dagger towards the heart of Rebecca Love. Rebecca struggled with all her might determined not to be an easy target. Catherine lunged forward with the knife just as Rebecca managed to loosen one of her bonds and dodge the oncoming dagger. The force of the knife as it struck stone instead of flesh knocked Catherine to the ground.

"Samuel, hold the bitch down," she said between gritted teeth as Eva helped her to her feet. There were murmurs of wonder from the faithful gathered around them. How could such a powerful witch be thwarted by a mere mortal girl? Catherine Deshayes was rumored to be the angel of death herself.

"Hold fast and stand away!" came a voice emerging from the forest. Jamie O'Roarke entered the clearing with pistols drawn.

"Why, Jamie lad," cried Eva in a relieved voice, "I knew nothing so simple as a small spell and a drawn cutlass could kill you."

"Aye, that's true enough, lass, and I can't be thankin' you enough for your part in it."

"Whatever do you mean, sweetheart?" said Eva as she sidled up to the pirate.

"Let's leave that for later shall we, m'dear?" said Jamie as he turned his attention to Samuel. "I'll thank you to release the girl, Reverend Brown. I'm sure your fine party can do without her."

"But of course, Captain O'Roarke, I'll be quite happy to as soon as you lower your firearms."

"I'll lower nothing, you blackguard," said Jamie laughing heartily. "Let her go and quickly or I just might take it into my head to shoot you anyway. There's many about Salem Town would turn a blind eye to that deed."

"Jamie, watch out!" cried Eva as she saw Samuel Brown draw a hidden pistol from his waistcoat.

The flash and report of the Reverend's pistol was echoed by another from the woodland behind Jamie. In a blast of smoke and gunpowder both men fell to the ground. Ian MacRae emerged from the woods and ran past the fallen Jamie O'Roarke to the sacrificial stone. With a slash of his cutlass Ian tore through her remaining bonds and freed Rebecca.

"Give me your sword!" she said with flashing eyes that challenged any of the gathering to come near them.

"Not so fast, little mistress," said Catherine rushing to the fallen Jamie. If Catherine was defeated now, in front of the faithful of Salem Town, all hope of holding this new land for Satan was gone. Cousin Samuel was dead, shot through the heart by that damned highlander. The Scotsman must pay. Those he loved must suffer. Blood for blood, soul for soul.

"One more step and yon O'Roarke dies, do you hear me?" cried the witch. "Leave the girl to me. That is the only way you and the Captain can keep your precious lives. Get in my way and you all die."

"If I must die then I might as well die for something," gasped Jamie.

"Hush now, love," said Eva cradling him tightly to her bosom. " 'Tis only a flesh wound. You'll be dancin' a jig in no time."

In answer to their words, Catherine summoned all the powers that she could and advanced on Jamie with death in her eyes. "Then die you shall," she screamed as two flashes of red fire sprang from her outstretched arms.

Eva leapt to her feet and blocked the volley of flame with her own less powerful beam of golden light. The fiendish glow of the fire encircled her body and in a scream of agony both flame and nymph disappeared.

"You'll pay for that, witch," said Jamie as he advanced on Catherine with his sword drawn and flashing. Catherine, weakened by her battle, turned on Jamie with dazed eyes.

"You can't kill me, pirate, no one can kill La Voisin."

"No one but the devil himself," cried Jamie as he impaled Catherine Deshayes against the sacrificial stone. Wiping his blade on the fallen Samuel Brown's coat, Jamie turned toward the people of Salem Town. "Make way you fools, that is unless there be anyone else who wishes to taste the blade of Jamie O'Roarke."

The silent crowd parted to let the three strangers pass. It was as if they were mesmerized by the sight of the dripping blood of the great witch of Monmartre, La Voisin. Satan had received a worthy sacrifice.

CHAPTER SIXTY-SIX

"Well done, laddie," said Jamie, as Ian draped an arm around the wounded pirate.

"It's the soul of a warrior you have, O'Roarke," said Ian laughing heartily.

"Well, I think you're both wonderful, but let's get out of here," said Rebecca smiling in exasperation at her two saviors. "There will be time enough for congratulations once we're clear of this place. Don't forget there is still a whole town of people who were more than willing to watch my heart be torn from my body."

"Right you are, lass," said Jamie with a merry grin that belied the ache in his side. All he wanted to do right now was to lay on the soft brown earth and close his eyes. Ian saw his faltering steps and tightened his grip around the older man. Together the three comrades made their way back towards Old Burying Point.

"Jamie, Ian, is that you?" came a voice out of the darkness. The bobbing lantern held by Arabella reflected the worry in her eyes.

"Yes, yes, it's us," said Rebecca rushing towards the motherly voice.

"Rebecca darling, what happened? Where have you been?" said Arabella handing the lantern to Peter and clasping the girl to her breast.

"Just a bit of a skirmish, Lady MacRae, nothing to worry about," said Jamie with a lightness in his voice that belied his weariness. "But it's high time we made our way out of these woods. No telling what else may be lurking about."

"Right you are, Captain O'Roarke," said Ian shouldering more of Jamie's weight.

"Did you find the dyad?" said Peter anxiously looking upward. The moon had moved across the sky and now shone directly overhead. "We must find her if we are to summon the forces we need to get us home."

"But there must be another way!" said Rebecca just beginning to realize the true price of her rescue. "Jamie and I made it here without Eva's help. Why can't he get us home?"

"Once we set foot on the soil of old Salem, I ceased to be a spirit," said Jamie wistfully. "Now I am only a man. There is nothing I can do to help you return."

"Then what I felt is true," said Peter grasping his staff. "I felt the power drain from the livewood as we followed you through the woods. It must have taken a great being to destroy such a presence. Eva was an ancient spirit, kin to the serpent of Eden himself."

"It was Catherine Deshayes, Peter," said Rebecca as she quickly told Peter of the strange scene that had taken place within the coven's circle.

"La Voisin," breathed Peter with respect. "To have destroyed the witch of Monmartre is a deed I would have not thought possible. Perhaps we may yet find a way to return home."

"What do you mean?" said Rebecca looking at Peter with a puzzled expression on her face.

"Surely you felt the magic within you, Rebecca," said Arabella realizing what Peter was getting at. "Something in the air here has awakened your own sleeping power."

"Power? What are you talking about?" protested Rebecca.

"Darling," continued Arabella, "We've all felt it coming from you. Don't deny that there has been something stirring within you for a long time that has finally been awakened by the atmosphere of Salem Town."

"I won't deny that," said Rebecca, "but no one is going to tell me that I'm some sort of a witch!" said Rebecca backing away from her friends in horror. Better to be dead than to turn into some horrible harpy like La Voisin.

"There are different sort of witches, Rebecca," said Peter looking at Arabella. The girl had been through a great shock this night and the look in her eyes was one of a small deer trapped by a pack of hounds.

"Oh darling," said Arabella touching the girl lightly, "I don't mean that there is any resemblance between you and that horror La Voisin. The true daughters of the Goddess are good and believe in healing the world, not destroying it. I've always been able to read the future. You don't think I'm evil do you?"

"Of course not," said Rebecca smiling despite herself. The dainty Arabella MacRae was the gentlest creature Rebecca had ever known. What she resembled most was some sort of fairy godmother, comforting all those around her.

"Then you see, there is nothing to fear. You too are a daughter of the Goddess through your mother. Many are and never know it. Some do. My powers are small. Yours, I believe, are greater. Perhaps they wouldn't have been if you had remained in your own quiet time but the moment you set foot on this soil the strength of the Goddess began to grow within you. And you will pass this power along to the unborn children I see in your eyes."

"How did...."

"Shh, listen," said Jamie interrupting Rebecca. "Do you hear that?" The pirate removed his black feathered hat and cocked his head to one side. From somewhere on the path to Old Burying Point came the low monotone sound of many voices moving slowly towards them.

"It seems the folk of Salem are still about this night," said Peter blowing out the lantern light. "We'll have to make our way in the dark if we want to avoid another meeting. Let's hope that the moon will give us enough light to see by. O'Roarke, do you know a way around the path that will lead us to the Point?"

"Aye, that I do, Professor," said Jamie replacing his hat and straightening his blue brocaded coat. "Ian lad, stand fast and guard the rear!"

With that the pirate parted the foliage to their right and quietly motioned for the party to follow him.

CHAPTER SIXTY-SEVEN

Old Burying Point stood proud and serene in the waning moonlight as Jamie mounted the summit and stood beneath the outstretched arms of the great oak tree. This had been the home he shared with Eva for three hundred years. He caressed the bark gently as he watched his companions complete the last few steps that would, if there was a Goddess, bring them home

"Eva, me darlin'," he prayed, "if there is any of you left come to old Jamie now and give him your strength." Jamie watched in silence as Rebecca gracefully climbed the last few steps.

"I can't believe we're actually here," she sighed, looking up at Jamie with heartbreaking beauty.

"Aye, that you are, lass," said Jamie giving her a squeeze around the waist. The gentle breeze that had been blowing suddenly picked up and tossed the leaves about them in a circular motion. "Can you feel the enchantment of the place? Many's the time I have stood by my mother's grave and felt the magic buried here. There was more than one enchanted moment when I could have sworn she answered me back."

"Oh, Jamie, is your mother buried here?" asked Rebecca suddenly reluctant to let Jamie go, despite her firm resolution. He was so alone. At least when Eva had been with him he had a companion. Now he had no one. Even his old shipmate Ezra was gone.

"She's buried right over here," said Jamie interrupting her thoughts. Jamie walked towards a magnificent headstone fashioned from the purest white marble. The grave of Rosie O'Roarke was set apart from the resting place of the more solid citizens of Salem Town by a lovely group of holly trees. Magnificent red roses had been trained to caress the stone.

"Why it's the most beautiful thing I've ever seen," said Rebecca enchanted by the finely chiseled features of the virgin and child. Standing atop the monument was the figure of Saint Michael with his sword drawn. The warrior angel seemed ready to do battle with any who dared disturb the grave. The simple inscription carved into the marble read:

Beloved Mother

Rose Ellen O'Roarke

March 12, 1636

December 13, 1662

"Oh Jamie she was only twenty-six when she died, how sad."

" 'Twas better to see her die young than to suffer anymore," said Jamie bitterly. "I was a lad of ten when the cough finally killed her, but that's not what really brought about her end. 'Twas the righteousness of the folk hereabouts. One by one they turned her from their doors as she came begging. All she asked for was a bit of warmth and some bread for her child. And what did the fine citizens do to her?" said Jamie with his eyes blazing, "they turned her away into the night because of her trade. If only I'd been a man I could have done something, but I was only a child. It was a bitter night a few weeks before Christmas when it happened. We had wandered all night and she could go no further. It started to snow and the wind battered our bodies. We tried to shelter in the church down in the town, but the Reverend drove us off. Finally we came upon the very bower where you and I tarried. We fell asleep in each others arms and when I woke to the bright morning sun she was dead. 'Twas the coldness of the town that killed her not the winter wind. I took a vow as I watched her being lowered into a paupers grave near Gallow's Hill that someday I would return and place my mother above them all," said Jamie with a smile as the tears coursed down his cheeks.

"You see before you the finest marble crafted by the greatest artisans of Italy. I carried it myself on my back up this very hill. Then Ezra and I made our way to Gallow's Hill and brought my mother here. Oh, it was a sight, I can tell you that, when the townsfolk discovered what I had done. 'Twas only the glow of gold in my hand that stilled their consciences. It took three bags filled with pieces of eight to turn a doxy into a lady, but I did it and never regretted a penny."

"Jamie, how wonderful you are," said Rebecca looking up at him.

"Not that wonderful, darlin'. I can't tell you how I regret bringing you here."

"Why, Jamie O'Roarke, what are you talking about?" said Rebecca, glaring at him in mock anger. "If you hadn't brought me here I would have never have known you and this wonderful place."

"Wonderful?"

"Yes, wonderful," said Rebecca giving Jamie a look that sent his heart singing. "Oh, I know it's dangerous and full of things I have yet to understand, but that doesn't matter. Don't you see that before you came into my life I was numb, living like the walking dead. You awakened me to the beauty of life and all it has to offer. If it hadn't been for you, Captain O'Roarke, I might have wound up some dried up old creature spinning her life away in the dusty bookshelves at the Peabody-Essex Institute."

"And now what are you?" asked Jamie taken aback by the fire of her words.

"I'm alive, gloriously alive. And more than that, for the first time in my life I'm not afraid of my own shadow. Jamie, my love," said Rebecca taking his hand and drawing him to her, "you have been my angel and my savior."

"A very unusual angel you must admit," said Jamie chuckling at the thought of himself with wings and a halo.

"But an angel just the same," said Rebecca putting both her hands on his face and drawing him towards her. The confusion she felt coursed through her as Jamie's powerful arms held her in their protective circle. His sigh as they parted brought the dreaming girl to her senses.

"I'm so sorry," she said as she backed away from the pirate in a panic. "I don't know what came over me."

"I quite understand, my dear," said Jamie wistfully. "Ye have made up your mind I see and it's not in old Jamie's favor, despite the barin you carry."

"I still don't understand how you know about that." said Rebecca softly.

"There's not much ye can pass by an O'Roarke, my darlin' girl," said Jamie crossing the space between them and placing his hand on her flat stomach. "I knew the moment the small soul took to ye, and now if I'm not mistaken he has company."

"You're quite right," said Rebecca blushing furiously despite herself. Damn Jamie O'Roarke, he always had a way of confusing her just when she thought she knew what she wanted.

"Oh, you are a case, Rebecca Love," said Jamie fondly patting her head. " 'Twixt dawn and the evening star ye went from virgin to wanton without nary a thought of the consequences. Don't you see? No matter where you go I'll always be with you, there's no leaving me behind now. What say you just forget this whole notion of doing what's right and settle down with me. Why, I'd build you the finest house in Salem, right in the middle of all those grand folk and we could raise a tribe of O'Roarkes to fill the place. 'Twould be a fine life I could give you, darlin'. There's more than one pot of gold that this leprechaun has hidden about. You would want for nothing, I promise on my mother's grave."

"But you're wrong, Jamie," said Rebecca sadly pulling away from him. "There is another child, and he belongs where I came from. They may have different fathers but their mother is the same She comes from the Salem I know. I will always love you Jamie, but it wouldn't work. Your place is not landlocked in some great house with a brood of children. You belong to the sea, you are part of it. You and I have different destinies. To deny what lies within us would be death. Captain Jamie O'Roarke has a job to do here. He must carve a mighty fleet out of the timbers of the new world. The ships of Salem were the first to sail to Russia and even made their way to China. That is where your greatness lies, Jamie my love, not enslaved behind some wooden door and fine lace collar. I know nothing of this place beyond my belief in its future greatness. You are a part of that future. Someday, hundreds of years from now your son will be born and see what you have wrought. Your greatness is too large to be confined by the narrowness of my time. This is an age where giants walked the earth. Now that you have your life, use that gold to take your rightful place amongst those giants. Don't forget that just as you and I have a path to be followed, so does your son. I haven't been able to see beyond the mist, but even with my clouded vision I have sensed marvelous things."

"Then it's true," said Jamie turning his face from her and gazing at his mother's stone.

"What?" said Rebecca.

"The prophecy my mother spoke of as she shielded me from the storm in O'Roarke's bower. She told me not to weep for her when she was gone. She said that she was happy because hers was to be a lasting legacy, one that would put the fine folk of Salem Town to shame. She told me that I would be a fine seaman and father a great line. It would be one that would serve the earth for generation unto generation until finally there would be an O'Roarke who would shine above all others. I dismissed it as the ravings of a dying woman because I died without issue. Now I understand."

"Rebecca," came Ian's voice as he stepped through the thicket, "Professor Hawking needs you."

Ian looked at Jamie anxiously as Rebecca quickly made her way towards Peter.

CHAPTER SIXTY-EIGHT

"It's time we spoke man to man, MacRae," said Jamie as he lowered his aching body to the ground and leaned against the stone of Rosie O'Roarke.

"Is your wound painful, Captain?" said Ian settling himself beside Jamie.

"Not as bad as some I've had," said Jamie rubbing his side carefully. " 'Tis more bothersome than anything else. I'll mend, laddie, don't you fear."

"I must say, O'Roarke, that in a way I envy you. Yours is a life any man would want."

"Aye, I suppose, but there's not many willing to pay the price. 'Tis a lonely life and a short one too, Ian. And the years at sea can be mighty sparse when it comes to companionship."

"But the freedom to be your own man is worth it," said Ian with blazing eyes. "The world that I come from hems you in and is often stifling beyond belief. You can't do anything without filling out a form and having it notarized. If you try you find yourself behind bars or ostracized by the powers that be."

"And what makes you think this place is so different?" said O'Roarke looking at the younger man in amusement. "I can't approach port without being boarded by some king's man eager to steal from me what I have gained by my very blood. Men have not changed, only their methods. If ye wish to be a pirate you must remember to always watch out for the politicians and the priests. One will steal your gold while the other claims your life for the good of your soul. Look not to follow in my footsteps, Ian MacRae, seek what I have sought."

"And what is that?' said Ian.

"Freedom, and respect from those that matter. The world's opinion of you may change, but as long as you stick true to your course then all's well. Your poet Wordsworth said it best, 'The soul that rises with us is our life's star.' That's something Eva would say to me when I would give into despair. How she loved the poets! Now then let's get down to business, MacRae, before the Professor has you vanish before my eyes."

"I don't know how much vanishing we'll be doing this night," said Ian anxiously. "The Professor is not having any luck duplicating the nymph's spell. He thought that if he reversed what she did then we had a hope, but nothing is happening and time is growing short. If it gets much later, you may have to find room for us upon the 'Red Witch.'"

"Don't get yourself riled up, Scotsman," said Jamie to Ian with a knowing wink. "I have a feeling our Rebecca may yet turn the tide in the favor of old Peter's Goddess. That girl seems to have more to her than even she knows."

"That's true," said Ian grinning at O'Roarke like a mate. "She is a woman."

"And what a woman," sighed Jamie. "Proud and stubborn as they come with beauty to boot."

"I see you've noticed," said Ian.

"Now, laddie, don't get your back up," said O'Roarke trying to keep his voice calm. "In a way the minx has made kinsmen of us, God save her, and like it or not that can't be changed."

"I'm afraid I don't understand," said Ian looking at Jamie in confusion.

"You don't have to," said Jamie, "leave that to the future.

For now rest content in my words. She belongs to you now, body and soul. That's the way it should be. You are from the same world, the same time. She only thought she was in love with me. It's you she has chosen for her mate. But you must promise me something, Laird Ian MacRae."

"What's that?" asked Ian wary of Jamie's sudden docility.

"That you will always make sure she is happy and protect her and her bairns with your life."

"Upon my honor, Captain, I swear," said Ian solemnly.

"Good," said Jamie springing to his feet. With renewed vigor he took his arm and gave Ian a resounding slap on the back.. "Now I believe it's time for you to be on your way, kinsman."

CHAPTER SIXTY-NINE

"I don't understand it," said Peter shaking his fist at the moon in frustration, "I've done everything exactly as the dyad did and nothing happens."

"Perhaps you are standing in the wrong place," suggested Arabella attempting to be helpful.

"I know I'm in the right spot, I can feel it." said Peter trying not to sound impatient. Time was growing short and he was making no progress at all. How he longed for his old brown leather easy chair and a good book. The thought of sitting before the roaring fire on a snowy winter's evening almost made him groan in anticipation. Never again would he curse the ancient furnace that banged and creaked in the cellar. What a blessed thing it was spewing forth comforting warmth during a nor'easter.

"Peter, you wanted me," said a lovely voice.

"Yes, my dear," said Peter cheered by the very sight of Rebecca's face. "I'm afraid we are in trouble. I thought that perhaps the touch of a true daughter of Salem might turn the tide. Hold my hands and repeat after me slowly:"

Oh Goddess,

Unto my hands bring forth the mystery of life,

Weave the past to the present and make them one.

Guard us, your children, on our journey through your sphere and take us safely home.

325

Rebecca placed her small hands in Peter's great ones and carefully repeated the words, praying that somehow his Goddess would hear them. At the finish of the incantation she opened her eyes and looked about. Nothing had changed. They were still standing atop Burying Point in Puritan Salem. Peter turned his back to her and gave a sigh.

"I can't think of anything else to try," he said picking up his staff. The wood no longer shimmered with the unearthly glow it had contained when the nymph had resided within its confines. Now it was just a finely wrought branch good for supporting weight and nothing more.

Peter raised it to the heavens and shook it at the stars. To his amazement, a strange comet shaped body appeared overhead that sent forth a shower of moonbeams. The beams filled the hilltop with light and gently formed an enchanted circle several feet from where Rebecca was standing.

"It wants you to follow it, Rebecca, me darlin'," said Jamie as he and Ian parted the holly thicket and joined the astonished Arabella. She was watching the shimmering beams with delight.

"But why?" asked Rebecca protective of her new state.

"To ready you for your journey. 'Twas the same when Eva passed over to me in yonder tree. The light is the soul of the Goddess making safe all those who journey in her realm. It's no wonder you couldn't leave as you were. Ye've changed, my girl. The Professor was calling for the same sphere that brought you here. Can't you see? That would mean you would have to abandon anything new within you before you left. You became a part of this old town and the Goddess knows it. Your very essence must be altered if you are to return in safety."

"My God, you're right," said Peter looking at Jamie in astonishment. "Why didn't I think of it myself?"

"Oh, don't feel bad, Professor. Remember I was locked up with a nymph for three hundred years. There was more than one trick she let slip during that time."

"I'll bet," said Ian.

"Now then, lassie, step into the magic circle and let the Goddess do her work." Jamie took Rebecca by the hand and ceremoniously led her to the spot where the glimmering light waited.

Rebecca stepped gracefully into the moonbeams and felt them shimmering through her body. They entered at her feet and slowly made their way up her legs, infusing her womb with a soft protective warmth. As the magic slowly creeped towards her bosom Rebecca was filled with a feeling of well being. The last of the light entered her mind and calmed the stirrings of fear. As it faded Rebecca felt rather sad to see it go.

"There now, Professor Hawking, she is ready," said Jamie sadly watching the fading light.

CHAPTER SEVENTY

Rebecca emerged from the moonbeams with a radiant look upon her face. Her beauty had been transformed into something beyond words. It almost took Jamie's breath away to look at her. It was as if she had been purified in the fire of the moon. She walked towards them like a maiden out of some medieval legend. To Ian's dismay, she approached O'Roarke.

"You too are a part of both worlds, Jamie O'Roarke. Why wouldn't the magic work for you as well as for me?" said Rebecca facing him and giving him a gentle smile.

"Rebecca, me darlin', surely you must see it's not the same thing," said Jamie evasively.

"Why not?" said Rebecca confused by Jamie's answer.

"Well you see, for one thing most of my mortal life has been spent here wandering about from port to port and scrounging what living I could make off the sea. For another, what would an old pirate like me do in your world?"

"Well for one thing," said Rebecca putting her hands on her hips and mimicking Jamie in a playful manner, "a man your age isn't that old in our times and for another there are as many pirates lurking about Salem in 1995 as there are around here. They're just called by different names. Think of it, Jamie! A man like you could be anything he wanted to be. I'll bet there is still plenty of your treasure left buried around the town. All you would have to do is dig some of it up and head towards Wall Street. That's where many of our pirates weigh anchor."

"You know, Captain O'Roarke," said Peter thoughtfully rubbing his chin, "the girl's not crazy. Can you imagine what just one pot of gold doubloons would be worth on the open market? Jamie, my friend, don't say no to the idea so quickly."

"I'm beginning to think you're all quite mad," said Ian praying that this nightmare would end soon. What chance would he have of holding Rebecca's love if Jamie O'Roarke came with them? He could tell from the look on her face that Rebecca still harbored deep feelings for the pirate, deeper than even she knew.

"Perhaps great wealth isn't the most important thing to the Captain," suggested Arabella trying to instill a calming voice into the discussion.

"Right you are, my lady," said Jamie relieved that at least one of these modern folk understood what he had been unable to put into words. "You see, Rebecca darlin', wonderful though your world may seem to you, to me it is a mass of confusion filled with people who don't know their minds and have little inclination to follow their hearts."

"I don't think I understand," said Rebecca trying to follow Jamie's explanation.

"Let me put it this way, sweetheart," said Jamie with a grin. "Do you really think old Jamie would be happy trapped in one of those glass prisons you call an office building? I would spend most of the time gasping for air and longing for a bit of green. And can't you see me all tricked out in one of those costumes you call a suit with a bit of cloth hanging about my neck like a noose? And what of my speech and manner. Wouldn't the folk of that place you call Wall Street think it a bit odd when I settled down to a meeting with a noggin of rum in me hand and a parrot perched on me shoulder? No, I think that here is where I belong and here I mean to stay. At least you can tell the pirates from the preachers in my Salem Town."

"Oh, Jamie," laughed Rebecca despite herself, "do we really seem so awful to you?"

"Not awful, dearest, just different. This man needs to feel the wood of the deck beneath his feet and the salt spray in his face to be really alive. There is precious little of that where you come from. I know you still have your fishermen and such but they are so bound up in rules and regulations that they might as well be dead, as I would be landlocked away from every thing I love."

"Everything?" said Rebecca searching his face for some sign of hope.

"No, darling, not everything," said Jamie realizing what he had said in the passion of the moment, "just those things that give me life and make me what I am. A man of the sea, just like you said, destined to follow every new horizon and explore this beautiful new world that you have given me. Don't you see? Can't you taste the adventure in the air? There are new ports opening up all over the world right now and I have to be a part of it. You opened my eyes to that, me darlin'. If I left now I would always regret turning my back on it."

"What do you see, O'Roarke?" asked Ian suddenly caught up in the vision.

"I see the great China Sea laying before me," said Jamie lost in his dream. "If I can recover enough of my gold, I mean to follow the routes that old Marco Polo took and land myself in the mysterious east. What is sugar turned into rum when compared to the vast treasure that await us there? Imagine the riches that could be bought and sold. Why Salem Town could become the seafaring capital of the world if Jamie O'Roarke has his way."

"Then follow your way, Captain O'Roarke, and build the future," said Rebecca giving Jamie a kiss on the cheek, "but don't forget those who have loved you and save a bit of your thoughts for them."

"Oh, lass," said Jamie as if his heart would break, "you are my heart, my very soul. Without you and the strength you have given me I would have ended my days a broken down old pirate spinning tales in some tavern for the rum it would get me. What I owe you is beyond measure, beyond words. I thank God and the Goddess and whatever else there is lurking about this town for you. You are my love, my life and everything I am is because of you."

CHAPTER SEVENTY-ONE

"Well spoken, Captain," said Peter Hawking coming up to Rebecca and gently putting his arm about her. "It makes me think that there was some reason for this madness after all."

"Of course there was some reason for it!" said Arabella looking at them as if they had lost their minds. "What of the curse of the MacRaes! It still hasn't been removed."

"My goodness," said Rebecca, "how could we have forgotten!"

"It's no wonder," said Peter for the first time realizing that not just Rebecca had changed. They had all been through a metamorphosis of sorts. Peter, Arabella and Ian had also journeyed through time to this strange land of Salem Town. Never would they forget what they had seen and done. Like it or not they were not the same people who had ventured out on All Hallow's Eve a short time ago.

"Now then, O'Roarke, what about the curse? If I have my facts right, it includes not only my Aunt and myself, but also any descendants of the Love brothers."

Rebecca looked at Jamie in astonishment. "That means that not only ourselves, but any children we may have," she said realizing suddenly that a strange twist of fate had resulted in Jamie's almost bringing about the downfall of his own child.

"Yes, my love," said Jamie reading the look on her face, "it seems that the old tale is true. One can never curse without becoming cursed three-fold. I've never removed a curse before and I'm not sure exactly how to go about it."

"Perhaps I can help," said Arabella in a comforting tone. "This is one thing that I have studied for many years. When Ian was a small boy I looked in vain for some way to remove the cloud that hung over him. All my searching eventually brought me to the same conclusion. He who places a curse must be the one to remove it. And only if he no longer wishes the object of his wishes ill. Can you truly say in your heart of hearts that you wish my nephew only good?"

"Why, 'twas this brave lad saved my life not an hour ago," said Jamie looking at Ian with respect.

"But, Captain, are you sure you do not harbor anything against Ian? You see, if you speak the words to remove the curse and hide any reservations within your soul, the whole thing may backfire on you. The mischievous spirits who first granted your wish don't like to be mocked. They would make you pay."

"I think I already know a bit about that," said Jamie staring past them to the old tree that had been his prison for three hundred years. "I can truly say, Lady MacRae, that all that stood between us has been removed. Your nephew, wild highlander though he may be, is now my comrade in arms. I am sure that in all broad Scotland there is not a braver heart or steadier hand."

"And what of Rebecca?" said Peter.

" She carries my soul in her hand, don't you, me darlin'?" said Jamie smiling at her.

"Then, Captain, I think you can safely remove your curse," said Arabella motioning towards where Rebecca and Ian stood.

Jamie solemnly looked back at the mighty oak and tipped his hat to its branches. He then turned and faced the last two descendants of the MacRae and Love families. "I wish I had the gift of a silver tongue, but plain speech will have to do," he said with unaccustomed humility. "Mistress Rebecca Love, Laird Ian MacRae, I wish to remove the curse that I so wickedly placed upon your heads. 'Twas in the heat of passion that it was done and I deeply regret it. May you be free of any but my good wishes for you and yours from this time forward and forever more. There now," said Jamie turning to Arabella, "is that good enough?"

"It was truly fine, Captain," said Arabella touched by the vulnerable look on Jamie's face. He looked so alone standing apart from them.

From somewhere overhead the rush of heavy wings battered the air about them. To Jamie's surprise old Nicodemus circled about his head three times and lightly landed on his left shoulder. The great hunter's talons gently sank into the padding of Jamie's embroidered coat and the owl gave a low hoot.

"Well I'll be," said Peter staring at the bird as if he'd just seen an apparition. "I've never heard of an owl doing such a thing."

"But you said yourself that Nicodemus was more than a mere owl," said Rebecca watching in amazement as Jamie carefully stroked the great bird. Nicodemus put his head against Jamie's cheek and closed his round eyes in sleepy contentment.

"It seems that he likes me," said Jamie flattered at the old owl's show of affection. "Perhaps we're birds of a feather, eh old fella," said Jamie shifting his weight so that Nicodemus could rest more comfortably. He looked up at the moon and gave a sigh that shuddered through his body. "Now, my friends, as much as I regret to say this, we are running out of time. Yonder moon is making its way rather quickly across the sky and it's high time you were on your way."

Jamie walked towards Ian and Rebecca. "It seems the time has come to say good-bye to you, my comrades in arms. Try to think kindly of old Jamie if you think of him at all."

"Oh Jamie," said Rebecca throwing her arms about the pirate, "how I will miss you!"

"There now, lass, how can you say that with such a fine highlander standing beside you?" said Jamie gently removing Rebecca from him and placing her hand in Ian's. "Take good care of our girl, MacRae. And don't be forgettin' that the path you follow this night can be traveled by others. If ever you find yourself in storm tossed waters just give a call for Captain Jamie O'Roarke."

With a sweeping bow and Nicodemus riding on his shoulder, Jamie turned his face towards the sea and burst into song.

> When the foes all surround me in battle,
> And I'm in the midst of all pain,
> To you I'll be true, lovely Becky,
> Fair maid of Lord Ian's domain.

PART SEVEN

THE LEGEND
OF
JAMIE O'ROARKE

CHAPTER SEVENTY-TWO

"Come on now," said Peter gazing overhead at the moon, "we have precious little time left if we ever hope to get home."

With that, the tall sorcerer placed his staff in the exact spot where Rebecca had stood a few moments before and motioned for the others to join him. He placed one hand on the staff and told the others to do the same. They formed a magic wheel with the livewood making up the center spoke. "No matter what happens, don't let go of the staff," warned Peter gravely. "It's this that will bring us safely home. The wood will seek its resting place on Burying Point and with any luck it will take us along with it."

Peter Hawking then closed his eyes and intoned the ancient prayer of homecoming. There were no words for the chant that ran through his heart, only a reweaving of the old souls to the new throughout the ages. The earth trembled slightly and they braced themselves for the journey. One by one the travelers began to shimmer in the moonlight until all that could be seen of them was a ghostly outline that marked the shape of their bodies.

Just as they began to fade entirely from sight, a great clap of thunder split the sky and the headstones of the Puritan folk of Salem town shattered into a million pieces. The only one left standing was the fine marble monument of Rosie O'Roarke. It had been protected by the thicket of holly trees that her son had planted. Rebecca was the last to catch a glimpse of the earth that was now floating beneath her. What she saw made her smile.

A tremendous rush of celestial wind caught the travelers up in its swirl as they lost any sense of earth and sky. Battered about by the force that seemed as if it would tear the very clothes from their backs, Ian and Rebecca fought valiantly to hold onto the staff. Peter and Arabella did the same as a huge wind tunnel sucked them into a narrow cavern-like space that drew them upward. The suction felt as if it were compressing the very breath from their bodies. Just as Rebecca turned her face and was about to say something to Ian, she felt her grasp come loose from the staff.

"Ian!" she screamed as she her body separated from the group. A strong hand held hers and clamped Rebecca's trembling fingers under his on the staff. As they were about to relax, another great gust of wind caught the Scotsman in its grasp and sent him hurtling into the dark nothingness that lay below them.

Rebecca watched in horror as Ian disappeared from view.

"Oh Mother of all things," she prayed with her broken heart, "grant me a miracle and restore your son to me." The tears coursing down her face stung her cheeks and caused her body to shudder with their violence. Rebecca battled the merciless winds and searched the air about her for some sign. The empty void of the rushing wind was her only answer. In great despair, Rebecca began to loosen her grasp on the staff. Better to die in the void with Ian than to face the lonely years ahead without him.

"No," yelled a voice in her mind as she felt some power outside herself gluing her fingers to the staff. Peter was glaring at her in anger. "Think of the life within you and live for that," came his command from deep within her mind.

Sadly, Rebecca knew that Peter was right. She must live for herself and for that which was to come. She held within her a sacred trust that she could not abandon. The blessed relief of death was to be denied her. Rebecca firmly grasped the staff and looked at Peter and Arabella in understanding. She must live for Ian now and find comfort in his son. Rebecca closed her eyes and felt the wind, that now took on the form of a gentle spring breeze, rock her into dreamless sleep.

Arabella turned to Peter forlornly and put her head on his shoulder. She too was soon lost in sleep. Only Peter remained awake watching over them with his wise eyes.

CHAPTER SEVENTY-THREE

"Wake up, Emily," shouted Danny as the shaking earth beneath him jarred the sleeping boy to his senses.

"Not yet, Danny, it's too early for school," said his sleepy sister. "Wait until Mommy's alarm goes off."

"Get up. Now!" said Danny roughly pulling the sleepy little girl to her feet. The ground beneath them had now begun to ripple and crack making any escape impossible. Danny held Emily tightly in his arms as he realized this moment might be their last.

"Where are we?" said the little girl hanging onto her brother for dear life.

"Don't you remember?" said Danny trying to make his trembling voice sound normal.

"The last thing I remember is dreaming about the big scary pirate and the beautiful fairy lady. It seems that Miss Love and the old professor were there too, along with some other people, but I can't remember what it was all about," said Emily staring at the remnants of the shattered oak tree.

"No, wait, I do remember something," said Emily pulling at Danny's arm frantically. "We have to be standing near that tree for some reason, I remember hearing a voice say that unless we are standing in the exact spot where the tree is, something terrible will happen."

"I remember, too!" said Danny giving his sister a hug and anxiously eyeing the shaking ground that lay between them and the shattered oak. Sure enough, the ground the oak fragments rested on was steadfast and calm. If they made a run for it they might be saved.

"Come on," yelled Danny as he grabbed Emily's hand and dragged her across the shaking earth towards the oak. As the two children made their mad dash, Emily's foot was caught in a fissure created by the shaking ground. The earth snapped open and then closed quickly again snatching the small red sneaker from her foot, but leaving her bare toes free.

"Made it," gasped Danny as he threw himself against the stump of the oak. Emily rubbed her pink toes and stared about her in wonder. Old Burying Point rippled and heaved with the pressure of the shifting earth below. Several headstones that had been there for hundreds of years toppled over, while others leaned this way and that at mad angles. One grave, that of the Honorable Samuel Brown, was completely unearthed by the force of the earthquake.

"EWWW," screamed Emily in horror as a bony hand clutching a tattered book landed a few feet from her wiggling toes. The hand seemed to quiver and then move towards Emily as she drew her legs back in terror. "Danny, make it stop!" she cried as the hand crept slowly towards the little girl.

Danny was more afraid than he cared to show his frightened little sister. He valiantly grabbed a huge piece of shattered wood that lay to his left and swung at the crawling thing with all his might. The bones of the ancient hand turned to dust as Danny beat upon them, but the fragments of the book remained. Danny carefully picked up the small black missal and turned it over in his hands.

"Don't touch it, it might be haunted," screamed Emily shrilly.

"Oh, Em', it can't hurt me," said Danny as he examined the strange markings on the cover. Opening the book, Danny was astounded to see a bit of ancient script.

"Why look, Emily, this book was some sort of gift. Somebody wrote in it. See, it's not haunted at all. After all, that was the grave of a reverend, not a witch."

"I suppose you're right," said Emily moving closer to Danny as he sat beside her and leaned against the oak stump. "Can you read what it says?" said Emily wishing she could make out the big words. There was not a single cap, hat or put in the strange writing.

"It says," said Danny tracing the lovely scrolled letters with his fingers, " 'To my beloved cousin Samuel, from your loving cousin Catherine. May you carry this treasure through the darkness so that we may once again be reunited to do the masters work.' "

"Is it some sort of a bible?" asked Emily trying to make some sense of the lines and curves that still remained on the cover.

"I guess so," said Danny tossing the book aside and watching as the earth about them gradually calmed itself.

The first rays of dawn could be seen appearing over Collins Cove as the heaving earth restored itself to quietness. "Do you think it's over, Danny?" said Emily taking a mitten from her coat pocket and pulling it over her cold toes.

"I think so," said Danny smiling at his sister's ingenuity. "I promise never again to yell at you for not tying your shoes," he said giving the small girl a hug. She might be a pest, but she was his pest.

The boy and girl stood up and looked about them. The old oak that had been shattered beyond recognition was a part of their lives. It had stood in its spot long before they were born. Danny stared at it and suddenly remembered everything that had happened the night before. He looked at Emily in excitement and saw his own awareness mirrored on her wise little face.

"You remember, don't you," he said in a whisper, afraid to speak too loudly.

"Yes, I remember. The pirate and the fairy were really real," she said watching the sun beams gradually creep up the hillside towards Old Burying Point. As the burning rays touched the roots of the ancient oak, a large shaft of sunlight formed itself into a pillar of fire. Danny and Emily watched in amazement as the pillar turned into a large burning staff. Surrounding the staff were three forms filled with golden light.

CHAPTER SEVENTY-FOUR

Rebecca felt an almost euphoric lightness fill her body as she roused from her dream like state. On either side of her Peter and Arabella were glowing pillars of light. They looked like some ancient king and queen out of a great legend. The sparkling light about their heads gave the illusion of halos.

"Don't be afraid, my daughter," said the magical Arabella in a comforting voice. "We are home."

The light was almost blinding as Rebecca turned her face towards Peter and was greeted by a peaceful smile. Home! They were really home, sang Rebecca's heart as she felt the energy of the light gently leave her body. Her feet touched something cool and restful. It was the earth of her very own Salem.

The gentle dawn creeping over Collins Cove stretched its misty fingers towards them as Rebecca, Arabella and Peter took on their earthly forms.

"Miss Love, Miss Love," shouted a small figure as it hurtled towards Rebecca. "You're back! I'm so glad. Danny and me thought that maybe you had become a ghost, too!" The small Emily hugged Rebecca with surprising strength.

"Well done, Danny my boy," said the professor putting a hand on Danny's shoulder.

"We really helped?" said Danny watching the last of the magical light fade from the three travelers.

"Of course you did," said Arabella. "It was because of you that our bodies found their way home. The staff heard the call of the old oak, but that was not enough to cause our spirits to reform into something that was of this earth. We needed a combination of physical and spiritual forces to do that. The wood lured our spirits and your hearts brought back our flesh. If not for you we may have returned, but only in ghostly form."

"Like the pirate and the fairy," said Emily looking about for some sight of Captain O'Roarke and Eva. "Wait a minute, where are they? And what about the other guy who talked with a fuzz?"

"Not a fuzz, a burr," said Danny surprised that with all that had happened Emily remembered his description of Ian MacRae's accent.

"Emily dear," said Rebecca gently, "Captain O'Roarke won't be coming back. We managed to free him from the tree. Right now he's sailing some fine ship on a great adventure. He's probably in China by now."

"Is the fairy and the other man with him? I know he liked the fairy lady, but I didn't think the Captain and the other guy got along so well."

"They did by the time we left," said Rebecca remembering Jamie's parting words to Ian. Then returning to the child's question, Rebecca said sadly, "I don't know where either of our friends are. They were both taken away by magic. We can only pray that somehow they will be restored to us someday."

"You mean they're dead, don't you," said Emily searching Rebecca's face for some sign of hope.

"I'm not sure, darling," said Rebecca trying to give the little girl an honest answer. "They probably are, but something deep down inside me feels they're alive.

"You came back, Miss Love," said Danny with youthful enthusiasm shining on his face. "That means that there still might be a chance, don't you see?"

"Oh, I hope so," said Rebecca turning her face to the sea as the sound of the bells from St. Peter's church began to ring. It was All Saints Day in Salem. One by one the other church bells in town joined in. The deep bell of St. Peter's was soon playing a counterpoint to the more lyrical sounds of St. Mary's carillon. In the distance, Rebecca could make out the steady tolling of the chimes of Grace church. With each new sound, Rebecca felt her heart lighten. Perhaps Danny was right. If they could find their way home then perhaps there was some way for Ian. What was it Arabella had said? The children had served as an astral link so that Peter, Arabella and Rebecca could return in body as well as soul. If Ian still existed, then there was a chance that they could call him to them. But how?

Rebecca watched as Peter approached the remnants of the great oak and surveyed the ruin. To her astonishment, the old man raised his staff and began smashing it against the trunk of the tree. The frustration on his face was echoed by the violence with which he attacked the wood.

"Peter, stop!" cried Arabella as she rushed to the man who had remained calm through so much.

"It's not fair!" said Peter as he threw what remained of the staff to the ground and put his hands over his face to hide the tears that sprang to his eyes. "I'm old. Why did your nephew have to be the one who was taken? It was my turn to go, not his. I would gladly trade my life for his if I could."

"I know you would, my dearest," said Arabella sadly, "but what's done is done. We must find a way to go on. As you said yourself, we must think of the living."

"Peter," said Rebecca softly, "what if Ian is not dead?"

"What do you mean?" asked Peter looking at Rebecca as if she were mad.

"You said that we need a spiritual and a physical link to return to this world. We have both right here. Just because Ian let go of the staff doesn't mean that he perished in the void. For all we know he may be floating in some sort of limbo, a soul without a body. What if all we need to call him home is a physical link?"

"She may be right," said Arabella excitedly. "I don't know why we didn't think of it before. Energy never really vanishes, it just transforms. What if we could bring together the right forces to recall Ian's spirit to his body and transport them here."

"But how?" said Peter. "It was a miracle that any of us returned at all. Without two very strong links it's quite impossible. The livewood lies here at our feet, but that is only half of it. Ian was the last of the true MacRaes. You my dear may call yourself his Aunt, but in reality there is no biological connection. Ian's only hope would be if there was another of his blood who could call him home. So you see, even though his spirit may still exist there is no way to summon his body to us."

"But, Peter," said Rebecca scarcely able to contain her excitement, "you're wrong."

"Why, what do you mean?" said Peter looking at Rebecca in confusion and then staring at her in understanding.

"Hurry, there is no time to lose," Peter shouted as he made his way back to the shattered oak.

CHAPTER SEVENTY-FIVE

The shattered wood that had housed the spirits of Jamie O'Roarke and the nymph Eva stood bathed in the light of dawn. Danny and Emily could hear the quiet breathing of the souls of Old Burying Point as they watched Rebecca, Arabella and Peter take their places amongst the ruins of the oak.

"What's that smell?" asked Emily as she watched the three people amongst the wood chips.

"It smells like the purple flowers in Mrs. Maloon's garden," said Danny sniffing the air about him.

"But, Danny, those are violets, they only come up in the spring. They're all dead by now aren't they?

"I guess so, Em'," said Danny as a light lavender mist began to encircle Rebecca, "but around here you never know."

The delicate fragrance of new autumn violets did indeed fill the air as the three friends held fast to each others hands. Rebecca felt as if she were a small girl standing between Arabella and Peter. She clasped their fingers in a mixture of fright and wonderment.

Arabella smiled at her gently and breathed out the violet mist that continued to envelope them. The magical violet cloud was coming from within Lady MacRae.

"You *are* a witch!" whispered Rebecca in awe.

"Aye, that's so lassie, but not one like that Catherine Deshayes. I have no dealing with any devils. Mine is the old religion, sanctified by the Goddess before time began. My work and hers are one on this earth. Healing is what we are about. Whist now, did you hear that?" said Arabella suddenly as the old tree shards began to creak and groan.

"What's happening?" asked Rebecca, feeling a spring breeze gently brush her body.

"I believe it's the Goddess entering her priestess," said Peter watching Arabella with loving concern.

Peter and Rebecca grasped Arabella's fingertips as the priestess received the ghostly presence of the Goddess that flowed through her. To Rebecca's strange delight, the peacefulness that had come to her in her dreams was rekindled, transmitted through the delicate line that had formed between the mortals standing on the Goddess's hallowed ground.

"Oh lady of the earth and skies, come unto me now and make me whole," intoned Arabella in a voice that oddly enough resembled the dyad Eva's.

Peter and Rebecca watched as the small Scotswoman was lifted a few inches off the ground, supported only by the lavender mist. Rebecca watched in astonishment as Peter soon followed suit. Rebecca found herself struggling to keep her hold on Arabella's ascending hand. Then to her delight, the mist flowed through her too and she felt a delicious weightlessness overtake her and elevate her to the level of her friends.

"Look, Danny," cried a child's voice from beyond the mist as Rebecca felt a rush of wind pass through her body.

Nothing in the fantastic experiences of the past few days could have prepared Rebecca for the sight that now met her eyes. She watched in astonishment as the bodies of Peter and Arabella merged into one androgynous whole. The creature that was forming within the mist was neither man nor woman, but a strange God/Goddess that seemed to represent the whole of mankind. The priest and priestess held within them the blinding light of the universe. Rebecca watched in awe as the light from above began to descend.

CHAPTER SEVENTY-SIX

"Rebecca," came a familiar voice from the light, "don't let go!"

"Ian," cried Rebecca as she lifted her face to the sound, only to avert her eyes quickly. The shinning brilliance that emitted from the God/Goddess was blinding. Rebecca tried in vain to connect with the voice.

"Patience," came the prayerful tones of the great one above her. "We are reweaving our world. Do not struggle so. You can become one with us if you wish."

Rebecca, lured by the seductive tones, relaxed and felt her body being drawn into the whole.

"There now, isn't that better?" came the sweet voice of Arabella.

"You're really here," said an awestruck Rebecca.

"Of course I am, and so are you and Peter and Ian and anyone else who chooses to believe. Pray with me now so that we may all rejoin the Gods."

Rebecca closed her eyes and felt a euphoric nothingness fill her body as she became one with the universe. The souls within her body reached towards Rebecca in perfect harmony. They took her heart and healed the pain within.

The light from overhead began to descend again and separate the three adventurers. Rebecca felt herself being lowered to the ground. She looked up and saw that Peter and Arabella had once again become man and woman, but there was still some sort of link holding them together. The light that covered their heads was forming into shimmering crowns.

"My children," came the voice from within the mist, "you have labored all your days in my service and asked nothing. Take from me now the greatest gift that can be bestowed upon those that choose to walk between the worlds. Your search is over. The gifts of the Queen and King now lay within your hearts. Use them wisely and cleave unto one another until your work on this earth is done."

Rebecca watched in respectful silence as Peter and Arabella joined hands and accepted the priceless gifts of Kinging and Queening from the Goddess herself. The babes within her moved gently as if understanding that which an earthbound mortal might question. As the light filled Peter and Arabella's bodies, Rebecca saw that they began to descend slowly. Their feet touched the ancient wood in unison as the lavender mist lightly entered the earth of Old Burying Point.

"But what of Ian? What was his part in all this?" wondered Rebecca frantically as she watched Arabella calmly look at Peter. The smell of lilies filled the air as Arabella spread her arms wide. It was as if the Scotswoman was embracing the whole earth.

"We thank you, Goddess, for your blessings and vow to make ourselves worthy of your sacred trust," said Arabella in a clear voice.

The glowing light about Peter and Arabella swirled through them and then gently descended into the earth, taking the magical aura with it. What it left behind was Professor Peter Hawking and Lady Arabella MacRae miraculously changed but somehow still the same.

The new guardians of Salem Town turned and smiled at Rebecca, Danny and Emily.

"I want the old perfessor," said Emily staring warily at the two figures as they approached her.

"But I am the old 'perfessor,'" said Peter sweeping the six-year-old into his arms as if she weighed nothing. Gone were all the infirmaries of old age and in their place was an energy that made Peter feel as if he could move mountains.

Emily gently touched his face and traced the sides of Peter's cheeks. "Where are your smilies?" she asked studying the old man intensely.

"Smilies?" asked Peter trying to understand the child.

"She means your wrinkles," said Danny looking back and forth from Peter to Arabella in astonishment.

"Why I do believe they're gone," said Arabella with a laugh. "How absolutely wonderful. I feel as if I were twenty again."

"So do I," said Peter tossing Emily into the air and catching her. "What say to a romp through cupid's grove my love?" said Peter setting Emily down and looking at Arabella with a young man's eyes.

"Not so fast, you two," said Rebecca. "What about Ian?"

"Ahh," said Peter searching Rebecca's face with an intensity that frightened her. "I forgot that you haven't wandered down our path. Rebecca, my dear, our boy is quite safe for the time being. The void that swept him away is merely a way station between this world and the many spheres that lie beyond. You can't possible imagine how many different levels there are to this universe. As long as he remains floating in the void no harm can come to him. It is only when he attempts to depart that we must be careful. There is an infinity of possibilities."

"I don't understand," said Rebecca irritated by the calmness that Peter displayed. Couldn't he see that it was getting lighter? What of the special energy that was produced by Old Burying Point on All Saint's Day? Hadn't the dyad said that it provided a focus point for returning souls?

"Yes, my dear, it does," said Arabella reading Rebecca's mind as she lightly touched Peter's arm in an attempt to bring him back to reality. "Peter, there might not be all the time you think there is. What if there are other creatures traveling in the void? A door could open at anytime if one of them chooses to depart. It could sweep Ian along with it into some strange world. We must try to find him now while we still know where he is."

"But that's the whole point," said Peter looking at Rebecca with dismay. "What we saw while the Goddess was blessing us made me realize the vastness of her universe and the smallness of this spot. To try to return Ian to our Salem might result in his destruction. I need time to think of how to anchor him here once his soul has been called. The cry of an unborn child might not be enough."

"I'm beginning to think all of this is some sort of evil nightmare," said Rebecca holding Emily close. The panic that was beginning to course through her was almost unbearable. Better to believe that Ian had never existed than to live with the madness of her grief. Why did she have to lose him to find out what he truly meant to her. The practical Rebecca Love had finally realized that sometimes the things you believe in were more real than anything that you could touch or feel or taste. Nothing was as real to her right now as the silent screams of her beloved lost in some dark land.

"Miss Love, it's going to be all right, really," said Emily trying to comfort the glassy eyed lady who was gripping her tightly. "There is always a miracle. The lady who sometimes comes to our house to make sure Momma is okay has a bumper sticker on her car that says 'expect miracles'. She's really smart and says that she sees miracles all the time."

"That's just a saying, Emily," said Rebecca loosening her grip on the little girl and giving her a gentle hug.

"No it's not," said Emily stubbornly. "Danny and me were in trouble right before you and the perfessor showed up. That crack over there was trying to eat my foot, wasn't it, Danny?"

"Yeah, so what," said Danny embarrassed by Emily's faith in the unseen.

"Well so, I remembered the bumper sticker and asked for a miracle. Danny thought the ground ate my shoe because I hadn't tied it, but you see I had; double knots. I made sure my shoes were tight today because I was planning to throw eggs at the Witch Museum later. I wanted to be able to run away fast. So you see, when my shoe came off it was a miracle. I just let Danny think it wasn't so that he would stop looking so scared."

"I wasn't scared, you jerk," said Danny looking at Emily with love.

"Yes, you were," said Emily wisely. "When my foot got grabbed you turned all white and yelled."

"But, children," said Rebecca looking from one small face to the other, "don't you see? You're both right. When you love somebody enough anything is possible, even miracles. Danny was scared that he might lose Emily. Somehow he found the strength to pull her from the fissure. Not even her tightly tied shoe could stop him. He must have ripped it right off her foot."

"Wow, I must be really strong," said Danny proudly.

"Nothing is stronger than true love," said Arabella as she turned to Rebecca and looked directly into her soul. "Somehow we must hope that the Goddess will accept yours in exchange for Ian. Are you ready, my dear?"

CHAPTER SEVENTY-SEVEN

Rebecca walked towards the ruins of the ancient oak. The courageous beauty that shone from her face transformed the very air about her. Was her love for Ian enough to save him? What of her infatuation for O'Roarke? Would the Goddess count that against her? How little her feelings for O'Roarke mattered now that Ian was in danger. Curse her wayward heart! She had gone from cloistered existence to a femme fatale in the course of a few hours and was still reeling from the transformation. How little she had known of her own nature and its longings.

"Hush now," she whispered to her beating heart as she thought of the caresses her body had received from the dashing Jamie O'Roarke. He had kindled a fire within her that Rebecca knew could never be extinguished. How she wished she could have come to Ian untouched in the mysteries of love. But it was too late for that now. What was done could not be undone no matter what her desires.

Rebecca placed herself in the center of the ruins and closed her eyes. It was strange how empty she felt. It seemed as if the events of the past few days had left her with nothing but memories of something that had happened to a girl she had loved long ago. Where was the passion and the lover that had brought her here? "Gone forever," she thought as she raised her hands to her face. Gone was the mate that should have stood by her side through every storm and joy. Why was it her curse to always be alone? The immensity of her solitude caused a great rage to course through Rebecca and carried her eyes upward.

"If you are all powerful, Goddess of the heavens and earth, then why did you take him from me in the first place? What good are you if all you grant is heartache and loneliness? I am not your slave. I am the child of Magdelene Love who chose a living death because her heart's desire was denied her. I will not be another sacrifice on the altar of grief. Bring back my beloved if you can, but don't ask more of me than I can give. I will not offer my soul up to you now or ever. If you are truly the benevolent Goddess you claim to be, my love and loyalty should be enough."

"And it is, my priestess," came a whisper from high above Rebecca's head. "I do not ask that you become my slave. You are my beloved handmaiden in whom I have entrusted a great gift. It was because of your strength that you were chosen."

"My Goddess," said Rebecca quietly, "I cannot carry this burden alone. Please don't ask it of me."

"To reject the gift of the Goddess is to abandon the soul you prize so highly, my daughter. Think well upon your words. If you wish, I will relieve you of your burden, but never again will my gifts be yours."

"Then it is a choice of doing your bidding or losing my soul?" asked Rebecca in a steady voice.

"Yes, my Priestess, it is as you say. Even I cannot promise you the return of your heart's desire. There are other forces at work against which I have no power. The babes within you, yet to be born, are two who will battle against the dark forces that have plagued mankind down through the ages. Reject them if you must, but think well upon the cost."

"What can I do?" said Rebecca as she sank to the ground amongst the ruins. "Use me if you must, oh Goddess, but please help me. I am out of courage and strength."

"Whist now, lassie," said a familiar voice from behind her. "I thought you were a brave one. What's all this carrying on about?"

CHAPTER SEVENTY-EIGHT

"Ian," cried Rebecca as she whirled around. The faint shadow of the Scotsman could be seen leaning towards her with outstretched arms.

Rebecca turned towards her beloved and tried to touch him, but to her dismay her searching fingers touched only the sunbeams shimmering throughout his transparent body.

"Is it really you, my love?" asked the desperate girl yearning to feel his strong arms about her.

"Yes, my dearest, it is," said the Scotsman looking about him in wonder. "How strange everything looks from here. There seems to be some sort of curtain standing between us."

"It is the veil," said Arabella, approaching the tree cautiously. Her greatest fear was that she might do something to cause her nephew to disappear forever. "Ian lad, can you see clearly or is the mist becoming thicker?"

"I seem to be moving farther away with every passing moment," said Ian trying to sound calm.

"The veil is becoming thicker. I fear that soon it will hide him entirely unless we do something quickly," said Peter grasping Arabella's hand.

"Rebecca, call the Goddess to you. Ask her to give her your strength," shouted Arabella as the wind around them began to blow loudly.

Rebecca closed her eyes and breathed a silent prayer to the Goddess. Gone was her pride. In its place was the voice of pure love beseeching the powers of the universe to rend the veil that lay between Rebecca and Ian.

The wind played with the hem of her skirts and Rebecca found herself being lifted from the ground in a violent wind devil. She battled against it with all her might but it was no use. The girl was thrown from the spot where Jamie O'Roarke had made his home. The last thing she saw was the ruins of the ancient oak swirling into a great column.

"Hold tight, lassie," said a dreamlike voice as Rebecca struggled up through the layers of her unconscious.

"I've lost him," she whispered as she opened her eyes.

"There now, sweetheart," said Ian stroking her brow, "you should know that there's no getting rid of a highlander once you have him."

Rebecca's eyes flew open as she heard Ian's voice and felt the touch of his arms holding her.

"My love," she said in a weakened voice as she attempted to sit up. The pain in her head forced Rebecca to lay back in Ian's arms.

"Rest easy now, lass. You've had a hard fall. I don't think anything's broken except maybe that hard head of yours. You are a stubborn one, my love. Imagine scolding the Goddess like that when all she was trying to do was help you. It was downright ungrateful of you," said Ian with a smile that caused the dimples in each ruddy cheek to flash brightly.

"A lot you know about it, Ian MacRae," said Rebecca struggling to sit up. "If it weren't for me and my temper you might still be riding about in some cloud right now screaming for help. And as long as we're talking about stubbornness let's not forget who got us into this mess in the first place. I've heard that Duncan MacRae only took the route that put him into Jamie O'Roarke's path because it might save him a few shillings. He dug in his heels and declared that the shorter way would get them home more quickly and win them a bonus from the wool trade. If he had taken the longer, safer route this whole adventure could have been avoided."

"And you would have never met me, my darling." said Ian planting a kiss on Rebecca's quivering lips. How lovely she was in her fury. Not even the large bump that was beginning to form on her forehead could detract from Rebecca's allure.

"Oh Ian, what are we doing?" gasped Rebecca as it began to dawn on her that the man holding her was not a vision. He was real, as real as the sun and the moon.

"Just being ourselves, I'm afraid, my darling. Something tells me that the ship we sail will be rocked by many a stormy sea, but don't you worry. I have a feeling that neither of us would be happy any other way."

"I suppose you're right," said Rebecca struggling to her feet and standing beside her beloved.

The swirling air about them had centered itself on O'Roarke's oak. Arabella and Peter were watching as the splinters of livewood circled around the most hallowed spot on Old Burying Point.

"Do you think they will fly away like the house in 'The Wizard of Oz?'" asked Emily as she shyly looked at Ian.

"I don't know, lassie," said Ian as he held Rebecca tight. Thank heaven all she had was a bump on her head and a bit of bad temper to go with it. When Ian had seen her lying on the ground as still as a corpse, he had almost given into despair. Rebecca would never be able to guess how much she meant to him. Rebecca Love had given him back his very being, his soul, and his life.

"Look," cried Danny as the livewood began to blur before their eyes. "What is it doin'?"

"It seems to be taking shape," said Peter holding out his hand. In his weathered palm rested a few splinters, part of the staff that had contained the spirit of the wood nymph Eva. The pieces of wood were dancing some sort of celestial jig that made them seem alive.

"Look at the perfessor's hand, Em," said Danny as he watched the motion of the livewood with delight.

Ian and Rebecca laughed at the children's amusement, but the smiles on their faces froze as the party of watchers turned their attention back toward the oak of the Goddess. The splinters that had formed the tree were dancing too, but their motions took on a far more sinister and dangerous aspect, Huge branches were cavorting around them destroying anything that stood in their path. Several power lines had gone down. The resulting sparks that began to fly from the live wires were dangerously close to them."

"Danny, Emily, don't move!" said Ian as he watched the cavorting wires come within a few inches of the children.

Then, as suddenly as the wind had been born, it died. Ian and Rebecca watched in amazement as the shattered oak reformed and now stood before them as tall and proud as it had ever been. Peter gave a gasp as the splinters in his hand shook suddenly and dove to the ground. Above them other shards of the oak rejoined their brothers. The livewood staff that had been destroyed now rested in Professor Peter Hawking's hand, as sturdy as the day he had found it.

CHAPTER SEVENTY-NINE

"Watch your step," said Ian as he gently lifted first Emily and then Rebecca over the wires that sparked about them. The whole graveyard was filled with the hissing and sputtering sound of live energy.

Peter rubbed the livewood between his hands and watched the sparking electricity enter the ground of Old Burying Point. "Just what we need," he said with tears of laughter running down his cheeks. "More energy in this place."

Rebecca, realizing what he had just said, burst into giggles that were echoed by the rest of the company. That was how the Salem police department found them as the screaming sirens surrounded the graveyard.

"Well, Professor Hawking," said patrolman Michael Beals as he surveyed the Point, "what have you been up to?"

"Nothing, I swear," said Peter as he burst into a fresh gale of laughter.

"It's true, officer," said Arabella trying to suppress her own merriment, "we were just taking a stroll through Old Burying Point when *woosh!*, this terrible wind came along and knocked everything down around our ears."

"We're telling the truth, honest, Officer Beals," said Danny holding Emily's hand and giving her the evil eye. If she started chattering about ghosts and fairies they would all be taken in for questioning for sure.

369

"And what are you doing here, Master Martin?" said the policeman taking in the odd assortment of citizens that stood before him.

"It's like the lady said, sir," said Danny politely. "We were just walking around the old graveyard. You should listen to the tales the perfessor can tell about it. They're really scary."

"I'm sure they are," said the policeman surveying the damage done to the old graveyard. It was certainly more than the suspects standing before him were capable of. What a night it had been!

"Did you see anyone else roaming about the Point this morning?" said Michael Beals turning his attention towards Ian. The officer could not recall ever seeing either the tall well built man, or the older woman around Salem before. But that was really meaningless this time of year. Since the parade on Friday the thirteenth there must have been thousands of strangers taking in the sights of Salem. These two were probably nothing but a few more tourists.

"No, officer," said Ian giving the patrolman a disarming smile.

"Well then," said Michael Beals giving a sigh, "be sure you watch your step. In fact it might be a good idea if you stayed right here while the electric company clears this up."

"Right you are, Michael," said Peter Hawking slapping the young patrolman on the back. "Say now how is that lovely wife of yours and the new baby? It was a little girl wasn't it?"

"Why yes, Professor," said Michael, his chest swelling with pride. "The most beautiful little girl that ever was born. We named her Eva Marie after her grandmother."

"Eva, what a lovely name," said Arabella warming to the handsome young officer. "Do you have a picture of her?"

"As a matter of fact I do!" said Michael, quickly pulling a small snapshot from his wallet.

"Why, her hair is like spun gold, Peter," said Arabella with delight," and look at those eyes, they shine like emeralds. Oh, she's destined to break many a heart. What a delight she must be to you."

"Most of the time, Ma'am, most of the time. But she has quite a mind of her own always toddling this way and that. Why only yesterday she escaped us and almost drove us mad with worry. You can't imagine our relief when we found her sitting under a tree in our backyard. She was singing and talking to it as if it were alive. She's quite a handful I can tell you that."

As they watched the men from the electric company carefully clear away the sparking wires and contain the damage, officer Beals took out his handkerchief and wiped his brow.

"You look tired, Michael," said Rebecca. She and Michael Beals had gone through school together and were old friends.

"It's just post Halloween syndrome," said Michael with a weary smile. "I don't know why, but this has been the worst year for trouble that we've ever had. Usually there is the regular things like eggs thrown at the Witch Museum and graffiti on the statues, but this year was different. It began just after the party at the Hawthorne hotel let out. All night long people kept calling in reporting strange sounds and ghostly sightings. At first we thought they were pranksters. It wasn't until the mayor's wife called complaining that she had seen pirates drinking rum in her garden that we took it seriously."

"It does sound strange, officer," said Peter, "but I've always known Elizabeth Burns to be a sober and sensible lady. Pirates you say? How curious."

"Not so curious as the reports from Collins Cove. Three different times last night we had to send a patrol car to answer complaints. It seems that there were screams coming from the caves. And to make it worse, every time one of us tried to investigate, a huge owl would attack us. My partner had no choice but to try to scare it away with a few shots. That did no good at all. The bird had no fear. Finally the owl headed out to sea towards the lights of some ship anchored in the harbor."

"How fascinating," said Arabella giving Peter a wink. "Perhaps there is something to the rumors about Salem. It certainly seems to be very busy around here on Halloween."

"Well now," said Michael Beals, "I've lived here all my life and have yet to see a ghost. I think it's all in people's minds. All this foolishness about witches and pirates might be good for the tourist industry but it has no basis in fact. I'm sure that everything has a logical explanation."

"Of course it does, Michael," said Rebecca. "You're quite right. It was probably some out of towners playing a joke. As long as no one was hurt it was really quite harmless."

"That's true, Becky," said the policeman giving Rebecca her schoolgirl name. "But I wish they would go somewhere else to have their fun. And besides, look at this mess. It was a lucky thing that none of you were hurt or killed by falling branches. Oh well, I guess we got off lucky at that. Now then it looks like they're done. Professor, Rebecca," said Michael Beals touching in hat in a rather old fashioned gesture, "enjoy your tour."

CHAPTER EIGHTY

"That was close," said Danny sitting down on the ground and leaning against an old headstone.

"I wonder what they really saw around here last night?" said Rebecca looking at Ian in wonder. "Do you suppose that the veil was so thin that they were catching glimpses of us? Jamie and I were in a tavern with a group of pirates and they were drinking rum. And what about the owl? Could it have been old Nicodemus?"

"I doubt it, sweetheart," said Ian. "And no matter what it was, I think it's time to begin to put all this behind us. I don't know about you, but I'm glad to be home."

"You're right, but it's going to be so hard to let go of what we've been through and go on," said Rebecca. "I've changed. I know there is no going back from what has happened. Like it or not I'm a different Rebecca."

"I like what I see just fine," said Ian grasping her around the waist and looking out over Salem harbor. "But there is something we must settle before we can go on. All that has happened in the past few hours can either bind us together forever or drive us apart. Don't you see? If we hang onto our adventures in old Salem and romanticize them, the memories will become more powerful with each passing day. Soon all that is ours right here and now will be lost. There is no way the sameness of everyday life can compare to the adventures we've been through. And there is no way, my love, that I can live up to the legend of Jamie O'Roarke. You must choose one of us. Living, the pirate Jamie O'Roarke is a formidable foe. Dead, he can't be beaten."

"But Ian, it's always been you, don't you know that," said Rebecca throwing her arms around the Scotsman's neck. "When I thought I had lost you I wanted to die, too. There was nothing left for me, no joy, no hope. It was only the thought of our child that held me back from throwing myself into the void after you. Oh my beloved, never for one moment think that I don't love you above all else."

"And what of O'Roarke?" said Ian taking Rebecca's arms from around his neck and walking away from her towards the stand of holly trees.

"Jamie is a man who will always fascinate a woman, but that doesn't mean I love him. He is like a flame that attracts and yet repels. I know now that to stay too close to his flame would destroy me."

"But do you love him?" shouted Ian not caring who heard.

Rebecca, taken aback by the violence of his feelings, closed her eyes and turned away from Ian. How could she ever ask him to be a father to Jamie's son if Ian felt this way. Better to try to manage alone than to watch the cruel war that would be played out in her own home. She had two children to care for, one the only son of the Laird Ian MacRae, and the other the miracle child of that will o' the wisp, Jamie O'Roarke. Even now Rebecca felt that the children who would spring from her womb would be very different. Ian's child would be a child of light, grasping at life as if it were his birthright to be handed all good things. Jamie's son would be different. He was a child of the night without a mortal father to protect him. It would be up to Rebecca to be both father and mother to such a child. If Ian could not accept Jamie, then how could he love and nurture his son?

Turning slowly to her beloved she stared at Ian and whispered a silent prayer. What she said now would follow her all the rest of her days. "Ian, my love, what I must tell you now I don't expect you to believe unless you love me enough to have blind faith in me." With that, the girl poured out all her feelings and fears about the future and Ian's part in it. The tears that flowed from her eyes could only be a mere echo of the torment her soul was going through. Rebecca felt as if her very being was being torn in two by what she must do. Oh why had she been handed such a task?

Ian, taken aback by the torment in the girl's face, felt humbled. What were his fears compared to what Rebecca must soon endure? Somewhere deep within him he was afraid that he would always have doubts about Rebecca's true feelings. He knew that she believed that she loved Ian above all things, but she had not seen Rebecca through Ian's eyes. He was a man not a saint. And what of O'Roarke's child? Rebecca was right to be afraid. Ian could promise to guard both little ones, but the son of Jamie O'Roarke would always stand between them. He was a living reminder of the stolen moments she had shared with the great pirate.

Ian turned back to Rebecca and beheld her tear stained face. His heart, strained beyond endurance, could no longer be denied. "My love," he said as he opened his arms to embrace her, "come what may we will face it together. Don't be afraid. I will always be here."

Rebecca rushed to Ian and felt herself being smothered in his powerful embrace. Her tears of sorrow had turned to tears of joy as Rebecca's lips met those of Laird Ian MacRae.

"Don't be afraid, my beauty," he said as they stood with hearts beating as one, "I will never leave you. No pirate in the world can take you from me, this I swear. And as for what is to come, it might be fun. Think of it lassie, two small hellions running about Salem Common or traveling to castle MacRae. I'm thinking that it will be quite a clamjamfry."

"A what?" laughed Rebecca as she stroked Ian's face.

"A clamjamfry lass. That's a happy battle amongst men. It's just the sort of thing O'Roarke would have loved, damn his hide."

"Now there you go talking about Jamie again," laughed Rebecca poking Ian in the ribs.

"Why so I was, lass, so I was," laughed the Scotsman ruefully.

———————

Ian and Rebecca walked arm and arm back through the holly thicket. The sunlight was now shining on O'Roarke's oak with an intensity that made its leaves shimmer like gold. Peter and Arabella strolled around Old Burying Point. They were lost in intimate conversation. The light of the early morning sunshine formed an enchanted circle around them.

"It looks like I won't have to worry about Aunt Arabella being alone much longer," said Ian watching the comfortable familiarity that passed between his widowed Aunt and the confirmed bachelor.

"Isn't it wonderful," sighed Rebecca. "I've never seen Peter look so young. Why he's almost boyish."

"Miss Love, Mr. MacRae," said Danny in an exasperated voice, "could you tell Emily one more time that the fairy and Captain O'Roarke are gone for good. She won't go home until she hears it from you."

"But they're not, Danny," said Emily tugging at the hand that Danny had imprisoned in his. "Can't you hear the sound?"

"What sound, dear?" said Rebecca stooping down in front of the little girl and searching her face.

"The twinkling sound, Miss Love. It's the same sound we heard right before that fairy showed up."

"I keep telling her it's just Laurie Cabot's windchimes, but she won't leave. Emily, you're driving me nuts," said Danny.

"Hush now, children," said Ian as the soft wind blowing from Collin's Cove brushed their faces. "I hear something too. It's coming from O'Roarke's oak. Emily, can you hear that?" said Ian looking at the small girl.

"Of course I can," said Emily, "that's what I've been trying to tell you. There are bells in the leaves, Danny." Emily ran towards the tree and began to search frantically for the source of the sound. She dived into a pile of red gold leaves at the base of the tree and came up laughing holding something shiny in her hand.

"See, Danny, I told you I heard something. The fairy left us a present."

Peter and Arabella joined the rest of the party beneath the oak and examined the round shiny objects in the little girl's hand.

"Why these are doubloons," said Peter turning the coins over in his hand, "and worth a fortune by the look of them. Finders keepers, young lady."

Ian MacRae held Rebecca close as the sun glinted off the old doubloons. "Long live the legend of Jamie O'Roarke," he said looking into her bonny blue eyes.

"And long live our love," said Rebecca turning her smiling lips to him.

EPILOGUE

HALLOWEEN 2000

CHAPTER EIGHTY-ONE

The portrait that hung over the white marble mantelpiece was Ian MacRae's greatest work. It was of two small boys, one dressed in black, one in white. The child dressed in white had dark red hair and emerald green eyes. His body, though only that of a five-year-old, showed promise of remarkable height and power. There was something almost mystical in the way his eyes scanned the horizon. It was as if the child saw something only he could understand. In contrast, the smaller lad in black, holding his brother's hand, was looking directly out of the portrait. His eyes seemed to challenge any who dared view his countenance. The boy had dark brown eyes and golden blond hair. There was a roguish dimple hovering near his smiling lips that made one think that he had just told a joke and was waiting eagerly for a response. These were the sons of Rebecca Love MacRae.

"Christian, Liam, hurry up. Grandpa Peter won't wait for us if we're late," cried Rebecca as she looked up the massive mahogany staircase. It was many years since Ian had moved Rebecca from her small cottage to the large Italianate mansion on Salem Common. The four floors of the beautiful structure were furnished with antiques that Rebecca and Ian had lovely collected during their travels through Europe. There were also several precious objects gleaned from the old Celtic castle in Scotland. Castle MacRae had now been completely restored, thanks to the success of Ian's work. His portraits of the people and places of Salem, past and present, had caused a sensation in the art world and brought about riches that Rebecca had never dreamed of.

Peter and Arabella now divided their time between Salem and the Isle of Skye. Rebecca would never forget the ecstasy on Peter Hawking's face as he left for Scotland. The old Professor who had always dreamed of touring the castles of the British Isles was now married to a lady who owned the great Castle MacRae. Rebecca kept a picture of Peter and Arabella, standing in front of castle MacRae, in a large silver frame on her dresser. Never had Peter Hawking looked more dashing. He was garbed in the full dress kilts that he had received from Arabella as a wedding gift. The gleam of the dagger tucked in his high knit stockings matched the one in his eyes.

"Boys, you simply must hurry. The sun is beginning to set." Tumbling down the stairs came two five-year-old boys. Red haired Christian was dressed as a Jedi Knight complete with an official Luke Skywalker light saber, and his brother was decked out as a pirate, sporting an eye patch and phony hook.

"Why, Liam, I thought you were going as a Power Ranger," said Rebecca in surprise. It was not the first time that the her tow headed son had changed his mind about his Halloween costume. He had spent the whole day rummaging through the attic where Rebecca stored all the odds and ends of the household. One corner of the cluttered attic had been entirely devoted to what Rebecca called "Liam's treasure hunts." The small boy had a passion for scavenging through the neighborhood on trash day and dragging home "treasures."

"Oh, Mom," said her sophisticated five-year-old son, "don't you know that Power Rangers are old stuff? This is much cooler."

With that, Liam whipped out his plastic sword and stuck Christian in the ribs. In response, the larger boy drew his light saber on Liam and they began to duel.

"Stop it, both of you, or there will be no Halloween," said Rebecca trying not to laugh. Both boys immediately sheathed their weapons and ran toward their mother in panic. "We're sorry, Mama," said Christian hugging Rebecca around the waist.

"It's all right," said Rebecca ruffling his ruddy hair lovingly, "but let's save the roughhousing for another time. Out the door with the both of you." Rebecca watched in exasperation as Liam gave Christian one last poke with his sword. How she wished Ian did not have to travel so much promoting his work. The boys, especially Liam, needed a full-time father.

The lights on Salem Common twinkled as Christian and Liam ran ahead of Rebecca. The two boy's frantic pace slowed to a respectful silence as Rebecca and her sons approached the Witch's Magic Circle. The sacred rites were taking place near the bandstand. The Temple of Nine Wells, a Salem Wiccan religious congregation, were celebrating Samhein. It was the eve of the Celtic new year. The magic circle ritual would be followed with a candlelight walk as soon as the sun had set. Rebecca and the boys paused and joined the other spectators as the worshippers of the Goddess concluded their rituals. Rebecca had often thought of attending one of their rites, but had been filled with fear at the thought. One journey close to the Goddess had been enough to last her a lifetime. In fact there were days when Rebecca had to concentrate with all her might to recall the events that had given her the life she knew now. It all seemed like some sort of dream that had happened to someone else. Rebecca would have forgotten the whole thing if it were not for the two boys holding her hands. "But how can these two scamps be denied?" thought Rebecca as she looked at the serious expression on her son's faces. Christian and Liam might resemble their respective fathers, but there was quite a bit of herself in them too. "Thank goodness for that!" breathed Rebecca quietly. If not for their shared similarities, the two boys would have been engaged in battle constantly.

Rebecca knew that deep down they shared many of her traits. They both loved to roam the graveyards of Salem and listen to Grandpa Peter's tales of old Salem Town, when witches and pirates roamed the streets. And each had a touch of Rebecca's clairvoyance. It never ceased to amuse her when a neighbor or stranger would come up to one of the boys and thank him for finding a lost object or reminding the adult of some forgotten event. Christian always seemed pleased with the praise while Liam would often act as if he didn't know what the grateful adult was talking about. Rebecca often wondered if O'Roarke's small son weren't hiding other powers of which she had no knowledge. He seemed to be able to read her mind, especially when she became weary of his constant antics. The small boy would stop whatever he was doing and put his arms around his mother's neck or sit in her lap as if performing an act of contrition. And then there was the almost eerie way the two of them could play or communicate without saying a word!

"Momma, why are you smiling?" said Liam as if echoing her thoughts.

"Oh, I was just thinking of how terrific the two of you look tonight," said Rebecca realizing that perhaps it was time she started to practice some sort of screening of her thoughts. She really should stop by Laurie Cabot's "Crow Haven Corner" and ask her if there was some sort of V chip available for a young mother of two mind reading five-year-olds. The followers of the Goddess in Salem were already quite aware of her children's special talents. More than once Rebecca had been approached with an offer of friendship and advice. But Rebecca had chosen to keep her distance and follow her path alone. She hoped that she was doing the right thing. If only Ian were here. There were times when she felt so alone.

CHAPTER EIGHTY-TWO

The Closing Circle celebration finished just as the last glow of the spectacular red sunset left the sky. The Common was filled with small costumed figures scampering under the twinkling lights towards one of the many events being offered around Salem.

"Come on, Momma, the lady over there promised me some magic dust if we talked to her," said Liam pulling Rebecca towards the "ask a witch" tent situated to the left of the bandstand.

"It's not really magic dust," said Christian regarding his brother with scorn. "It's just that sparkly stuff that you get at 'Jokers Wild.'"

"So what," said Liam angrily, "it sounds like fun. Besides you never let us talk to the witches. Why not, Momma?"

"You know I don't want you talking to anyone who is a stranger, young man," said Rebecca, "especially this time of year. Most of the visitors to Salem are nice people, but it only takes one dangerous one to hurt a little boy. Liam, you must promise to stop roaming about without telling me. If I lost you it would kill me."

"Would it kill you if you lost me, too?" asked Christian, already aware of his mother's more protective attitude towards Liam.

"Of course it would, my love," said Rebecca hugging her little ones close. "Don't worry, Liam, you'll get plenty of chance to talk to a real witch up at Old Burying Point. The Wax Museum had hired a few of them to roam the graveyard tonight. I hear they're even bringing their broomsticks!"

"And can we stop by the 'Hall of Haunts' on Derby street and watch them bring Houdini back to life?" asked Christian.

"Oh, that's about as real as the witch's magic dust," scoffed Liam, getting his own back for his brother's teasing.

"I'm afraid he's right," said Rebecca steering her sons through the Common and turning them towards Sweet Scoops. "Besides, it's time to stop for Emily and go to the Point. You wouldn't want to be late for Grandpa Peter's lecture and the real ghost tour now would you?"

"Will Danny be there, too?" asked Liam, barely able to contain his excitement.

"Yes, he will," said Rebecca wishing once again that Ian were home. All day long she'd had the strangest sensation of being watched.

———

Fourteen-year-old Danny and eleven-year old Emily had changed quite a bit in the past five years. Peter Hawking had taken the two children under his wing and provided them with a security they had never dreamed of. The sale of the gold doubloons had brought enough to help Mrs. Martin and give her some happiness for the first time in her life. Little Emily's asthma had disappeared soon after Peter and Arabella had provided the Martin family with a small home of their own and a modest yearly income. But the highlight of Danny's life was his yearly forays around the ancient graveyards of Salem with the old professor.

Rebecca and the children dodged the overfilled Salem Trolley as they crossed Essex street and walked past the Peabody-Essex museum towards Old Burying Point. Rebecca had deliberately avoided going down the small brick lined path that led to several of the many museums that were open all night. The ancient rites of Samhein had taken on the flavor of a carnival. There was the usual mixture of ghosts, goblins and witches wandering the enchanted streets. It was strange, but ever since Rebecca had visited the real site of the witch trials she had lost her enthusiasm for celebrating All Hallow's Eve. Rebecca's small sons, however, fit right in with the other children who ran excitedly from exhibit to exhibit. A small "princess" almost knocked Christian over in her enthusiasm to show her parents the smudgy gravestone rubbing she had made of Judge Hathorne's gravestone.

"Momma, why is Salem so special?" asked Christian as he watched the little girl running among the stones with envy.

"Because you're here," said Rebecca evasively as she looked about. The strange feeling that had haunted her all day had suddenly become stronger. She could not shake an ominous feeling of foreboding. To Rebecca's great relief, Emily spied Peter.

"There they are," said the eleven-year-old pushing her black cat mask over her face. "Let's sneak up on Danny and scare him."

With that the three children slipped away from Rebecca and attacked the unsuspecting tour guides with laughter. Peter, Arabella and Danny each claimed a child and gave hugs all around.

"Where's your mother?" said the still lovely Arabella. Her sea green dress was interspersed with silver threads. The gown gave her the impression of a land-locked mermaid whenever she moved.

"Here I am," said Rebecca drawing her dark red velvet cloak about her. The mild afternoon air had become chilly with the setting of the sun. How she wished Peter and Arabella were alone right now so that she could speak to them privately. The force that had begun to surround Rebecca was moving closer.

"Good, now we can begin," said Peter eyeing his two small step grandsons warily. It was only last year that Christian had insisted on going home before the tour was finished. Something had frightened the child into an almost hysterical state. Liam, on the other hand, had been delighted with every spooky tale and flickering light.

"Samhein is a pagan festival celebrating the eve of the Celtic new year. The ancient worshippers of the Goddess and Gods believed that on this night the veil between the living world and the spirit world became so thin that anything was possible. Even today the worshippers of Wicca gather together on this, their most sacred night, and celebrate the power of the Goddess. Many of the customs of that ancient time still exist, such as storytelling, trick or treating and gathering around bonfires until dawn. The harvest is gathered and the year is turning towards the dark times to come. On this night we acknowledge the power of the stars and the elements over us all."

As Peter's voice droned on, Rebecca separated herself from the crowd and wandered towards the old stand of holly trees that stood on the edge of the burying ground. She almost stumbled over the still gleaming stone of Rosie O'Roarke in the dark. Rebecca cleared away the brush that had grown up around the ancient stone and lovingly traced the etched carving with her fingers.

"What's that, Momma?" said a small but surprisingly deep voice behind her. Liam James MacRae had an unsettling habit of appearing out of nowhere at the most inconvenient times.

"Why, it's just a gravestone," said Rebecca trying to keep her voice steady. The last thing she wanted was for Liam to start asking questions now. The fact that Rosie O'Roarke, not Arabella MacRae, was the child's true grandmother had never dawned upon Rebecca until this very moment.

"It's so far away from everything else," said Liam touching the white marble delicately. "Is it because it's so pretty?"

"I suppose so," said Rebecca looking at her little pirate lovingly. "Don't you want to hear Grandpa's lecture?"

"Oh, I've heard it before," said Liam sitting down at the base of the stone and staring at the full moon overhead. "I'd much rather look around on my own like you do."

"I do that a lot, don't I," laughed Rebecca as she sat next to her small son and put her arm around him. Liam had a strange way of comforting her at the oddest moments. He was just a small boy, but even at his tender age the manliness of his spirit was strong.

"I like it up here," sighed Liam listening to the Halloween sounds around him.

"So do I," said Rebecca feeling at peace for the first time all day.

"Momma, can we visit the pirate museum, just you and me? I'm tired of the tour. Could we please?"

"Why not?" said Rebecca tousling her son's bright hair and thinking not for the first time of how charming he could be.

"You wait right there while I tell the others," said Liam jumping to his feet and hurrying off before his mother could change her mind.

"Be sure to tell Grandpa to have your brother home by midnight," cried Rebecca as she watched her little pirate in sneakers disappear through the thicket.

CHAPTER EIGHTY-THREE

"Har Har, me fine beauty, so you dare to enter our world," chuckled the old man dressed up as a pirate as he held the door open to the New England Pirate Museum, for Rebecca and Liam.

"If only you knew," thought Rebecca as she stared up at the black skull and crossbones that was mounted over the entrance. Inside the small museum Rebecca and Liam joined the rest of the tourists as their guide led them from exhibit to exhibit. They learned that New England's first great explorer, Captain John Smith, came to Salem searching for gold to pay his men. The venerable New Englander had stated that "privateers in time of war are a nursery for pirates against a peace." They also learned that the financial partner of the famous Captain Kidd had been none other than the Earl of Bellomont, Governor of Massachusetts, New Hampshire and New York.

"Now," continued their guide, "let me show you something that will amaze you. Cape Ann itself was the home for many well-known pirates. This recreation of the Blue Anchor Tavern in Lynn shows the famous judge, Cotton Mather, consorting with such dangerous local pirates as Jack Quelch and of course the notorious Captain Jamie O'Roarke."

Rebecca let out a gasp as she gazed at the life-size wax replica of Jamie O'Roarke complete with a noggin of rum in his hand. The artist who had formed the statue had done a masterful job.

"The likeness of Captain O'Roarke," continued their guide, "is quite accurate thanks to a certain tavern wench named Melinda Briggs. The lady went on to marry the respectable magistrate, Isaiah Wolf, but she kept many momentos of her former profession. It seems that Mistress Briggs had been on quite intimate terms with our friend Jamie O'Roarke the pirate. Many years after her death a descendant of Melinda's found a small locket that had been tossed in an old sea chest. It was buried beneath some clothing that must have been put in there in more modern times. Standing before you is Jamie O'Roarke as he actually looked in the year 1695. This was, of course, at the time of his famous trial."

"Was he hanged,?" asked a portly man in a red devil costume.

"Oh, no sir," continued the guide warming to the story. "Captain Jamie O'Roarke received a full pardon and went on to become a privateer. He was one of the first men to open up the famous trade routes to China and Russia in the new world. You might say that he was the father of Salem's great age of sail."

"Momma, that's the man with the bird," said Liam staring at the likeness of Jamie O'Roarke in wonder. The resemblance between the man and boy was remarkable. From the gold in their hair and deep brown of their eyes, down to the gracefulness of their muscular bodies and twinkling dimples, they were mirror images. Rebecca had forgotten the forceful physical impact that Jamie could have on her. Could it be that she still loved him despite her protestations to Ian? How could she be in love with a man who had disappeared from her life so long ago? What she was clinging to was nothing but a dream. Jamie O'Roarke had gone away with a vision of the sea and distant ports in his head. The faraway cities of St. Petersburg and Hong Kong had beckoned to him even as he kissed her farewell. Even if they met again it would not be the same. In the slow relentless march of time she had become a different woman just as he had become a different man. Any hope of recapturing whatever she had with Jamie O'Roarke was nothing but a hopeless dream. Jamie had been dead for almost three hundred years. And what of Ian? She loved him, she knew she did! It was only the insistent shaking of her arm by her small son that broke the magic circle of love, solitude and shade that had descended upon Rebecca.

"The bird, Momma, the bird," repeated Liam in a desperate effort to get his mother's attention.

"Oh yes, he's quite nice," said Rebecca trying to regain her senses and focus on what her son was saying.

"No, Momma, he's not nice," said Liam staring at the replica of old Nicodemus that was perched on Jamie O'Roarke's shoulder.

"What are you talking about?" said Rebecca grabbing Liam's shoulders as the rest of the tour advanced to the next exhibit.

"That's the man with the bird who plays down in the caves."

"What's this all about, sweetheart?" asked Rebecca having to remind herself that Liam was still a very small boy.

"There's a man who lives in the caves in Collin's Cove. It's right near where they have the bonfire tonight. That's the bird who lives with him. The man talks to me, but whenever anyone else comes near he disappears. I tried to show him to Christian but the bird chased him away."

"Did the man tell you his name?" asked Rebecca, sitting down on a nearby stone bench to keep from collapsing.

"No, Momma, he just said he was a friend. He also said I wasn't to tell you about him because you might cry. Why did he say that?"

"I don't know, darling," said Rebecca. The intuition that sleeps in every woman's heart suddenly awoke a hopeful dread within Rebecca.

CHAPTER EIGHTY-FOUR

Rebecca's eyes sought the darkening heavens as she and Liam hurried towards Collins Cove. Perhaps Liam's visions of Jamie O'Roarke were only the result of his psychic powers. Rebecca had known for quite some time that her blond haired son had the gift of second sight. There had certainty been enough forceful energy in the shade of Jamie O'Roarke to cause some sort of celestial aftershock. Perhaps that was what Liam had seen.

Salem Common was alive with excitement as Liam and Rebecca retraced their steps. The revelers from the Monster Mash Bash, being held at the Hawthorne Hotel, could be seen through the windows dancing with wild abandon. The sound of the music was echoed by the many other parties being held around the Common. There was even a group of Halloween carolers going from door to door demanding treats.

"Hurry, Momma, we don't want to miss the lighting of the bonfire," said Liam as he urged his mother across Washington Square and turned down Forrester Street. The bright yellow of Mrs. Maloon's house was a cheery sight. As usual, the Maloon family had decorated their seventeenth century house with skeletons and black cats. The two carved pumpkins that guarded the entranceway were works of art. Rebecca waved to Mrs. Maloon as she and Liam hurried past. The massive tree that guarded the house stretched its limbs upward towards the ever blackening sky. Rebecca looked at it and felt a sudden shiver go through her body. There was something about the tree that beckoned her to sit beneath its branches. Once again the strange sensation of being watched filled Rebecca with fear.

"There they are!" shouted Liam as he spied a group of Salemites heading towards the beach with torches.

"Liam, come back!" cried Rebecca as her small but swift son took off after the revelers. Rebecca realized she was just wasting her breath as she watched Liam, oblivious to her cries, being swallowed up in the crowd. Rebecca began to run. She was afraid that she might lose sight of him. She could feel the beating of her heart match the sound of her footsteps pounding the brick pavement. As she turned the corner onto Briggs street, Rebecca caught sight of Liam holding aloft a torch. Walking next to him was Will Montana, a well-known storyteller in the Salem area. The devilish look on her son's face told Rebecca that man and boy were swapping some sort of Halloween lore. Either that or Will was telling Liam about the secret passages and smuggler's treasures that were rumored to be buried in the Cove. "That's all I need," thought Rebecca seeing the look in Liam's bright eyes.

To her great surprise it was Liam she heard leading the conversation as she caught up with them. "Thank you for taking care of my son, Will," said Rebecca as she firmly took hold of Liam's hand. "One more stunt like that, Liam James MacRae, and we're going home."

"He was no bother, I assure you," said Will looking over Liam's head at Rebecca. "In fact I found Liam's story quite interesting."

"What story?" said Rebecca looking at her son warily. There was no telling what he might have said to the unsuspecting man.

"Why, his story about the fairy and the pirate," said Will surprised at Rebecca's attitude. The child had a remarkably creative imagination.

"Oh yes, that story," said Rebecca firmly taking Liam's arm. "Give Mr. Montana back his torch, sweetheart, you know Momma doesn't let you handle fire." Liam reluctantly handed the flaming torch back to Will and smiled up at his mother.

"I'm sorry, Momma, I won't run away again. Please let me watch the bonfire." The heartbreakingly sweet look in Liam's eyes almost brought Rebecca to tears as she hugged him.

"Of course you can watch the bonfire. Just stay close to me. And Liam," said Rebecca as they watched Will rejoin the large group of adventurers, "what is all this about fairies and pirates?"

"Oh just something I dreamt," said Liam with a faraway look in his eyes.

"What was your dream about?" asked Rebecca.

"It was about a great big pirate and a little fairy, only she wasn't like the tooth fairy. She liked the pirate a lot and kept teasing him about losing something. It was like she wanted to make him mad."

"What did the fairy look like?" asked Rebecca feeling the earth and sky around her begin to swirl.

"Well," said Liam, "first she was little and then big and then little again. And there was this funny stick thing she lived inside of. That made her mad, but not as mad as the pirate."

"Why, darling?" said Rebecca quietly.

"Well, the pirate said he had to find his treasure and the fairy couldn't come along. Then she got real mad and made the pirate disappear. All I can remember after that is waking up and hearing the bells at St. Peter's. Only they sounded funny, kinda' high instead of low. It was that same day I saw the strange man with the bird playing in the caves. I can't wait until you meet him, Momma, he's neat."

CHAPTER EIGHTY-FIVE

Rebecca and Liam took their places around the bonfire as the revelers solemnly lit the old branches that had been gathered for the occasion. Soon the firelight cast an eerie glow upon those captured in its light.

" 'Twas on a night such as this, over three hundred years ago, that witches and pirates trod this very soil," began Will Montana. "Some say that the devil himself still keeps company in the caves of Collins Cove. Hard to believe you say? Well, think again. Who in this town has not heard of the strange tales of La Voisin the witch and the wood nymph Eva who brought about the evil witch's destruction? And what of the old owl that haunts these shores ready to slit the throat of any who dares to intrude upon his abode? These are but a few creatures that lurk in the shadows of Salem Town. Then there are the tales of the greatest pirate of them all, Captain Jamie O'Roarke. It is said that his restless spirit still prowls these shores searching for his lost love."

"Oh how sad," said a heavy set woman dressed as Hester Prynne, complete with a scarlet "A" emblazoned on her ample chest.

"Yes, it is indeed a sad tale. For you see, all the riches in the world did not bring the great Captain O'Roarke happiness. He sailed the seven seas and visited many ports. But he never found the treasure he sought. Some say that his beloved died young. Perhaps she was a victim of the Salem witch trials, but there is no real evidence of that. I think she left him for another or was already married when they fell in love. The fact that he spoke of the lady but never mentioned her name points to that conclusion. It seems to me that he hid her identity to protect her honor."

"Perhaps it was that Melinda Briggs, you know the one who had his portrait in her old sea chest," offered a man dressed as a Puritan preacher.

"Many have thought so, but I don't believe it," continued Will. "You see, Melinda Briggs and Jamie O'Roarke had known each other for years. She was a serving maid at the Blue Anchor Tavern. They could have married anytime they wished. No, the lady in question was unattainable. I'm sure of that. The only evidence we have of his beloved lies in the lyrics of Jamie O'Roarke's favorite song:

> But farewell till bonny Lifford where the sweet
>
> Mourne waters flow.
>
> And likewise until my brownhaired girl, since I
>
> from her must go.

Suddenly, to Rebecca's astonishment, Liam joined the storyteller and helped him finish the lovely Irish sea chantey. The little boy's pure soprano lent a purity to the melody that was eerily beautiful.

> As down Lough Foyle the waters boil, and my
>
> ship stands out from the land.
>
> I'll say farewell and God bless you, my flower
>
> sweet Strabane.

Will Montana looked at the little boy in wonder. Will was quite proud of the fact that it had taken him extensive research to uncover Jamie O'Roarke's favorite song. He had followed some rather elusive clues he found after hours of research at the Peabody-Essex museum library. His research had led him to an old dust covered notebook. The notebook had belonged to a companion of Jamie O'Roarke's who had recorded the only known personal facts about the pirate. Amongst these was the fact that Jamie had never married, and the lyrics to the old song. Will had not even been sure of the melody. He had tried his best to match the words to some tune that followed the style of the times, but he had never been sure. And now that strange little boy, Liam MacRae, had bested him. The melody coming from the child's lips had rung strong and true. The tune was close to the music that Will had chosen, but it contained subtle changes that fit the words perfectly.

"Thank you, Master MacRae," said Will trying to cover his embarrassment graciously. "It is a lovely tune, isn't it?"

"Whatever happened to all of Captain O'Roarke's treasure?" asked "Hester," who was becoming bored with sitting around the bonfire. The Cove was a bit too cold and damp for her taste.

"Ah, the treasure," smiled Will. "Gather round and I will let you in on the greatest mystery that still surrounds Salem Town. For many years, the citizens of Salem would hold a celebration in the early spring. They would call it Harbor Day. Many outsiders thought it strange that seafaring folk would bring shovels and picks down to the Cove for a seaside celebration, but as Salem was known for its odd ways so no one really interfered. The fact was they were looking for the lost treasure of Jamie O'Roarke. It seems that he left quite a bit of it buried about the town. He often teased the citizens about where he had buried his treasure but he never told them exactly what he had done with it. It was more fun for him to watch them search frantically for it than it was for Jamie to spend it. The game he played with the good folk of Salem Town was a cruel one that has lasted over three hundred years. The townsfolk never found any of his gold."

"Then it must still be buried around here," said the "preacher," jumping to his feet.

"Oh, of that I'm sure," said Will with a smile, "but I doubt if you would ever find it. O'Roarke was a clever one and it is obvious that he never meant for anyone to find his treasure. It was worth more to him buried."

"I don't believe any of this," said the stout "Hester," joining her husband in disgust. "Come along, Harold, this is just a waste of time. I told you we would have more fun at the Monster Mash, but no, you had to find out about that silly pirate. Treasure and lost love, it's all just a show for the tourists." With that, the disgusted woman dragged her husband away from the bonfire and waddled off down the path that led through the woods. As they disappeared from sight, Rebecca heard the hooting of an owl and the rustle of wings overhead.

"But it is true, Momma, all of it. The man in the caves said so," said Liam earnestly.

"Did he teach you that song too, darling?" asked Rebecca with tears in her eyes.

"Oh yes, Momma," said Liam proudly.

CHAPTER EIGHTY-SIX

Rebecca and Liam helped Will Montana smother the last remaining embers of the bonfire as they watched the tourists make their way towards the path that would lead them back to the Common.

"Do you really think there is buried treasure in Salem, Will?" asked Rebecca as she kicked a glowing ember with her toe.

"Absolutely," said Will picking up his knapsack and hat, "but only the ghost of Jamie O'Roarke knows where."

"I think I know a ghost," said Liam proudly.

"Well that's just fine," said Will, not overly anxious to be bested by a five-year-old twice in one night.

"No, really, I do," said Liam earnestly, sensing Will's reluctance to listen.

"Now look, Liam," said Will looking at Rebecca over the top of the small boy's head, "I'm sure you think you see a lot of things around here, especially during Halloween. But don't get too carried away or folks will stop believing what you say. Haven't you ever heard the story about the little boy who cried wolf?"

"But I'm telling you the truth, Mr. Montana," said Liam, truly hurt by the storyteller's words.

"I'm sure you think you are, Liam, son, but perhaps you should start keeping some of your thoughts to yourself until you are a little older."

"They're not just thoughts, and I'm not your son, I'm not anyone's son!" said Liam pulling away from the friendly hand Will attempted to put on his shoulder. Before Rebecca could stop him the little boy turned towards the woods and took off at break-neck speed.

"Liam," cried Rebecca, as she gathered her crimson skirts and proceeded to run after her precious child for the second time that night.

Liam MacRae knew the path leading back towards the Common very well. Ever since he had been able to walk, he had been exploring the area that lay between his house and Collins Cove. Sometimes he had been able to persuade his brother to follow him down the overgrown path that promised untold adventures, but most of the time Liam would wander off on his own. Rebecca had almost given up hope of ever being able to control the adventurous spirit that was contained in his small body. Many the time she had awoken to find his small bed empty and his jacket gone from the hook by the front door. The first few times this had happened she had left the house in a panic calling his name, but after learning that all her searching only resulted in exhaustion for her and no Liam, she had resolved herself to the hard truth that anytime the boy wanted to elude her he could. He always showed up a few hours later with his face smeared with berries and treasures of sea shells and bird's feathers in his pockets for the whole family. Rebecca had tried in vain to explain to her small son that what he did was both naughty and dangerous but her words fell on deaf ears. Even punishing him had no effect. Whenever she confined him to his room, Rebecca felt like a jailer keeping a small wild animal in a cage. Liam would accept his punishment quietly and with good grace but the look on his stricken face told Rebecca that he had no idea that he had done anything wrong.

The moon that shone on the path cast strange shadows on the surrounding foliage. It was very confusing to the small boy. He had always wandered these woods during the day. The nighttime made everything seem different and unfamiliar.

"Momma," whispered the little boy turning first this way and then that. Somehow he had taken a wrong turn and actually left the path.

The low hanging branches from the trees that surrounded him scratched at his face and arms mercilessly. Liam sat down on a soft bed of fallen leaves and looked about. He knew he shouldn't have run away, but how dare that man tease him. What did old Will Montana really know about ghosts and witches? Even someone as young as Liam knew that most of it was made up stories. Besides, the ones that Will told weren't even very good. The ones that the fairy lady told him in his dreams were much better. His favorite time of day was that moment when Christian lay lightly snoring in the bed next to his and he was truly alone. It was then, as the last light of day was leaving the sky, that the fairy lady would come to him. She was almost as beautiful as Momma in her greeny goldy dress and she always smelled of springtime, even at Christmas time.

Liam would never forget the first time she had come to him. He had cried himself to sleep because of Christian's teasing. Daddy had read them a book about a little boy who had been stolen from his crib and replaced with another. The strange child had been called a changeling. He was unaccepted by the family as he grew older because it was obvious that he didn't belong. Christian had said that Liam must be a changeling because he didn't look at all like Daddy. Liam had been glad when Momma had made Christian go to bed early with no dessert, but it had not helped the aching feeling inside. Liam had always known that he was different. He knew he was a little like Momma, but nothing like Daddy. Christian had just put into words what Liam had felt all along. It was that night that the fairy had come to him for the first time and crooned him to sleep with her lovely voice and promises of great adventures and happiness. She had told him that there was someone who loved him as no one else could. This someone thought that Liam was the most wonderful boy in the world.

Overhead, the hooting of an owl awakened Liam from his thoughts.

"Nicodemus," he cried as the great bird gently circled his way down to the small boy. "Show me how to get home, old fella'," said Liam scratching the top of the bird's head.

Nicodemus gave the child a golden eyed wink and took off slowly. The stately owl looked back from time to time to make sure that his young godchild was following him.

CHAPTER EIGHTY-SEVEN

Rebecca stepped into the clearing and looked about frantically. When she had lost Liam's trail in the woods she had headed towards the Common. She hoped against hope that Liam had merely beaten her home. Rebecca looked up the street towards her house and prayed for some sign of life. There was none. The windows were as dark as she had left them. Mary Maloon waved to Rebecca as she gave out the last of her Halloween treats to a small "Pocahontas" and her father. Rebecca saw Mary blow out the light in her pumpkins and close her door. The enormous elm that stood in front of Mary's house looked like an inviting refuge to Rebecca. From there she could watch her own unlit front door and still be able to see Liam if he happened to emerge from the woods.

It had been many years since Rebecca had rested underneath the old elm's spreading branches. The tree cast a shadow of blood red as the moonlight shone through its fiery leaves. The night had become strangely quiet. Too quiet for Rebecca's taste. She loved the excitement that coursed through the town during the fall and in a way it made her sad to see it go. Tomorrow would bring the downward slide towards the cold New England winter.

Had it only been six years ago on this very night that Rebecca had met both Ian MacRae and Jamie O'Roarke? It seemed like a lifetime ago. How far she had come since then.

Now she was a married woman with two little boys to care for and a husband to love. Her handsome, talented husband was often a bit too demanding and left her alone more often than she would like, but the passion that had first drawn them together was as strong as ever. How she would have liked to be lying beside him right now, cuddled in his muscular arms and breathing in his masculine scent of aftershave mixed with the oil paint and turpentine he loved so dearly. Ian was everything a girl could ever want and then some. So why was she so restless?

The answer of course was simple. It was Rebecca's curse to be haunted by the memory of Captain Jamie O'Roarke. She would never love him as she did her flesh and blood husband, but O'Roarke was always there lurking in the corners of her mind ready to spring into her thoughts. Up until now she had hidden the fact from Ian. But how much longer could she play such a dangerous game? Damn Jamie O'Roarke! All he had ever done was confuse her and make her doubt everything that mattered to her. If only the apple peel she had thrown over her shoulder in O'Roarke's bower had given her the answer she needed. But not even that was to be. The top half had formed what could have been mistaken for either the letter I or J, while the bottom half of the peel had been trampled by the feet of the soldiers who had come to take Jamie into custody.

Nothing was ever finished or final where Jamie O'Roarke was concerned. Once he put his mark upon you it stayed.. Not even the powerful wood nymph Eva had escaped his allure. In the end she had given her very life to save Jamie. And for what? Rebecca felt that though he had been fond of the dyad, Jamie had never really loved her. It was just that in some mystical way Eva belonged to Jamie the same way Rebecca did.

"Well I won't have it any longer, do you hear me, Jamie O'Roarke!"

The wind battered the leaves and branches of the elm as if in reply. Rebecca knew that her son Liam would have to fight the same battle as she did when he grew older and she must be strong enough to help him. Her son must find happiness in this world. Liam must not spend his life chasing after some rainbow image that could never hold or love him. Ian loved the boy as much as he did their own son Christian and had accepted Liam as his second child. Yes, it was time Jamie O'Roarke crawled back into the history pages and stayed there. Rebecca thought that perhaps it was time to leave Salem for a while and go back with Peter and Arabella to Scotland. Up until now Rebecca had been reluctant to leave her hometown, but for Liam's own good she must.

"Oh, where is that child!" thought Rebecca anxiously as the wind suddenly surged again. Her skirt and cloak rippled furiously in its power. The strange gust seemed to be coming from above Rebecca's head. Rebecca looked up just in time to see old Nicodemus come to rest comfortably in the sturdy branches of Mary Maloon's elm.

CHAPTER EIGHTY-EIGHT

To Rebecca's relief Liam burst through the underbrush and headed straight for her.

"Did you see the bird, Momma?" asked her small son breathlessly.

"Of course I did, darling," said Rebecca hugging Liam tightly to her breast. There would be time enough later to chastise him for running away. Right now all she wanted to do was hold him close and convince herself he was unharmed.

"That's the bird that belongs to the man who lives in the caves. Isn't he wonderful?"

"Yes, darling, he is. Old Nicodemus has always been a king amongst birds."

Now it was Liam's turn to look at his mother in wonder. "You know him, Momma?"

"Oh yes, quite well," said Rebecca enjoying the astonished look on her son's countenance. "Nicodemus and I are old friends."

Liam made a face and slunk down against the elm.

"What's wrong, darling?" asked Rebecca looking at the deflated little boy.

"I thought he was my special friend," replied Liam. "But if you already know about him it spoils everything."

"No it doesn't," said Rebecca putting a protective arm around Liam. "Nicodemus chooses his friends very carefully. As far as I know you are the only little boy he has ever liked."

"Really?" smiled Liam looking up into the branches of the tree. "Then I suppose it's alright. But maybe he just likes me because I'm your little boy."

As if in answer to Liam, old Nicodemus left his perch and approached the son of Jamie O'Roarke. The huge bird walked right over to Liam and nuzzled against him.

"See how much he likes me, Momma?" whispered Liam as he stroked the bird.

"Well, now you see? You must be his favorite," said Rebecca watching her son fondle the killer owl. "He never did that to me."

Liam said nothing, but the proud look on his face almost broke Rebecca's heart. What a man her son would make!

Nicodemus soon became tired of his inaction and began to strut around in front of them. He preened his magnificent feathers and walked towards an indentation in the tree. The enormous bird gave a loud hoot as he focused on something imbedded in the bark.

"What's this, Momma?" said Liam as his fingers traced what looked to be leaves and letters.

"Why it's just an old love token someone must have carved," said Rebecca watching her son try to make sense of the initials Jamie had carved for Melinda Briggs three hundred and five years ago. Even in the dark she could still make out the J.O. and M.B. The flowers and leaves of the woodbine that wove the two sets of initials together were still visible in all their loveliness. What was it Jamie had said? "Wherever the woodbine twineth shall be Jamie O'Roarke forevermore."

Somehow the carving was clearer than Rebecca remembered it. The last time she had visited this spot it had barely been visible. Now it shone in the moonlight like a freshly cut work of art. "I must be seeing things," thought Rebecca with Jamie's words still echoing in her mind.

"Who do you think did this?" asked Liam studying the tree carefully.

"I don't know, sweetheart," said Rebecca realizing that soon the time would come when she would have to answer Liam's searching questions. His instincts were as sharp as Rebecca's, perhaps sharper. But for now an "I don't know" was all she could manage.

To Rebecca's relief she saw Peter and Arabella walking down the street swinging a delighted Christian between them. The huge orange and black bag that Peter carried with his other hand was bursting with Halloween candy.

"Come on, Liam! We collected double so you could have some too!" yelled Christian to his brother as he hurried up the large granite steps to the heavily carved mahogany doors of their home. Rebecca heard the bells of St. Peter's begin to chime as Liam ran to join his brother. It was midnight.

"I'll be there in a minute," cried Rebecca as Peter waved to her. He opened the door and ushered Arabella and the children inside. "Don't be too long," he said, "who knows what may be lurking about on a night like this."

Rebecca watched the old man fondly as he closed the door. How she loved Peter Hawking. Perhaps he was right, it wasn't safe to be standing around after midnight under the old elm. Who knows when one of those "strangers" she was always warning Liam about might appear.

Rebecca turned toward the house. A cup of hot cocoa was just what she needed to chase away the ghosts haunting her thoughts. As she took a step forward she found her path blocked by Nicodemus the owl. He spread his wings and began to flap them furiously.

"What is it, old friend?" said Rebecca alarmed at the violence of the bird's motions. "Don't you remember me? I'm not going to harm you."

At the sound of her voice Nicodemus slowed his flapping and began to hoot at her. He circled Rebecca three times and came to rest directly below Jamie's carvings. To Rebecca's amazement the old bird began to claw at the earth.

"What's the matter, Nicodemus? Is something wrong?" asked Rebecca knowing better that to ignore the owl.

In answer the bird nipped at her leg and cocked his head. He was pointing to something shiny that was buried at the base of the ancient elm. Rebecca got on her knees and began to scratch at the earth.

How could she have forgotten! The old owl gave a triumphant hoot as Rebecca uncovered her beloved garnet cross. Beneath it Rebecca could see the wooden top to an old sea chest. So that's where he had buried it! Rebecca broke into almost hysterical laughter. Leave it to Jamie O'Roarke to bury his treasure in the middle of town. Why it was right under everyone's nose. Rebecca's laughter turned to tears as memories of the noble pirate flowed through her heart. Like it or not she loved him with a love that was eternal. How on this earth would she ever be able to go on? The torment in her heart was unbearable.

"Oh, Jamie tell me what to do," said Rebecca as her tears fell upon the cross.

"There is naught to do but live, me darlin'," said a voice from within the elm. "Feel the sea spray upon your lips and the wind in your face. The fire of our kisses cannot be extinguished by any mortal mist. There will be time enough for darkness between this life and the next. Guard our child, my love, and use the treasure of Jamie O'Roarke to bring him to manhood. I'll not have it said that he received charity from others. And remember that where you have found love once ye will find it again. Our lives are many and our destinies entwined."

But farewell till bonny Lifford where the sweet
Mourne waters flow.
And likewise until my brownhaired girl, since I
from her must go.
As down lough Foyle the waters boil, and my
ship stands out from land.
I'll say farewell, for now, my love, my flower
sweet Strabane.